THIRTEEN
ORPHANS

TOR BOOKS BY JANE LINDSKOLD

Through Wolf's Eyes

Wolf's Head, Wolf's Heart

The Dragon of Despair

Wolf Captured

Wolf Hunting

Wolf's Blood

The Buried Pyramid

Child of a Rainless Year

Thirteen Orphans

THIRTEEN ORPHANS

JANE LINDSKOLD

A Tom Doherty Associates Book

New York

This is a work of fiction. All of the characters, organizations, and events portrayed in this novel are either products of the author's imagination or are used fictitiously.

THIRTEEN ORPHANS

Book design by Spring Hoteling

Illustrations by Jackie Aher

A Tor Book
Published by Tom Doherty Associates, LLC
175 Fifth Avenue
New York, NY 10010

www.tor-forge.com

Tor® is a registered trademark of Tom Doherty Associates, LLC.

Library of Congress Cataloging-in-Publication Data

Lindskold, Jane M.
    Thirteen orphans / Jane Lindskold.—1st ed.
        p. cm.
    "A Tom Doherty Associates Book."
    ISBN-13: 978-0-7653-1700-1
    ISBN-10: 0-7653-1700-1
    1. Astrology, Chinese—Fiction. 2.Folklore—China —Fiction. 3. Mah jong —Fiction. 4. Fathers and daughters —Fiction. I. Title.
    PS3562.I51248T45   2008
    813'.54—dc22
                                                            2008034085

First Edition: November 2008

Printed in the United States of America

0 9 8 7 6 5 4 3 2 1

For Pati Nagle and Chris Krohn, in cheerful memory of the Christmas Eve they taught me mah-jong, and unknowingly planted the seeds for this book.

And for Jim and Mom, in thanks for all those three-handed games.

ACKNOWLEDGMENTS

Since *Thirteen Orphans* begins a new series, there are a lot of people to thank. Some have already been noted in the dedication, but many others aided in the creation of this book in ways large and small.

My thanks to Judith Baker and Sage Walker for discussions on Pill Virgins; to Walter Jon Williams for sharing his enthusiasm for Chinese martial arts weapons; to Lupe Martinez for helping me track down a host of obscure texts, including the original Babcock on mah-jong; and to my cousin Diane Watkins Fellenz for showing me Japantown.

Many thanks to my first readers: Jim Moore, Julie Bartel, Yvonne Coats, Sally Gwylan, Alan Robson, Phyllis White, and Bobbi Wolf.

Special thanks to my agent, Kay McCauley, who made my enthusiasm for this project her own.

At Tor Books, my thanks go to Patrick and Teresa Nielsen Hayden, the self-proclaimed "uncle and aunt" of this new venture; to Tom Doherty for asking many questions and suggesting bringing Brenda to the fore. Extra special thanks go to Melissa Singer, who came on board as editor at the eleventh hour. She has shown a true gift for applying both the spur and the rein. I've enjoyed having her along for the ride.

THIRTEEN
ORPHANS

PROLOGUE

Albert Yu scattered the mah-jong tiles with restless hands, not liking what they were showing him. They clattered softly against each other, sparrow-voiced protest against this rough handling.

With dexterity too automatic to be graceful, Albert sorted the tiles, flipping them to hide the bone faces, each with its own intricately incised pattern. When all the faces were hidden, Albert lightly touched his long-fingered hands against the smooth surfaces of the bamboo backs and shuffled the tiles against the printed fabric spread over the tabletop.

The tiles clicked and clattered when they touched each other, their voices softer, mollified. After a long while, when even the tiles themselves might have been confused as to which was which, Albert began stacking them two high, arraying the stacks into lines, the lines into a perfect square.

From a small, round cloisonné bowl, Albert scooped two ivory dice. He rolled them in the center of the square, observed the number, counted off the walls until one of the four was selected. Then he rolled again. This time he counted from one end of the previously indicated wall, found his place, and broke the wall by carefully lifting free two tiles.

The cloth that covered his table was printed with a dozen stylized animals positioned in a circle around the square. A thirteenth animal was in the center.

Moving quickly, not stopping to analyze the developing pattern, Albert set a tile on each of the twelve animals. A thirteenth tile was placed in the exact center of the square. The fourteenth was set, facedown, on an ideograph printed on the lower right interior margin of the square.

Albert studied the tile he had placed on the first animal—a sharp-nosed, grey-furred rat. He nodded as if the tile had told him something he already knew. His gaze flickered to where the next tile rested upon the depiction of a water buffalo. He frowned.

Next around the circle was the tiger. The tight lines around Albert Yu's mouth softened when he read the tile there, softened further when he shifted his attention to the tile set upon the rabbit.

Tightness returned as he read the tiles set upon the dragon, the snake, the horse. The tightness increased, etching lines between his brows as he read the tiles set upon the ram and the monkey. Hastily he shifted his attention to the tiles upon the rooster and the dog. Whatever he read there did not increase his tension, but neither did it ease it. The tile set upon the pig made his frown return.

Lastly, he examined the tile set upon the picture printed on the center of the cloth. The picture depicted a house cat sitting upright in perk-eared alertness, its gaze angled as if observing a bird just out of reach.

Albert spoke aloud for the first time as he looked at the tile. "Well enough there, but then I knew it would be."

He turned over the fourteenth tile and held it between three fingers, staring at it for a long while, his expression holding mingled fear and disbelief.

He was setting the tile down and reaching for the nearby telephone when a door behind him opened.

Albert swung around and lurched to his feet, the phone still in his hand.

"You! Why did you come here unannounced? Have you also received inauspicious omens?"

"All well for the Cat?" the other said, then gestured to where the fourteenth tile sat on the printed cloth. "Or perhaps not . . . perhaps not . . ."

Albert dropped the phone, moved to put the table between himself and the intruder. The other raised one hand. Nestled in the palm was a small sphere that caught the light, and gave back twisted images. Then the intruder reached into a jacket pocket and came out with a strip of pale yellow paper upon which Chinese characters had been painted in black ink.

Albert ducked, but there was no dodging what was coming after him. He saw his name twisting out to wrap around him, and then he saw nothing more.

Brenda Morris shifted uneasily in the passenger seat of the car her father had rented at the airport.

"Move the seat back if you're not comfortable," her father said without removing his gaze from the road. "The manual is in the glove compartment if the controls don't make any sense."

Obediently, Brenda pulled out the manual and leafed through the glossy pages, but her discomfort was something other than physical. Indeed, the car seat was comfortable to the point of ridiculousness, the result of a double upgrade her father had finagled at the rental counter. He was good at things like that. The strange thing was that people always liked Gaheris Morris, even when he'd just taken advantage of them.

Brenda's mother frequently said her husband and her eldest were alike in their ability to make people like them. Although she always said this with a smile, the comparison usually made Brenda uncomfortable. It didn't seem quite right that people should admire you for being smart enough to take advantage of them.

Brenda slid the manual back into the glove compartment, and leaned back in the seat without making any adjustments.

Her father glanced over at her.

"It's all right if you change the seat, Breni."

"I'm fine."

He shrugged one shoulder and turned his attention back to the road. "If you say so. I just can't figure out where you put all that leg. You seem to grow an inch every couple of months."

"Not quite *every*." She laughed. "Actually, I'm not growing nearly as fast as I did in high school. I did need to buy new jeans last week."

"I know." Her father gave a mock sigh of exasperation. "I saw the credit-card bill."

I just wish the rest of me would catch up with my legs, Brenda thought. *I'm tired of being flat-chested. Other girls complain about their hips and big butts, but at least they don't get taken for a boy from the back. I think the only thing that saves me from being embarrassed more often is the length of my hair.*

Brenda liked her dad a lot, but she wasn't going to say something like that out loud. He was a man, after all, and he'd probably be embarrassed.

Or worse, he'd say something witty, and she'd be the one to get embarrassed.

So she turned her gaze out the window. She could see enough to know that northern California was a lot different from South Carolina.

My hair wouldn't save me here, she thought as she watched two men with pony-tails bike by on a side path. *I'd have to wear a skirt all the time, and then I'd look like a stretched-out nine-year-old, or worse, a boy in drag.*

"Dad, why are we here?"

"You mean in California, or has the local vibe given rise to existential thoughts?"

Brenda swallowed a grin. She'd tried to ask her father the reason for this trip several times over the preceding week. Gaheris Morris traveled on business a lot, and he hadn't felt the need to take his eldest and only daughter with him on other trips. When he'd gone out earlier to meet with a client, he'd left her back at the hotel, so he wasn't indoctrinating her into the family mercantile business as a prelude to some sort of summer internship.

Each time Brenda had asked, Dad had found a way to put her off or distract her. She wasn't going to let him do it this time, even if that line about existential thoughts was a pretty good one.

"I mean here in California, at this time, heading wherever it is we're heading."

Dad sighed deeply. He drove in silence for a long moment, but Brenda held her breath, refusing to say anything he might use to turn the conversation in another direction. Only after he had navigated a complicated turn did he speak.

"We're going to see an old friend . . ." He interrupted himself. "Actually, 'old' isn't the right word. Albert Yu is about my age, mid-forties. 'Friend' isn't exactly right either. We've had plenty of disagreements. How about this: We're going to see someone I've known just about my entire life, and the reason we're going is because I want you to meet him."

"Albert Yu?" Brenda frowned. "I don't think I've ever heard you mention him."

"No . . . I probably wouldn't. Like I said, I've known him pretty much all my life, but we . . ."

He paused again. Brenda found herself startled to silence by her usually articulate father's strange inability to say whatever it was that was on his mind.

"Brenda," he began again, "humor me, would you? One of the reasons I brought you here was to meet Albert before I talked about him, before I biased you in any way. Just because . . ."

He almost visibly bit off his words in midstream.

"Would you humor me, Breni?"

Brenda had a distinct feeling that she was being "gotten around," the way her dad got around so many people, but what could she do? Besides, seeing Dad so flustered had *her* flustered. She had to admit that she was now eager to meet this Albert Yu so she could figure out what it was about him that made Dad so edgy.

"Okay," she said, "but I'll hit you up for something later."

"Anything," he promised in the tone that indicated he meant it, "as long as it isn't chocolate."

On that startling note, he fell silent. Except for comments on their surroundings, he maintained that silence for the rest of the drive.

Brenda had no idea what she had expected their destination to be, but a high-class, higher-end, high-tech shopping plaza was not it. The buildings were crafted from exposed steel set with sweeping sheets of tinted glass. Most were smoke grey, but interspersed with these were randomly placed strips of bronze or gold. Roofs rose at odd angles that reminded Brenda of old science-fiction illustrations of cities of the future, yet there was a feeling of "village" about the complex as well, created by meandering paths between buildings, immaculately groomed potted plants, and individual storefronts with signs swinging over their doors.

There was plenty of parking, but Dad didn't pull into any of the available spaces. Instead he guided the rental car down service alleys meant to be over-looked, so that mundanities like trash disposal and stock delivery would never smear this retail paradise.

"Does Albert Yu work here?" Brenda asked as her dad pulled the car into a space near a series of door-lined alcoves.

"He . . . does, in a way. He has an office here. Look, sugarplum, no more questions for now, all right?"

Brenda blinked. Her father had stopped calling her "sugarplum" sometime when she was in high school. This Albert Yu must really have him rattled.

"Right, Dad."

When they got out of the car, Dad moved more slowly than usual, checking and double-checking locks, glancing at his watch more than once. When he started moving, though, he strode along swiftly enough that, long legs or not, Brenda had to trot to keep up.

He led the way to one of the door-lined alcoves, and selected the central door. It must have been unlocked, because he was swinging it open almost before Brenda caught up. She had time enough to glimpse the legend "Your Chocolat-ier" written on the door with gold ink in a thin, elegant script before her father was inside and heading up the stairs.

The stairway was so startling that Brenda could hardly make herself ascend the treads. She'd done her time in retail and knew that elegance rarely extended behind the scenes. Here, however, instead of grey painted metal and harsh light-ing was a narrow stairway paneled in ebony. Light so dim that it hardly qualified as such reflected off tiny silver nailheads bordering wall panels and stair treads. When the door at the base of the stairwell swung soundlessly shut behind her, Brenda had the impression that she was walking through the night sky, held up only by the stars.

"Dad?" she said softly.

"Here," he said. "Come on. It's strange, but nothing to be afraid of, pretty even, in its way."

Brenda had to agree. She concentrated on forgetting her surroundings and let her feet carry her up as she would have at home. In moments, she was behind her father, close enough to catch his familiar scent, one that mingled sharp after-shave and the mustard he inevitably slathered on almost anything he ate.

She heard Dad rap his knuckles against the door, but instead of someone coming to answer the door, it swung open of its own accord. Fleetingly, Brenda thought this was another element of the mysterious Mr. Yu's eccentricities. Then her father stepped forward and exclaimed in wordless shock.

Brenda slipped past him and into an office that was, in its own way, as odd as the stairway. She had no attention for the peculiarities of the decor because, like her father's, her attention was riveted by the empty room, and the evidence that it was probably not empty by choice of the occupant.

A table showing what at first glance looked like a mah-jong game in progress dominated the room, as an executive desk might a more usual office. This table had been shoved to one side. It was too large and too heavy to have been knocked over, but some of the tiles had been spilled from the squared-off wall that still stood mostly intact on a cloth at the table's center.

Other pieces of furniture had been moved roughly aside. Papers had spilled from stacks on cabinets to drift on the thick Oriental carpet that covered most of the polished hardwood floor. A chair was shoved into a corner.

Brenda had watched enough television to know that you didn't interfere with a crime scene, so she was almost hurt when her father said sharply, "Don't touch anything!"

Then he pulled out his cell phone, but instead of hitting 911 or Operator or something, he punched in a string of at least ten numbers. She heard the faint sounds of someone answering on the other end.

"Pearl Bright, please," her father said briskly. He waited a moment, then said, "Auntie Pearl?"

His next words, to Brenda's complete astonishment, were in fluid, unmistakable Chinese. She knew that Auntie Pearl—one of her father's oldest friends—was part Chinese, but Dad had never spoken to Pearl Bright in that language before, at least in Brenda's hearing.

Brenda knew enough Chinese to thank a waitress or follow the occasional line of dialogue in a foreign film, but that was it. She recognized the sound, though, because her parents had a fondness for foreign films and always insisted on watching them subtitled. She'd never had the least hint that Dad understood a word of what was being said, but here he was quavering and fluting away like a native.

Deciding she'd had enough of weirdness and miracles, Brenda steadfastly turned her back on her father and tried to figure out what had happened in this room.

She'd thought of the room as an office, because that's what her father had led her to expect, but it was certainly unlike any office she had seen before.

Her first impression had been that the room was windowless, but now she saw that it had windows, front and back. The one in the rear was smoky grey, clearly one of the exterior panels of the building itself. It began about seven feet from the floor, then angled upward sharply to become part of the ceiling for about three feet, before a more standard, solid ceiling took over.

The front window was even stranger. At first glance it was more grey, nearly opaque glass, but as Brenda stared at it, she realized that what she had taken for dim reflections of herself and her father were actually people moving around on the other side. She studied them for a moment before turning to her father.

Gaheris Morris was pocketing his cell phone, his expression mingling concern and relief.

"Dad, there are people out there! A shop, I think."

Dad nodded. "That's right. That's the shopfront for Your Chocolatier, Albert's business."

"He sells candy?"

"He sells candy the way Ferrari sells cars. Your Chocolatier is where movie stars and millionaires buy their Valentine chocolates. Individual truffles can cost twenty dollars or more. A box small enough to fit in your jacket pocket can set you back two hundred dollars."

His tone held respect tempered with something Brenda couldn't quite identify. Resentment? Envy?

"That window," Dad went on, "is one-way glass. There's a control somewhere that makes it almost clear—from this side only."

"I guess he doesn't trust his employees," Brenda said. "I'm not sure I'd blame him. They could eat about five hundred dollars' worth in about two minutes."

"Actually, Albert claims the window is for market research, not spying. It enables him to see what attracts shoppers, what turns them off. Employees are coached to step on a button when prize clients come in. Then Albert can use the window to see who is there, and 'accidentally' come out to greet them."

"He sounds manipulative."

"That's about right," Dad agreed. Again, Brenda caught that odd note in his voice. Dad went on, "I've reached Auntie Pearl. We're in luck. She was in the area today, and thinks she can be here in about twenty minutes or a half hour."

"Dad, why did you call Auntie Pearl?" Brenda asked, her gaze shifting to watch the ghostly forms of the staff going about their business. "Why didn't you call the police?"

"Too soon to call the police," Dad said. "We don't even know if Albert's really missing. He knew I was coming by, but something could have called him away."

Brenda looked at the messed-up office, and thought her father was being disingenuous. Albert Yu clearly valued order accented with a certain amount of beauty. The office walls held the file cabinets one would expect, but they were crafted from dark, polished wood, the fittings in mellow bronze. The wall space above the cabinets was adorned with elegantly simple ink-brush landscape paintings after the Chinese style.

There was an expensive computer workstation, but it was tucked away in a back corner. Cabinet doors were neatly folded to either side. When they were folded shut, the modern era would be gone, hidden behind polished mahogany inlaid with a pattern of cranes worked in mother-of-pearl. Waist-high cabinets that didn't precisely match, but were similar to the computer workstation in their ornate beauty, balanced the file cabinets.

"What are we going to do if someone in the shop buzzes?" she said.

"They won't," Dad said. This time his voice held absolute confidence. "Albert would have told them he was not to be disturbed, not even if the First Lady herself arrived to shop for White House party favors."

"Because we were coming?" Brenda asked, impressed despite herself.

"Because he was doing this," Dad said, sweeping his arm to indicate the mah-jong tiles scattered on the table. "Albert would not have wanted to be interrupted."

Brenda turned her gaze from ghosts in the shopwindow. "Don't tell me he was playing mah-jong by himself! You need at least three players."

"I won't," Dad said, forcing a grin. "I'll let Auntie Pearl explain. Come on. Let's go meet her."

Brenda glared at her father, but she knew she'd get nothing more from him. His gaze had fallen to the scattered tiles on the cloth-covered table. His grin had vanished, and his expression was very, very worried indeed.

★

Pearl Bright instructed her driver to drop her off at the main entrance of the largest building in the shopping mall that was quite proud to host Your Chocolatier.

By habit more than vanity, she inspected her reflection in the mirrored surface of the smoked-glass door as Hastings moved to hold it open for her. The reflection gave her back an older woman—no doubt of that—but an older woman who still carried herself upright and moved briskly. The elegance of her attire turned heads in this age when casual dress had gone so far that thongs were worn on both feet and backsides, doing, in her opinion, no credit to either.

"Hastings, I will phone when I wish to be picked up."

"Yes, madam," he replied with formality, standing straight as he held open the door.

He didn't tell her he had a book and a lunch in the trunk of the car, but she knew, just as she knew he would find himself a nice spot under some shady tree and spend a leisurely interlude waiting for her call. There were worse jobs, far worse, than chauffeuring a rich former movie star.

As was often the case with older people, Pearl's vision had actually improved as she had grown older, so that the spectacles she once had worn had become no longer necessary. As she advanced into the mall, she inspected the people who lingered in the tiled atrium, looking for the two she was to meet.

Pearl had known Gaheris Morris all his life, and sometimes she had to remind herself that he was no longer the eager young boy she so fondly remembered. His family had moved to the Midwest when he had been something like six. It wasn't until after Gaheris's grandfather's death and the attendant ugliness that she and Gaheris had resumed more than casual contact.

Then Gaheris had been reeling from everything he had discovered about himself and his heritage, all that had been thrust upon him through his father's denial. He had turned to her as a source of stability.

"Auntie Pearl" had been happy to oblige, even if the attention she paid to Gaheris had made young Albert less than pleased. She wondered how Albert would feel when he knew that his sparring partner had been the one to discover his absence.

She wondered if Albert was in a position to feel anything at all.

Glancing to the right, she spotted Gaheris standing next to one of the smooth stone columns that punctuated the open reaches of the foyer. Lean and slim, his curling reddish-brown hair untouched with grey, his skin ruddy with sun, he looked like what he was, an American male of indeterminate ethnic heritage. The young woman standing beside him had similar features, but her coloring was taken from a different palette: browns and ivories, rather than her father's redder hues. The white pantsuit she wore set those colors off nicely.

At nineteen, Brenda Morris was already as tall as her father, her legs seeming impossibly long in proportion to her torso. Her dark brown, almost black, hair was thick and straight, long enough to fall past her breasts. She wore it unstyled, except that the part was slightly off-center, a nice, if possibly unintentional, touch that kept her appearance from rigid symmetry. Her eyes were the same dark brown as her hair, slightly slanted under perfect brows.

Brenda was not pretty, nor would she ever be so, but she was something far better—she was exotic and interesting. Pearl wondered if Brenda realized how lucky she was, and decided she probably did not. Brenda was still young enough that "difference" meant separation from the parental generation, but not from the peer group.

Gaheris raised his right hand in a lazy wave. If Pearl hadn't known him so well, his manner would have been the perfect form of a nephew greeting an elder relative. She knew him, though, and saw the tension in how he gently nudged Brenda forward.

Brenda moved lightly, only the tightness of her shoulders showing how much she disliked being steered. The smile she turned on Pearl was equal parts shy and warm. Pearl knew why. Pearl was a celebrity who was somehow family. The role gave her a certain mystique—a mystique Pearl had refused to relinquish, staying in hotels when visiting the Morris family, and never being seen disheveled or informal.

After greetings had been exchanged, Gaheris said, "I locked both Albert's office, and the stairwell. I don't think anyone will bother them before we can get back. Do you want to stop for something to eat or drink?"

Pearl smiled. "I was finishing lunch when you phoned, but if you and Brenda need to eat, I would be happy to sit with you."

Gaheris shook his head. "We got sandwiches from one of the outrageously expensive places here. I charged it to Albert's account. I figured we're here on his business."

Pearl shook her head in mock reproof, but such behavior really was typical of Gaheris. He was financially well-off, but he never stopped looking for an angle, especially if it would get him something for nothing. Maybe having three children to support was the root of his scheming. However, she suspected it was part of his integral nature. His father and grandfather had been the same way.

Brenda was looking at her father with affectionate dismay. She clearly knew this aspect of her father's personality, but thought he carried it too far. Pearl wondered what the girl would be like when she came into the full force of her inherited nature. She hoped they would have a long time before they found out.

"Very well," Pearl said. "Since we have all eaten, then we should go up to Albert's office. Is his staff aware anything is amiss?"

"They know nothing," Gaheris said. "I sent Brenda into the shop, and as far as she could tell everything was normal. They sold her something the size of a Hershey's kiss for ten dollars."

"It was delicious," Brenda said. "Absolutely wonderful."

The young woman's smile faded, and she gave Pearl the full force of her gaze. "I don't know what's worse, knowing something is wrong or not knowing why Dad won't call the police. He said you'd explain."

Pearl nodded. "Your father did the right thing. However, these are not matters we should discuss here. Shall we go to Albert's office? I would like to see for myself what Gaheris described."

She turned and led the way to the elevator. She was spry for her age, but there was no need to overdo things, and Albert *would* insist on having his office on an upper floor.

Brenda covertly studied Auntie Pearl as they made their way through the mall to one of the discreetly placed service corridors.

Pearl Bright had to be old—she'd been a child actress when Shirley Temple was still popular—but she moved with energy and grace. Moreover, although she didn't look old, she didn't look fake young, either. She hadn't had face lifts or injections. That was for sure. There were lines on her face, and her once-dark hair was silver, but neither made her look old. This made her look weirdly beyond time, as if Time had touched her, and she'd slipped his noose.

Brenda knew Auntie Pearl was at least half Chinese. That had been in the biography Brenda had read a few years ago. Her birth name had been Chinese: Something Ming. Ming meant "bright," and was one of the few Chinese ideographs Brenda recognized on sight. Auntie Pearl didn't look Chinese, though, or at least she didn't look *too* Chinese. In her early films, she looked like a cute little girl whose straight dark hair was a nice contrast to Shirley Temple's golden curls. In her later films Auntie Pearl looked more exotic. Did a person grow into ethnicity?

Thinking back to the phone call she'd heard him make, Brenda found herself wondering for the first time if her dad—and that meant Brenda herself—was part Chinese. Maybe Auntie Pearl really was his aunt or great-aunt or something.

Dad didn't look Chinese. He looked American. His mother had been Scotch-Irish, or at least mostly so. His father had been German, but now that Brenda thought about it, he hadn't looked all German. But then, what did anything look like? Brenda had seen pictures of Navajos who looked more Chinese than many of the Chinese movie stars and models she'd seen.

Dad led them unerringly down service corridors to a door that opened into the top section of the weird ebony and silver staircase into Albert Yu's office. He motioned them in, then carefully locked the door behind him. The stairway was narrow, but he squeezed by them and led the way up. Auntie Pearl followed, and Brenda came last. She felt like she'd been appointed rear guard, until she noticed that when Dad got to the top, Auntie Pearl stopped and waited until he had unlocked the door and motioned for them to come ahead.

I guess Auntie Pearl is watching out for me, not the other way around.

Brenda didn't know whether to feel annoyed or relieved by this, and decided she could settle for a little of each.

Albert Yu's office was unchanged from when they had left. Auntie Pearl moved immediately over to the table and studied the scattered mah-jong tiles.

"It looks as if he had just completed a reading into the status of the Thirteen Orphans," she said. "Whoever interrupted him deliberately scattered the tiles, so I can't guess what Albert saw."

Brenda waited for her father to laugh or say something like "Be serious," but instead he nodded.

"I couldn't tell anything either," he said. "I didn't realize the tiles had been deliberately scattered though. I thought they'd just been displaced when the table was moved. It's usually parallel with the front window, the one into the shop."

"Look at how the tiles rest," Auntie Pearl said, pointing to the bone and bamboo rectangles with her index finger. The fingernail had been polished bloodred, and was absolutely perfect. Brenda would have killed for nails like that. "If the tiles had simply shifted when the table was pushed, then some tiles would have remained on their marks. Not one does. Moreover, one side of the wall would have collapsed more completely than the other according to where force was applied. This wall has been completely broken. You can tell, however, that the tiles were in wall formation because the majority still remain facedown."

"I didn't notice," Gaheris Morris admitted.

"You were shocked by what you found," Pearl Bright said matter-of-factly. "Moreover, I have an eye for such things."

Brenda had listened in silence, but as the sensation built that she had entered a madhouse, she broke in.

"Why are you talking this way? I mean, it's odd that this guy was playing mah-jong by himself. Fine. I've got that. But why aren't you calling the police? Why are you standing here studying a messed-up game board?"

Auntie Pearl looked at Gaheris Morris.

"How much does Brenda know?"

"Not much. Letting her know was the reason for this trip. I wasn't going to do to her what my dad did to me, but I didn't think I should tell her too soon. Look what knowing too much too soon did to Albert."

"I have long held," Pearl Bright said, "that it was less the knowledge than his father's refusal to act that marked Albert. However, that old argument is not worth reviewing now."

She shifted her gaze to Brenda, and the young woman fought not to squirm under its unrelenting scrutiny.

"Brenda, what do you know about mah-jong?"

Brenda replied promptly. "It's a game, sort of like gin rummy, only it has trump suits, too. They're called winds and dragons. There are bonus tiles called flowers and seasons. Those can do a lot to help your score if you have a cruddy hand. Oh, and instead of four suits, like in a regular card deck, mah-jong has only three: dots, bamboo, and characters."

"You play?"

"Sometimes, mostly with Dad and Mom, and one of my brothers. We don't play as often now that the boys are getting older. Only four can play, at most, and my brothers don't like being coached, but they don't like being left out either."

"That wouldn't make for a very good game," Auntie Pearl agreed. She beckoned with those long red nails. "Come here and look at what Albert left."

Brenda moved obediently to the woman's side, her curiosity overwhelming the almost unconscious trepidation that had kept her at a distance from the table.

"You know a good deal about mah-jong," Auntie Pearl said. "What do you make of this cloth on which the tiles are set?"

"I can't see much detail," Brenda admitted after a moment, "not with the tiles all over it. There are animals on it, block-printed, along with lots of what look like Chinese characters."

Auntie Pearl started moving the tiles to one side, evidently so Brenda could see what was printed on the fabric.

"Hey!" Brenda said. "You shouldn't do that. The police wouldn't want a crime scene disturbed."

Pearl Bright continued moving the tiles. "This is not a crime scene, at least not one the police would recognize as such. Now. Tell me how this cloth fits in with the game of mah-jong."

Brenda glanced at her father, but his face was expressionless. She decided she'd better go along if she wanted to understand anything. She hadn't missed Dad saying that apparently having her learn something was the whole reason for this trip. Could this be what she was supposed to learn?

"The cloth doesn't fit in with any version of mah-jong I know," Brenda said, bending to inspect the cloth since Auntie Pearl clearly expected her to do so. "Mah-jong's more like a card game than a board game. You make the board out of the tiles. I mean, everybody grabs tiles from the shuffled batch, then builds the tiles into the Great Wall. Only then do you deal them out."

"Why go to all that trouble?" Pearl asked. "Why not just deal from the shuffled batch?"

"To keep anyone from cheating," Brenda replied, feeling weirdly like she was reciting catechism lessons. "We didn't gamble at home, but mah-jong is like poker. Lots of people bet on it. When dealing from the wall, it's just about impossible to stack the deck."

"Why?"

"Because no one knows where the wall will be broken," Brenda said. "One person rolls the dice to indicate which wall will be broken. Most of the time, another person rolls the dice to indicate where the wall will be broken. So, for someone to stack the deck, they'd need weighted dice, and to get both rolls."

"Very good," Pearl said. "Now, tell me why if mah-jong is a game that does not need a board, Albert Yu was setting up his 'Great Wall,' as you call it, on this cloth."

Brenda looked where Pearl's red fingernail was pointing and understood instantly. Although the tiles had been scattered, much of the base of the wall remained in place. There was sufficient to see that the tiles had been set within one pattern printed on the cloth. Another pattern was printed within the wall.

"He was, wasn't he?" Brenda mused aloud. She was pleased when no one pushed her to answer quickly. Her father and Auntie Pearl seemed quite willing to let her figure out the details for herself.

The Chinese characters printed on the cloth mostly meant nothing to Brenda, although she recognized a few, mostly from Chinese takeout menus and playing mah-jong. Instead of trying to figure them out, Brenda studied the figures printed in what she was thinking of as the "outer ring." They were so stylized it took her a moment to recognize what they were, but when she did, she was so pleased she muttered aloud.

"They're animals. The ones at the top are a pig and a rat, then there's a bull or something . . ." She traced her way around, as if reading the face of a clock. "Big cat . . . tiger from the stripes. A bunny, a dragon, a snake, a horse, a sheep or goat, a monkey. Is that a chicken? Then a dog and back to the pig."

She frowned, chewing the inside of her lip in thought. "That sounds familiar . . . Why am I thinking of food?"

Brenda straightened and looked at her dad and Auntie Pearl, punching her fist into the air in triumph.

"I've got it! They're the animals from the Chinese zodiac. I've seen them on menus. That's not a chicken. It's a rooster. The bull is usually called an ox. This one sort of looks like a water buffalo."

Then Brenda frowned. "But what are they doing mixed up with mah-jong tiles? That makes no sense. The zodiac and the game aren't related, except that both are Chinese."

Auntie Pearl said gently, "But apparently they are related, at least for Albert Yu."

"And for you," Brenda said, "and Dad. You knew what you were seeing here. You talked about the tiles like this Albert Yu had been reading tarot cards or Ouija boards."

Her dad gave her something like his usual grin. "And where did you learn about those? Been messing about with the occult, have you?"

"Dad! You can buy tarot cards in the bookstore in the mall. They're not occult. They're just kind of cool."

"Occult," interjected Auntie Pearl, her tone saying she did not care for them to be distracted, "means 'hidden' or 'secret.' It is derived from the same root as 'occlude,' I believe. Sometimes, the best way to hide something is to hide it in plain sight."

"You're saying that mah-jong hides something?" Brenda challenged.

"I am indeed, but for you to know what was being hidden, and why, you would need to subject yourself to a long and rather complicated story, a story that begins with the exile of the Twelve and the creation of the Thirteen Orphans."

Brenda stared at her. "A true story?"

"Perfectly true, I assure you. I heard it from my father, and he was one of the Twelve."

Brenda almost expected what came next.

"Your great-grandfather was also one of the Twelve," Pearl went on. "He was the Rat. My father was the Tiger."

Brenda looked at her dad, but he was no help at all. He was nodding seriously, and when he saw Brenda looking at him he managed to twist his lips around into a smile.

"It's true, Breni," he said. "My grandfather was Exile Rat, and I'm the Rat now. The reason that I brought you here is because all the omens say that you will be the Rat after me."

"I don't get it," Brenda said, looking at the printed image on the cloth. "I don't even like rats. I don't think that's my year anyhow. I'm a rabbit or a sheep or something. Something not really cool, anyhow. Not like a tiger, or a dragon, or even a horse."

Pearl said calmly, as if Brenda wasn't talking crazy, "The designations to which you refer are comparatively modern, hardly more than a thousand years old. The Twelve Earthly Branches were not originally associated with animals at all. The Twelve Animals that we are speaking of don't have specific counterparts on Earth at all. They belong to the Lands Born from Smoke and Sacrifice."

"Smoke and Sacrifice," Brenda repeated woodenly. "Twelve. Thirteen. Zodiac animals off a restaurant place mat. I don't get it. And I still don't understand why you aren't calling the police. Albert Yu was supposed to meet Dad and me here a couple of hours ago. He wasn't here, and his office has been messed up. He's a wealthy guy, I bet. Someone might have kidnapped him for ransom or something. But instead of calling his wife or the police or something, you two stand here and talk about mah-jong tiles being messed up."

Her voice had shifted from stiff to tense, almost shouting, before she finished.

Dad came forward and put a hand on Brenda's arm. She shrugged it off, but didn't move away.

"Brenda, listen to me," Gaheris Morris said. "I did call Albert's number, both at home and his cell. No answer. He doesn't have a wife. He's divorced. He has kids, but they don't live near here. He has an invalid mother who probably wouldn't be helped by knowing we can't find him."

"Does old Mrs. Yu know about Tigers and Rats and stuff?" Brenda asked. She knew she was sneering, and she knew she sounded nasty, but she couldn't help herself. This was all too much.

It wasn't too much because she couldn't believe it. It was too much because somewhere deep down inside she did believe it. Her dad could be a rogue and he could be a rascal, but he had never been the sort of mean practical joker he would need to be to pull a trick like this on her.

So either Brenda had to accept that all these impossible hints were real, or she had to accept that her dad was nasty beyond belief. She knew what she was going to believe, and she drew herself up. Taking a deep breath, she quirked the corner of her mouth in an apologetic smile.

"Sorry. I lost it there. I'll try not to again. Do we have time for a long story or should we try and find this Albert?"

Her dad squeezed her shoulder, a quick sort-of hug he'd adopted when she'd gotten as tall as him.

"How about we do both?" he said. "Auntie Pearl, Brenda's right. Knowing why we had come here today, seeing the tiles out and messed up—and, honestly, knowing that Albert is intensely security-minded—made me jump to conclusions. How about I go and make some sensible inquiries? I'll check Albert's schedule with the folks in the shop. I'll go by Albert's house and make sure he didn't somehow forget our appointment. If that doesn't tell me anything, I'll call hospitals and police stations for accident reports. Meanwhile, you two can stay here and wait for Albert to come trailing in, making excuses. While I do that, Brenda, Auntie Pearl can fill you in just like she did me when my granddad died."

"You'll be careful, Gaheris," Auntie Pearl said sharply.

"I will be very careful," he promised. "And you two lock the doors. I'm going to leave the spare keys with you and ring from below to be let in. That way, if you hear anyone at the door . . ."

He trailed off, and Pearl Bright continued the thought.

"It will probably be Albert. I will expect to hear from you every half hour. If you do not call within thirty-five minutes, I will call you. Understood?"

Brenda expected Dad to protest, say something about being a grown man, but he didn't.

"Understood." He squeezed Brenda's shoulder again. "Listen carefully, Breni. I didn't really believe any of this the first time I heard it, but I do now. Okay?"

"Okay."

Brenda watched Dad vanishing down that ebony and silver stair. She felt suddenly terrified, but she fought the terror down. Everything was going to be fine. Albert Yu would come trailing in. They'd talk to her dad every half hour. Everything was going to be fine.

Nonetheless, Brenda watched fixedly as Pearl Bright locked Dad out. Then Brenda licked her lips.

"Is there a bathroom?"

"Through there," Pearl said, nodding in the direction of a door. "And I'm going to want something to drink. Do you drink jasmine tea?"

Brenda nodded. When she came out of the bathroom, her face and hands freshly scrubbed, she was feeling a lot calmer.

Pearl had opened one of the waist-high cabinets, revealing a two-burner stove. Water had been set to heat and Pearl was unwrapping a package of short-bread cookies.

"Where do I begin?" Auntie Pearl said. "I could go all the way to first causes, but I don't think you need that quite yet. Would you settle for events more intimately connected to our families?"

"You mean us, here and now?" Brenda said. "I think that would be best."

"Very well," Pearl said, "then suffice to say that in a land so far away that you will not find it on any map, there was an emperor, and that emperor had twelve advisors, all of whom were scholars, skilled in the arts of magic."

Brenda opened her mouth to protest, then stuffed a piece of shortbread in instead. She saw Pearl Bright give a small smile, and realized that it was the first smile she had seen from that elegant lady. Oddly, it made her feel a great deal better.

Pearl noted the water was boiling, rinsed the pot, then poured more water over the tea leaves.

"Now, this emperor had advisors other than the Twelve, and not all of them were as devoted to their master as were the Twelve. Several were, in fact, traitors."

★

Pearl noted Brenda's restraint with pleasure. Smart girl. More of a Rat than she knew. Clever enough to know that Pearl wouldn't lightly invite ridicule. Clever enough to swallow a cookie to cover swallowing her words.

"These traitors," Pearl went on, "devised an elaborate plan to overthrow their emperor. It went very well, so well that soon all that stood in the way of the new emperor and his allies were these twelve advisors. The Twelve were offered the opportunity to go into exile if they ceased fighting on their deceased emperor's behalf. They elected to do so, even though this meant abandoning their families and homeland forever."

"Tough choice," Brenda said sympathetically.

"Very," Pearl agreed. "My father never stopped wondering what might have happened if the Twelve had chosen to continue their battle. He usually arrived at the same conclusion. They might have defeated the usurpers, but in the course of doing so much of what they sought to preserve would have been destroyed—including their families. And they might have lost. And there would have been even more destruction, because battles among the powerful are terrible indeed."

"Their families," Brenda said. "How did they know their families wouldn't be destroyed after they weren't there to protect them?"

"Permitting the families and their property to survive untouched was one of the terms of surrender," Pearl explained. "If the usurpers had violated that term, the Twelve would have had tremendous incitement to return from exile."

"I see," Brenda said. "Still, I bet those people who had to stay behind didn't have an easy time of it, even if they still owned their property. There are lots of ways to make someone miserable without touching either of those things. Any school bully knows that."

"I agree, but when the alternative is total obliteration, accepting social ostracism and other such penalties seems a reasonable option."

"Still, I bet the wives and children didn't like being left behind."

Pearl checked the tea, and found it to her liking. She poured the pale liquid into two of Albert's translucent antique Chinese teacups, wondering how much more she should tell Brenda at this point. The young woman was taking the tale very well, but perhaps that was because she was viewing it as a tale, nothing more.

"Those who were left behind certainly didn't like it much," Pearl agreed, "but they weren't given a choice. The usurpers wanted insurance that the Twelve would not violate the agreement. The families were that insurance. Their role as hostages was specifically written into the treaty—as was the reverse, that if anything happened to their families, the Twelve would be free to return.

"However, as careful as the usurpers were, they were unaware the Twelve had one remaining advantage. It was a small advantage, and if the Twelve had been ruled by the spirit of their surrender agreement, they certainly should have given it over. However, they decided not to do so."

"That was taking a big risk," Brenda said. Her expression was very severe. "What could be worth the risk of having their families killed, and probably starting the war all over again?"

"The emperor," Pearl replied, "or, rather, his very young son by a lesser wife. The usurpers thought they had wiped out anyone with a better claim to the throne than that which was held by the man they had elevated to emperor. However, the Twelve had succeeded in keeping this boy—he was only two years old—in hiding. When they went into exile, they took the child with them. Only after they had arrived at their destination did they arrange to let their enemies know."

"I bet the new emperor and his supporters weren't happy."

"They were furious. However, they could not do anything about what the Twelve had done without risking that word would leak out that a legitimate claimant to the throne lived. So they decided to let the Twelve keep their child emperor, and concentrate on the future, or so the Twelve believed."

Brenda sipped her tea. Her fingers were very long, and wrapped around the bowl-shaped cup almost hiding the device painted on the porcelain.

"Believed?" the young woman asked.

Pearl nodded. "The Twelve had good reason for their belief. For the first several years, they were left in relative peace, but this was not because they had been forgiven or forgotten. Rather, the new emperor was solidifying his rule. Only when the assassination attempts began did the Twelve realize their danger.

"As you must have guessed, the land of the Twelve's exile was China. Ethnically, the Twelve could blend in there fairly well, and they had chosen to reside in a bustling region that was attracting people from all parts of not only the Middle Kingdom itself, but of greater Asia and the world. In a village, their oddities of speech and custom would surely have been detected. In a teeming metropolis, they were not.

"When the attempts on their lives began, the Twelve fled, first to other cities in China, then briefly to Japan. Eventually, they emigrated to the United States, because there was room enough to spread out. The relocation also put an ocean between them and their enemies. With this last and greatest move, they found some peace."

Pearl glanced at Brenda, but the young woman offered no question or comment. However, she was not in the least bored. Her listening silence was so alert that Pearl imagined her whiskers twitching.

"After one of their number was slain, and several others severely injured, the Twelve also took precautions to preserve and enhance their greatest single asset—their ability to work magic."

Brenda's perfect eyebrows rose, almost involuntarily, but she said nothing. Pearl poured herself a small amount more of the jasmine tea, took a fortifying sip, and went on.

"The details of that great assault must wait for another time, but by the time it came, the Twelve had learned much about hiding. They had also learned that multiplicity and a veneer of openness were their greatest protections. As long as their enemies believed that killing the Twelve and their young ward would end their problems, they would persist. However, if the power the Twelve held could be passed to another, and if the tools for utilizing that power would be readily available, the task would be much more difficult. Therefore, from various Chinese card games, the Twelve adopted mah-jong. Encoded into the one hundred and forty-four tiles is a wealth of magical lore—including the ability to ascertain the well-being of each of the Thirteen Orphans."

"And that's what you and Dad think Albert Yu was doing," Brenda said. Although she was obviously attempting to sound matter-of-fact, doubt crept into her voice.

"That is what we *know* he was doing," Pearl said with faint emphasis. "I have told you that I am the Tiger, and your father is the Rat. The other ten advisors also had designations that corresponded with one of the animals now associated with the Chinese zodiac."

"Now?"

"As I mentioned earlier, the association is relatively recent," Pearl said, knowing she was getting off on a tangent, but feeling she must not reject Brenda's questions. "Long before that, the animals already were associated with various traits. Only later were they linked to the Twelve Earthly Branches of the astrological calender."

"And so the wizards called themselves by those animal names."

Pearl nodded, although the reality was far more complex.

"You keep saying twelve," Brenda said, "but there were thirteen animals printed on that cloth, and you keep mentioning the Thirteen Orphans. Since there are thirteen exiles in your story, I can guess that the last animal—the cat—must stand for the boy emperor."

"Precisely," Pearl said. "Just as none of the original Twelve are alive, but their power has been inherited by their children or, in far more cases, grandchildren or great-grandchildren, so the original boy emperor grew to be a man. He had a son, and that son had a son. That son is Albert Yu."

As if the name had been a prompt of some sort, there was sound from the door leading into the ebony and silver stairwell.

"Dad must be back," Brenda said. "I'll go let him in."

She rose, but before she could take more than a few steps, the door to the stairwell swung open and a man who was very clearly not Gaheris Morris entered.

He was dressed in a dark suit that showed its expense in perfect tailoring rather than ostentation. His shining black hair was worn longer than a typical businessman usually would permit himself. His close-cut beard and mustache gave him something of the look of a stage magician—albeit, one who hailed from the mystic Orient, not any place in Europe.

He had been holding an umbrella, and this he dropped into a tall porcelain urn, before turning to greet them. Pearl noted that Albert did not seem to find it the least odd that they were in his private office, without his having let them in.

"I am sorry I am late," he said affably. He gave Pearl a polite bow and extended a hand to Brenda. "You must be Brenda Morris. I am Albert Yu. Will Gaheris be along soon?"

Pearl felt something inside her tighten as she listened. The voice was right, as were the clothing and the appearance, but something else was very wrong.

Brenda did not know Albert Yu, so she answered politely.

"Dad drove over to your house," Brenda said, "when you didn't come for our appointment. I could call him. Let him know you're back."

"Whatever, whatever," Albert said vaguely. He glanced over and noted the scattered mah-jong tiles on the table. "Having a game while I was out?"

Pearl stiffened, forced herself to relax. Brenda, who had pulled out a cell phone, paused with her fingers above the keypad. She glanced over at Pearl and Pearl signed her with an almost imperceptible shake of her head. Brenda let the phone fall shut.

"Actually not," Pearl said. "You know you need at least three to play mah-jong. The tiles were much like that when we arrived."

"I'm sorry the office was left in such a mess," Albert apologized. "Still, no harm done. I see you found some tea and shortbread. Did you get any chocolate?"

"Dad bought me a piece," Brenda said. "It was lovely."

"Let me get you a sampler," Albert said.

Before they could comment, he had breezed out the door that went into the shop. They heard one of the staff members saying "Oh, Mr. Yu, I'm so glad you are here! The dowager of Longleaf . . ."

The words were cut off by the closing door.

Brenda looked at Pearl, and Pearl, who had expected to see doubt or accusation in the younger woman's eyes, saw only apprehension.

"That's Albert Yu?" Brenda asked.

"That looks like Albert Yu," Pearl replied. She moved quickly over to the table and began gathering up the mah-jong tiles. "I have known Albert all his life. This man does not act like Albert Yu—especially Albert Yu among the Twelve. He reserves that breezy manner for customers, and only for those customers that formality would drive away."

Brenda came over and helped Pearl collect the tiles.

"What are we going to do?"

"Will you follow my lead?"

"If I can ask questions later, and get straight answers."

"Done."

They had most of the mah-jong tiles stacked into their case when Albert returned. He held a long, flat box in one hand.

"Sorry for the delay," he said. "A client who is ordering favors for five hundred guests at her granddaughter's wedding wants to rearrange everything—at the last minute, of course. My manager needed to brief me right away."

He extended the box to Brenda. "This is a sampler I reserve for clients who are coming in with a big order. I hope it will serve as an apology for my tardiness."

Brenda accepted the box with stammered thanks. Pearl saw her heft it surreptitiously, and knew that Gaheris's daughter shared her father's tendency to automatically estimate price. Whatever figure she arrived at, Brenda was impressed.

Albert extracted a small, deep box of truffles from his pocket and handed it to Pearl.

"Your favorites. I do apologize. Do you still have time to visit?"

Pearl dropped the last mah-jong tiles into their places in their lacquerware carrying case.

"Actually, I think we should leave you to attend to your business. We'll go out and call Gaheris, then reschedule our visit for later this week. We'd love to stay, but we have another appointment."

"Of course, of course. . . ." Albert glanced toward the telephone, visions of expensive wedding favors clearly claiming his attention.

They said their good-byes.

As they were leaving, Pearl said, as if in afterthought, "Albert, might I borrow your mah-jong set? Brenda was admiring it earlier, and we might while away the evening with a game or two."

"Take it, take it," Albert said.

"It is an antique," Pearl said, looking for the least sign of hesitation on his part.

"Don't worry," Albert said. "I know you will take good care of it."

Pearl motioned for Brenda to pick up the case containing Albert's mah-jong set. With easy, housewifely efficiency, Pearl herself folded up the printed cloth and tucked it into her purse.

They took their leave, exiting through the shop into the mall. Brenda pulled out her phone and looked at Pearl.

"That was Albert Yu?"

Pearl frowned. "If that was Albert Yu, then he has forgotten everything he ever knew about himself, or he would not have let me take this away with me. Call your father. We must talk."

Paradoxically, the manner of Albert Yu's return was what pushed Brenda into accepting that something like truth lay behind Auntie Pearl's strange story.

Auntie Pearl seemed to sense this. When they were back in the mall's grand foyer, waiting for Auntie Pearl's driver to bring the car around, she gave a small, understanding smile.

"Not here," the older woman said. "There's my car."

The car was long and dark blue, trimmed with silver, and like everything else associated with Pearl Bright, both expensive and quietly elegant.

The driver came around and opened doors for them.

"Tell Hastings the name and address of your hotel," Pearl said.

Brenda did. Then she slid into the car's vast backseat. As Hastings shut the door behind her, and moved around to take his place behind the wheel, Auntie Pearl touched a button on the armrest beside her. A thick glass partition slid into place between compartments.

Auntie Pearl gave the slightest of smiles.

"An indulgence, yes, but even at my age I still find myself discussing business that I do not wish my driver to know. Tell me. You had never met Albert Yu before. I had the impression that your father had not spoken of him to you. What made you sense that something was wrong?"

Brenda looked down at the box of chocolate she now held in her lap. The box was metal, tinted a muted shade of bronze and embossed with what she thought of as "Chinese-type" flowers, hand-painted in artistically natural colors.

It was a beautiful piece, and helped her frame her thoughts.

"He wasn't right," she said. "The man who designed that office, who commissioned this box to hold his candy, wouldn't have spoken the way the Albert we met did. The Albert Yu we met would have had signed photographs of himself with famous clients framed on the office walls, not ink-brush art. He would have boxed his candy in something not necessarily flashier . . . This is flashy in its own right, I guess. But something that hinted at dreams of moving his product into, you know, high-end department stores. Sort of like Godiva did. That kind of thing."

Brenda looked up from the box, expecting to see Auntie Pearl looking amused, but the older woman was listening intently. Brenda was reminded of a great cat, frozen in the tall grass near a watering hole, waiting with perfect patience.

Brenda went on, her words tumbling over each other.

"And how he acted was all wrong, giving us the chocolates like that. And I could tell he didn't remember he had an appointment with my dad, or maybe that he did, but he didn't remember why. And he should have, shouldn't he?"

"Oh, yes," Auntie Pearl said. "Albert should have done so. Meeting you is very, very important to him. You are, after all, your father's heir apparent. You don't realize quite yet how important that is, but I promise to explain. For now, accept it."

Brenda felt both scared stiff and relieved. She wanted to know why all this Rat stuff was important, but she didn't, too. It was like waiting for the teacher to give out grades after a test where you had no idea at all how you had done. You wanted to know, but then again, you didn't.

"Albert Yu shouldn't have let you take that mah-jong set, should he?" Brenda asked, more to cover her indecision than because she had any doubts about the answer.

"He should not have done so," Auntie Pearl agreed. "There are thirteen original mah-jong sets. This is one. They are more than antiques, more than family heirlooms. The Albert Yu I know would no more let me walk out carrying his set without comment than he would have let me walk out with his head.

That argues that either that man was not Albert Yu or Albert Yu has completely forgotten who he is."

Brenda pursed her lips, then asked, "Did he look like himself?"

"Looked, dressed, sounded, even smelled like himself," Auntie Pearl replied. "What he did not do was speak like himself—and even that is not completely correct. I have seen him adopt that manner with some of his clients, usually movie stars or nouveau riche who would be intimidated by his usual, much more reserved manner."

Pearl Bright paused, and when she resumed speaking, Brenda could tell that the older woman was thinking aloud. Rather than being offended, Brenda found herself deeply flattered. That great cat she'd envisioned crouching in the grass never forgot her surroundings.

"I think Albert's deepest core," Auntie Pearl said, "is centered around the knowledge that he is the great-grandson of an emperor. He never forgets that, not for a moment. I have known royalty. True royalty can be as human and flawed as the rest of us—more so, perhaps, because they know that no one can take from them their titles and prestige. Albert, however, knows all too well that titles can be taken, that he is an emperor in exile, not a reigning monarch. Therefore, he never lets his dignity slip."

"But this man we met didn't have that reserve," Brenda said. "Are you sure he wasn't off his guard because we were, well, sort of family?"

"Family? Never that." Auntie Pearl coughed a hoarse laugh. "Honored and privileged advisors, but except for a few who had blood ties to the emperor—and distant ties at that, for the old emperor was wise enough not to let both bloodlines and power close to his throne—none of the Twelve were family."

She sighed deeply, and for the first time since they met, Brenda thought that Auntie Pearl looked old. The car was curving into the wide driveway of a nice hotel of the sort that catered to business travelers.

"We will discuss this further when we have met up with your father," Auntie Pearl said.

Gaheris Morris was waiting for them, and joined the driver in helping them out of the car. His eyebrows rose when he saw the box of expensive chocolates Brenda held, but his gasp of surprise was audible when he saw the box of mah-jong tiles Pearl Bright carried.

"Shall I help you with that?" he asked.

"Please," Auntie Pearl said. "They are quite heavy, and I would not drop them."

"No," Gaheris agreed, taking the box with what Brenda thought looked like reverence. "I think not."

Hastings was told that they would be some time, and so he could have the next several hours for his own business.

"I may not drive back home tonight," Pearl said. "If I take rooms here, I will call you."

The driver nodded. "I had thought this might be the case, madam. Call if I am needed."

He bowed, slid into the car, and drove off.

"Polite fellow," Gaheris commented. "Where did you get him? Central casting?"

"Just about," Pearl agreed with a light laugh. "Young would-be actors always need work. Driving for me is not terribly onerous, and I am understanding if a casting call comes up suddenly. Sometimes, I even unbutton enough to reminisce about my successes. Hastings has dreams of understudying the lead in a traveling Broadway show. I do not doubt that he will ensconce himself somewhere and memorize lines until I call."

The idle chatter had carried them to the bank of elevators. As they shared the elevator car with a couple of earnest-looking young men in suits, further talk waited until they arrived at the suite Gaheris had taken for himself and Brenda.

It was a nice set of rooms, not unduly lavish, but roomy. The front room was comfortably furnished with a sofa and two chairs with a low coffee table stretched between them. Off to one side was a small kitchenette. A square table, about the size of a card table, sat surrounded by four chairs, ready either for meetings or meals. Brenda knew that later she and her dad would flip a coin for which of them got the bed in the other room, which would sleep on the sofa bed out here.

"There's tea," Gaheris said, glancing at a narrow wicker basket beside the two-burner stove, "and coffee. I can get sodas and ice, or order room service, if you'd like."

Dad must be rattled, Brenda thought, feeling herself smile. *He never orders room service. Or maybe he wants to be kind to Auntie Pearl. But, looking at him, I think he's rattled.*

"I see Earl Grey there," Auntie Pearl said. "I think I can settle for that. I also have a box of absolutely overly rich chocolate truffles here. I hope you two will share them with me."

Brenda felt a momentarily selfish joy that she wouldn't have to share her own treasure trove, then ashamed of herself.

"I have my chocolates, too," she said. "Dad, I think I'd like coffee rather than tea. We got up really early this morning to fly out here. My head's muddled with everything that has happened."

Dad moved to set up the coffeepot, and when Brenda put her box of chocolates on the table in front of the sofa, Auntie Pearl waved for her to put them away.

"Keep those for later," Pearl said. "That's an expensive treasure, and one to be savored. You may never have anything like it again. I assure you, these truffles will be more than enough for us all."

Gaheris turned from setting up the coffee, and glanced at the two boxes with their "Your Chocolatier" labels.

"You decided to raise Albert's profit margin?"

"No," Auntie Pearl said, and her tone held a challenge Brenda could not quite understand. "Albert gave them to us by way of an apology for his being late."

"Gave you?" Dad turned and picked up Brenda's box. "This is a half-pound sampler! Those run something like two hundred dollars, especially in that box. I remember thinking about getting Keely one for our anniversary, and decided that if I was spending that much she'd prefer something more permanent."

Auntie Pearl nodded. "And Albert didn't even offer you a discount, did he? Yet he gave Brenda and me our little gifts with a smile. That's not the only odd thing he did."

Succinctly, she summarized the events that had followed Albert Yu's return.

"You're sure that was Albert?"

"Albert or his twin," came the tart reply, "and he does not have a twin. I may be elderly, but my vision remains perfect. My doctors are quite impressed. I simply explain that I have an excellent heritage."

Gaheris frowned. "Auntie Pearl, is eating that chocolate wise? You said Albert wasn't behaving quite like himself. Maybe he had some ulterior motive for giving you those chocolates."

Pearl smiled a thin, catty smile. "Gaheris, I think you're jealous . . . but that doesn't mean you're being unreasonable. As far as the chocolates go, I think we're safe. I watched through the hidden window, and saw Albert tell a shopgirl to make up the boxes. She took the chocolates directly from those in the larger display case."

"I wish I had been there," Gaheris said. "Here's your tea. I hope I didn't let it get too strong."

Brenda moved to pour herself some coffee. Auntie Pearl was opening the box of truffles, and cutting them into thirds with a very sharp folding knife she pulled from her purse.

The coffee wasn't bad, and the truffles were like the divine ideal of chocolate. Brenda let a piece of one melt on her tongue and felt instantly restored.

"You said Albert Yu doesn't have a twin," she said. "Does he have any brothers? Any cousins? Anyone who might be able to pass for him?"

Auntie Pearl shook her head. She wiped a minute bit of dark chocolate off her lip before speaking.

"No. Albert is an only child. His own father was the only son of the boy I told you about earlier, the last survivor of the old emperor's line."

"The first Cat," Gaheris added. "Has Auntie Pearl told you about the twelve animals?"

"A little," Brenda said. "I know that each of the twelve wizards was associated with an animal, and that those animals are associated today with the Chinese zodiac. I know that the boy emperor, Albert Yu's grandfather, was called the Cat, but I don't really know why."

Auntie Pearl said, "There are many stories about how the different animals were chosen for the zodiac, and each of them gives a different reason for why the cat was left out. Personally, I think it was because there was already one cat in the zodiac already, in the tiger, but that is neither here nor there. What my father told me is that someone started calling the boy—remember, he was hardly more than a toddler—the Cat as a joke. When the magics associated with the mah-jong were developed, they considered their options.

"Normally, the emperor is associated with the dragon, but there was already a dragon among the Twelve. Had the child been a girl, they might have chosen the phoenix, the Red Bird of the South, but that would not do for a boy."

Brenda longed to ask why not, but decided she'd probably learn soon enough.

"As I told you, mah-jong was adopted when the Twelve realized that their enemies were still pursuing them with intent toward harm. Someone, the Dog, I think, pointed out that cats were really quite good at hiding and at slipping away, even when you believed them cornered. Cats were as fierce as tigers in a fight, and nearly as cunning as rats. Everyone agreed that as the little boy already was on his way to identifying with the cat, they could do far worse, so the symbol of the emperor in exile became the cat."

"Oh." Brenda ate a bit of raspberry truffle and nearly dissolved at the rich levels of flavor.

She wished her mother were there to share. Thinking of her mother reminded Brenda of something that had been niggling at the back of her mind ever since Auntie Pearl had begun her tale.

"Were all of the Twelve men?" she asked. "Were any women?"

"Half were women," Auntie Pearl said. "The Ox, Hare, Snake, Ram, Rooster, and Pig were all women."

"Ram and Rooster?" Brenda asked. "But those are male animals."

"They are male animals, but yin principles," Auntie Pearl replied. "I'll explain about this later, I promise."

"Now isn't the time for esoteric theory," Dad agreed. "We need to figure out what happened to Albert. I have a suggestion. Why don't we lay out a reading? We might learn whatever it was he saw, and even if we don't, Brenda will have a bit of her necessary education filled in."

"Did you bring your set?"

"I did."

"Good. I don't want to use Albert's, not until we know more." Auntie Pearl glanced at her watch. "I think I should stay here, at least for tonight. Let me call the front desk and see if I can get a room."

Brenda watched as her father went into the bedroom and came out with a box like, but unlike, the one that held the tiles Auntie Pearl had taken from Albert Yu's office. The lid of this box was ornamented with the stylized image of a rat. The other, of course, was decorated with a cat.

For a last, blessed moment, Brenda could pretend that they were simply going to play a three-handed game. Then her father opened the box and took out something that looked like a compass, except that it had a much more elaborate graph drawn on the surface. He held the device in his hand, slowly turning as the needle turned.

"That way is north," he said. "Breni, help me orient the table so one side faces directly north."

"Okay, Dad, but why does it matter? Mah-jong directions aren't real—they're not even right. East and west are reversed."

Gaheris grinned. "Or south and north are. It's a matter of perspective, but I know what you mean. On the 'real' compass, the directions are north is on top, then south on the bottom, with west on the left, east on the right. Mah-jong flips that, so east and west change places. All the more reason for making sure north is properly aligned."

Brenda didn't argue further, but she felt reality flee as Gaheris carefully shifted the table so that the four sides were precisely oriented to the compass points.

Auntie Pearl hung up the room phone with a click.

"Are we ready?" she said.

"Ready," Dad agreed.

Brenda wished she could agree. All she could manage was silence.

★

As Pearl came over to join Brenda and Gaheris, she noticed that the earlier un-easiness had returned to Brenda's expression. Well, there was nothing like doing something—anything—to distract an unhappy mind.

"All right, Gaheris, spill out the tiles and we'll all build the wall. Brenda, have you seen this mah-jong set before?"

"A couple of times," Brenda admitted. "We had a plastic set to play with, but Dad brought this one out sometimes, just to let us look at them."

Gaheris would have, Pearl thought, *looking to see which of his children was to follow him as Rat. Two sons and a daughter, just like my family, but I bet his reaction to learning his daughter would follow him was very different from my father's.*

"The tiles are made from bone and bamboo," Pearl continued, and shot a glance at Gaheris from beneath her lashes lest he give away precisely what type of bone. Brenda was not ready for that. "The bone holds the carving, and the bam-boo protects the bone. Each element has symbolic significance as well, but that can wait."

"Lots of things seem to wait," Brenda muttered.

"Isn't that the way of life?" Pearl agreed pleasantly. "Now, you told me ear-lier that you knew about building the wall to start a game. That is the first step for what we are going to do as well. However, there is a different reason for building this wall than to avoid cheating in a gambling game."

Pearl reached out and touched the tiles lightly, shuffling them, the motion just a bit sluggish because of the loose fabric beneath the polished bone.

Gaheris did the same, and, after a moment, Brenda reached over and joined in. Their hands were very different: Pearl's with their elegant nails, the knuckles slightly swollen from arthritis; Gaheris's narrow and long, the nails neatly trimmed; Brenda's a feminine version of her father's, the nails short and a little ragged, traces of old polish near the cuticles.

"What's the reason for building the wall then?" Brenda asked after a mo-ment. "I mean, if not to keep someone from cheating?"

Pearl stopped shuffling and started building the wall. The other two followed her lead almost automatically.

"Like the altered directions I heard you and your father discussing a moment ago, it has to do with Chinese cosmography," Pearl said. "The majority of an-cient Chinese descriptions depicted the world as a square—or a cube. That detail depended on which theorist was doing the describing. Cube or square isn't important. What is important is that whatever the description, those doing the describing agreed on one thing. China was in the center of the square."

"Lots of cultures were like that, weren't they?" asked Brenda. "I mean Galileo got in a lot of trouble for not putting the Earth at the center of the universe, right?"

"Lots of cultures were—and are—egocentric," Pearl agreed, "but few went so far as the Chinese. Their word for what Westerners came to call 'China' translated as 'center country' or more eloquently, Middle Kingdom. Even more poetically, the translation could be extended to mean 'Celestial Kingdom' or 'Heavenly Land,' because by an extension of that same cosmography, by being placed at the center, China was directly under heaven and so specially blessed."

Gaheris added, "Brenda, remember when I showed you the Chinese character that means 'middle' or 'center'?"

"The rectangle with the line through it," Brenda said. "The same as on the red dragon tile."

"We'll get back to the red dragon later," Gaheris promised. "What I want you to remember is that the character that we translate as meaning 'center' isn't simply made up from a random assortment of lines. It is a drawing of how the entire universe was perceived as being shaped."

Brenda drew a finger around the now completed square they had constructed from the double-stacked mah-jong tiles.

"So when we build this square out of the tiles, we're building the world—the universe?"

"That is correct," Pearl said.

Brenda looked at how the square was positioned on the printed fabric. "The way we've built the wall puts the cat inside the world, and the other twelve outside. Is that deliberate?"

"It is. The Twelve were exiled, shut out of the world. The Cat left, but he was not formally exiled. Therefore, he is still inside the world."

Gaheris cleared his throat. "That pattern also permits the twelve animals to remain correctly oriented as to their symbolic directions. Squeezing the cat in would have thrown everything off."

Brenda looked as if dozens of questions were competing to get out of her mouth, but she only said, "What do we do next?"

Gaheris smiled at his daughter. "Because randomness has its benefits in divination as well as in gambling, the next thing we do is roll dice to break the wall."

"Just as if we're playing mah-jong?" Brenda said. "Well, if we're going to do that, we need to choose seats. Usually we draw winds for that, but the wall's already built. Do we bust it up and start over?"

Pearl shook her head. "When working an augury, it is best that those involved sit in the direction most closely associated with their zodiac animal."

Brenda looked very much like she wanted to ask, "Associated directions?" but she kept her lips pressed tightly shut.

Gaheris spoke into the uncomfortable pause. "North is the direction associated with the Rat, so I will take that chair. Auntie Pearl?"

"The Tiger's direction is east-northeast," Pearl said. "Since Gaheris has north, I will cover the east. Brenda, can we impose on you to be both south and west?"

Brenda moved to the chair opposite her father in reply.

Gaheris rolled two dice.

"High roll starts," he said, both in invocation and explanation. "Four."

Pearl rolled a seven. Brenda rolled a nine, and therefore was the one to start. She looked uncertainly between the others.

"Start like you're playing mah-jong," Gaheris prompted.

Brenda rolled the two dice in the center of the square. They came up a three and a five, totaling eight. Pearl had played so many games, cast so many auguries and even more complex spells that she knew where the wall would break, but she waited patiently as Brenda counted off the walls, starting in front of herself, and moving counterclockwise in the approved fashion.

". . . Six, seven, eight," Brenda concluded. "East rolls next."

She picked up the dice and handed them politely to Pearl. The younger woman's earlier trepidation seemed to have ebbed. Her dark brown eyes were bright and interested.

Pearl rolled the dice. They came up twelve. She added twelve to nine, then counted off from the wall in front of her, until she reached the twenty-first pair—which happened to be in the wall directly in front of her.

"As in a usual game, we remove this pair of tiles, and the pair beside them," Pearl said, following words with appropriate action.

"I've always wondered," Brenda said, "about the rules for breaking the wall. Doesn't all that adding eliminate the lower pairs completely? I mean, you're never going to roll a one, because you're rolling two dice, but adding together means you'll never get lower than four, and that would be so rare as to be almost impossible."

It was the same question Gaheris had asked when Pearl had taught him, and he gave the same answer.

"Overlap covers the eliminated sets," he said. "You said you knew tarot cards."

"A little."

"Well, a tarot reading starts by pulling out the signifier for the person for whom the reading is being given, right?"

"Right."

"So that eliminates that card, and all its meanings. It seems to me that could be rather important, since the signifier is usually selected from among the face cards."

"But there are other cards with the same basic meaning," Brenda said, "and a good reader keeps that in mind."

"Exactly. The same principle applies here," Gaheris said. "There's lots of duplication in a mah-jong set. There are four of each tile in each of the three suits. There are four of each of the four winds, and four of each of the three dragons. Only the flower and season tiles are unique, so, for that reason, we grant them extra emphasis if they appear in a reading."

Brenda blinked as if pressing the information into her memory, then nodded. "Okay. So we've broken the wall. What next?"

"Next," Pearl said, "we deal out the tiles, except instead of dealing hands out to each player as we would if we were playing mah-jong, we place one tile on each of the animals. We begin with the rat, who is the first animal in the zodiac, and end with the cat."

"We don't use those first tiles, the ones we used to break the wall?" Brenda asked.

"No. Those are used later if needed. Gaheris, since we're using your mah-jong set, you place the tiles."

Gaheris did so, moving quickly, and not pausing to look at the results until he had placed the thirteenth tile. The pattern that developed was not precisely reassuring.

Pearl stared at the arrangement. She read it through, then read it again, knowing that in this case the numeric value of a tile could be ignored, that only the suit mattered.

Rat: bamboo. Ox: character. Tiger: bamboo. Hare: bamboo. Dragon: character. Snake: character. Horse: character. Ram: character. Monkey: character. Rooster: dot. Dog: dot. Pig: character. Cat: character.

Pearl's brow wrinkled with confusion as she absorbed the significance of the reading. Then, with the automatic force of long habit, she smoothed the confusion away lest she get wrinkles.

"Auntie Pearl," Gaheris said, "I'm not sure I understand."

"You understand," Pearl said. "You simply do not want to believe, any more than I want to believe. This makes no sense—or perhaps it makes too much sense."

Brenda interjected. "There's something weird here. I get that. I mean, that's a really weird array for a random drawing, but it's not impossible. I mean, even drawing mah-jong is not impossible. Would you like to tell me what's going on?"

Pearl shook her head in disbelief. She touched the character tile that rested on the ox with one fingernail.

"In this type of reading, the character suit," she explained, "stands for overwhelming danger."

"Is that a polite way of saying 'death'?" Brenda asked.

"No. It means just what I have said: a tremendous danger that has not resulted in death touches the people on whom a character tile rests."

Gaheris interrupted. "Breni, death readings are rather more difficult to do with this system, for reasons I will explain later. What these tiles are saying is that of the Twelve, seven are in overwhelming danger."

Pearl nodded. "The dots resting on the dog and rooster show that they are threatened, a state milder than indicated by the character suit. Bamboo shows that Hare is fine for now, as are Tiger and Rat."

"That's a relief," Brenda said. "I mean, since you're the Tiger and Dad's the Rat."

"You haven't mentioned Cat," Gaheris interjected. "Cat is severely threatened, too, but you and Brenda saw Albert just a little while ago."

"It is possible," Pearl said, "that whatever is threatening him has not yet materialized."

"But you don't believe that," Gaheris said.

"No," Pearl agreed. She could see Brenda studying her and knew she was going to need to offer more detailed explanations. "Another thing that is very strange is that I believe Albert had been doing a similar reading to this one when he was disturbed. Two tiles lay next to Cat when I was picking them up. One probably fell from the wall when the table was knocked into, but both were dots tiles."

"Showing that when Albert Yu did this reading," Brenda said, "he was like the Dog and the Rooster—facing a threat, but not in real danger."

"Yes," Pearl agreed. "He was threatened then, but now Albert is no longer threatened—according to this reading, the threat has materialized. He is in danger of his life—or worse."

Brenda didn't need to be told that whatever this threat was had nothing to do with the fact that someone who seemed to be a perfectly healthy, even happy Albert Yu had spoken to her not more than a few hours ago, and had given her a half-pound box of expensive chocolates.

She took another wedge of truffle from the plate. Dark chocolate with toasted almond. Pure bliss.

"Something worse," Brenda speculated aloud. "Like how Albert Yu didn't know why we were there, or why the mah-jong set should be important to him. Something has touched his mind, his memory, even though his body's still around."

Pearl nodded. "That's what I think. The advantages of such a tactic for someone who wanted to render the Twelve ineffective would be astonishingly high."

Brenda decided to test her own guesses. "You've been talking about my being the next Rat. That means there's some sort of mechanism in place to allow for inheritance of the abilities. Right?"

"Right," said Gaheris with a crisp, approving nod. "That's why readings for 'death' are hard to do with this system. The individual may die, but the Rat or Tiger or whoever remains."

Brenda nodded to show she understood, but she didn't want to lose her train of thought, tenuous as it was. She feared that if she thought too hard about all of this, the inherent craziness would destroy her ability to believe in any of it.

"Kidnapping someone could cause lots of problems," Brenda went on. "I mean, remember how I wanted you to call the police when we found Albert Yu's office all messed up? Try and pull off twelve kidnappings without the FBI finding connections between the people involved. It might take a while for them to do so, but I bet they'd find them."

"Definitely," Dad replied. "In many cases, the connections would be obvious. Auntie Pearl is a friend of our family. She has been something of a professional mentor to the current Rooster. I do business with both the Dragon and the Pig."

Brenda started moving restlessly in the limited space offered by the suite. "Okay. The same restrictions would apply for murder, but the consequences would be even worse. I mean, murder gets the law interested, especially when famous people like Auntie Pearl are involved."

"Or Albert Yu," Dad said almost grudgingly. "And several of the rest of us at least qualify as pillars of our communities."

"Fatal accidents might work," Brenda said, "but twelve accidents that don't get taken for something else . . . that would be tough. Tougher given that even if the law was fooled, that doesn't mean the other members of the Twelve would be. And you keep track of each other, or at least some of you do of some of you."

Auntie Pearl raised a hand in almost regal interjection.

"Murder or fatal accidents would offer another problem," she said, "one you touched on before. Inheritance. Murder would not eliminate the member of the Twelve. It would simply pass their abilities to their heir apparent. In a few cases, that could provide a great inconvenience. The Hare's heir . . ."

Pearl noted the inadvertent pun, but went on, "Her heir apparent is a small child, no more than two or three years old, ineffective as a tool, and if something happened to her mother, she would be very carefully watched."

Brenda felt a sinking sensation blended with apprehension that turned the chocolate truffle's lingering sweetness sour on her tongue.

"I'd be almost as useless," she said, "but a lot more vulnerable. I mean, I know nothing about any of this or almost nothing. If someone had come after Dad, say, a week ago . . ."

Brenda shivered. She'd been going after this as an intellectual problem, like something the professor might present in an ethics class. When she thought about something happening to Dad, suddenly, she found it hard to think at all.

She moved over to where Gaheris stood staring down at the mah-jong tiles and pressed up against him as if she were about six, not a grown woman in college. He put his arm around her and squeezed, and Brenda had a sudden insight as to why her dad might have taken so long to bring up this whole Rat thing. It would be admitting there would be a time that he, like his own dad, wouldn't be there, when he'd need to pass a responsibility along to her.

Brenda swallowed hard, and looked at Auntie Pearl. The older woman was studying them with a look that mingled compassion and something like envy. Brenda wondered how that original Tiger had felt about his beautiful and talented daughter. Brenda had figured Pearl's father would have been proud of his daughter, but maybe he hadn't been. Men could be weird about strong daughters.

Auntie Pearl glanced at the face of the slim diamond and emerald wristwatch that adorned one wrist. "It's getting on to dinnertime here, which means that I can still make a call to the Rooster. Des lives in Santa Fe. I'll warn him to be careful of strangers."

"How would Des know the difference there in Santa Fe?" Dad said. "They're all strange there."

He grinned as he made the joke, but the expression was forced. "More seriously, doesn't Des work in retail? It's going to be hard for him to avoid strangers completely."

"He can be careful," Auntie Pearl said. "I'm more worried about what we'll do about the Dog. However, let me make a call where it may do some good."

"Why don't you use the phone in the bedroom?" Dad said. "I'll get on my cell out here and call Deborah Van Bergenstein and Shen Kung. Those are the Pig and the Dragon," he added to Brenda. "I'll ask a few questions, see how they respond."

Auntie Pearl nodded. "Good. We should also look to getting someone out to Denver. That's where, according to my last report, the Dog lives. I'll call my travel agent after I talk to Des."

Brenda bit her lip to keep from asking any of the thousand questions this strange exchange evoked.

"Dad, I'll step out in the hall, call Mom and let her know we got here safely."

"Good," Gaheris said, his own phone already in hand. "I'll call her later when we know better what we're doing."

When Brenda came back from making her call, she found Auntie Pearl and her dad in deep discussion. They stopped the minute she came in, but not, she felt, because they were trying to close her out.

Dad turned to her. "Breni, we're going to Denver tomorrow, you and me. Auntie Pearl is going to make some further inquiries into the well-being of the other members of the Twelve. However, since there's nothing more productive we three can do for the rest of this evening, I think now is the time for you to ask Auntie Pearl every question you can think of."

"And listen to the answers, as well," the older woman said with a thin-lipped smile. "Pleasant as this hotel room is, I could use a change of venue. Brenda, with your father's agreement, I have made reservations at Hour's Deserve. The food is excellent, and the menu varied enough that we should all be able to find something we'd enjoy. Hour's Deserve has the added advantage of being accustomed to hosting guests who wish to be given their privacy. We can talk freely about the most outré matters."

Brenda mentally reviewed the clothes she'd packed. She thought she put together an outfit respectable enough to pass in a good restaurant. They agreed to meet in the lobby in half an hour.

"I am not as young as I once was," Auntie Pearl confessed. "Fifteen minutes to rest my eyes would be useful."

⭐

Pearl Bright's eyes were shut, but her mind was racing. The results of the phone calls she and Gaheris had made between them had been disturbing. Des had taken her warning seriously, but several of the others had shown evidence of that same peculiar amnesia that she had witnessed in Albert Yu.

They had remembered whatever ostensible reason they had for knowing her, but of the deeper mysteries that bound them they had remembered nothing at all.

All of these were people Pearl had known all their lives, and, in some cases, for much of her own. She was among the oldest of the Twelve, the only surviving first-generation descendant of one of the original Orphans, but several of the others had held their positions for decades. The Exile Tiger had been the youngest of the Orphans. Some of his older colleagues had passed their heritage on to their children within a few decades of their being exiled. This had, of course, created problems of its own. Orphaned orphans had not always cared for their inheritance. Some had rejected it outright, but it would not reject them.

"I didn't ask for this either," Pearl said aloud to the empty hotel room. "I didn't ask, yet here I am. Now with Albert gone . . . Is it worth going on?"

But Pearl knew she would. For one, even if she were to resign her role, that did not mean whoever had gone after the others would leave her alone. Moreover, the Tiger had an interesting problem. The Tiger did not have any children. There was a serious question as to whether or not she had an heir. The auguries Pearl had cast had been more than a little ambivalent on the matter. Probably the Tiger's power would pass to one of her brothers, or to one of their sons and daughters. Probably.

Did that ambivalence make Pearl's life safer, or at greater risk? She wasn't about to wait quietly and find out. Unfortunately, Albert was not available to coordinate the Twelve as he should. Pearl would need allies. Would the others assist her? Would they accept the leadership of an old toothless tiger as once the Orphans had accepted her father?

Are you laughing, Old Tiger? she thought. *Your challenge was that your allies considered you too young. Here I am, wondering if I am too old.*

Pearl looked down at her hands. The once-elegant fingers now showed swelling around the joints. She'd let the jetty hair whose blue-black highlights had been her private pride go silver. She'd resisted the urge to get "just a little bit" of plastic surgery: a tuck, a nip, an injection.

I've let myself grow old outside. Have I grown old inside as well? Can I still lead my people into battle?

Pearl moved restlessly, feeling all the aches of joint and muscle that were her daily companions. Then she smiled.

Of course I can, even if only to spite you, Old Tiger.

She fell asleep with that tiny, infinitely happy smile on her lips, knowing, as an actress never stops knowing her face, how that joy made her face young again.

Pearl's travel alarm beeped a reminder and Pearl opened her eyes. Years of practice had made her skilled at touching up her hair and makeup with a few quick strokes. Tonight she went for the shadows and tints that would accent the features she had inherited from her Chinese father, rather than those from her Hungarian Jewish mother. Tonight was a night to remind her audience, ever so subtly, of her connection to the mystic Orient.

Once the reverse had been the law by which Pearl had ruled herself, seeking to blend into the general population, but the older she became, the closer that old Tiger stalked her, ruling her life in death as he had never wished to in life.

Pearl put her father from her mind and hurried down the corridor to the elevator. Gaheris and Brenda were waiting for her on the ground floor. Brenda's eyes were alight with questions, but she asked not a one until the three were settled at their table at the Hour's Deserve, and the waiters had finished their awed hovering over the faded celebrity and her guests.

However, once drinks were ordered and the gentle hum of conversation and music assured their privacy, Brenda leaned slightly forward.

"Dad told me about the calls, how the people you reached didn't seem to know, well, you know, about Things." She paused, obviously embarrassed, but nonetheless determined. "Then he told me about why we're going to Denver. He said you'd explain how this Dog we're going to find doesn't even know he's a Dog."

Pearl decided not to glower at Gaheris. He couldn't be blamed for briefing his daughter. Pearl would have liked to handle that briefing in her own fashion, but she could adapt the script.

"I said I would answer your questions," she said. "The answer to this one is among the most simple, yet the most complex. I have already told you how the original Orphans were six men and six women. I have also told you how their families were not permitted to come with them into exile."

Brenda nodded, and reached for the cut-crystal water goblet beside her plate. The young woman did not drink, her concentration so intense that she seemed to forget the glass as soon as her fingers wrapped around the stem.

"To understand why the Dog and many of the other lineages became separated from their heritage," Pearl said, "you need to understand that despite the care the Twelve took to make certain their abilities were fixed in their family lines, the refusal of just one heir apparent to learn his or her duties would be enough to complicate matters."

Pearl paused when a waiter arrived with their drinks. Over Gaheris's protests that she need not go to such expense, Pearl insisted on ordering several appetizers for the table. They needed time to talk, and she felt more at ease here than she did in the sterility of a hotel suite.

When the waiter walked away, Gaheris took over.

"Brenda, our family came pretty close to being one of the 'lost' lines. My dad, your grandad, was one of those who resented the tutoring his father had forced him to accept. My grandfather, the Exile Rat, lived until I was eight, and when he died my dad found himself in a real bind. Basically, according to the terms of his father's will, he couldn't inherit his father's estate—and it was a good one—unless he filled me in on what it meant to be the Rat. Moreover, Dad had to pass this information on in front of witnesses, one of whom was Auntie Pearl.

Now, your grandad may have wanted to deny he was a Rat, but he shared the rattish love for gain. He gave in, just as his father had known he would."

Pearl felt a bitter smile rise unbidden as she remembered how the Rat had been beaten by his own nature. "Gaheris's discovery of our shared heritage was not a pretty scene. And at the end of his recitation of family history, your grandfather shoved the mah-jong box at Gaheris and said, 'The damned thing is yours now. May it do you as much good as it ever did me.' Or something like that."

"Pretty close," Gaheris said. "My head was spinning with fairy tales of emperors and magical lore, and then I had this box in my hands with a rat looking up at me from the lid. I'd never even played mah-jong. My dad had been determined that we were going to be the all-American family. We played poker, Go Fish, and Old Maid but I don't think there was as much as a box of dominoes in the house. Auntie Pearl tutored me in what I needed to know, and my dad never stopped resenting that. I think that ate him up. He was a sour man, older than his years, when that heart attack finally got him."

Brenda looked at him. "You decided a middle ground for me, then, right? No sudden revelations, but no childhood indoctrination either."

Gaheris shrugged, and Pearl saw all over again the little boy who had held that heavy box of tiles in his hands and stared up at his father in disbelief.

Brenda seemed to see something, too, because she said softly, "Not too bad, Dad. Not too bad."

Pearl decided they'd better return to the subject of the Dog. This family bonding was lovely, but she wanted Brenda to have more than Gaheris's point of view.

"Not all the Orphans were as fortunate or as conniving as the Rat," Pearl said. "The current Dog is a young man several years older than you are. His father was a soldier, and died before he could tell his son about his heritage. Albert has periodically talked about the need to seek out and educate this young man—Charles is his name—as to his inheritance, but Albert has always shied away from actually acting."

"It wouldn't be an easy thing to do, would it?" Brenda said. "I mean, I'm having a hard enough time accepting this, and my dad is here, and I've known you for as long as I can remember."

"And," Gaheris added, "Albert might have been an egocentric, self-opinionated, pompous ass, but he wasn't one to disrupt someone else's life without reason. The Orphans had sought to pass their abilities on with the direct intention of someday returning to what they thought of as 'home.' However, over a century has gone by. Is there a home for any of us to return to? Perhaps the time for the return home the Thirteen Orphans dreamed of is forever over. What remains is a curious family heritage, but nothing else."

"So I might have agreed," Pearl said, "until now. Someone is hunting the Thirteen Orphans. Someone sees a value in the heritage the Orphans retained. I, for one, have no desire to lose any part of my memory—and I am greatly apprehensive as to what else this stalker might want from us. Will he stop with memories, or will there come a time when he—or she—wants something more?"

"You're making my skin crawl, Auntie Pearl," Brenda said.

"Mine, too," Gaheris said, "but I don't disagree. That's why I'm willing to go to Denver to try and find the Dog, and then take on the nearly impossible task of convincing him he's in danger of losing something he doesn't remember ever having."

"For my part," Pearl said, "I am going to Santa Fe to brief Des Lee—that is, the Rooster. There are things that should not be discussed over the phone. Denver and Santa Fe are an easy day's drive from each other. We five should be able to meet up and share counsel after that."

Appetizers arrived, and with them a waiter hoping to take their entree orders. Pearl discovered she had far more appetite than she had imagined. She decided she could handle a rare filet mignon, and noted that Brenda, who had ordered something to do with scallops and mushrooms, seemed impressed. Gaheris ordered lobster, something he did every time they dined together. He always said that this way, between them, they managed surf and turf.

"Does this 'Des Lee' know about all of this?" Brenda asked.

"Des knows," Pearl said, "and believes. Unlike many of the Orphans, his grandmother married a Chinese. So did his mother. He was raised within the culture, and is inclined to take all the talk of Orphans and zodiac signs as a sort of special family fairy tale. He knows a considerable amount, both theory and practice, but has never really had to utilize all that knowledge for anything serious."

"How old is he?" Brenda asked.

"A bit younger than your father and Albert . . . Somewhere in his thirties. I have trouble remembering. Years go by so quickly."

Gaheris had been methodically sopping a bit of toasted bread with a large spoonful of buttered crab. Now he stopped, the dainty half raised to his lips.

"I've been thinking about that divinitory reading we did. Of the unaffected signs, most were yang: Rat, Tiger, and Dog. Rooster is yin, true. Hare is yin, Tiger's partner. I wonder if there is any significance in that?"

"Possibly," Pearl said. "It also might be a matter of ease of access. If you look at a map, you will see that the unaffected signs also live farther west. Albert is the first of the victims to be touched in this part of the world."

"But the Hare lives in Virginia," Gaheris protested.

"But Nissa is a very social person. She lives with her sisters in an extended family arrangement. Unless she is working, she has her small daughter with her. Nissa would not be one to be conveniently approached by a stranger."

"Dad," Brenda said, "you'd better eat that before it disintegrates."

"Oops!"

Gaheris gulped down the sodden bit of bread, and Brenda looked at Pearl.

"Nissa . . . That doesn't sound Chinese. Who is she?"

"Nissa Nita," Pearl said. "She is the great-granddaughter of the original Hare. She is about your age, a little older, I think."

"But she has a daughter?"

Pearl couldn't decide whether Brenda sounded impressed or appalled.

"A very rabbitlike accident," Gaheris said, trying not to laugh. "The story I heard was that Nissa was on the pill and still managed to get pregnant. She won't tell anyone who the father of her daughter might be, and her entire family is so in love with the little girl that no one cares."

"Noelani," Pearl said, dredging the name from her memory. "That's the baby's name. Every indication is that she will be the next Hare."

"Noelani really doesn't sound Chinese," Brenda said. "I've been wondering. Except for Des Lee's family and maybe that Shen Kung, it sounds like most of the Orphans didn't marry Chinese. How come? And weren't cross-cultural marriages, well, frowned on, back then?"

"You have a Rat's nose for detail," Pearl said, and was glad to see that the young woman took this as a compliment. "The Orphans not only did not marry Chinese, in most cases, they actively sought to marry outside that ethnic group. They were hiding, you recall, and even an immigrant Chinese community was not large enough to hide them. As for the problem of racial intermarriage . . . Well, they tended to find ways around it."

"They changed their appearances," Gaheris explained. "They couldn't eliminate all elements that made them look Chinese, but they could minimize them. Some of the changes were cosmetic or surgical, others were, well . . . wizardly. The alteration wasn't perfect, but it was enough. However, since they couldn't completely alter their genetic heritage, not without eliminating the very traits they were seeking to preserve and pass on, there are throwbacks."

Brenda glanced at her reflection in one of the polished serving pieces. "I'm a little bit of a throwback, aren't I? I always wondered why I'm so dark-haired when all the rest of you have reddish-brown hair."

"That's it," Gaheris said. "You still look enough like both me and your mother that no one really thinks about it, but there's some of the old blood cropping up in you. Your heritage won't be denied, even when you try to deny it."

The waiter was approaching with their entrees. He made a bit of a production out of clearing away appetizers, then setting their selections in front of them.

Pearl sniffed appreciatively at the perfectly cooked rare filet in front of her. "Quite honestly, I have no desire to deny my heritage."

Brenda looked up from cutting a scallop with the edge of her fork. "Your father didn't like that you were going to be the next Tiger, did he?"

"He did not," Pearl said. "The Chinese have never been comfortable with female tigers. Your father mentioned yin and yang signs earlier. There are six of each, but some are, you might say, more yang—or yin—than others. Tigers and Horses are very yang. Hares and—yes, I know it's odd—Rams are very yin. It is a mistake to equate yin with female, yang with male. That is only one of many paired oppositions, but many people do make that equation. My father was a warrior, and he was far from happy that his heir apparent was—as he saw it—unsuited to follow him. He fathered two sons, but no matter how many times he cast the tiles, the omens told him that I was his heir."

"That's so unfair!" Brenda said sympathetically. "Dad, you never felt that way, did you?"

"Never," Gaheris said honestly. "I mean, my dad was a male Rat, and all that yang did was make him hardheaded. I figured a mixture of traits was all for the best."

Brenda smiled lovingly at him. Pearl fought down a distinct sensation of envy. Brenda seemed to sense this and returned her attention to Pearl.

"So, Auntie Pearl, what you're saying is that even though the Orphans manipulated things so that they could pass on their abilities, they didn't have much choice as to who got them."

"That is so. Mostly the firstborn inherited. In a few cases, when a second child was born, the ability slid down the line, as if finding a better fit. That is what my father hoped would happen. When it did not, rather than holding back all I should know, he tutored me with tremendous intensity, but the heart and soul of every lesson was that I was not learning for myself, I was learning in order to be a dutiful daughter and pass on my knowledge to my unborn son, my father's rightful heir."

Pearl cut a bit off her steak and ate it with satisfaction. Brenda kept silence and concentrated on her own meal, then studied Pearl from those amazingly clear eyes.

"You got even with your dad, though, didn't you?" Brenda said. "You don't have any children. What's going to happen to the Tiger after you?"

"I have brothers," Pearl said breezily. "They have sons and daughters, grandsons and granddaughters. One of them will be revealed as my heir when I die."

Or will they? she thought. *I have cast auguries on the birth of each niece and each nephew, and none show promise. Will there be another Tiger, or have I really gotten the old man good? Will the Tiger end with me, and so also end all hopes that the gates between this place and the Lands Born from Smoke and Sacrifice will ever again be opened? Will I know or will I simply be dead? Do I care?*

Pearl knew one answer among all those questions, and considered that answer as she deliberately cut into her filet and watched the red blood seep out and pool on the whiteness of the plate.

She did care, even if not for reasons her father would understand. She did not want to be the one who failed the ancient trust, the one whose stubbornness determined that the Thirteen Orphans could never go home again.

Seated in another rental car, speeding along the open Colorado highway from the airport into Denver proper, Brenda stared down at the photo Auntie Pearl had given her and Dad earlier that morning before they had left the hotel for the airport.

Auntie Pearl was driving—or rather being driven—home to San Jose. There she would do some more research into the status of the "missing" members of the Thirteen Orphans, then take a flight to New Mexico, where she would meet with Des Lee, the Rooster, brief him, and await their report.

"This is the Dog," the old woman had said. "Charles Adolphus, nicknamed Riprap. He was born on a military base in Germany, and in the best tradition of the 'army brat' has lived all over the country, occasionally overseas. Charles was recruited to play professional baseball while he was still in college. He even made it up into the majors for a short time before a shoulder injury put him out of professional sports for good. After that, Charles served a hitch in the army. He got out a few years ago, and has held various odd jobs.

"You two don't have an easy job in front of you. To the best of my knowledge,

Charles knows nothing at all about the peculiar heritage he shares with us. His father was not antagonistic to his role as the Dog, but as far as we know, he had not told his son anything before his death. The inheritance passed rather oddly, so it is possible that Charles Senior didn't know much—but we did confirm that he owned the Dog mah-jong set, and that it's likely Charles Junior owns it now."

"You told us that this Charles's father was a soldier," Brenda had said softly. It was hard for her to imagine not having a father around. She'd felt inclined to like this Charles, sight unseen, even to feel a little sorry for him. Then she'd seen the photo and had gotten a distinct shock.

Charles Adolphus was black. Not coal black, just dark brown, with that soft, fuzzy-looking hair black people had.

Brenda wasn't prejudiced, at least she didn't think she was, but she'd never really had any black friends. The schools where she lived in South Carolina were integrated and all that, but kids tended to hang out with their own kind. Nobody made them. It was just the way things were.

With a nickname like "Riprap," this Charles Adolphus sounded like he might be into gang stuff. Suddenly, Brenda felt not only very young, but very provincial. Semirural, mostly really suburban, South Carolina was not much preparation for meeting a big-city guy, especially one who was called "Riprap."

Brenda looked at the picture again. Auntie Pearl had said it was a few years old, taken when Charles had been discharged from the military.

"Dad," she asked, "what are you going to say to this guy when we find him?"

Gaheris gave her a quick grin, then returned his attention to the road. "I've been wondering that myself. One angle would be to come out and show him some pictures Auntie Pearl has promised to forward to me from her files. She has copies of old photos, pictures of his grandparents and parents, going all the way back to the original Orphan Dog. Then I could explain I'm interested in genealogy, and go from there. What do you think?"

"Possible," Brenda said, trying to imagine how she'd feel if someone came up to her and started talking a similar line. "Maybe."

"Another angle," Dad offered, responding to the hesitation in her voice, rather than to the words, "would be to take the business approach. I did a bit of research while we were waiting for our plane, and apparently Charles Adolphus is seriously involved in sports. My company sells some nice novelty items, nothing tacky."

Brenda nodded, reserving her opinion on the tacky. Those bobble-headed cheerleader dolls in her high-school colors had been the source of lots of teasing, especially when someone had joked that parts other than the heads should be bouncing.

"And if Mr. Adolphus says 'no thanks,' and starts to close the door?"

Dad didn't pause. "Then I go from there to saying that his name sounds familiar, and was his father such and so, and didn't I know the family from this and that. Might work."

"Might."

"You have any better ideas?"

Brenda shrugged. "I guess I keep thinking that if all we had to tell him was the genealogy stuff, then that would be okay. Weird, but okay, but all this other stuff, magic mah-jong boards, exiled emperors, renegade wizards . . . I mean, that's just too weird."

"We don't need to tell him that weird stuff," Dad said, "at least not all at once."

"Why not? I thought that's why we're making this trip."

"We are and we aren't. We're making the trip because the reading Auntie Pearl and I did showed that both Charles and Des were in some sort of danger. As I see it, our job is to put Charles wise that he shouldn't be too trusting of strangers."

"Like us."

"Like anyone other than us. Breni, you're being difficult."

"I'm just trying to understand—understand stuff that I'm not sure that I understand myself."

"You've had to take in a lot, Breni, I know," Dad said. "I never planned to leave you ignorant as to your heritage. Now that all this has started, I'm gladder than ever I didn't delay. The situation is confusing, sure, but better you learn from me than not."

For a moment there was something in her father's tone that made Brenda think he was trying to tell her something more, but when she glanced at him, she decided she was mistaken.

"Read off exit signs for me," Dad said. "I've got to concentrate on this traffic. The way people are driving, you'd think we were in the Wild West."

They planned to go looking for Charles Adolphus later that evening. After they'd arrived at their hotel and checked in, Dad had gotten online, then on his cell phone. He'd confirmed that Charles was working at a nightclub somewhere in a part of downtown Denver that the locals referred to as LoDo.

"But, Dad, I'm not packed for going to a nightclub." Brenda looked at the contents of her open suitcase and frowned. "I'm not really packed for Denver. I'm packed for northern California."

"Your mother said the same thing when I talked to her," Dad said with a grin, "about Denver, that is, not about nightclubs. Look. I still have a living to earn, so why don't you take the rental car and go shopping? I'll trust you not to overspend, but you will need a jacket at night here. The West is pretty informal, so you can probably get by at the club with one of your new pairs of jeans, but if you really need something else . . . just keep the spending reasonable, okay?"

"Do you need a jacket or anything?"

"I have a couple of blazers that should pass. In any case, I'm hoping we won't need to stay at the club very long. We're just using it to make first contact. We'll go from there."

For a cowardly moment, Brenda thought about asking if she could just stay behind, but she banished the temptation. How often had she protested being treated like a kid, even though she was in college? Now Dad was treating her like an adult, and she was trying to weasel.

Or rat, Brenda thought glumly, jingling the car keys in her cupped palm as she rode the elevator down to the ground level. *But doesn't "ratting" mean telling on someone? We sure don't give animals much of a break, equating them with our all-too-human failures. Dog. What does "dog" get stuck with? Dogged. That isn't too bad. Stubborn. Persistent. Better than a rat.*

The man at the front desk drew Brenda a map to a nearby mall. There she found a lined jacket on such a good sale that she didn't think even Dad would mind if she splurged on a new shirt to dress up her jeans. The fabric was one of those brocade prints that said "Chinese," even if she had no idea why. The rich reds and golds went really well with her coloring.

Humming David Bowie's "China Girl," Brenda roamed the mall, trying to get a feel for what made the West, even the modern West, so different from her own Southeast. It had something to do with cows, and with thinking that Native American stick-figure drawings were artistic—which they were once her mind got over comparing them to drawings like a kindergartner might do. It had something to do with brown and turquoise, and a bit with mixing leather and lace.

Brenda enjoyed herself so much, she had to hurry to get back and meet Dad for dinner. They took their time eating, and then Brenda put on her new top and did her hair.

"You look good," Dad said when she emerged from the bathroom. "I feel a little strange taking you out after the time I used to be trying to get you to go to bed, but things change. Always remember that Breni. Things change."

Again Brenda heard that note in his voice, the funny one that seemed to tell her he was saying more than he'd say right out. She had noticed that the box that held the Rat's mah-jong set had been out when she got back, and wondered if her dad had been messing with the tiles.

And what he'd seen if he had been. . . .

But somehow Brenda couldn't bring herself to ask. When Dad was in the bathroom, she sidled over to the box and studied the rat on the lid. The depiction was ornate, full of curves and twisty lines. The rat looked inquisitive and intelligent.

When Brenda heard the toilet flush, she darted into the adjoining room, pretending to have been browsing through a booklet on the attractions offered by Denver and the surrounding area.

"There's a lot to do out here," she said. "More than skiing, I mean."

"Your mom and I have talked from time to time about taking a family trip out this way. Think you'd like to come back later this summer?"

"Depends on if I get that job I applied for, but, yeah, it might be nice."

They drove to the area where Fatal Boots, the club where Charles Adolphus worked, was located. They found that parking nearby was impossible, even though the area looked like one that invited walking. Dad finally slipped the car into a multilevel parking garage, despite the fact that to Brenda the facility looked closed.

"Then no one will mind us parking here," Dad said, but Brenda noticed he was more careful about checking the locks than usual.

If the music pouring out the door onto the street was any indication, Fatal Boots specialized in electrified country. Although Brenda found the night air a bit cool, even with her new jacket zipped to the neck, the locals didn't seem to share her opinion. The pavement in front of the club was crowded with men and women, many of them smoking. A few were dancing under the benignly watchful gaze of a security guard who stood about halfway down the block.

Although she'd gone clubbing at school, Brenda felt self-conscious about walking up to the door with her father. A man seated on a stool near the door checked their IDs.

"No minors in the bar area," he said. "Dance floor is fine. Any sign she's drinking, even a sip from your glass, mister, and we toss you both out. Lady over there will take your cover. Have a good night."

Gaheris paid the cover charge for both of them, and the lady at the register had Brenda stick out her wrist. She slipped a plastic strap printed with the words "Fatal Boots" on it and zipped it snug but not tight.

"Have fun," she said cheerfully. "Band should be on again in just a few minutes."

Perhaps because of the break, they didn't have any trouble finding a table. Gaheris ordered two iced teas and a mixed snack tray from a waitress wearing a red bandanna print skirt that swirled out just below her knees and an artistically faded denim shirt. A matching bandanna was fastened around her neck with a slide closure in the shape of a cowboy boot.

Brenda shrugged out of her jacket, and saw her Chinese top attract a few glances that she thought were admiring rather than otherwise. The club was warm, but not uncomfortably so, and from where they were sitting, the music was muted enough to permit conversation.

When the waitress returned, Dad asked, "Is Charles Adolphus working tonight?"

The waitress shook her head.

"Riprap?" Brenda interjected. "How about Riprap?"

The waitress grinned. "He's here, be back when the band starts up. Want me to tell him you're here?"

Dad scribbled a note on a napkin.

"Sure."

"Run a tab?"

"Let me settle. Don't know how long we can stay, been traveling all day."

From the waitress's expression, Brenda guessed that whatever Dad had slipped into the folder was more than her usual tip.

"I'll let Riprap know you're here," she said.

The band came back before Brenda had done more than sip her tea. They hadn't yet completed their first number, "Big Girls, Big Hair," when a tall, broad-shouldered black man loomed over their table.

He wasn't at all what Brenda had imagined. He wore no gaudy jewelry, not even an earring. His hair wasn't much longer than it had been in the military discharge photo. His Western-style shirt was two-tone denim, trimmed with a narrow border of red bandanna fabric.

"Are you the couple who were asking for Riprap?" he said politely.

His voice had no trace of the accent Brenda had mentally filed under "black." If it had any accent at all, it was a touch of a Western twang.

"That's right," Dad said, getting to his feet and putting out his hand. "I'm Gaheris Morris, and this is my daughter, Brenda. I was wondering if you had time to talk."

"I'm working," Riprap replied politely, shaking Dad's hand, then Brenda's. His fingers were dry and she could feel calluses. "I get off when the club closes, but that's not so late during the week, usually about eleven."

"Do you get a break?" Dad asked.

"Just had one."

Dad nodded, and Brenda could almost see him deciding he had to put his cards on the table. Knowing Dad, he'd have chosen which ones with care.

"Mr. Adolphus," Dad said, "this is going to sound ridiculous and melodramatic, but I was wondering if you would do me the favor of making sure you don't go anywhere alone until I have a chance to speak with you. I've come all the way from California for the express purpose of doing so."

Riprap's polite expression flickered, incredulity showing for a moment. Then he became very, almost too, polite.

"And might I ask why?"

"I have reason to know you may be in danger," Dad said, and Brenda could practically feel him pouring all the force of his personality behind the statement. "I came here to warn you, and to explain, but I understand you need to finish your night's work. Brenda and I will wait, and, if you will permit, we will speak with you after closing."

This time Riprap grinned, a broad, friendly grin that balanced disbelief and amusement.

"Well, if you've come all this way to warn me, least I can do is listen. I usually need time to wind down anyhow. I'll meet you out front a bit after eleven."

Brenda was feeling the drag of two long days, but the music was lively enough to keep her going. She switched to coffee rather than tea, and convinced her dad that a slice of incredibly dense chocolate cake was a necessity, even at a price that would buy an entire cake at the grocery store.

To Brenda's surprise—she was sitting there with her dad, after all—she got several offers to dance. While she was laughing and joking with her various partners, working her way into the unfamiliar dance steps, she took the opportunity to observe Riprap going about his job.

He seemed to be a bouncer, but a bouncer like none Brenda had ever seen before. He broke up one fight just by looking at the two men, and managed to walk one particularly obnoxious drunk out in such a way that Brenda bet that the man thought leaving was his own idea.

A kicking-scratching match between two overly made-up women gave Riprap a little more of a challenge. He didn't seem to want to risk laying hands on them, but he convinced the floridly handsome young man in the oversized cowboy hat who was one of the young women's escorts that he really needed to get his date out into the air.

Brenda didn't hear a word of what Riprap said to convince the other man. It was like watching a silent movie, but she had enough imagination to provide the dialogue.

The end result was that when the band finished playing and the club started clearing out, Brenda found herself anticipating rather than dreading talking to Mr. Charles "Riprap" Adolphus.

She'd seen Riprap glance their way from time to time as the evening had stretched on, and she guessed that he was pretty curious about them, too.

Riprap met them out in front of the club about a quarter after eleven.

"There's lots of places that will still be open," he said, "if you want to grab a cup of coffee and tell me what this is about."

"Sounds good," Gaheris said. "Lead on."

Brenda's nerves were already jangling from too much coffee, so when they got to the all-night diner she ordered a milkshake instead. It came in a tall glass and was topped with melting whipped cream that started running down the side of the glass even before the waitress put the tray on the table. A metal canister contained even more milkshake. Contemplating the probable calories contained within, Brenda began to be very glad she had spent much of the last several hours out on the dance floor.

Dad ordered a slice of cherry pie and coffee. Riprap ordered a towering burger, fries, and a side salad.

"Don't get to eat much after about seven," he explained, starting in on the salad, "at least not on busy nights. Usually grab something while the kitchen staff is cleaning up. Now, Mr. Morris, what is this danger you want to tell me about? Why do I need to watch my back?"

Brenda had wondered what clever angle her father had decided to use to answer that question. He'd carried a briefcase with him, and had sat with it between his feet in the nightclub. She figured Dad had his laptop with him, although the case seemed rather bulky for that, but when he rummaged inside, what he pulled out was the box containing the Rat mah-jong set.

He set it on the table with a dull thump, his gaze fixed on Riprap's face. He opened it to show the contents, then closed it again.

"Have you ever seen one of these?"

Brenda thought there was something guarded in Riprap's expression.

"A mah-jong set? Sure. Guess the game's not so popular as Scrabble, but people still play it."

Dad shoved the heavy box across the table. "I meant a set like this one. Go ahead. Open the box. Take a look. It's an antique, but it's seen lots of use. Those pieces were made for handling."

Riprap opened the lid of the box with one broad thumb against the edge. He examined the pieces inside without touching them. His expression remained neutral. Too neutral, Brenda decided. Either he should be asking questions or he should be thinking Dad was crazy and making excuses to get away. Instead, his demeanor had settled into something like guarded watchfulness.

"Nice," he commented at last, when neither Brenda nor Gaheris broke the silence. He picked up one piece—a three of characters—at random. "You're right. It's old. Bone and bamboo pieces, not plastic like most of the ones I've seen. Even those sets can run over a hundred dollars. This set must be a lot more expensive."

"Priceless," Dad said. "It's one of only thirteen such sets ever made. I had word that you might own one of the others, Mr. Adolphus."

Riprap looked at him, "And owning an antique mah-jong set is going to put me in danger . . . how?"

"You do own it?"

"Time for you to answer a question or two, Mr. Morris. Otherwise, I think I'll just enjoy my burger and chat with Ms. Morris here about how well she did out there on the dance floor."

Riprap's burger was just arriving then, and he took a big bite and chewed thoughtfully, his gaze never leaving Gaheris Morris's face.

"Very well," Gaheris said. "I'd like to say that I let my fondness for the melodramatic get away with me, that by 'danger' I meant getting robbed by an unscrupulous antiques dealer or some such, but I only spoke the truth."

Riprap ate another bite of his burger. Brenda, impatient to get things moving, but not knowing exactly what she'd say if she did speak, sucked on her shake. It was good. Real ice cream, not powdered whatever like fast-food milkshakes.

"I mentioned that only thirteen of these mah-jong sets were made," Gaheris went on. "I should be more precise. Each set is unique, but the thirteen sets were related, made for a group of thirteen friends. My grandfather was one of those. Your great-grandfather was another."

"This set is Chinese work," Riprap commented, gesturing toward the still-open box with a French fry before dipping it in ketchup, "made for the Chinese, or possibly the Japanese market. You can tell because there are no Arabic numbers on the tiles. Sets made for issue in Europe and the United States had Arabic numbers printed on them, and sometimes letters printed on the 'wind' tiles. Chinese and Japanese sets didn't need those indicators because they could read the tiles."

Riprap ate the French fry, then went on, "You don't look Chinese. Your daughter . . . Maybe she does a little if I stretch my imagination. She could be part a lot of ethnicities, though. There are Eastern Europeans who have those same long eyes. And me, I don't look at all Chinese, yet you're saying my great-grandfather was Chinese?"

"I'm saying your great-grandfather had a mah-jong set made specifically for him," Gaheris countered. "And, yes, his heritage was more Chinese than otherwise."

Riprap had finished his burger, but he continued on his fries. "Go on. You were talking about danger, back before you started talking about mah-jong."

"Are you familiar with generational feuds?" Gaheris went on.

"Sure."

"Well, being the descendant of your great-grandfather has set you up to be targeted by one such feud."

"Me? And what about my sisters? What about my cousins? My grandfather wasn't an only child, you know. Neither was my father. There are lots of Adolphus kin out there."

"That's why I asked you about the mah-jong set," Dad said. "Did you inherit the mah-jong set?"

"Do you want it?"

"No! I just want to know if you have it."

Brenda looked at Riprap, watching his expression so intensely that she didn't realize that she'd emptied her milkshake until a rude sucking noise broke the waiting silence. She jumped, and felt her cheeks get hot, but neither of the men looked at her. Their gazes were locked, and she could feel the tension between them as if it were something physical.

At last, Riprap spoke very softly. "Tell me what would be on the lid of the box holding my great-grandfather's set."

Brenda heard herself answering, "A dog. The Dog."

"And yours has a rat. The Rat." Riprap looked back and forth between them. When he spoke next, to Brenda's surprise, he spoke to her. "I've got the set. The lid's the match to yours, but it shows a dog on it. Big dog, sort of like a chow, but meaner-looking than most chows I've seen. Tiles inside are a lot like yours. Now, what of it?"

Dad countered, "What do you know about why these sets were made?"

Riprap seemed to relent all at once. "I know more than you think I do, that's clear enough. My dad left letters for me, along with the box. He knew a soldier couldn't count on coming home. I know why those mah-jong sets were made is something we shouldn't discuss here, not if I want these nice people who run the diner to think I'm sane, and I do because I like how they cook. I also know that there hasn't been a wink or whimper of trouble for several generations. Why should there be now?"

"I don't know," Dad admitted, matching frankness with frankness. "If you would come to our hotel, I could show you what alarmed me enough to end my holiday in California and come here to warn you. Or I could send you off with a warning and tell you to check for yourself. All I ask is that you take us seriously."

"Interrupted your holiday?"

Impulsively, Brenda dug into her purse and came up with the stub of her boarding pass.

"Look for yourself. I can show you my driver's licence. We live in South Carolina. I've been up since way too early, and my body doesn't even know what time zone I'm in anymore."

She heard a trace of a whine in her voice, and hated herself for it, but she couldn't help it. She was suddenly all too aware that it was closing on midnight here, which was probably something like after two at home, and she'd been on and off planes two days running, and up at dawn both days. Caffeine and sugar were making her feel like her brain and body were disconnected. She wanted to sleep, and at the same time felt like she'd never manage to sleep again.

Riprap studied the stub of the boarding pass.

"Where are you parked?"

"In a garage a few blocks over," Gaheris said.

"Right. Let me walk you to your car. Then you can drive me over to mine, and I'll drive straight home with the car doors locked. Consider me warned and careful, but Ms. Morris is not the only one who has had a long day."

"You want to confirm what I've told you," Gaheris said. "I have no problem with that."

He reached and picked the check up off the edge of the table, took out his credit card, and waved for the waitress.

"Here's my phone number and the number of the hotel," he went on, sliding one of his business cards and one of the hotel's across the table. "Can I have a phone number for you?"

Riprap wrote neatly on a paper napkin.

"Sure. Cell and home. I check my messages."

"When can we call you?"

"I'll call you around noon. I want at least eight hours' sleep."

"Noon then."

They made the walk to the parking garage in a near silence that felt like a screamed argument. The night was distinctly cold, and Brenda pulled her jacket closer around her.

The parking garage was dark, lit mostly by a few security lights and the red glow of Exit signs.

"Gate's up," Riprap said, "but I don't think they're exactly open for business."

"Couldn't find a place," Dad said, "and just pulled in."

"Should be okay," Riprap said, but Brenda was aware that he was looking from side to side, checking the shadows. His gaze was alert, and Brenda had the feeling that if he really were a dog, his hackles would be up.

The rental car sat alone in a pool of pale yellowish white light near a concrete pillar. Almost alone. As they advanced toward it, their three pairs of shoes sounding sharply against the pavement as they unconsciously sped up to get to the safety of the car, someone stepped out from behind the pillar.

Even in the poor light, there was no doubt he was Chinese. He wore long robes of dark green fabric. They were embroidered with elaborate designs and possessed voluminous sleeves. His hair was sleeked back, nearly hidden beneath a round cap with a button on top. He was clean-shaven, but that was all Brenda could make out of his features, for he held his face averted. The stranger's hands were crossed in front of him, hidden within the wide bells of his sleeves.

Brenda stopped midstep in astonishment and fear, aware that on either side of her, her dad and Riprap had stopped as well. For a long moment, no one moved; then the stranger whipped his hands free of the concealing sleeves and made a throwing motion.

Something long and yellow snapped through the air toward them.

"Brenda, down!" Dad yelled.

6

At Dad's command, Brenda dove for the pavement. Her hands caught on the concrete, but most of the impact went into the sleeves of her new jacket. She felt the fabric shredding, but she was too scared to feel regret. Instead she rolled to one side, putting one of the concrete support pillars between her and the strange man over by the rental car.

Neither Dad nor Riprap had followed her down, instead splitting wide. She could hear the soles of their shoes against the bare concrete as they ran for cover. She realized she was listening for something else, the report of a gun, the clatter of a knife, something to indicate what it was the man in the Chinese clothes had thrown toward them. There was nothing.

She peered cautiously around her pillar. She couldn't see either Dad or Riprap, so she figured they'd gotten to cover. The Chinese man was just standing there, his hands back within his sleeves, his back against the driver's side of the car. His posture was the embodiment of watchful patience, and something about it chilled her to the bone.

It's like he's got all night, she thought. *All night and all day, like no one is going to come in here and interrupt this standoff. Like we won't just pick up and leave.*

"Dad!" she called. "Let's get out of here!"

There was no answer. Brenda's words echoed for a moment in the empty space, then left the parking garage emptier than before. Brenda pulled herself up a little higher, trying to see where her dad and Riprap had gotten to. They couldn't be too far.

Then she spotted her dad. He was down at ground level, crouched so low that he was almost on all fours. He was moving from shadow to shadow, each step taking him a bit closer to the Chinese man by the car.

Brenda's vision blurred, and she rubbed her eyes against her torn jacket sleeve, but when she looked again the blurring was still there. It surrounded Gaheris Morris, a grey mist denser than the surrounding shadow. It took form as she stared at it, resolving so that her father seemed swallowed by the mist, leaving only a grey rat creeping across the pavement.

Brenda stifled a scream. She forced herself to look, and when she did so she could see her father again. He was there, inside the rat, or rather he was the rat, or somehow he wasn't really a rat, not changed into one, but he'd worked things so that he was no more noticeable than a rat would be.

Dad isn't running, she thought. *Why isn't he getting out of here? It can't be he wants to protect the rental car. It must be . . .*

With a flash of insight, Brenda understood. Her dad wanted to capture the Chinese man, wanted to talk to him. They already knew something bad was going on, but they had no idea why or what. If they ran, their enemy would be free to stalk them again, with them none the wiser. But if they could get hold of the stranger, learn something from him . . .

Go for it, Dad, Brenda thought. *And you're not going to do it alone. I don't know where that Dog went, but I'm here, and I'll just . . .*

She rose to her feet, and walked out from behind the concrete pillar. Somehow she felt completely confident that whatever the strange man wanted, she was relatively safe. After all, she wasn't one of the Thirteen; she was only the daughter of the Rat.

And he didn't hurt Albert Yu, at least I don't think he did, not physically. So I'll just provide a distraction for Dad.

Brenda shot a quick glance over at Dad, and thought the man within the rat was trying to warn her back.

Don't worry, Dad. I'm fine. Just do your thing.

"Wow," Brenda said, weaving a little. "Is there an after-hours costume party going on around here? You look just marvelous. Maybe you need a date? I've got a Chinese top. I mean, it's sort of Chinese. I got it at a department store, but would it do?"

She was unzipping her jacket as she moved, acting a little drunk. The Chinese man reacted for the first time, turning his head to look in her direction. He was younger than she had thought, and drop-dead gorgeous. His eyes were dark and mysterious, and he had the most sensuous mouth she'd ever seen. Suddenly, it wasn't at all hard to act unsteady on her feet.

"My dad was here, and his friend, but you look like a lot more fun. I wonder where they went?"

Brenda let her voice go a bit high, like she was musing aloud, and moved a few steps closer. The Chinese man removed his hands from his sleeves. His right hand held what looked like a long strip of very heavy paper, or maybe lightweight cardboard, ornamented with Chinese writing, green ink against black paper. The writing seemed to glow, the last glimmer of thought against a night-dark sky.

"You can see me? How can you see me?"

The young man spoke perfect English, but with a music Brenda had never heard before.

"I can see you, honey," she said. "No problem."

"You should not be able to see me." He started moving away from her, sliding alongside the car. "That cannot be. Only thirteen should be able to see me, and you are not one of them."

"I can see you," Brenda repeated, wondering where her dad was, what had happened to Riprap. Should she just tackle this guy? It didn't sound like a completely bad idea. Looking at him made her tingle.

What is wrong with me? Maybe that milkshake was spiked.

The Chinese man had reached the front of the car and was pivoting, apparently getting ready to run. As he turned, Gaheris Morris stepped out from behind a pillar. The mist was gone, but Brenda thought she could see traces of it clinging to him.

"Hold on, young man," Gaheris said. "I want to talk to you."

"Me, too," came Riprap's voice. He stepped out and blocked the young man's forward escape route. "I'm wondering where you got those threads. They're cool."

The young man's expression changed. All traces of nervousness left him. He went from stillness to motion without a hint of transition, charging directly toward Gaheris Morris. He flung out his right hand, and the piece of paper flew from his fingers, cutting through the air like a knife blade.

Brenda screamed as it wrapped itself around her dad's face, covering his left eye, the bridge of his nose, sealing one corner of his mouth.

The Chinese man continued his forward motion, and Brenda thought she saw him touch her dad with something small and round, but she couldn't be sure. Too much was happening. She kept expecting her dad to reach up and rip the paper off his face, but he just stood there. Then the paper started sinking, melting into the flesh of Gaheris Morris's face.

Brenda stifled another scream with her clenched fist and ran forward, not knowing whether to grab the Chinese man, or to root out whatever it was that was burying itself in her father's face. She managed to do neither. Although she crossed the intervening space with the speed born from pure panic, the black paper was vanishing like frost on a windowpane with the first touch of sun.

The Chinese man was vanishing too. She caught a glimpse of his features as he faded away, as if his very existence had been tied to the paper he had thrown. Her only comfort was that his expression held raw confusion. Clearly, events had not gone according to plan.

"Dad!" Brenda said, keeping herself from screaming with an effort, reaching up and touching his face. "Dad! Are you all right?"

"I'm fine," he said. "Are the muggers gone? Are you all right? I'm sorry I pushed you down, but I thought one of them had a gun."

"There was only one," she said, beginning to understand with a horrible certainly what must have happened. "A young man, maybe a bit older than me."

"That may be all you saw, Breni," Dad said, patting her arm. "I saw more. I'm certainly glad Mr. Adolphus decided to walk us back to the car. Denver is a lot more dangerous than I realized."

Riprap was staring at them both. Then he bent and picked up something from the pavement near the car. It was another of those strips of paper, the yellow one the young man had thrown first. Although the green writing on it looked like Chinese to Brenda, it seemed to decide something for Riprap.

"We'd better get out of here, Mr. Morris, in case the muggers come back. I'll tell you where I'm parked."

"Good idea," Dad said. He looked at Brenda again. "Sorry you ripped your jacket, Breni. I'll get you a new one."

"No problem, Dad," she said weakly.

During the short drive over to where Riprap had parked his car, Brenda asked a few questions, but it was the thing with Albert Yu all over again. Mention of neither mah-jong nor of the number thirteen brought any hint that her father remembered them as significant.

Finally, in desperation she said, "But, Dad, what about the Thirteen Orphans?"

"Isn't it a little late to go to a movie, Breni? In any case, you know my feelings about first-run theaters. They're really too expensive."

Brenda wanted to cry. The only thing that kept her from feeling she was going crazy was the look Riprap gave her when he got out of the car. The look said, *I remember. You're not nuts.*

What Riprap said aloud was "I'll call you in the morning, Mr. Morris, so we can discuss that business offer."

"I'll look to hear from you about noon," Dad replied cheerfully.

Brenda hid a shiver. That reference to "noon" showed how selective whatever had happened to Dad's memory was. He remembered that Riprap had said he'd call around noon the next day, but not why the other man was going to call.

"Or earlier," Riprap said, getting into his car. "Maybe much earlier."

Then he slammed the door. Brenda heard the locks snap shut before he started the engine.

Gaheris Morris pulled out into the street, and headed for the hotel, but for all his cheerful chatter along the way about the tourist sights they might hunt out and what souvenirs they should buy for her mother and brothers, Brenda couldn't help but feel that a complete stranger was driving the car.

The rest of that night and the early morning was a nightmare. Exhaustion let Brenda sleep, but it was a sleep tormented by nightmares. In the morning, she tried to prompt her dad's memory, even going so far as to pull out the mah-jong set and ask him for a game.

His answer chilled her. "Not now, Breni. I can't think why I brought that heavy old thing with me. It should be in a safe, or maybe a museum. Old man's folly, I suppose. Let me get my slides in order. I think Mr. Adolphus might make a good client."

So Brenda left her dad to organize slides of custom bobbleheads and other sports paraphernalia that she suspected Riprap Adolphus would have as little interest in as she did. She thought about asking to take the car out shopping, but didn't want to risk missing Riprap's call.

Anyhow, she was a little scared. What if that Chinese man was out there, stalking them? He'd looked startled right before he'd done that queer vanishing act, but whatever he'd done to Dad might have given him confidence.

Instead, Brenda took the mah-jong set and vanished back into the bedroom section of the suite. The room was equipped with a desk, probably in case two people were traveling together and both needed a place to work.

Setting the box on the desk, Brenda studied the ornamentation on the lid. Although the lid of the case was a masterpiece of elaborate inlay, the style in which the rat itself was represented reminded her of Chinese paper cuttings she'd seen. The lines were curved and sinuous, really quite lovely. The rat looked neither cute, like the rats and mice that seemed to be just about omnipresent in kiddie stories, nor sleazy and sinister, like rats in horror fiction.

For all that it was depicted in a few rather simple lines, the rat presented an impression of flexible strength, of tenacity. Brenda found herself thinking that if one had to be the Rat, perhaps this was not too bad a rat to be.

Dad was still busy at his computer, so Brenda opened the box and inspected the tiles stacked on top. The box held a row of ten across, and five down. There were three such layers, with a few empty spaces, making for a total of 148 tiles—four more than were needed to play the game.

Brenda sat cupping one of the red dragon tiles in her hand, remembering how Dad had implied that there was more to the red dragon—to any of the mah-jong tiles—than he had time to explain at that time. He and Pearl had made really clear there was lots you could do with a set of mah-jong tiles. Brenda knew one of those things now. You could use them to divine how twelve other people were doing. What other things could you do?

What other . . . Brenda almost hesitated to frame the word in her mind . . . other magics could you work?

She stared down at the red dragon tile, letting her imagination wander. Her eyes blurred and her vision became unclear. For a moment it seemed like the rectangle stretched out, elongating in all four directions. The image became three-dimensional. The line in the middle no longer touched the sides, but went directly though the center of the square, pointing toward something.

Brenda leaned forward to see . . .

Dunt-da-da-dunt-da-da-dunt-dunt-dunt!

In the other room, her dad's cell phone chirped out a brief rendition of the Lone Ranger's theme, and Brenda jumped. The tile in her hand was nothing but a bit of bone and bamboo.

"Yes? This is Gaheris Morris."

Brief pause.

"Mr. Adolphus! You're up early. Would you like to come by our hotel or is there somewhere you would prefer to meet? Okay. Do you know where . . ."

Brenda stopped listening as her dad started giving directions, concentrating on fighting down relief that Riprap hadn't decided they were crazy Southern whites having on an honest black man. He was coming. Maybe they'd get a chance to talk. How quickly things had changed. Yesterday she'd wondered if she'd know how to talk to a black person. Today she couldn't wait for a chance to talk to this particular one.

Brenda set the red dragon tile back beside its companions in the box, and tried to think how she'd manage to arrange a private chat with Riprap. A few ideas came to mind, but she knew she'd need to refine them when she had a sense of how Riprap was reacting to the situation.

Dad had come to the door of the bedroom.

"Breni, that was Mr. Adolphus. He's going to be here in half an hour, maybe twenty minutes if traffic isn't too bad. I thought I'd show him my presentation, then offer to take him to lunch somewhere. Least I can do, even if we don't make a deal."

Brenda nodded agreement, then decided to try jogging Dad's memory one more time.

"Hey, Dad. I was looking at these again. Do you remember which are the flowers and which are the seasons? This set is different from our set at home."

He moved over to her side. Brenda pointed with her finger at the flower and season tiles, the only tiles in the mah-jong set that could be considered unique, because, although there were two groupings of four tiles each, each flower and season was unique in itself.

Gaheris Morris pointed, "Those would be the flowers, Breni. You can see that there are four distinctly different plants. Therefore, the others would be the seasons. Our set at home does have different pictures, doesn't it?"

He leaned forward. Brenda held her breath, hoping something was awakening. She concentrated on keeping him looking, begging for one of those ancient tiles to contain something that would break through to his real memories. However, when after a few moments of studious inspection Dad stood up, his words were disappointing.

"That one tile definitely shows a bamboo, but as for the others, I can't tell. We should compare with our set at home."

He tousled her hair, and then went briskly back to his computer. She heard him humming what sounded like a college fight song.

Brenda stared down at the tiles. The flowers and seasons were marked with characters in Chinese that she was willing to bet said which was which. Her dad had been speaking Chinese just yesterday, fluently even. Had he forgotten how to do that, too? Or wasn't he interested enough to make out faded signs inscribed into old bone?

As she stared down at the tiles, once again the figures blurred and her vision became unclear, but this time the reason was nothing more than her eyes flooding with tears.

When Riprap arrived, closer to the twenty-minute mark than the half-hour, Brenda had put the mah-jong set away, washed her face, and combed her hair. The hotel room was comfortable enough that the clothing she'd packed for California would do.

Riprap greeted them both with the exactly right measure of friendliness and formality; then he let Gaheris put him in a chair where they could both look at the computer screen. Brenda sat on the small sofa to one side, trying to read the book she'd brought for the plane, and listening to them talk.

She gathered that Riprap played several sports, but that these days he was mostly a coach for various teams of junior-high and high-school-aged kids. Most of these were not affiliated with schools, but with organizations like church groups or the Y or Boys and Girls Clubs of America.

That was why Riprap worked as a bouncer, so his afternoons and early evenings would be free, and so he would have a flexible schedule on those occasions when one of his teams went on the road. It also became clear that he was passionate about what he did.

"Denver is not New York or L.A., Mr. Morris," Riprap said. "In fact, there's a saying around here that you know you're from Denver if you think Five Points is a slum. Even so, we have our problems with drugs and gangs. Sports can fill some of the same need to belong, to be a part of something. Shirts like these your company sells, even hats or decals, those can substitute for gang signs, give a sense of belonging that has nothing to do with crime."

Brenda wondered if her dad was disappointed that Riprap didn't have any big account to draw on, but he didn't seem to be. Maybe he hoped the Boys and Girls Clubs or the Y would come through. Maybe he was just being nice. Dad supported similar groups back home. No matter how prosperous an area was, there were always those at risk.

"Why don't we go out to lunch and talk about this more?" Dad said. "Is there anyplace near here you can suggest?"

Riprap suggested a Mexican place. "It's going to be different from what you get at a Taco Bell, but it'll be good."

It was, and over the meal Brenda found herself drawn into the conversation.

She had played some sports, mostly soccer and volleyball, in high school. Riprap had a way of listening that made her want to tell a few of her favorite stories. By the time they were finishing their meal, she'd almost forgotten the craziness of the night before.

She remembered, though, when Riprap said, "How long are you going to be in Denver, Mr. Morris?"

"A few days, give or take," came the reply. "We're driving to Santa Fe to meet up with an old friend of my family. You might have heard of her. She was a famous actress once. Pearl Bright?"

"Shirley Temple's rival? Or was she her successor as the big child star? Sure. I've heard of Pearl Bright."

Brenda, marveling that Dad remembered that they were to meet Auntie Pearl, even if he had forgotten why, nearly missed what Riprap said next.

"Listen, it's going to be pretty dull for Brenda to sit around the hotel room while you work out that proposal you want to give me. Why don't I take her and show her some tourist sights. Our natural history museum is pretty well known, and there's a nice open park right next to it."

Dad looked at Brenda. "What do you think, Breni? I know you had a late night last night, so if you want to catch a nap?"

He was giving her a way out, if she wanted one, and Brenda appreciated that Dad didn't expect her to entertain someone who clearly he thought of as nothing more than a business contact.

"I'd like to get out, Dad, if you don't mind."

"I don't. You have your cell phone?"

They made arrangements. Back at the hotel, Brenda made an excuse about needing a few things from the room. Feeling like a thief, she grabbed the Rat mah-jong set and bundled it into her backpack. She thought Dad would be okay, but she was worried that the mysterious Chinese man might come back for the set. She remembered, too, how Auntie Pearl had taken Albert Yu's set.

Maybe the mah-jong sets weren't important. Their enemy seemed not to think so, but if Auntie Pearl thought Albert's set had been worth having, Brenda would follow her lead. Brenda stuffed her torn jacket on top of the mah-jong set and hurried down. She found Dad and Riprap leaning on the hood of Riprap's car, sketching some sort of sports logo.

Five more minutes of that, then Dad was on his way inside, and Brenda was in a car with a man who she'd not known existed two days ago, but who was connected to her by shared memories of the strange events of the night before.

"Your dad seems like a nice guy," Riprap said once they were on the road.

"He is a nice guy," Brenda responded a trace defensively.

"Hey, easy." Riprap glanced over at her. "Am I right that something happened last night that, well, changed him?"

"Yeah." Brenda ran a hand through her hair, searching for words. "The weird thing is, the only things that have changed are things that I didn't know existed until two days ago. Superficially, he's Dad like he's always been."

"Would you tell me what's missing?"

Brenda began. Then she realized that to do so, she'd also need to tell about what had happened to Albert Yu.

"I'll tell you, promise, but first I'd like to hear your story."

"You mean about my connection to all of this?"

Brenda nodded. "Until two days ago, I didn't know anything. From what you said in the diner, you know a lot more."

"Okay. Fair enough. I was going to tell you today anyhow. My dad was in the army. He was an officer, and we traveled a lot, especially when I was younger."

"Is yours a big family?"

"I've got two sisters, both younger."

"Hey! I've got two younger brothers . . . Dylan and Thomas. Dylan's going to be a junior in high school. Thomas will be in seventh grade. It's sort of a mirror image of your family."

Riprap didn't take his eyes off the road, but she saw him smile. "My sisters are both grown. Lily's a nurse. Tammy does computer data entry. They both are married and have little kids."

He changed lanes. "Especially after Tammy was born, we didn't always travel with Dad. Sometimes he had posts in places that weren't great for families. Then we'd come back here to Denver and stay. My mom's from here, and her family's all through the area. My folks had gotten married pretty young, and so I'd already moved out on my own when, five years ago, the word came that Dad wasn't coming back from his current tour."

Riprap's voice slowed and got choked up on that last sentence, and Brenda didn't know what to say.

"I'm sorry," she managed at last, feeling completely inadequate. "Really sorry."

"Thanks." Riprap drove for a couple of blocks in silence, maybe just concentrating on the increasing traffic, maybe not. Then he went on. "After the funeral was when I learned that the stories my dad had told me and my sisters when we were small, basically, for as long as we'd listen, weren't fairy tales like we'd thought. They were history. Family history.

"Dad left each of us something personal. I got the mah-jong set. When I took it home and opened it up, remembering how Dad would only let us play with that set on special occasions because it was an antique, I found there was a little envelope inside the case. The envelope contained the key to a safe deposit box, and in that box was . . . well, it was sort of like a stack of letters, and sort of like a journal. I still remember the first part. I read it over and over, unable to believe it.

"It began, 'Dear Riprap. Remember the stories I told you, the ones about the brave Dog who came from China, and how his enemies chased him, and how he lost his master and one day hoped to find him again? They're true. Each and every one of them. They're part of our family history, a part that has a special place for you.' "

"That had to have been . . ." Brenda paused. "Amazing. Astonishing. Did you believe it?"

"Not at first," Riprap admitted. "I thought he'd written a novel or something, and wanted me to get it published for him. I kept reading, waiting for Dad to tell me that the stories were 'real' to him the way a good book or movie gets real if you really sink yourself into it. He didn't though. After repeating a lot of what had been in the Brave Dog stories, he started telling me about the mah-jong set, and how it could be used for a few things, like telling who was to be the next Dog.

"He ended up by saying 'Riprap, you're probably wondering why I didn't tell you this before. I guess the truth is, I didn't want to alienate you. I'd meant to tell you all along. That's what those stories were for, so you'd have a foundation. Then when I was about ready, something would come up. I'd be gone, or you'd have a test, or there was some big game and I didn't want to rattle you. I thought I'd have a long time. I'm not that old.

" 'I have a bad feeling about this upcoming tour, though, and so I'm not taking any chances. Here it is, with my apologies that I didn't do more to prepare you.' "

Riprap hit the turn signal with unnecessary force and turned his car in to a paved lot on the edge of a park that bordered a pretty large pond, maybe even a small lake. Signs indicated the direction to the natural history museum.

Riprap muttered softly, "My dad didn't need to apologize. He did just fine."

"I'm sorry," Brenda said again. She heard the echo of her words to Dad that night when they'd gone out to dinner with Auntie Pearl, and Dad had told her about his dad.

Her heart ached for Riprap. At least she'd gotten to tell Dad in person that he hadn't messed up. She fished around for something else to say. "When you were repeating what he wrote, you had him call you 'Riprap.' Is that what he called you?"

"My nickname from the first time Dad had to go away and leave the family back in the States," Riprap said, easing the car into a parking space and switching off the engine. "You know what riprap is?"

"I don't," Brenda admitted. "I thought maybe it had something to do with rap music maybe."

Riprap laughed and got out of the car. "Nope. Nothing like that, though you're not the first to think so. You've seen riprap, even if you've never looked twice. Riprap's those heaps of stones that are used to curb erosion or for the foundation of something, loose rocks, piled tight. They hold things together, even though nothing is holding them together."

"Oh."

"When Dad first went on a tour where the family couldn't go along, I wasn't more than about eight. People who meant well kept saying things like, 'Charlie, you're going to have to be the man of the family now, and help your mama.' I got pretty scared. I went to my dad and asked him if he really had to go, because I wasn't at all sure I could hold even myself together. He took me for a walk, and showed me where some riprap was, and then he said, 'Charlie, what's holding those rocks together?'

"'Nothing,' I said, 'except that they're all together.' And Dad said, 'That's right, and yet they are so strong in that being together that they can hold up whole buildings, and keep rivers from eating away their banks. That's all you need to do while I'm gone, Charlie, be riprap. Hold yourself together, hold on to your mama and sisters, and everything will be fine.'"

Brenda shook her head in disbelief. "That's a lot to put on a kid."

"Not really. All Dad was saying was that I just had to be myself, and the rest would follow. He was saying I didn't need to be the man of the family. He was saying I could just be me—or Riprap. That's what he started calling me before he went, and pretty soon everyone else was too. I liked it. Charlie's a family name, and being called Riprap made me feel like a unique me, not just one of the Charlies."

"I guess, but it still seems like a lot."

They'd left the car and started walking while Riprap told his story, going through the parking lot, and down through some plantings of roses toward the lake. The air blowing off the water was brisk, and Brenda's long-sleeved shirt didn't seem quite warm enough.

"Hang on a minute. I want to get my jacket on."

Riprap waited, standing politely, and not looking to see what else was in the daypack, although Brenda bet he'd guessed.

"That jacket got pretty torn last night," he said. "Did you hurt yourself when you hit the pavement?"

"I'm a little bruised," Brenda admitted, "but less than I thought I'd be. I've been helping my brother Dylan practice his soccer scores. Goalies do a lot of diving."

"Good. You want to walk, or go into the museum?"

"Let's walk a bit. It's easier to talk without being overheard."

"Right."

And it might be harder for someone wearing Chinese robes to sneak up on us, Brenda thought.

"I haven't forgotten that I promised to tell you about what's changed with my dad," she said, "but would you answer a couple questions?"

"Ask. I'll tell you if I can."

"Okay. You said your dad said the mah-jong set could be used to do other stuff than play the game. Can you tell me what?"

"Sure, but I don't know much. One is that it can be used to check the well-being of twelve other people."

He glanced at her, and she nodded that she understood.

"The other thing Dad knew how to do was read who would inherit being the Dog. Apparently, it doesn't always shift to the current holder's kid. That's part of the reason my family lost touch with the other Orphans. My dad inherited from an aunt, and that aunt wasn't sure she liked that her kids were being passed by. She told my dad the bare minimum, and, of course, the mah-jong set didn't come to him until after her death. My great-aunt didn't even tell Dad who the other Twelve Orphans were.

"My dad did a lot of research, though, and asked his mom, whose older sister this aunt was, for family stories and such. That's the material he used to create the Brave Dog stories. To be honest, I'm not sure how exaggerated the Dog's deeds might have been. Good stories tend to grow in the telling. What's your other question?"

"I saw you pick something up last night. It looked like the piece of paper that man threw at my dad. Was it?"

Riprap hesitated, and Brenda thought he wasn't going to answer. Then he said, "I've got it with me. Come over to that bench out of the wind while I pull it out."

Brenda obeyed, and Riprap fished a small folder out of the long pocket on the inside of his windbreaker. He opened it, and let her examine what it held. On the surface, it was not very impressive: a long strip of pale yellow paper on which had been written in bright green ink five or so Chinese characters.

"Do you know what they say?" Brenda asked.

"No, and, sort of, yes. You see that one character there? The one that looks like a small 't' walking with a raindrop next to it?"

"Yeah."

"That's the character for 'Dog.' I think that man was throwing this at me."

Looking at the slip of yellow paper and thinking how a similar one had melted into her father's face made Brenda shiver, never mind that her torn jacket was perfectly warm. She sprang to her feet and started walking.

As soon as Riprap joined her, Brenda told him everything she could recall, starting with going to see Albert Yu, and what had happened there, then repeating what Auntie Pearl had told her.

Riprap was a good listener.

"So your dad really hasn't changed a lot," he said when she had finished.

"No," Brenda agreed. "That's what has me so crazy. I mean, a week ago, he'd just seem like Dad. Now he seems like Dad, but not . . . What scares me is how well he fits things together around what must be holes in his memory. Like this morning he remembered meeting you, even remembered that you were going to call around noon, and he made up a reason why. But he didn't remember the real reason that meeting had been set up. I'm sure of it."

"And if you hadn't been there, and he hadn't confided in you, no one would know the difference."

"That's right. No one but Auntie Pearl, I guess, and some other members of the Thirteen—if they remember anything about anything. If this had happened some other way, Auntie Pearl might not even know, not for weeks or probably even months. It's not like we live in the same city and get together a lot."

"I'd like to meet this 'Auntie Pearl,'" Riprap said. "The notes my dad left talked about the Tiger, but they never mentioned who she was. Actually, I thought the Tiger was a he."

"I wonder if your dad knew," Brenda said. "Auntie Pearl inherited from her father, and your family might have been already 'lost' when she took over."

"True. Tell me. If I found an excuse to get to Santa Fe while you're there, do you think you can arrange introductions?"

"Count on it. The plan from the start was for all of us to meet up and talk. Dad may have forgotten, but I haven't."

Pearl Bright walked briskly along the sidewalk bordering the east side of the Santa Fe plaza, glancing into the shopwindows as she went along, but seeing very little of the colorful chaos displayed within.

The store that was her destination was adorned with, in comparison to its neighbors, relatively sedate window displays, but this did not mean that the clothing that was the focus of those displays was any less expensive. A relatively simple men's shirt might be had for several hundred dollars, a woman's skirt for three or four times that amount.

Pearl paused in the cool depths of the doorway, looking to see if Des was within. He was not difficult to locate. In a city where the majority of the population was either Hispanic or Anglo, a pure-blooded Chinese stood out. However, Des Lee would have been noticeable in the heart of modern Chinatown—although not in the Chinatown of a hundred or so years before.

Taller than the average and quite lean, Des wore his shining black hair in a long braided queue that reached past his waist. His forehead was shaven so far back that from some angles he appeared completely bald. As if to balance this, he wore a long mustache and a wispy chin beard. Neither of these concealed beauti-ful cheekbones and a strongly sculpted face.

Pearl remembered a time when Des's employers hadn't permitted him to shave his head. He'd had to make do with theatrical makeup when he'd taken part in plays and authentic historical re-creations. His interest in theater was how Des had become friends with Pearl. When Des became involved with historical re-creation, the Rooster had not hesitated to call upon the Tiger for advice.

These days, Des's employers didn't mind his odd style, partly because outré fashions were "in," especially in trendy places like Santa Fe, partly because Des had become quite well known, at least among collectors of Western art.

Des had posed for numerous paintings and had been the subject of one life-sized bronze. Hanging on the shop's walls, Pearl noted, were prints featuring Des as a gold-rush miner, a railroad worker, even a cook. Des Lee was listed in the credits of numerous Hollywood movies, and was thanked in the small print of Broadway programs. His home was packed with photos, costumes, and other props, and he was not averse to wearing historical clothing on the street.

Today, like all of those who worked in the store, Des was attired in an ele-gantly simple shirt and trousers meant to glorify the expensive attire he was sell-ing. It said something about his personality that Des Lee looked neither ridiculous nor even particularly out of place, only exceptional.

A saleswoman who exuded "friendly and approachable" from every pore moved toward Pearl when the Tiger crossed the shop's threshold.

"Welcome! Are you looking for anything in particular?"

Too early in the spring for summer visitors, too late for snowbunnies. She's hungry for a commission, Pearl thought, but she returned the woman's smile with one equally warm—and equally false.

"I'd like to speak with Des, but I see he's with a customer. I'll just look around until he's free."

The saleswoman faded back, promising help if help was needed, but too well-trained to poach on her associate's customer. But then Des was more than a mere salesman. He might work the floor, but he was also one of the store's buyers. His choices, although often superficially peculiar, never failed to sell, so the man-ager paid him well and tolerated those times a modeling gig called Des away.

Des gave no sign he had noticed Pearl, but continued to focus on his current client, giving him perfect attentiveness that never became fawning. Suit jackets, trousers, and silk ties were stacked by the register. When the customer turned to pay, Des gave Pearl the most infinitesimal of bows. Only when the client had departed did Des cross and bend to give Pearl a feather-light kiss on one cheek.

"Pearl," he said cordially. Then he dropped his voice and spoke in Chinese, "I was hoping you would arrive today. Your phone call left me very uneasy. The research I have done since has only served to make me even more so."

"I spent yesterday making phone calls," Pearl replied, "before I realized that what I could learn over the phone would tell me little. Have you had any difficulties?"

"Not here," he said, "but . . ."

He switched to English. "I have a break in about fifteen minutes. Perhaps I can take you for some tea."

"I'd like that," Pearl said. "I'll go wander under the portal at the Palace of the Governors. Come look for me there."

She left, knowing that Des would be as good as his word—and that the young saleswoman would in the meantime be thrilled with tales of just who that upright old lady had been.

Had been. I still am . . . Toothless tiger. I'll show them. Whoever "them" is.

Pearl crossed the street and made her way through the crowded space beneath the portal. The area had never been wide, and now with over half the narrow walkway filled by Indians—or did they prefer "Native Americans" these days?—their handicrafts spread out on blankets, hardly enough room was left for walking.

Pearl looked at the turquoise and coral, the blues and reds so familiar from her childhood in San Francisco's Chinatown. The Chinese had never favored silver as much as gold, though, for reasons that had little to do with relative degrees of expense. White is the color of death, the paleness left when the blood ceases to move beneath the chilling skin.

Pearls were white. She'd often wondered if her name held any hidden significance for her father. "Pearl" wasn't an uncommon name among the Chinese, but still . . .

Chinese brides wore red, and weighted their arms with gold and jade. Pearl Bright was all American, but if she had married, that old conditioning remained. She would have worn red.

Des met Pearl within the promised quarter hour, and escorted her to a little café a block or so from the plaza. He seated her at one of the tables scattered under an awning along the sidewalk, and gave her a slight bow—Chinese style, with hands pressed together in front of him.

"They have learned to make an excellent pot of tea here," he said, his voice rising and falling in the singsong cadences of a stage Chinese. "This most humble one has had the smallest part in their success. If I might beg to order for the beauteous lady?"

Pearl mimed throwing something at him, but found herself smiling nonetheless. She needed to smile. Very little of what she had to report would make either of them smile.

Des emerged from the shop a few minutes later, and seated himself across the small, round table from her.

"The tea will be out in a few minutes," he said, his accent now wholly that of northern California, with only the faintest hint of a Chinese accent for flavor. "I ordered some almond wafers as well. They are wonderful."

"Thank you."

Almost unconsciously, Pearl replied in Chinese. Des had that influence on her. Besides, it would be safer if they held their discussion in a language that few eavesdroppers would understand.

Pearl folded her hands in front of her. Many, many years ago, when she was still on the stage, her mother had taught her how the posture of the body could influence the mind.

"Seem calm, and you will be calm, Pearl. Seem a lady of quality, and you will be a lady of quality. The Greek philosophers and those who followed their tradition argue eternally over the separation of mind and body. Those of us who escaped their influence know that mind and body are inseparable."

Pearl had taught Des that same wisdom, and knew from his expression that he understood what she was doing.

"So things are very bad," he said, taking a seat across the table from her, and accepting, as she had known he would, her wordless suggestion that they speak Chinese. "I suspected as much from my own readings."

"Then they confirm what I told you?"

"Yes. I did as you requested and did not review the e-mail with the details of the reading you and Gaheris Morris had done, nor of the ones you had done on your own until I had my own results. Mine were unsettlingly similar. I have written them down for you."

He reached inside his jacket pocket and pulled out a sheet of white paper. The writing on it was in Chinese, but he had eschewed the elaborations of an ink brush and written in ballpoint pen.

"Very similar," Pearl said. She glanced at the date and time of one reading, and felt a thin-lipped smile shaping her lips. "However, I am certain you wondered about this one. What it says about the fate of the Rat does not match the earlier readings."

"I did wonder, but I agreed with you that such matters were not to be discussed over a telephone. You do not look in the least surprised. Therefore, you know something."

"I had a phone call from Brenda Morris," Pearl said. "Yesterday. She and her father found the Dog, but in the process they seem to have lost the Rat."

"Tell me."

Pearl elaborated what Brenda Morris had told her over the phone, including the meeting with Charles "Riprap" Adolphus and what she had learned about him. The cell-phone connection had been far from perfect, the signal relayed over several mountain ranges, but Brenda had been willing—even eager—to repeat herself, as if in telling Pearl what had happened, she had handed over responsibility to the other woman.

"Brenda concluded," Pearl said, "by saying that her father planned to drive to New Mexico from the Denver area today. They should arrive in Santa Fe either late today, or early tomorrow, depending on whether Gaheris makes many stops."

"If Gaheris no longer remembers he is the Rat," Des asked, "how does he justify making this trip? How does he rationalize his sudden departure from California for Denver?"

"Brenda says that Gaheris seems to think the entire thing is a combination business jaunt and holiday with his daughter. She says the rationalized continuity is frightening. Gaheris has even managed to make deals with various contacts he already had in the region."

Des chuckled. "Gaheris may have lost the memory of being the Rat, but he has not lost one iota of the Rat's head for business nor its appreciation of an opportunity. You say that the Dog is accompanying them?"

"Yes. Gaheris thinks the young man is someone he met specifically in order to do business. This Riprap has convinced Gaheris that he can introduce him to others who are involved with nonprofessional sports. Gaheris is delighted to have him along."

"And can Riprap make good on his promise?"

"Brenda thinks so. She seems quite taken with Riprap. He apparently behaved with great poise after Gaheris was attacked."

"Romantically attached?" Des said, raising his eyebrows.

"I don't think so," Pearl said. "Rather she is attracted as many are attracted to the Dog, for his stability and strength."

"Good. We don't need Gaheris to decide that he needs to protect his daughter from her impulses. That would complicate matters greatly."

"I agree."

A pot of tea and a plate of cookies had been delivered while Pearl was report-
ing what Brenda had said, and now she sipped gratefully of the steaming, pale
green liquid. The cups were Chinese style, rounded, without handles, and she let
the heat sink into her arthritic knuckles. Santa Fe was cooler than San Jose. The
lack of moisture in the air, combined with the higher altitude, was something
she felt in her bones.

"Where have you left your luggage?" Des said.

"At La Fonda. I've taken a room there."

"Will that be safe?"

"As safe as staying with you at your house, maybe more so. After all, I will be
surrounded by many people."

"Yet will they be able to see a threat to you?"

Pearl smiled. "They will be able to see an old woman acting crazy. That will
bring interference—or at the very least people who could report to you that I was
in distress. If we are alone together at your house, it may be that Brenda and Riprap will arrive only to discover that two more of the Thirteen are lacking their
memories."

"True."

Pearl frowned. "I cannot help but feel that there is more to be learned from
what Brenda heard Gaheris's attacker say before he vanished."

"That bit about her not being able to see him? That only thirteen should be
able to do so?"

"That."

"Thirteen only," Des said thoughtfully. "That is curious. He must have
meant the Thirteen Orphans. How very strange that his proposed victims should
be the only ones who could see him."

"How very strange, if this was supposed to be the case, that Brenda Morris
should be able to see him."

"Perhaps the spell our enemy worked to render himself invisible was not as
complete as he believed," Des offered. "Perhaps the heirs to the Orphans, who
are connected, if only passively, to our heritage, were not excluded."

"Maybe so. Des, will you be safe at your house? I could take a room for you
at the hotel."

"No need. My house is warded, and I have a couple staying with me. Historical re-creationalists from Tombstone. They are in the area to do some shopping, especially for antiques. They are not around all the time, of course, but they
are home most evenings, and are unpredictable with their comings and goings
during the day."

"As good as anything, then," Pearl agreed.

"Have you spoken to Nissa?"

"I have, and I spoke with her again when I heard from Brenda Morris about what happened to Gaheris. Nissa has promised not to leave herself vulnerable. When I expressed concern, she just laughed and said that time alone, rather than the other, is what is hard for her to find. Noelani—she calls her Lani—is at that age where she follows her mother everywhere, including into the bathroom. Now that Nissa is attending school again, as well as working a full-time job, Lani has become very clingy."

"How much protection can a toddler be?" Des said.

"Perhaps quite a bit," Pearl said, "especially if, like Brenda, she can see anyone strange who approaches her mother. Nissa offered to come out here, but I told her there was no need. It is possible that whoever is stalking the Thirteen Orphans is able to travel anywhere at a whim, but I think he is operating under more usual restrictions."

"Because of how those in other parts of the country were affected first," Des said. "Why then didn't he go for Nissa when he was in the East?"

"I checked that," Pearl said. "The explanation is almost too simple. Nissa was away from home. She'd taken Lani to one of the Disneys. I forget which, but locating her would have been difficult."

"And Gaheris brought Brenda to California," Des mused. "I wonder if our stalker knew he was coming here, and chose to bag the Cat and the Rat at one time . . ."

"And the Tiger," Pearl said. "Remember, I was coming to San Francisco from San Jose to help with Brenda's indoctrination. So many of us so close together may have been quite tempting."

Des poured himself more tea, then warmed Pearl's cup.

"There is so much we don't know. We can speculate and wonder, but we have no idea who this stalker is—and without knowing that, we are limited indeed."

Pearl smiled mischievously. "Shall we speculate more then? There are various categories into which our stalker might fall. Most obvious is, of course, that this is a renewal of the old trouble."

"But that is not the only possibility," Des said. "There are other magical traditions than our own. Our stalker could be from one of those."

"He was dressed as a Chinese," Pearl objected.

Des looked at her and stroked his old-fashioned beard, a reminder than many enjoyed dressing up as other than they were.

Pearl conceded. "Very well. You have a point. Another possibility is that we have a disaffected member of one of the thirteen lineages. The Dog's line is not the only one that possesses members who have been discontented with how the heritage has passed."

"The Ram," Des said, nodding, "and the Monkey as well. Perhaps others. As the Dog's story has shown us, we cannot be certain that all is forgotten, even when we have every reason to believe that it has been. There is another possibility as well."

Pearl tilted her head in mute inquiry.

"The stalker could be one of us," Des said. "The stalker could be one of the Thirteen Orphans."

★

Meeting up with Auntie Pearl and Des Lee but getting rid of Dad so he wouldn't wonder about the subject matter of their conversation proved easier than Brenda could have imagined.

Auntie Pearl was staying at some expensive place right off the Santa Fe plaza, a place with a name that reminded Brenda of "fondue," though she knew it was Spanish and almost certainly had nothing to do with dipping things in cheese and chocolate. Dad, being Dad, had found them a much less expensive place built in what seemed to be the parking lot for a failing outlet mall. Their hotel was at the edge of the city, and, other than the mall, had nothing to recommend it as a tourist attraction.

The evening of their arrival in Santa Fe, all three of them had dined with Auntie Pearl at the restaurant in her hotel. That's when she'd suggested that Brenda and Riprap come into town and use her hotel as a base from which they could tour some of the more famous sights.

Dad had agreed with alacrity. Riprap was going with Dad to some of the educational and charitable organizations where he had contacts, but the earliest he had been able to set up appointments had been for late the next day. Dad, however, had his own projects to pursue, and was thrilled that Pearl Bright was willing to take over the role of guide.

"Oh," Pearl had said, "our actual guide is going to be Des Lee."

From the way she'd looked at Dad, Brenda knew this was a test of his memory. Dad had nodded and smiled.

"I remember him, your protégé, the artist's model and historian. Des is an interesting fellow. Brenda, you know what's the most interesting thing about him?"

Brenda had stopped with her forkful of pie halfway to her mouth, hoping that Dad was remembering.

"What?"

"His first name."

Riprap took the role of straight man when Dad paused, obviously waiting for a cue.

"Isn't it Desmond or, maybe, Desi?"

"No. It's 'Desperate.'"

"You're kidding," Riprap said. "Desperate?"

Dad beamed, pleased at the response. "That's right. Auntie Pearl, correct me if I have this wrong. Des's family is ethnically Chinese, although he was born here in the U.S."

"As was his father," Auntie Pearl had said. "I believe his father's mother was originally from elsewhere."

She put a lilt under the word that told Brenda that the "elsewhere" she meant was that land from which the Thirteen Orphans had originally come. Riprap gave a short nod to show he understood. Brenda found herself mirroring the gesture.

Dad, happy to have a good tale to tell, simply took this as encouragement.

"Now, like Auntie Pearl said, Des Lee's father was American-born, but he'd married a woman from China and she spoke only Chinese. She'd had a couple of girls, but like any traditional Chinese woman—sorry, Auntie Pearl . . ."

"No problem, Gaheris. You're just telling things the way they happened. Go on."

Brenda drank hot coffee to warm away a sudden chill to her soul. The alteration to Dad's memory had been so perfectly done. He remembered that Auntie Pearl resented her father's rejection of his daughter, even if he didn't precisely remember why the old Tiger had reacted so strongly.

Gaheris went on. "Well, anyhow, this traditional Chinese woman had wanted to have a son desperately. Apparently, she'd been saying that—or the Chinese equivalent of that—over and over again during the pregnancy: that she 'desperately' wanted a son. Anyhow, Des was born a few weeks early, and his father was out of town on business when his mother—Des's that is—went into labor. A cousin who spoke some English, but not a lot, took her to the hospital.

"Apparently, the birth wasn't the easiest, and by the time Des was born and considered safe, everyone was exhausted. This cousin, trying to explain how happy the new mother would be, said something like, 'She wanted desperately,' but the staff nurse or whoever was taking down information, and knowing the woman's surname was 'Lee' heard it as 'She wanted him named Desperate Lee.'"

Riprap guffawed. "And that's what went on the birth certificate? Somehow, I can believe it. You should hear the names of some of the kids I coach. I think their parents hold competitions to make up weird names."

"And remember," Dad said, "this was northern California thirty-some years ago. Strange names were practically the rule."

Auntie Pearl smiled, but Brenda thought there was something sad beneath the expression. She was probably remembering days when Chinese residents of the United States had been forced to deal with a lot more prejudice than a "mistaken" name on a birth certificate. Dad hastened to finish his story.

"Anyhow, when Des's father learned what had happened, he decided to make the best of it. The boy was called 'Des,' and in an odd way, I think Des is rather proud of his name. He's certainly never changed it."

"He's a rather odd fellow," Pearl said. "But you'll see that for yourself tomorrow."

When the next day came, and Brenda did meet Des Lee, she had to agree that he was odd. However, after about ten minutes of conversation, she also knew she was glad to have him as part of the group. She decided that Des Lee was one of those rare people who were so far gone into affectation that the affectation was more natural than the role society would have assigned to them.

Or something like that. In any case, it's his hair. Why should I care how he wears it?

Brenda had always thought of herself as a fairly open-minded person. The last three or four days had awakened her to just how much she defined as "normal" according to the fairly limited standards of upper-middle-class suburban South Carolina.

And those are probably not the standards of all of South Carolina, just of the part I know best.

Midmorning in Santa Fe, even in late May, was cool enough that sitting outside wasn't an attractive option. Instead, they had met in a small café where Des apparently knew the owners well enough that they were happy to let him wait on their group while the paid staff handled the steady stream of people coming in for their early-morning caffeine fix.

The corner table by the plate-glass window in the front of the shop was sufficiently isolated that Brenda and Riprap were not constrained when Pearl asked them to repeat what had happened on the night Gaheris Morris had lost his memory.

"You are certain," Des Lee asked when they indicated that they were finished, "that you did not see this Chinese-looking man at any time earlier in the evening? He was not, for example, in the nightclub? You did not glimpse him on the street?"

"I didn't," Riprap said firmly, "and it's my job at the club to notice as much as I can about the patrons. Given how that man was dressed, he would have created a sensation."

"I didn't notice him either," Brenda agreed. "I don't think I could have missed him." She took a deep breath and went on, inviting teasing, "And not just because of the clothes, either. Even if he'd been in jeans and a work shirt, he still would have been absolutely gorgeous."

No one teased her. Riprap gave a little nod, confirming her assessment of their assailant.

"But the man was waiting for you where Gaheris had parked the rental car," Des said. "Interesting. I wonder when he started tracking you? Had he followed you from California?"

These were not questions that demanded answers, simply musing aloud. Auntie Pearl added to the list.

"He was prepared for Riprap, as well as for Gaheris. That piece of paper with 'Dog' written on it is proof."

"He threw the 'Dog' paper first," Riprap said. "It was the one he had ready in his hand."

Pearl smiled. "I would have tried to neutralize you first as well. Physically, you are much more formidable than Gaheris. Also, a Dog would be a greater threat than a Rat in such a situation. Unless cornered, rats are not known for their fighting spirit, but dogs are."

"Dad had me to worry about, too," Brenda said. "That guy couldn't be sure Riprap would be as distracted."

"Good points," Riprap said. "Now, I've noticed that none of you three seem to find it at all odd that this fellow attacked by throwing pieces of paper at us. I've got to admit, I find it very strange. Is there something I'm missing?"

Pearl raised her elegant brows and tapped her cheek with the tips of her long fingernails as if gently rebuking herself.

"I am sorry, Riprap. You came to us so much more aware of your heritage than I had dreamed possible, that I had forgotten that you would not necessarily be aware of the larger cultural context. How much do you know of Chinese legend and magical traditions?"

"Not much," Riprap said. "My dad never really placed the Brave Dog stories in any context. They were sort of 'once upon a time and far away,' if you know what I mean. Brave Dog defended his master, and sometimes Dad referred to the master as an emperor, but sometimes not."

Riprap looked a bit uncomfortable. "Honestly, given my obvious ethnic heritage, when I read the letters Dad left for me after his death, I thought that Brave Dog might have been a slave, and that the master in question was, well, maybe, his owner. It didn't make me feel very comfortable. I shied away from learning more about that particular angle. Hope you don't think the worse of me for that."

"Not in the least," Pearl Bright assured him, reaching across the table and patting his hand. "My father always expressed a very low opinion of me for a different accident of birth—in my case, gender, rather than ethnicity. Having grown up with that hanging over me, I can see why you, a modern, forward-looking American, would choose to look to the future rather than being overshadowed by the past."

"Thanks. So, anyhow, you're right. I know something about my personal heritage, but very little about Chinese lore."

"The roots of Chinese writing," Pearl began, "quite likely come from divination. Will you trust me on this?"

"Sure," Riprap said.

Pearl went on. "Perhaps because Chinese writing evolved from attempts to tell fortunes, it has never lost an association with magic. I'm not saying a grocery list or directions to someone's house would be magical, but words written with magical intent, by a person who knew what he or she was doing, were considered capable of remarkable things."

"In the beginning was the word," Riprap said softly.

"Truer than you know," Des said, and Brenda thought he might have said more, but Pearl gave him a really sharp look and he fell silent.

Brenda decided that she wasn't going to ask what that was about. Probably Des had been about to go off on some esoteric tangent and Auntie Pearl was forestalling him. Already, just in ordering tea and cookies, they'd heard more about the various types of tea than Brenda had known existed.

Instead, Brenda turned to Riprap. "If you want, we might be able to find a movie that shows some of this kind of magic in action. Mom and Dad love foreign films, and I remember seeing some Chinese martial-arts fantasy things where spells were written on pieces of paper. You see it in Japanese anime, too. I guess they got it from the Chinese."

"Chinese culture," Des said, "permeated the developing traditions of many lands—Japan, Korea, and elsewhere."

Again, Brenda felt certain that "elsewhere" must be the same as that place Auntie Pearl had already mentioned—those "Lands Born from Smoke and Sacrifice." She was about to ask point-blank where this place was on the map when Auntie Pearl asked:

"Riprap, do you have the paper the man in the Chinese clothing threw at you?"

Riprap nodded, then pulled a long envelope out of the inside pocket of his jacket. He slid it across the table to Pearl Bright.

"Here. This is a copy. There was writing on both sides, so I made copies of both sides."

Pearl accepted the envelope with a tight smile that, nonetheless, was not without a degree of appreciation.

"You do not trust us."

"I saw what happened to Mr. Morris when that paper hit him in the face. I'm not giving it to anyone."

"Did you destroy it?" Des Lee asked.

"No. It's in my safe deposit box, back in Denver. Thought we might need it for some reason, but I thought I'd get to know you folks a bit before handing you what might be a loaded gun."

"Wise," Auntie Pearl said. This time there was no mistaking the approval in her voice. She opened the envelope and unfolded the piece of paper onto the table where they could all see it. "Let us see what this can tell us."

Pearl was pleased by the intelligence and forethought demonstrated by this new Dog. Riprap had even gone so far as to write neatly at the bottom of the page: "Originally written with what looked like green ink on pale yellow paper. Paper was heavy, but with no watermark."

Riprap looked at his notes and amended them verbally, "At least there was no watermark I could detect. I don't claim to be an expert. The paper looked hand-made, though. My sister Lily was into making paper for a while, and you learn how to tell the difference. It was good paper. Heavy. Thick. Textured, although with a texture you felt rather than saw."

"What does the message say?" Brenda asked, leaning forward. "It looks like different things were written on the opposite sides."

Des traced the line of characters on the side less written upon. They were beautifully ink-brushed onto the paper, the brushstokes art in themselves.

He read aloud. "This side says, 'Dog.' Then it adds 'Eleventh Earthly Branch.' Are you two familiar with the Twelve Earthly Branches?"

Riprap shook his head. Brenda tapped her right index finger on the tabletop as if the motion might conjure thought.

"Auntie Pearl said something about Branches when she was telling me how the association of the twelve animals with the signs of the zodiac was a sort of modern thing. She said the Twelve Earthly Branches came earlier than either the animals or the zodiac, that they came to be associated with the animals first, then with the zodiac. Is the Branch that's written there the one that's associated with the Dog?"

Des nodded. "So, effectively, the combination of the two sets of characters limits this to one Dog in particular, the Dog who is the current incarnation of the Eleventh Earthly Branch among the Thirteen Orphans."

"Me," Riprap said.

"You."

Des traced his fingers along the longer series of characters. Pearl knew Des could read them as easily as she herself could, but was delaying so he could have a moment to think about the ramifications of what he was reading.

"This side says, in rough and not very poetic translation: 'Silence the Dog's mind. Send it forth into the Dragon's care.'"

"The 'Dog's mind,'" Pearl repeated, nodding her agreement at this translation. "That is, then, the part of the person's memory specifically associated with being the Dog. The rest would remain untouched, thus explaining the partial amnesia we have personally witnessed in both Albert Yu and Gaheris Morris. I remain impressed that the memory remains sufficiently intact to permit the level of justification that Gaheris has been demonstrating. He remembers me teaching him to play mah-jong, for example. He simply does not remember why."

Brenda interrupted anxiously, "Dragon! That's one of the twelve signs of the zodiac. It's one of the signs you mentioned earlier, when we were talking about those who hadn't lost the family tradition. Is the Dragon the one behind this, then? Could he—Shen something—or whoever, just be pretending not to remember?"

Brenda had pushed back her chair while speaking, almost as if she was preparing to set off in physical pursuit. Pearl gently pushed Brenda back into her chair.

"The dragon is perhaps the most prevalent magical being in Chinese myth and legend. The Dragon of the Thirteen Orphans is but one of many associations with the dragon of myth and legend. Think, my dear. There are three dragons associated with mah-jong alone. Certainly, we will investigate the possibility that Shen Kung has turned to treachery, but we must be careful when we do so. After the Rat, and in some capacities the Tiger, the Dragon is probably the most scheming of all the signs."

"But not evil," Des protested. "The Chinese dragon is little like the dangerous monster of Western Europe. The dragon is most definitely dangerous, especially if one fails to treat it with appropriate respect, but it is not a monster. Dragons are intelligent, wise, powerful, and highly magical. Not only can they change shape, but the very parts of their bodies may confer magical blessings. As in the West, dragons guard treasures. They are not only the source of earthquakes, but of enormous waves as well."

Brenda lightly stroked the string of ink-brushed characters with the tip of her finger, as if that might help her remember what was written there.

"So when this says 'Send it forth into the Dragon's care,' it doesn't necessarily mean that Shen Kung. It could mean one of those dragons that guard treasures."

"That's right," Pearl said. "However, even if we admit that the simplest solution is not necessarily the only or best solution, this does not mean that we should eliminate it completely."

"Where does the Dragon—Shen Kung," Riprap said, "live?"

"In New York City," Pearl said. "Shen is one of the older members of our company, although the grandson of the original Dragon. His mother, the Dragon's first heir apparent, did not survive her son's birth. Shen was taught by his grandfather, and so, like me, is well-schooled in our traditional roots. Yet, when I spoke with him over the phone, he remembered nothing."

Pearl caught her breath, trying hard not to show how much Shen's loss of memory had bothered her. When she was certain her voice would be steady, she went on.

"I spoke with Shen's wife, and she confided that she suspected Shen might have had a serious stroke. I hated myself for not letting her know what we suspected, but how could I?"

Riprap was making some notes on the envelope from which he'd produced the copy of the stalker's spell.

"You keep mentioning the Thirteen Orphans. Can you tell me a little about them? Who's in the game, who's not? Who has training, who doesn't? I want a sense of what we have going for us."

Not much, Pearl thought, but aloud she said, "It will be easier to keep them straight if we go in order. Rat comes first."

"Rat is Gaheris Morris," Riprap said, scribbling on his envelope. "We know he's out of the game."

"Next," Des said, "comes Ox. The current Ox is a woman named Clotilde Hilliard. She is in her mid-forties, and lives in Boston. From what we read in the augury, she has lost her connection—what we have been calling 'memories'—to the Thirteen Orphans."

"Out of play, then," Riprap said. Next?"

"Next is Tiger," Pearl said. "Very much in play. Tiger is followed by Rabbit or Hare."

"You've mentioned her," Riprap said, glancing back and forth between Des and Pearl. "Lives in Virginia, right?"

"That's right," Pearl said. "Nissa is only a few years into her inheritance. Her mother died a few years ago—a car wreck. Very sad. However, Nikki had taken her responsibilities seriously, and Nissa knows the lore. I do not think, however, that she believes it. My impression is that Nissa considers the stories her mother told her a charming family eccentricity. I had never seen a need to convince her otherwise."

Brenda cut in, grinning. "This woman's name is Nissa? Her mother's was Nikki? No wonder she figured her mother was simply eccentric."

Pearl found herself grinning in response. "Every female in that family has a name beginning with 'N.' Nissa's daughter is Noelani, although she is commonly called Lani. Noelani is her mother's heir apparent, as you are Gaheris's."

Des noted that Riprap had finished writing, and said, "Next comes Dragon."

"Shen Kung," Riprap said. "Trained but out of play."

"Then comes Snake," Pearl said. "The current Snake is named Justine Bower. She is eighty-three and lives in an assisted living community in Duluth. Our auguries show that she, too, is 'out of play,' but since she never knew very much, this is hardly a loss."

Riprap looked discouraged, and Pearl thought that the next several entries on his list were not going to provide much encouragement.

"Horse, Ram, and Monkey," she said, "should go on your list as out of play—and also as never trained."

Riprap dutifully made his notes. "It doesn't seem like much effort was made to maintain the Thirteen Orphans."

"Not in recent generations," Pearl admitted. "No. There hasn't been. Someday, when we're not being stalked, I'll explain a bit more of why the various lineages dropped away."

"But what you must remember," Des said, "is that trained or not, the link to the Earthly Branches is there. These people are members of the Thirteen Orphans, even if they don't know it."

Brenda leaned over and counted the entries on Riprap's list. "That's nine. Four to go."

"And simple enough to answer," Des said. "Rooster comes next. That's me. In play. Dog comes after. That's Riprap. In play."

"But," Riprap said, "pretty much ignorant as to the rules of the game."

"We'll fix that," Des promised. "Next comes Pig. Her name is Deborah Van Bergenstein. She could have been quite helpful as she is fairly well-trained. Unhappily, our auguries show that, like Shen, she has already been taken out."

"Like Dad," Brenda reminded. "Like Albert Yu—who as the Cat is number thirteen. Riprap's right. This looks really bad."

"It is," Pearl agreed, "and all the more reason why we should decide what our next move will be."

Brenda frowned. "Move? I suppose by that you mean who do we talk with next? Who do we warn? Well, there's something I want more than that. I want to know what I am supposed to do if that man appears and tries to do something weird to one of you. I'm not flinging myself to the floor again and waiting for someone else to turn into some shadow of him or herself. Once was enough. Once was *more* than enough."

"And next time," Riprap added, "that strange man might not be content to overlook Brenda like he did this time. He seemed surprised that she could see him. In fact, I think that's what drove him to retreat. He'd been at least partially successful—with Mr. Morris, I mean—and he left to regroup."

Pearl nodded. "Brenda, you have a point. Des, is there anything we can do to safeguard ourselves?"

Des thoughtfully stroked his long mustaches and beard.

"There are spells," he said. "Defensive and offensive both. None of them have been much in use in recent years, since they are meant to be used against sorcery, and there has been no such threat for decades, but I suppose we could teach Riprap—and maybe Brenda. The question is whether Brenda will have any capacity for such arts. Her father remains the Rat, although his memory is gone."

"Stolen," Brenda said firmly. "Stolen, and what is stolen can be found. Nothing's going to stop me from trying to get Dad's memories back for him—nothing I can prevent anyhow—but it's going to be hard to do if all the rest of you turn vague."

It would be even harder, Pearl thought, *if you were killed. Not all the original Thirteen Orphans died peacefully.*

Aloud she said, "Des, you are more skilled in sorcery than I am. Would you take these two on as students?"

"If they are willing. Pearl, there's something else we haven't considered, something you may not have thought of because it doesn't really touch you."

"And that is?"

"Jobs. Riprap and I have jobs. Brenda?"

"Not yet, but I was going to get one for the summer. I've only been done with exams for a few weeks, and even Dad believes in giving a breather now and then."

Pearl nodded. "Actually, I had considered the problem of those of you who need to hold jobs. We could all go our separate ways, but I think that would be playing into our unknown enemy's hands. I thought to offer Riprap and Brenda some sort of employment with me, but I had not worked out the details."

Riprap frowned. "My job isn't much, but I was planning on working on several summer sports programs. Still . . . I don't know how much good I'd be as a coach, looking over my shoulder all the time. I met Gaheris before whatever happened to him happened to him. I didn't know him well, but I know enough to know he's not himself. I know that by definition I can't miss what I don't know's not there, but the idea of standing by and letting someone amputate a part of my mind, my heritage . . . I don't like it. The kids may need to do without me until this is solved."

Brenda nodded. "Dad might let me take an internship or something like that with you."

Pearl could sense Brenda working the angles.

"I'd need to figure out the best way to approach Dad," Brenda continued, "but I think we could work something out that would suit. Like I said. I've got to do what I can to get Dad back his memories. The way he is now . . . It's creepy."

Pearl nodded. "Then we'll do our best to work out an internship for you. Riprap, your giving up your job would provide you with more difficulties, I suspect. You have rent or a mortgage to pay. Arrangements will need to be made for your utilities."

"I have a roommate. Teacher at the local grammar school. I can work out to have him actually write the checks, but you're right. My bank account's not so huge that I can go without working indefinitely."

"I will handle the financial end," Pearl said firmly. "I assure you, I have the means, and, like you, I have no desire to have my memories tampered with. I have a great many more memories than you do, and good or bad, they are mine. If the need arises, I will make similar arrangements with you, Des. For now, at least, Santa Fe may as well be your base of operations. You have room at your house for these two?"

"My house guests leave today," Des replied. "But what about you?"

"Now that I know I need to be careful," Pearl said, "I will take care to defend myself. I am also the logical person to go to see Nissa Nita, since she and her sisters know me as a family friend. These are not matters to discuss over the telephone, and we need to learn how much Nissa knows of her heritage. Even more, we need to convince Nissa to take what she does know seriously. Meeting Riprap has shown me that I know all too little about the younger members of the Thirteen. It is time I became better acquainted, before it is too late to do so to any effect."

★

Dad proved far easier to convince than Brenda had imagined possible.

"It's time you saw a bit more of the world, Breni," he said when Pearl Bright left father and daughter to discuss her proposal that she take Brenda on as a paid intern for the summer. "I know you've only had a couple of weeks home, but Auntie Pearl will introduce you to another world."

For a brief, hopeful moment, Brenda thought her dad meant that mysterious place that had been alluded to a time or two before, the homeland of the Thirteen Orphans, the Lands Born from Smoke and Sacrifice, but his next words had dashed her hopes.

"Auntie Pearl travels a great deal, especially for someone of her age. You'll see cities all over the U.S., maybe even parts of Europe. More importantly, you'll move in social circles into which I could never introduce you—and she'll be paying you for the privilege. I hope you'll seriously consider taking her offer."

"I will, Dad. What do you think Mom will say?"

"Let me present the idea to her. I know you have applied to work for one of my associates, but Auntie Pearl isn't young. An offer like this might not come again. The family will miss you, of course, but this is a once-in-a-lifetime offer."

Mom did come over to Dad's point of view, although perhaps not as quickly as Dad had thought she would. Brenda knew her mom had been looking forward to having another woman around the house. Ever since Brenda started college, Mom's comments about living in an otherwise "stag" establishment had been frequent and cutting.

But Mom had finally agreed. When she got Brenda on the phone her long list of things Brenda needed to watch out for—especially in the presumably fast and loose circle of Pearl Bright's Hollywood friends—showed a considerable amount of knowledge about all manner of vice.

Brenda was relieved that Auntie Pearl had not mentioned that Riprap was also becoming part of her entourage. Mom might have had serious second thoughts if she'd known there would be a young, unmarried man traveling with Pearl and Brenda. Brenda didn't know whether the fact that Riprap was black would make him more or less of a threat in Mom's eyes. Des might be traveling with them, too, but Des was too old for consideration.

Any homesickness Brenda might have entertained was quelled by the sound of her youngest brother, Tom, now in junior high and certainly old enough to know better, piping in the background, "Can I have her room? It's bigger than mine!"

Brenda knew the rearrangement only made sense, and surrendered gracefully. After a few cautionary words regarding the storage of those things she had unpacked, Brenda asked if her mom would send on some clothes and personal items to Des's address in Santa Fe.

"Auntie Pearl has said we'll go back to California maybe in a few weeks," Brenda finished, "but I can't get by here on what I've packed until then."

Mom agreed, and Brenda hung up, feeling, despite her excitement, a bit choked up.

Thank heavens for cell phones, she told herself. *I can call Mom every day if I want.*

Almost as if he'd been waiting for something like this to happen, Dad finished up his business. He left for South Carolina the next day.

As soon as Gaheris Morris had left, Brenda and Riprap relocated to Des Lee's house.

Pearl made reservations on a morning shuttle to the airport, promising to call when she arrived in Virginia. She suggested that if Gaheris asked, Brenda simply imply that Pearl had remained in Santa Fe.

"Otherwise, it's going to be a bit difficult explaining why I abandoned my new intern almost as soon as I acquired her."

"What if Dad calls and asks to talk to you?"

"I trust you to be creative. I am napping. In a meeting. 'Indisposed' is always a good word to use. Especially when said to a man with just the right inflection, it can stop all questions cold. Then you call me, and I'll call him back. I don't expect to be in Virginia long, so we won't need to maintain the charade for more than a few days."

Brenda grinned. "I've done things like this for roommates who were staying the night with boyfriends, but I never thought I'd be making excuses for a movie star."

"Get used to it," Pearl said, patting her hand. "Making excuses for others is the backbone of middle management."

Des Lee might have lived by himself, but his house was roomy enough for a family and there were pictures of the same kids at various ages, ranging from babies to young adults, displayed in the living room. Brenda saw others when she peeked into Des's room.

"Are those your kids?" she asked.

"Yep," Des said. "Three of them. Two girls and a boy. They're about your age, give or take. My son is in grad school. My elder daughter is in college, the younger finishing high school."

"Man," Riprap said. "You got an early start."

"I did," Des agreed, "part of the reason the marriage didn't work. We were young and thought we knew everything. Got married in college. My wife had our son before we graduated. Time passed, we grew apart. She got custody on the grounds that I was less fit to provide a stable home environment, but the kids always visited me and I made sure to let them know I cared about what was going on in their lives. That's why I kept this big house—wanted them to have their own rooms when they came."

"So you've lived here awhile," Brenda said.

"That's right," Des said. "I fell in love with the West—not the geographic west, the idea—when I was a boy. I wanted to be a cowboy in the worst way. Then I started noticing that there were very few Chinese cowboys. The Chinese you saw on TV and in movies were usually cooks or doing laundry, maybe running a shop. I started reading and discovered there had been Chinese working the railroads, punching cattle, panning for gold—all the 'leading man' roles. Sometimes they did them so well that they came to odds with both their own people and the dominant 'white' population. Putting the Chinese back into the story became my personal obsession. Didn't do my marriage much good. Like me, my ex was ethnically Chinese, but she was interested in blending in, in assimilating, not standing out."

Des sighed and shrugged, a gesture that involved his shoulders rising almost as high as his ears before dropping back.

"Sorry. I've lived alone too long, I guess. The kids are beyond custody agreement mandatory visits. My friends here already know my sad song."

"That's all right," Brenda said. "I really did want to know."

Des showed her to a tidy room at the end of a long hallway.

"This bedroom has an attached bath, so why don't you take it. Give you an element of privacy. Riprap . . ." He turned to face the other man. "I'll put you here. You'll have to share a bathroom with me, but you get the better view."

Riprap followed Des into the indicated room. Brenda, moving into her own temporary quarters, heard him say, "Those the Sangre de Cristo Mountains?"

"Yep, and a good view of them, too," Des said. "I couldn't touch this house at today's prices, but back when I bought it, this part of town was considered too far from the Plaza to be convenient and not in the least fashionable."

The men's voices continued in quiet conversation. Riprap, it turned out, was interested in the buffalo soldiers, as the black army units had been dubbed by the Indians. The two men were out in the living room and deep in a discussion of the Indian Wars by the time Brenda finished unpacking.

Des offered her a choice of drinks, and Brenda accepted oolong tea. Her host produced a lovely tea set after the Chinese fashion, the cups small and round, nestling into her hand as a bird's eggs would into a nest. In Riprap's big hands the cup completely vanished but for the thin trail of steam rising into the air.

"Now," Des said, "why don't we start your first lesson? There's a tremendous amount of theory involved, but I'm going to try to keep to the bare minimum. If I skip too much and start confusing you, stop me."

Brenda nodded, and Riprap said, "Right, coach."

"Good. Now, first of all, I'm not going to try and explain what magic is. You've seen it at work. You've seen its effects. That's enough to go on. A child learns about gravity by dropping things and watching them fall. You can learn the principles of magic in a similar fashion."

"Seems to me," Riprap said guardedly, "that a child also learns about gravity by falling. I wouldn't teach a little kid to play baseball with a hard ball and wooden bat. I'd use a whiffle ball and a plastic bat."

"You're one step ahead of me," Des said, his tone pleased, although Riprap had just challenged him. "In sorcery, there is no equivalent to that plastic ball and bat, but there are more and less dangerous types of spells. There are also more and less dangerous ways of casting spells.

"Brenda expressed an interest in knowing how she might protect herself—or someone else—if our mutual enemy was to reappear. That's where I'm going to start, by teaching you a sequence called the Dragon's Tail. You can envision the end result as a barrier that will completely surround you on all sides, but not above and not below."

"Sort of as if a dragon wrapped its tail around you," Brenda said, setting down her teacup to gesture.

"That's right. The first thing that you need to realize is that this isn't any force wall or magical barrier. You really will be summoning a dragon to protect you. To the uninitiated the dragon will not be visible, but you will see it, and, sadly, so will those who attempt to attack you with magical force."

"Sadly?" Brenda said. Then she understood. "Oh, because they'll see it, they'll know the zone of protection isn't complete."

"Precisely," Des said. "Later, if either of you proves particularly adept, I can teach you other routines, but this one is comparatively easy."

"Why easy?" Riprap said. "From what you said about dragons earlier, I wouldn't think they'd much like being summoned at someone's whim, especially when that summons involves putting themselves between the summoner and danger."

"Easy, because all that you are doing is turning something that's available to your service," Des replied. "Chinese dragons are elemental creatures. In one sense, they are omnipresent. In this part of New Mexico, you're going to find earth and cloud dragons. There are some really powerful dragons nearer to the ocean, but I think starting with weaker dragons is all to the good."

Brenda and Riprap traded glances. She saw anticipation and apprehension in his eyes, wondered what he saw in hers.

"But won't the dragons turn on us?" Brenda asked.

"Not if you prepare the spell correctly," Des said, "and I'm here to make sure that you do. We are going to work this spell the hard, slow, tedious way. The end result should be reliable. It will, however, serve for only one summons. Neither of you know enough to prepare a multi-use summons."

Riprap set down his teacup. "Got to perfect making baskets before you can learn trick shots. I'm with you."

Brenda finished her tea. "What first?"

Des gave a crisp nod of approval. "Let's move into the dining room. A wide flat surface will be helpful for the first part."

Once they were in the dining room, Des opened a locked drawer in a tall, ornate cabinet. Like all but the most utilitarian furnishings in the house, the cabinet was crafted in a Chinese style, the carved front worked with peonies and songbirds. From the cabinet, Des produced the Rooster mah-jong set. He set this next to his seat at the head of the table, then went to a chest in the corner. He came back with two perfectly normal, modern plastic mah-jong sets. These he placed to either side of him and motioned for Brenda and Riprap to take these seats.

"Eventually, you'll use your own family sets," Des said, "but the glory of the magical system our ancestors constructed is that the magics can be worked with any mah-jong set at all. When you are skilled, you can dispense with the tools entirely. They were meant as an aid, not a crutch. When you are skilled, you will not be some wizard in the Western tradition, easily disarmed by the removal of your staff or wand. You will be scholars. No one will be able to take away your power, for your power will be rooted in knowledge."

Des's voice had risen to a triumphant note, but now it fell and he sat rather heavily.

"That is, of course, as long as no one tampers with your mind. Then, unhappily, as you have already seen, you will be completely helpless."

Des broke the awkward silence that followed his statement by opening the box containing the Rooster mah-jong set. Brenda looked at the tiles with interest. They resembled those in her dad's Rat set, but she could tell that another hand had carved the characters. She wondered if each set had been made by the original Orphan to pass along to his or her descendants, or whether there had been a few gifted artisans who had made the sets among them.

It did not seem to be an important question to ask now. Des had spilled out his tiles and was sorting through them.

"I'm going to put up a powerful protection," he explained, "because two novices at work is going to raise quite a lot of noise."

Brenda understood without asking that he meant "noise" in a metaphorical rather than literal sense. Doubtless she and Riprap would be clumsy in their early efforts to do whatever it was Des intended to teach them. If dragons could be summoned deliberately, what might come of its own free will if it thought the pickings might be good? Monsters would probably be the least of it. From the fairy tales her parents had read to her, Brenda recalled that humans were usually more dangerous than any monster.

Brenda realized she had dozens of questions. If she and Riprap could learn magic, did that mean anyone could, or could only those who shared their strange heritage? Were the Chinese the only culture with "real" magic? Des had spoken of "Western wizards," and not as if he were speaking of characters from fantasy fiction. Did that mean there were lots of people out there, working magics of various types? If so, why didn't more people know about it?

Looking down at the top layer of tiles in the plastic mah-jong set, Brenda knew these questions were just a diversion for what was really bothering her. Would she be able to learn any of these spells or routines or rituals at all? Riprap was the Dog, even if he didn't know much more than she did, but she wasn't the Rat. As far as she knew, her dad was still the Rat, even if he couldn't remember those things that had made him the Rat.

Brenda swallowed a sigh. Maybe Des was only having her sit in on these lessons to test her, but maybe he believed she had the ability to learn something practical. Either way, she'd do better to be patient and attend to her lessons. A few nights ago, she hadn't believed that a piece of paper could be a weapon. What other things didn't she know?

Des had been selecting a long row of tiles, fourteen in all, Brenda noted, exactly as in a winning hand of mah-jong. He laid them in a straight line, facedown.

"Our ancestors chose to use mah-jong as an aid to memory not because they created the game, but because it already existed and therefore could not be taken away."

"Like a wand or staff," Riprap said.

"Right," Des agreed. "I've always thought of their use of mah-jong as a sort of Purloined Letter approach. As I said before, our type of wizard is a scholar, and a scholar's ability is rooted in knowledge. Inborn aptitude helps, even as perfect pitch is an asset for a singer, but just as a singer can learn music without possessing perfect pitch, so someone who does not have an inborn talent can master the knowledge that will, in turn, lead to the ability to work magic. With me?"

Both Brenda and Riprap nodded. Brenda wondered if her relief showed in her expression, for Des's mustache moved as his lips twisted in a knowing smile.

"Then can anyone learn how to work magic?" Riprap asked. "If so, why isn't magic as common as knowing how to drive a car?"

"I didn't say anyone could learn to use magic," Des said, "but that one did not need an aptitude. Let me extend the singing analogy. Some people are naturally gifted. They don't need to be taught to sing; they only need to be taught songs. A larger group of people can learn to sing, if trained. Then there are those who cannot ever sing. They are tone deaf or simply have bad voices."

"Still," Riprap said, "it seems to me that even that analogy would allow for a lot of people doing magic. Why don't they?"

"Lack of knowledge," Des replied promptly. "Very few people will try something they know is impossible. I wouldn't doubt that there are those out there who, when playing a hand of mah-jong, have felt something when the tiles were arrayed in a certain fashion. However, without the knowledge of how to interpret that sensation, of what to do to stir potential into actuality, they would simply ignore the sensation and get back to play.

"However, we're straying farther than I want into theory. Brenda was right yesterday when she reminded us we have at least one enemy, and that we should take precautions to protect ourselves against him if—or perhaps I should say 'when'—he returns."

Des gestured to the line of tiles set in front of him. "When our ancestors were exiled into China, they found a number of gambling games in common use. Already familiar with these, for variations on the same games were played in their homeland, they adapted one to their use.

"One advantage," Des said, "to using the mah-jong set to encode spells was that the same tiles could be rearranged into various patterns. Today, in the game of mah-jong, many of these patterns have come to be known as 'limit hands.' Therefore, you may be familiar with the pattern I am about to show you."

He turned over the tiles, displaying three each of the tiles for south wind, west wind, green dragon, red dragon, and a pair of white dragon tiles. None of these tiles pictured either winds or dragons. Instead, Chinese characters were inscribed on the surface.

"That's the hand called 'All Winds and Dragons,'" Brenda said. "You can form it with any of the wind or dragons tiles, so in a way it's one of the easier limit hands to do—if you're lucky and no one else is collecting the same tiles. It's also closer to a standard mah-jong hand than lots of the limit hands are, so you can back out and regroup if the tiles you need don't come through."

"However," Riprap said with a grin that showed he'd tried that gamble at least once himself, "someone else is likely to be collecting those same tiles, which is why I learned early not to try for this. Des, are you saying this mah-jong hand is a spell?"

"A spell of protection," Des agreed. "When I work it, I will be calling on two winds and all three dragons to protect us. Because of our location, I have chosen the south and west winds. Were we somewhere where other winds dominated, or at a different time of year, I might have chosen differently. However, any combination will work."

"When you play mah-jong," Brenda said, "you can use sets of three—pungs—or sets of four—kongs. Is it the same when you do spells?"

"It is," Des said, "but the more tiles you use, the more you need to concentrate, the more patterns you need to hold in your mind. I only extend to four when in great need. Three, especially with an already powerful combination like this, is ample."

"I'm beginning to understand," Riprap said. "So these tiles are not, in themselves, magical. What is magical is what you—or whoever is doing the spell—know they represent. It's like the words written on that sheet of paper. Words are magic."

"Pretty much," Des agreed, "although you'll learn that making words do what you want them to do isn't always easy. Now, what I'm going to do next isn't very showy, but I want you to watch. Don't say anything until I indicate I'm ready for questions, just watch."

Des raised his hands above the tiles, lowering them until his fingers almost brushed the surface. Then he moved his left hand until his index finger rested above the leftmost tile in the line—the first of the south wind tiles.

He didn't seem to be doing anything, but Brenda watched closely as Des moved his index finger to the next of the south wind tiles, then to the third. It was as he was holding his finger over the third tile that Brenda thought she saw something—a pale pearlescent glow—manifest between the tile and the pad of Des's fingertip.

It wasn't as if Des was projecting the glow, but as if the space between his finger and the tile had filled in.

Now that she knew what to look for, Brenda could look back and see that the glow extended back into the spaces between the previous two tiles. When Des moved his finger forward and continued concentrating, the glow moved forward until, when he finished his concentration with the pair of white dragons, a pale, nacreous band hovered above the tiles.

It remained when Des turned his outspread hands on their sides and made a cupping motion. He pushed against the glowing band, and it contracted, then burst apart into fourteen small components. Brenda could have sworn that some of them looked like tiny Chinese dragons, but they moved so quickly that it could have been her imagination.

Des dropped his hands, and relaxed back into his chair.

"Don't say anything," he commanded, shoving toward each of them a couple of sheets of paper and pens he had set ready. "Write down what you saw. Don't leave out any details, no matter how odd."

Brenda obeyed, aware as she scribbled of Riprap's pen moving with deliberation across his own sheet of paper.

I guess neither of us flunked that test, she thought with satisfaction.

Des waited with perfect patience until they finished. Then he read each report carefully, his gaze flickering back and forth between the written accounts, obviously comparing details.

"You both did very well," he said. "Brenda, you are not to become competitive over this, but Riprap saw more and saw more quickly. However, the fact that you saw anything at all—especially since not only have you not come into your inheritance, but that inheritance seems to have been sealed from the Rat himself—speaks exceptionally well of you."

"What did Riprap see that I didn't?" Brenda asked, hoping she didn't sound contentious.

"A little more detail at the end is all," Des said. "You thought you saw tiny dragons. He did with enough detail to describe a bit about their traits. He also saw faint manifestations of the winds—a much more difficult thing to see, since wind, by its very nature, does not have a form."

Brenda decided she could live with this, and gave Riprap an approving nod and a thumbs-up, just so he'd know she wasn't sulking.

"Now," Des said, "if that has not exhausted your patience, I would like to start teaching you the Dragon's Tail. The protection I cast should keep us safe for several hours at least."

"I'm game," Riprap said.

"Me, too," Brenda agreed.

"Good," Des said. "You just witnessed me casting a spell that was immediately needed. What I'm going to do is teach you to cast a spell in a manner that will permit it to be stored for later use. As you saw, casting a spell takes concentration. If our unknown enemy comes walking down the street toward you, a bit of paper in his hand with your name on it, stopping and concentrating isn't going to do you much good. He'd have you before you could get the first element in focus."

"I'd wondered about that," Riprap admitted. "Are we going to write something out?"

"Not quite," Des said. "For one, I doubt that either of you write Chinese well enough to manage an accurate transcription with the tools needed. An ink brush takes considerable practice to learn to handle correctly. Secondly, throwing the paper toward a target is a special skill."

"I'd wondered about that, too," Riprap said, a deep chuckle underlying the words. "I've had nightmares about the moment the paper came at me. It moved like a knife. I think the only reason the man missed is because I'm pretty good at getting out of the way of things heading at me. . . . Baseballs hurt if they nail you anywhere but your glove."

"There's one drawback to what I'm about to teach you," Des said. "The item you create is good for one use only."

Brenda remembered how the strip of paper had melted into her father's face. Would these do something like that? She covered a shudder of aversion with a nod. As Riprap would probably say, they had to learn to play the game by its own rules, not by the ones they'd like.

"Okay," Brenda said, hearing her tone a bit too bright. "What's the first step in making this Dragon's Tail?"

"First you're going to lay out the tiles so that they'll aid concentration," Des said. "Either of you have the Dragon's Tail limit hand memorized?"

Brenda tilted her head to one side. "I think I do. It's a hard one, requires a run of one to nine in a single suit, and then a pung of dragons and a pair of winds—or is it a pung of winds and a pair of dragons?"

"Either," Des said. "Remember what I said about the Chinese dragon being associated with the elements? In this spell, the winds can stand in for a dragon. There are reasons for the variations, having to do with tailoring the spell to certain types of protection, and to the specific traits of the caster. Today we're going to focus on a protection from magical attack, since that's what you're likely to face. For that you want not a grouping of three dragons, but of the winds most closely associated with your sign."

"I am confused," Brenda admitted. "Do you mean our birth year, or our, well, wizard year?"

"Wizard," Des said, "and in your case, we're going to do everything we can to emphasize your relationship to the Rat. Your father has acknowledged you as his heir, and although he may have forgotten, you have not. It is possible that some connection remains."

"Why winds?" Riprap asked. "I mean, why winds when there are dragons?"

"Because the dragons are not quite dragons," Des said, "not in the way you think. Trust me on this. We'll have time later to talk about the evolution of symbols."

"Okay," Riprap said. "So, what's the Dog's wind?"

"West-northwest," Des replied. "Since there is no such tile, we will use west."

"And Rat?" Brenda asked.

"North," Des said. "Do you two know those tiles?"

In answer, they each picked out three of the appropriate tiles from the selection in front of them.

"Good," Des said. "Now, we're going to emphasize the dragon's head with its two 'horns'—the paired tiles Brenda mentioned. For these we will use the dragon tiles. The Rat's color is black. The Dog's color is yellow. Since neither of those are represented in the three dragons, we will make do with red instead. Red is the color of celebrations, luck, and joy."

Brenda and Riprap each extracted two red dragon tiles from the box. Brenda looked at the rectangle with the line through it that was printed on the tile.

"Center," she said aloud. "That's another good reason for using this one, isn't it? We're going to be at the center of the protection."

Des's eyebrows shot up and he beamed at her.

"Very good, Brenda! You're on your way already to understanding the nature of the dragon tiles—and why they can be complicated to use."

Brenda felt very good, and set the red dragon tiles in place with a satisfying snap.

"Now," Des said, "our last choice is which of the three suits to choose for the dragon's tail. In the West, the suits are commonly called dots (or balls or circles), bamboo, and characters. If you don't mind, I prefer to avoid the rather vulgar contractions that became popular in the 1920s."

"Dots, bams, and cracks," Riprap said. "Yeah. I never liked them either."

"I'm fine with it," Brenda said. "Those terms don't mean anything, the others do."

"Okay, Des," Riprap said, shifting a bit impatiently in his chair. "So which suit do we pick for the string of nine?"

Des answered promptly. "The suit I would choose for your purposes would be the bamboo. Either of you want to guess why?"

Brenda shot her hand in the air as if she were in class, but neither of the men mocked her—although Riprap's eyes held a distinct twinkle.

"Bamboo is flexible, and we want our dragon's tail to bend."

"Right. Anything to add, Riprap? I'm not trying to pester you, but considering the depths of symbolism each tile may hold can contribute greatly to the power of a particular spell."

Riprap shuffled through his tiles until he came up with the eight of bamboos. He studied it for a while, then said, "Okay. How about this? Bamboo is not only flexible, but it's evergreen and very strong. Evergreen is symbolic of life, and we want to stay alive. Strong is another advantage. A weak barrier wouldn't do us much good."

"Very nice," Des said. "Let's take a stretch. When we come back, I'll show you how to cast a spell."

Brenda took advantage of the break to call home. Mom was vice-president and treasurer—that meant bookkeeper and accountant—for Unique Wonders, the company Dad had started before Brenda had been born.

Dad had a partner at first, but had bought the other man out when Brenda was still in grammar school. This meant more travel, but Dad liked the personal contact with the clients, and Mom was very good—better than Gaheris would have been, as they both admitted—at the administrative side of things.

Mom was glad to take a break herself. She was doing payroll, and the various government forms always drove her crazy.

They talked about a bunch of things, but although Brenda wanted to ask if Dad was acting odd, she refrained. She wondered just how much Mom knew about the family's weird heritage, but this really didn't seem the time to ask.

Besides, both Des and Pearl had told them not to discuss particulars over the phone, and had hinted at dire consequences if they were caught doing so.

As she was walking back to her room to stash her cell phone, Brenda heard Riprap making arrangements to have someone cover for him as coach of some team.

"I know it's sudden, Larry, but it's a chance I couldn't pass up—and it may pay off for the kids one of these days. Sure. Call me anytime."

When they settled around the dining-room table about half an hour later, Des had assembled a curious array of items. None of them looked particularly arcane. In fact, Brenda thought it rather looked as if Des expected a group of kindergartners to arrive any moment.

"Now," Des said, "not only are you going to learn how to cast a spell, you are going to learn how to fix that spell in an item so that you can draw upon it at need."

Brenda, whose American soul had been getting just a little tired of Des's praise of all things Chinese, couldn't resist.

"But isn't that just what you were sneering about 'Western' magics for doing—locking the wizard's power into a staff or wand?"

Des looked momentarily indignant. Then he grinned.

"Sure sounds like it, doesn't it? The difference here is, if you continue to follow the art, you're going to reach the point where you can dispense with such assistance, whereas the Western wizard becomes increasingly bound to items of power."

Brenda grinned back. "Fair enough. What do we do?"

"Something that is quite difficult for most of us raised in modern America: concentrate on doing one thing at a time. I don't suppose either of you has studied meditation?"

Brenda shook her head. "All the books I ever looked at started with 'clear your mind,' and whenever I try to clear my mind, it only gets busier."

Riprap said, "I haven't tried even that much."

"Don't worry," Des said. "Skill in meditation might have been useful, but we can manage without it. What you're going to do is make the physical representation of the fourteen tiles that represent the elements of the spell. While you're doing that, you're not to let your mind drift. If you find yourself daydreaming, think about something related to the spell: the meaning of the tile you're crafting, what dragons look like, even why you want to be protected. Obviously, the more focused you can be on the specific tile the better, but what you don't want to do is think about something completely unrelated—how well you slept last night, what Pearl is doing, how much you'd like steak for dinner. With me?"

"So," Riprap said, "we're not making an item into which we'll later put a spell; the two tasks are intertwined. Well then, I'd better tell you, I'm no artist. I'm no better at carving bone than I am at meditating."

Des patted the largest of the packets in front of him.

"Not to worry. This is where modern technology comes in. What I have here is polymer clay—the basic white modeling compound. I also have molds that will let you form the tiles, and help them hold their shape while you inscribe them. The molds even have marks to show where to pierce them so you can wear the finished tiles as beads on a bracelet. You need to concentrate on the act of inscribing the characters, not on making perfect tiles."

"We're going to need to write Chinese?" Brenda asked.

"Copy it," Des corrected. "The hardest tiles are going to be the winds. The red dragon is a simple ideograph—a rectangle with a slash. Except for the one of bamboo, the bamboo are represented as cylinders marked with lines. The one bamboo should resemble a bird, but it doesn't need to be elaborate."

"Do we get time to practice first?" Brenda asked.

"I think not," Des said. "I want your concentration pouring into the task."

He spent a few minutes showing them how to fit the white polymer clay into the molds, how the various trimming and inscribing tools worked. He explained that they could color the inscribed tiles after they were baked. He gave them a short time to see which tools worked best in their hands; then he rose to his feet.

"Dogs and Rats are, each in their own ways, quite competitive, so I'm going to have Riprap move to a table in the living room. You'll both be where I can see you, and offer help when needed, but you won't be able to see each other and start racing."

Riprap rose obediently, and helped Des gather up what he'd need. Brenda arrayed the fourteen tiles in order. On a whim, she arrayed the three winds that were the dragon's head into a triangle, set the red dragon tiles to the sides of that head in roughly the place that an Oriental dragon's horns would be, and then nudged the others so that they made a curving dragon's body, swimming sinuously through the air.

Des looked at what she done and nodded approval. "Anything you can do to help you concentrate is good. If either of you need me, just stick a hand into the air. Take your time. I have a good book, and I won't mind having time to read."

"What if we have to get up, like to use the bathroom or something?" Brenda asked. She knew she was being argumentative, but she couldn't help herself.

"Go now," Des said, "and if you need to go later, go, but I think you'll find that you won't."

A little sheepishly, Brenda obeyed. When she headed back to her place in the dining room, she heard the other toilet flush and felt a little comforted that Riprap had decided to take precautions as well.

Settling into her chair, Brenda used a dull-edged plastic knife to cut a chunk off the large block of polymer clay. She'd played with the stuff before—an experience that gave her an edge over Riprap, whose interests had been almost wholly restricted to sports. Polymer clay was basically the perfect beginner's modeling medium: flexible and nondrying, able to be hardened in a kitchen oven without cracking. Des had repeatedly reminded them that if they messed up, a line could be rubbed out with a fingertip and drawn in again.

"And as long as your characters are close to those on the mah-jong tiles," he reassured them, "don't worry. I'll make sure you don't write the wrong word, and there are variations in handwriting styles for Chinese calligraphy, just as in Western script."

Brenda settled in. Packing the clay into the molds wasn't difficult. Des had recommended they inscribe the sequence in order, so she started with the north wind, the character for which always reminded Brenda a little of the New York Yankees' logo. The first wind needed to be redrawn repeatedly, but by the third she felt her confidence growing.

Compared with the north wind, the red dragon tiles were simple, so simple that Brenda had to force herself to pay attention. She looked back over the five completed tiles before moving on to the first of the sequence of nine bamboos.

Her peacock looked a bit cartoony, but Brenda stopped reworking lines when she realized she was obsessing. Drawing columns that represented stalks of bamboo was easier. She quickly grasped that the best technique was to etch each in faintly, then even out the shape, giving it a hint of dimension.

When Brenda reached six bamboo, fitting the lines of bamboo onto the increasingly tight space became an obsession in itself. She realized she was sweating, although Des's house, with its thick adobe walls, was not in the least warm. Other than that momentary awareness, however, she completely forgot her body. Each stalk of bamboo in the increasingly complex patterns became a part of a forest, and through that forest a long-bodied dragon moved, ready to come to her aid, ready to place itself as a wall between her and any danger.

Brenda hadn't realized that Des was standing behind her until she looked up from completing the crowded array that represented the nine of bamboo. She tapped the tile from the mold and ran a bit of wire through the marks on the sides, so that when the tile was baked there would be a hole.

"Looks good," Des said. "Want to stretch while I bake them?"

"Are they right?" she asked. "I don't mean the shapes, I mean, well, will they work?"

"I'll test them," he promised. "Stretch. Riprap's outside shooting baskets. You'll need to get the kinks out of your muscles before you do the coloring and sealing."

Brenda nodded. Sparing one more proud glance for her creations, she went out through the front door. Riprap was in the driveway along the side. There was something rhythmic about how he bounced the basketball, and she smiled to herself.

And he says he knows nothing about meditation. . . .

Brenda strolled down the street for a few blocks, enjoying the evidence of spring's rapid transition into summer.

When she came back to Des's house, it smelled faintly of cooking plastic.

"The tiles are nearly done," he said, "and they all look great. Are you ready to start painting? Those inks will go on equally well on warm or cool tiles."

"I want to finish," Brenda said. "Do the inks wash off if I mess up?"

"With some effort," Des said. "But don't think about failure. Think about dragons."

Brenda had no trouble understanding. A few minutes later, fresh from the bathroom, she was back at the table. Using the mah-jong tiles as guides, she colored in the various tiles. The ink flowed easily, creating the irresistible image of blood flowing through veins. By the time she was done, she could sense the dragon and its connection to her.

She could sense something else as well. There was Des's spell, the winds and dragons creating a mesh that protected the house and its surroundings. Outside the mesh, things swam in the air and through the earth. She sensed no direct menace from them, but rather a peculiar curiosity.

The curiosity reminded Brenda of how she and her brothers would examine boxes at Christmas. She knew without a doubt that if Des hadn't crafted his protections well, something might decide to lift a corner of the wrapping and take a poke at what was inside. Pokes weren't meant to hurt the contents, but once she had put a run in a silk blouse. Dylan had chipped a crystal model of a train engine his grandmother had sent him.

Brenda shivered and concentrated harder on feeding the colors into the lines she'd etched into each of the tiles that would make her dragon. She imagined it curving its tail between her and whatever was out there, poured herself into the image, until she knew the dragon would come when she called.

Come. But only once. And judging from what else was out there, once would not be enough.

Pearl stood in the aisle where she could watch the activity at the pharmacy counter without being observed herself. Upon her arrival at her hotel in this small town in the Blue Ridge Mountains of Virginia, she had called Nissa Nita's home. A cheerful female voice—one of Nissa's many sisters—had informed Pearl that Nissa was at work, and from there she would be going directly to school, but that she'd be home in time to tuck Lani into bed.

"Do you want to leave a message? I could give you her cell."

Pearl had declined both offers, preferring an opportunity to inspect her subject unseen. As a young woman with fluffy strawberry blond hair moved into view, Pearl had her wish.

Nissa Nita had rosy, lightly freckled skin that went well with her hair. Her figure was rounded, probably overweight by the emaciated standards of current fashion, but pleasant and feminine by those of an earlier day. She wore a white lab coat over a pale blue dress, small sparkling earrings to match, and, from how she moved, what were doubtless sensible shoes.

Nissa was only a few years older than Brenda Morris, but there was a balanced gravity about her as she discussed a prescription with a man old enough to be her grandfather, maybe even her great-grandfather, that made the older man pay attention. He had questions, but they were asked politely, without any sense that he thought he'd better check up on the competence of this young person.

Pretending to inspect an array of toothpastes, Pearl continued to watch as Nissa assisted a middle-aged woman with what was obviously a regular refill, a boy in his teens who was embarrassedly purchasing a prescription acne treatment, and a woman about her own age who wanted advice on what shade to color her hair. This last was obviously a personal friend, and the two chatted for a moment.

At last the pharmacy counter was empty, and Pearl took a tube of toothpaste and a small bottle of aspirin up to the counter. Nissa, her badge giving her first name over the legend "Pharmacy Assistant," turned from where she was putting tags on a box of gaudy sunglasses.

"May I help . . ." she began with a warm smile. Then the smile faded and her eyes, a startling turquoise shade, widened. "Oh, it's you! I mean, Miss Pearl, Miss Bright I mean . . . I didn't expect you to come all this way."

Nissa Nita had a touch of a Southern accent, something musical, rather than drawling, as if adding an extra syllable to the words only contributed to the pleasure of speech.

At Nissa's exclamation, a dark-haired man whose badge read "Bob" over the legend "Pharmacist" turned from where he had been counting out pills. His eyes widened when he saw Pearl.

"Pearl Bright!" he exclaimed, carefully setting down the bottle he'd been holding and hurrying over to the counter. "As I live and breathe! I love your movies. I have all the recordings. I even have a first-edition copy of that children's book you did. What a great pleasure!"

Pearl shook the hand he extended to her, and smiled, saying all the right polite things.

Nissa beamed. "Pearl's a longtime friend of my family, Bob. She knew my mama, and my grandmama, and even my great-grandmama, although you'd never know it to look at her. I told you that."

"I know, I know . . . I know you even said you could get me her autograph if I wanted, but meeting her face-to-face. What a tremendous honor! What will Maddie say when I tell her?"

His face, ordinary before, was suddenly handsome in his pleasure. Pearl, accustomed to California where she was a very, very minor celebrity, if one at all, realized she was actually blushing.

Thankfully, after the busyness a short while before, almost no one was in the store, and Bob, obviously a courteous man, dampened his enthusiasm to appropriate levels.

"Ms. Bright," he said, "would you mind if I took your picture—I mean, if Nissa took your picture with me? I don't have a camera, but I could run to the photo counter and get one."

Pearl, who realized that having Nissa's immediate supervisor's cooperation would be very helpful, agreed, although she did reach up and touch her hair.

"I don't look my best," she said. "I only arrived in Virginia a few hours ago, and decided to surprise Nissa."

Bob assured Pearl that she looked radiant, and bounded away to acquire a camera. Nissa smiled, moved back a few steps, and shook the pills out of the bottle Bob had been filling.

"He'd better start over," she said. "He won't know his right hand from his left, he's so excited. Well, now, you said you'd meant to surprise me, and you've done that."

Nissa's tone was serious now, her initial astonishment damped beneath a hint of fear. "Is this about what you told me on the phone a couple days back?"

"It is," Pearl said. "There have been developments that I didn't want to discuss over the phone. Yesterday, I was able to get a flight from New Mexico to D.C. I hired a car this morning, and drove here. Do you have a break coming up?"

"Not really," Nissa said. "I don't usually take a long break when I'm leaving early for class, and I can't cut, not tonight. We're having a question-and-answer session to prepare for finals."

"I thought exams would be over," Pearl said.

"We're on a different schedule," Nissa said. "The college survives by catering to nontraditional students, people like me who need to work."

"Can I take you to dinner?"

"I have to go home right after class and tuck Lani in," Nissa said. "She's having trouble getting used to the fact that Mommy isn't around all the time. I could meet you after that, probably about seven-thirty."

Bob returned then, bearing a camera he must have purchased on the spot, and trailed by a handful of people who had heard there was a real, live movie star in the drugstore.

Pearl posed for pictures and signed autographs, amused despite herself at this momentary return to the limelight. Then she drew Nissa aside.

"It is possible that my coming here may have increased the danger I spoke with you about over the phone. Will you promise to continue to take care?"

"Only if you do yourself," Nissa said. "I've got a funny feeling about all of this—and it's not from watching Bob turn starstruck."

"I'll go back to my hotel and get some rest," Pearl said. "Then I may go over and visit with your sisters. It would look strange if I only looked in on you."

"They'd love to see you," Nissa said, "and that will make it easier for us to go out to dinner alone. I can make them understand. Somehow."

"I'll help," Pearl said. "After all, by then you'll be the only one I haven't spent time with."

"Sounds good," Nissa said. "And take care."

Pearl did, although it seemed impossible that anything could happen on this small town's main street in broad daylight. Still, she wasn't about to overlook the younger woman's caution. Whoever had attacked Gaheris Morris had been very confident that he would not be seen. Such confidence might lead to anything.

She napped, and then, as promised, visited with Nissa's sisters. There were several at home, watching over a brood of children, some their own, some in day care for other working mothers. The Nita sisters followed a similar template: fair, with eyes of various shades of blue, and hair ranging from dubiously natural blond to undoubtedly natural flame red. They were cheerful and intense, their intensity of the kind that invigorates rather than drains.

Wanting to assure herself of time alone with Nissa, Pearl left, rather reluctantly, when the children were settled to dinner. Later, Nissa came over to Pearl's hotel and the two walked over to have dinner at a "home style" restaurant a few blocks away.

"The food at the hotel," Nissa said apologetically, as if she herself was somehow to blame, "isn't very good. They can get away with it because they're the only place in town that rents rooms."

"Did you have any problems with your sisters?"

"None. They were in heaven because you stayed so long, and the kids were so good. They kept going on and on about how you had them all charmed."

"Well," Pearl said with a dry smile. "I did spend a lot of time with children, both when I was one myself and later. Maybe because I was expected to be a professional as well as a child, I've never made the mistake so many adults do of underestimating just how smart and curious even a very little child can be."

When they arrived at the restaurant, it was clear that the small-town grapevine had been at work, and that the owners knew exactly who their guest was. However, rather than exploiting this, they seemed prepared to bend over backward to assure that Pearl and Nissa would not be troubled by the other patrons. They were put in a booth near the back, and waited on by the owner himself.

"His wife is the head cook," Nissa said, "and everything here is delicious."

Pearl ordered free-range grouse with homemade bread stuffing, and was told that the birds were raised by a relative of Nissa's. So, it turned out, were the salad greens. Another relative made the cheese and butter.

"Post-hippie commune," Nissa said. "The commune part didn't stick, but the interest in organic food and not working for 'the Man' did. Now, tell me what brought you here all the way from California."

"Via Santa Fe," Pearl amended, and launched into an unedited account of the events of the last several days.

There was a great deal to tell, and they had finished slices of strawberry pie and were sipping cups of some exotic blend of herbal tea when Pearl finished.

"So," Nissa said, "of the Thirteen Orphans, only four seem untouched: you, me, the Dog, and the Rooster. The Rat is taken, but his heir apparent seems to be shaping up into someone who will be a help. Have you gone to visit any of the other heir apparents?"

"I haven't," Pearl admitted. "Only a few might prove useful. I know the Dragon did not leave his son untutored, but, frankly, most of those who knew of their heritage did not cultivate the skills that went with it."

"Why should they?" Nissa said reasonably. "I'm the fourth generation since the first Rabbit—or Hare—or whatever. Nothing has happened to any of us since my grandmother's day, and I'm not sure I really ever believed any of the stories I was told by Grandma."

"But you believe what I've just told you," Pearl said, hating the pleading note that crept into her voice.

"I believe it," Nissa replied firmly. "My ears are twitching and my nose is wiggling. I can scent the hawk on the wing. And I'm a mama, too, and I don't want anything coming after me or my baby. I believe you with my gut, and my brain is going to have to take second place until it catches up."

"I cannot express with sufficient eloquence how relieved that makes me," Pearl admitted. "Are you willing to accept further training?"

"Training, yes," Nissa said, "but I'm not in a position to drop everything like you say young Brenda and Riprap have done."

"Riprap," Pearl objected mildly, "is older than you are."

"Older in years, maybe," Nissa said, "but I'm old in living. I've got a two-and-a-half-year-old daughter to care for, and she's having a tough enough time dealing with me being away at work and school. I'm not packing up and leaving her."

"Fair enough," Pearl said. "We'll do what we can to work something out. Maybe I can stay a few days, teach you a few tricks. Tonight I am too tired to begin."

"Let me walk you back to your hotel," Nissa said. "My car's there anyhow."

"Good. Maybe you can stop up in my room. I made some notes for you that should give you a start on your studies. When you get a moment, you can review them."

Although Pearl's room was only on the third floor, they took the elevator. Nissa admitted that being on her feet for hours at a time took away most of her extra energy. They discussed exercise and diets as they walked down the hall toward Pearl's room.

"Funny, isn't it?" Nissa said. "Despite my title, 'rabbit food' just isn't enough to keep me going."

Pearl had been digging out her key card, preparatory to sliding it into the electronic lock, but now she paused and raised one hand, holding her index finger to her lips. Nissa froze. Pearl swore she could almost see rabbit ears twitching.

"Something is not right," Pearl said, not so much whispering as moving her lips so that the younger woman could read them. "Talk normally. I'm going ahead."

Nissa blinked at her, but obediently started chattering again. "I mean, my sister grows these fantastic vegetables, but I want to coat them in butter. Nancy is always swearing if I'd just give myself a chance to learn . . ."

Pearl whispered to her wind—the wind of the east-northeast, which ruled her sign. They had been friends a long, long time, and the wind flicked obediently ahead. As Pearl requested, it slid beneath the door, touched what was within, and came back to her. It was agitated, so much so that Pearl had to frame its report as words in order to understand.

"You were there already?" she asked. *"How is that possible?"*

The wind insisted that it had gone through the door and sensed no one but itself. Pearl felt a prickling along her back and she paced closer.

"I can't find my key card," Pearl said aloud. "I prefer good, old-fashioned metal keys. These cards may be more secure, but I don't trust them."

"Give me your purse," Nissa said. "You check your pockets."

Pearl appreciated the young woman's facility for deception. Because she would need her hands free, she gave over the tidy black leather bag she'd carried to dinner, then dropped one hand to cover the doorknob.

A long, long time ago she'd learned a charm for opening locks. Now she visualized the appropriate sequence in her mind, touching each shape with her paws. She felt the lock release and, without delay, pushed open the door.

Nissa came after, closer behind her than Pearl would have liked, but then the Hare had always followed close on the Tiger's heels.

Standing across the hotel room, wrapped in wind, stood a young man dressed in full, long-sleeved robes after the Chinese fashion, the green fabric embroidered with stylized animal figures. Pearl registered two things about the intruder at once: he was very handsome, and he reminded her of someone, someone her mind told her she knew very well, and yet had never seen.

The young man moved with fluid grace as Pearl and Nissa crossed the threshold, two long strips of paper held between the fingers of his left hand. Both pieces of paper were green, the writing on them in a green ink so dark it was almost black. He grabbed the first strip of paper in his right hand, and threw it like a dagger, directly at Pearl.

She, however, was ready for him. Her wind was waiting, and she used it to divert the paper dagger from her. She snatched it from the air, noting that it was inscribed on one side with the character for "Tiger."

The young man was already throwing the second piece of paper, but Nissa, quick as a Rabbit must be, had darted back into the hallway. The paper hit the doorframe, then clattered to the floor as if it was, at least at that moment, something far more solid than a sheet of paper.

The young man cursed, not at them, but at himself. He spoke a peculiar form of Chinese Pearl had never heard spoken by a stranger.

However, unlike when he had failed in the parking garage, the young man—for this must be the same as had attacked Brenda, Riprap, and Gaheris—did not flee. Instead, he drew a long slim sword, its blade inscribed with many characters, from a sheath worn close to his side. With the same motion, he released the winds that had hidden him, commanding them to seal this area so that no one would hear noise and be tempted to interfere.

Pearl felt a growl low in her throat. Perhaps this young sorcerer/warrior did not fear two women—one of them bearing quite a number of years on her slim shoulders—as he had two men. Perhaps he was unwilling to fail again. Whatever the reason, he was coming at them, his dark brown eyes narrowed, bright with intensity.

Hearing Nissa reenter the room, Pearl knew she must protect this untutored young woman. Pearl had been a young woman of attractive appearance, and long ago she had committed to memory those spells that would permit her to get the upper hand over impulsive young men, especially if they would be left in a position that would not lead them to talk about the situation later.

Many years had passed since she had needed such a spell, but Pearl remembered well the sequence that culminated in releasing the Winding Snake. Stepping back as if in retreat, she released the spell. The young man must have had very good training, for he saw the snake coming for him as none of her would-be swains had ever done.

He altered his sword stroke so that he might cut at the Winding Snake, but did not adapt quickly enough. Pearl's snake knew what to do. It entwined the young man's legs and ankles, making him unsteady. The tactic also had the advantage of rendering him quite reluctant to use his sword, for were he to do so, he would likely slice into his own body.

Nissa was standing in the doorway, her turquoise eyes wide. Pearl wondered just what she was seeing. Did she see a young man stumbling about, waving a sword ineffectually? Did she see the snake that was causing him to stumble, to drop his sword, to tear at his legs with both hands?

Looking on with satisfaction—and catching her breath, for casting a spell from memory with little time to store the ch'i in advance took energy from even the strongest sorcerer—Pearl had a flash of memory. She knew who the young man had reminded her of, and acted upon the impulse.

The green slip of paper with "Tiger" written upon it was still in her hand. She spoke the Dragonfly charm to stiffen it and make it fly straight and true; then she released it.

Seeing it coming, the young man gave a wordless cry of terror, raising his arms as if to defend himself, but Pearl's dragonfly dodged and darted, driving the paper solidly against the young man's forehead. The written charm sunk in, vanishing into his flesh, just as Brenda and Riprap had described the Rat charm vanishing into that of Gaheris Morris.

Then a curious thing happened, curious even in this moment when all things were strange. The young man reached into his sleeve and brought out a small crystal sphere, perhaps three inches in diameter. He cupped it in his palms and a leaf-green light shone forth from his hands, filling the sphere, then solidifying within into the shape of a great cat—of a frozen tiger.

Nissa reentered the room. Pearl noted with approval and amusement that the pharmacist's assistant held a long-legged occasional table in her hands, clearly ready to use it as either weapon or shield.

The young man did not seem to notice either Nissa or Pearl, staring instead at the sphere he cupped in his hands.

"What's wrong with him?" Nissa whispered.

"I threw his own spell back at him," Pearl said. "Apparently, the stolen memories are sealed within one of those spheres. The sequence must have been set in advance, and once it began, he could not break it. That is one of the problems with stored spells. Now he is trapped. In a moment, he will probably stop staring at that sphere. I would guess that right now the spell is rewriting his memory to allow for the gaps. I think it best that our unwelcome guest sleep while we decide what to do with him."

Nissa gestured as if to wallop the young man with the table she still grasped between her hands, but Pearl made a dismissive gesture.

"I think I have one more spell in me, although I will not be good for much thereafter."

She did the spell called Moon, which among its abilities contains that of bringing sleep. The young man's eyes closed and he slid to the floor, the sphere that held his memories clasped between his cupped hands.

Nissa helped Pearl lay the young man on one of the beds in Pearl's room. She returned the occasional table to the hallway, and brought back with her a can of soda.

"You looked exhausted."

"I am, rather," Pearl admitted. "It is many years since I cast so many spells in quick sequence."

"But how did you know his spell would work against him?" Nissa said. "Wasn't it the spell meant to trap you?"

"Meant to trap the Tiger," Pearl corrected. She looked down at the crystal sphere and the green tiger within. "From the first moment I saw that young man, I was reminded of someone. Oddly, I did not recognize him in concentration, nor in impulsive anger, but when he was there, struggling to keep his balance and looking all the fool, I knew him."

"Knew him?"

"Rather, I knew who he reminded me of," Pearl amended. "Our young visitor looks very like my father did when my father was a young man."

"Your father?"

"My father," Pearl repeated, feeling an odd satisfaction. "My father, the warrior Tiger."

Only Nissa's faith in Pearl's arcane abilities made the young woman agree to return to her home and daughter.

"We can't have your sisters coming to find you," Pearl said, "and you know they would wonder if you didn't get home to Noelani."

"Noreen certainly would," Nissa said. "She'd be sure I have another boy-friend. She'd snoop and pry. Nadine wouldn't, but . . . are you sure he'll sleep all night?"

"I'm sure. That is no normal sleep. It is the Moon. Try pinching the back of his hand."

Nissa did, and the young man didn't even stir.

"They could use that trick at the day care," Nissa said, trying to make a joke of her unease at the man's lack of response. "Fine. I'll be back to help you in the morning."

"By then I will be rested," Pearl said. "I plan to rebind him, then see what he can tell me."

"I'll be back," Nissa repeated. "You're going to need help, even if only with explaining to the hotel staff how he got here."

"I don't plan on explaining," Pearl said loftily, but she knew the situation wasn't going to be resolved that easily. This was a small town in Virginia, not Hollywood, or even San Francisco or San Jose.

The young man slept through the night, as Pearl had known he would. When dawn washed away the last of night, he stirred. Pearl had been awake long enough to shower, dress, and eat what had proved to be a very nice breakfast she had brought up from the hotel restaurant. Now she poured herself a second cup of cof-fee and watched her young would-be assassin become aware of his surroundings.

As a precaution, she had removed his sword, along with the dagger he had tucked in his sash. Up close, the stylized animals on his robes proved to be tigers. She was not surprised.

Other than disarming him, Pearl had left her guest much as he had been, curious to see what he would do when he awoke in an unfamiliar setting. She had seated herself on a window seat, where she could observe without being readily visible.

He moved, shifted, and then opened a pair of absolutely lovely dark brown eyes. His lashes were long and thick, without being in the least feminine. Her father had possessed lashes like that. Pearl, although hardly less gifted in that de-partment, had always envied him.

The young man's jet-black hair was worn long, bound up beneath a small cap with a single button. His skin was golden, showing the touch of the sun without the abuses of weathering. His cheekbones were perfect, and his build muscular and athletic while still possessing a certain feline litheness. Pearl guessed his age at between twenty and twenty-five. She was good at estimating ages, but without cultural clues and body language she would not bet any closer.

Those brown eyes were open now, studying their surroundings with increasing apprehension and rising panic. The young man forced himself upright, swinging his feet to the floor. The sound of the springs under the mattress startled him and he froze. His gaze drifted to the tasteful carpet, a dark red figured with curving lines in golden brown. That seemed to fascinate him as well.

Pearl could tell when the Moon's hold lapsed, for the young man surged to his feet and began to look wildly about. Pearl had told the winds to keep sound from escaping when the young man began to stir. Now she was glad, for he let out a bellow that was part defiance, part fear, and completely without words: the panic of an animal, not of a man.

To this point, Pearl had held very still. Now she set her coffee cup into its saucer with an audible clatter. The young man started at the sound and again when he saw her. His eyes widened as he took in her neat Chanel suit, her tidy, low-heeled pumps, and all the other accessories and accouterments of a modern woman of some years who, while not feeling she necessarily need try to look young, had not decided that age meant she must look decrepit.

"What manner of creature are you?" he asked in his peculiar dialect of Chinese. "Where is this place? Into which of the hells have I stumbled?"

"My name is Pearl Bright," she replied in the same language, "and this is no hell. As for how you came here, I should be asking you. I returned to my room and found you here. What do you have to say for yourself?"

The young man had seen the sword and now he leapt toward it. His lithe grace was admirable, but did him no good. Pearl had adapted a spell for Wriggling Snakes to hold the sword to the dresser. He might grasp it, but he could not lift it, and the dresser was very solid. Cherry, she thought, or walnut.

"Who are you?" Pearl persisted. "What kind of man are you who needs a sword to defend himself against an old woman?"

He stopped in midmotion, before, Pearl noted with interest, his hand touched either sword or matching dagger. His expression turned puzzled, his right hand raised to lightly touch his forehead. Then he raised both hands and stroked his face. He looked down at his robes, studying the elaborate patterns with fascination. At last he looked directly at her.

"I don't know who I am," he said. "I can't remember my name, although I know I must have a name. I can't remember my parents or where I live or where I got this clothing. I can't even think why I would reach for a sword. Who am I?"

"A good question," Pearl said. Her cell phone rang, interrupting the conversation. She held up her hand to the young man and answered it.

Nissa was on the other end. "Did everything go all right last night?"

"Fine. He slept like a baby until dawn. He has been awake just a short time now."

Pearl had spoken in English and noted that the young man did not seem to be able to understand her.

"We have a problem," she went on. "The memory spell seems to have hit him very hard."

"Worse than Gaheris?"

"Far worse. My young visitor does not seem to remember anything about himself."

"He's faking it," Nissa said. "He's trying to cover."

"I wish I thought so," Pearl said, "but I don't think he's acting. I think he has genuinely lost his memory. If so, we've lost our best chance at learning who sent him."

"You don't think he's in it on his own?" Nissa asked.

"Now that I've met him, no," Pearl said. "I'll explain why later. Are you coming over?"

"I've called in to work. Bob understood perfectly why I needed a sudden holiday. All I had to do was promise I would get you to autograph a stack of paraphernalia from his collection."

"Gladly. Can you leave Lani at home?"

"Yes, if she thinks I'm going to work. She knows the rules."

"Then come when you can. Meanwhile, I'm going to talk to my young guest. Maybe something I say will jog his memories."

"Take care," Nissa warned. "It could be someone will come looking for him—and that someone cannot be counted on to make the same mistakes."

Des's phone rang early, while Des was over at the stove stirring a pot of rice congee for his breakfast. Reassured by more normal foods available, Brenda and Riprap had promised to try the rice porridge, but it didn't look very appetizing—especially as Des apparently planned to eat it with hot and spicy pickles.

"Get that for me, Brenda?"

"Sure. Hello. Des Lee's residence. May I help you?"

"Brenda? This is Pearl Bright. Are Des and Riprap near?"

"Right here," Brenda replied. "We're having breakfast."

"Ask Des if his house phone has a speaker."

Brenda did and Des nodded. "Sure. Right there."

When the connection was established, Pearl launched into a report of what had happened the night before.

Remembering how she and Riprap had been ordered not to discuss anything related to magic over the phone or via e-mail, Brenda was impressed how Pearl managed to talk around the fact that magic had evidently been used.

Had anyone been tapping in on the call, they would have thought that Pearl and Nissa had had an encounter with a particularly obsessed fan—one of those who could be dangerous—but certainly not odd beyond the fact that in the shock of his encountering his idol he had somehow lost his memory.

Pearl's listeners, of course, had the necessary information to fill in the gaps.

When Pearl stopped for breath, Des cut in.

"Pearl, do you think the amnesia is real?"

"I do. My young 'guest' honestly doesn't remember a thing about himself, where he is from, or why he came here. He only speaks a form of Chinese, which is rather a help, as I'm the only one here who understands him, and so he can't tell anyone that I'm, well, effectively holding him captive. I think the best thing would be for me to drive cross-country to my place in San Jose."

"You wouldn't dare fly," Des agreed. "You couldn't get him through security, but why go all the way to California?"

"Because I can control everything—including him—much better both in a car and then in my own home," Pearl replied sharply. "I also have resources in my home that might enable me to figure out how to alleviate his amnesia."

Riprap leaned toward the phone. "Ms. Bright, would you like me to fly out and join you on the drive? If I understand correctly, Ms. Nita is a young woman responsible for an even younger child. I might be of more help if your 'guest' decided to cause trouble."

"Riprap, I would," Pearl said. "I hate to interrupt your studies, but Nissa admits to being reluctant to subject Lani to a week where the child would be strapped for hours on end in a car seat. I must say, I agree."

"But Nissa does want to come to California?" Des asked.

"Very much so," Pearl said. "She was hesitating before, but now she's quite certain she'd like to be one of this summer's interns."

"I'm surprised she wants to bring Lani," Des went on.

A new voice cut in, its notes colored with a Virginia drawl. "This is Nissa. I can use the chance to take a California internship as an excuse to get my professors to let me take my exams early. However, my sisters would never believe I'd go away for what might be weeks and leave Lani. Anyhow, I think all that emphasis on secrecy might have made the Thirteen vulnerable. Lani might as well pick up what she can. She's at the age where she'll accept anything, and no one will believe her if she talks about magic and spells. They'll just think she's mixing up some book I read her with reality."

"That makes sense," Des agreed. "Pearl, even if we're lucky enough to find

Riprap an open flight, he can't get to Virginia immediately. Can you handle things until he gets there?"

"I think we can," Pearl replied. "Nissa is quite resourceful, and, at least for now, our young visitor is completely overwhelmed. He looked out the hotel window earlier and saw a couple of cars driving by. That nearly sent him under the bed. He's not a coward, but right now he's convinced he's in some supernatural hell. Nissa and I are his closest anchors to reality."

"That's weird," Brenda said. "If it's the same man, we met him first in a parking garage, I mean. He should know about cars."

Nissa asked. "Brenda, can you get pictures on your phone?"

"Sure."

"I'll send one. Tell us if it's the same man."

When the picture came through, Brenda studied it for a minute, then turned her phone so Riprap could see it. He nodded.

"It's the same fellow," Brenda said. "He's not dressed the same, but as best as we can tell from such a small picture, it's the same man."

She didn't mention that the young man looked even better with his hair loosely gathered at the nape of his neck, or the weird mixture of fear and attraction she felt as she looked at him. Covertly, she saved the picture on her phone so she could look at it later.

"Our guest showered this morning," Nissa said, "and while he was in the bathroom, we took his Chinese clothes. They're sort of noticeable. He wasn't thrilled with our style of clothing. I'm glad I thought to buy him button-fly jeans—a zipper would have stumped him. He's not dumb, but he sure isn't sophisticated."

Des frowned. "If he's that naive, he's not likely to enjoy traveling by car."

"He's not going to have much choice," Pearl replied tartly. "If he will not cooperate, I will compel him."

Riprap asked, "Do you think he has allies?"

"That's a pretty good bet," Pearl said. "There were 'items.'" Her inflection indicated that these were other than normal, and Des mouthed "probably amulets," to clarify. "I think the wisest course of action is to assume that our boy is the front man for someone more sophisticated."

"Any thoughts?"

"Let's just say I think we may have a return to old troubles."

"Pearl," Des said, "we'll call as soon as we know what flight we can get Riprap on. Let us know what arrangements you make for Nissa."

"We will," Pearl said. "Be careful."

"We will. . . . Talk with you later."

Had the world been at all normal, Brenda knew she would have protested against what the others were doing. What Pearl Bright was doing amounted to kidnapping, and probably a bunch of other illegal things. However, the memory of Gaheris Morris's face as his memory was taken from him, of the vacancy Brenda sensed whenever they talked, seemed to have burned every residue of pity from Brenda's soul where that young stranger was concerned.

By the next phone call, Pearl and Nissa had christened their amnesiac visitor Foster, which seemed to be appropriate, given his role as their charge. Brenda tried to accustom herself to referring to him by such a prosaic name, and found herself wondering what his real name was. Maybe the spell's hold on him was like in a fairy tale, and when they learned his true name, his memory would come back to him.

After breakfast, Brenda listened in when Des called his travel agent. "Patricia? Des Lee. I have a friend visiting who needs to get to a small town in Virginia's Blue Ridge Mountains as soon as possible, family emergency. From what I know of his eventual destination, he might do better to fly into D.C., then drive from there. Can you find me anything—a cancellation, even a good bet at standby?"

Des listened, then nodded. "Yes. My friend can drive. Okay. Book that flight, and arrange for a rental car, something comfortable for at least four. He's probably going to need to drive relatives around.

"My friend's name is Charles Adolphus. Thanks a bunch, Patricia. By the way, keep your eyes open for good fares either to San Jose or San Francisco, for two, probably sometime next week. Thanks . . . You're an angel."

Des hung up the phone, rubbed his eyes, and stretched. "Okay. Riprap, we have a nonstop flight for you out of Albuquerque tomorrow leaving fairly early. It will get you into Washington National—I can't stand the new name for that airport—midday. There will be a rental car waiting. I'll let you judge whether you'll drive to Pearl in Virginia then or wait for morning."

"That afternoon, if I'm not too beat from the flight," Riprap said. "I know Pearl Bright is a tough old tiger, but it makes me nervous thinking of her there pretty much alone with that young thug. I'm itching to leave right now, but I know it won't do any good."

Des grinned mischievously. "Well, since it won't do any good for you to sit around and fidget, I plan to keep you and Brenda pretty busy tomorrow morning."

Brenda wrinkled her nose. "Making more tiles? Des, I'm not sure I could concentrate."

Des shook his head. "I know. However, I've tested the tiles you and Riprap made, and they look good. I think we'll go out and show you how to use them."

★

Pearl hung up the phone and turned to Nissa in time to see the younger woman apologetically patting back a yawn.

"Sorry, Pearl, but I had trouble sleeping last night. I was worried about you here, alone with him."

She tossed her head to where Foster sat as if mesmerized in front of the television.

"That was sweet of you," Pearl said. "Des has arranged for Riprap to take a flight that will get him into D.C. by tomorrow afternoon. He'll drive down here to meet me. I think we'll leave as soon as Riprap can bear to get in a car again, although I'll drive to give him a chance to rest. Now we need to make arrangements for you and Lani."

"I don't want to leave until after Riprap is safely here," Nissa said.

"That's fine," Pearl agreed. "I was actually thinking that since we're driving, and Des and Brenda are still in Santa Fe, you could have a few days here to tie up your affairs and come up with a reason why you're going to California on such short notice."

"I've already been working on that," Nissa said with a faint smile. "Bob, my boss at the drugstore, already has it in his head that you came out here to scout Lani for the movies and TV. The rumor got home before I did."

"Aren't your sisters upset that I'm overlooking their kids? Several of them are very cute. I realize that you're biased, but I think they're at least as cute as Lani."

Nissa shook her head. "Not much. Not really. Most of them are seriously into the home-schooling, natural-foods way of life. Hollywood doesn't match with that at all."

"Good," Pearl said "If that's our excuse, I'd better make some calls. It wouldn't hurt to at least do a portfolio and some screen tests. I have a friend I can call. . . . But first, let's see about getting you a flight."

There were plenty of available seats on nonstop flights from D.C. to San Francisco, fewer available directly to San Jose at such short notice.

"But if you don't mind," Pearl said, reviewing the options she'd copied down, "I'd like to put you on a late flight five days from now. That will get you into San Francisco early in the morning. I'll arrange for my driver to pick you up."

"A night flight would be best," Nissa said. "Lani's much more likely to sleep on a night flight."

"That was what I was thinking, too. You can drive my rental car to D.C. and return it," Pearl said. "Des said Riprap's bringing a larger, more comfortable car with him."

"Sounds as if you and Des have everything covered," Nissa said. "But isn't this going to be expensive?"

Pearl glanced at where Foster sat staring at the television.

"Not nearly as expensive as if we pay with our memories, not nearly as expensive at all."

★

"Okay, folks," Des said. "If I'm going to show you how those bracelets you made work, I need a little time to set up. Can I leave you to review this list of limit hands?"

He put two copies of a short list on the table: name of hand, combination of tiles needed, and a short description of what the hand could do.

"These are good basic attack and defense spells," he went on. "You'll find it easier to craft them onto tiles—and later to work them from memory if you have the sequences down cold."

Brenda still felt awash with the tension and confusion of the last few days, and she'd have preferred a chance to go for a walk or see some of the local tourist sights.

And get jumped like Pearl nearly did? the querulous voice of her inner self asked her.

"Sure, Des," Brenda said.

Riprap took out the spiral-bound notebook that Des had—with some reluctance, for apparently it was traditional for students to learn without written cribs—given each of them.

Riprap looked up from the notebook he'd spread open on the table, his large brown eyes warm and nonjudgmental. Brenda went to her room to get her own notebook, but when she was seated across from Riprap at the table and saw that he was now carefully copying each sequence over ten times, something in her snapped.

"You're determined," she said. "Don't you want to give it a rest? We're in

one of the tourist capitals of the country—if not the world—and here we are doing lessons."

"I don't think I can give it a rest," Riprap said almost too mildly. "You see,
whoever's after us has got what they want from the Rat's line, but they didn't
quite manage with the Dog's. More than that, I'm still burning over letting that
man get to your dad—especially since Pearl managed to stop him. I'm not going
to let anyone go down while I'm standing by—not if doing a bunch of lessons
will let me know what to expect."

Brenda flushed. "Yeah. Me either, I guess. I'm sorry. I guess this has all
caught up with me. I'm not sure what difference getting to Auntie Pearl's is going
to make, but I feel like it should make some."

Riprap raised his broad shoulders in a casual shrug.

"Maybe. Maybe not. One thing I've learned though, from playing and
coaching both. You can't control the rest of the team. You can't control the
weather or home-field advantage or any of that stuff. What you can control is
yourself, and as I see it, we're seven innings into this game, and the other side has
scored lots of points. If we're going to pull a save, I can't be expecting one of the
star players to do my part as well as theirs."

Brenda blinked. "That's quite a lecture."

Riprap grinned sheepishly. "You should hear me when I get all inspirational
on my players. Don't get me wrong, Brenda. I don't think these tricks I'm learning will let me do anything spectacular. I just don't want those who can use the
big guns to be kept from doing so because they're busy pulling my butt out of
the fire."

Brenda, remembering her father yelling, "Brenda! Down!," remembering
how both men had moved to protect her against the "mugger," thinking how her
own cockiness might have made matters worse, not better, flushed again.

"You've got a point, coach. I'll remember. I guess I've been thinking that the
'game' will start when we're there. You're right. It's ongoing, and we're not winning. Thanks."

"No problem."

When Des arrived about forty-five minutes later, though, Brenda was glad
for a chance to stretch.

"Come out into my yard," Des said. "I've set wards, so even if someone
catches a glimpse of us, they'll not see anything odd."

Brenda, accustomed to the open yards of the Southeast, understood his
"even" better when they were outside. Des's yard was completely walled, the
thick adobe uneven and picturesquely crumbling in places. Along parts of the

wall, red and yellow trumpet vine spilled over in a wild wash of color that relieved what was otherwise dirt brown.

The yard itself showed that Des wasn't much of a gardener. Near the walls
there were scattered shrubs and off in one corner was an apple tree that even
Brenda's untrained eye could see needed pruning. Dominating the enclosed area
was a flat area of smooth packed earth, neatly swept clean of any debris.

There were benches on one side, and on these Brenda saw an assortment of
oddities, including the tiles she and Riprap had made two days before. These had
been strung on parallel bands of thin elastic.

"Put those on," Des said. "I strung them for you last night after I checked to
be sure the spell was live."

Brenda's bracelet fit a little loosely, but Riprap's had to stretch to go over his
big hand and fit very snugly around his wrist.

Des frowned. "In later versions, we can incorporate a few beads to give you
more play, but this will do for now. Who wants to go first?"

Brenda glanced at Riprap, and the big man shrugged. "Your call."

"I guess I will, then," Brenda said. "What do I do?"

"Move to that open area," Des said, "and when you're comfortable, take off
the bracelet and smash it onto the ground."

"Won't it break?"

"More easily than you imagine, especially if you throw it with the intent that
it will break and so release the ch'i—that is energy, in this case, magical energy—
you trapped within. Ready?"

In answer, Brenda moved to the open space. The bracelet slipped easily over
her hand. With a decisive snap of her wrist, Brenda threw it hard onto the packed
dirt. As soon as the bracelet hit the ground, the fourteen tiles immediately vanished, leaving a trace of white dust against the brown.

Brenda was still struggling to accept this phenomenon—polymer clay didn't
break that easily, and when it did, it didn't explode into dust; it cracked or chipped—
when a translucent dragon's tail swirled around her and took her into its embrace.

The dragon's tail was colorless, and yet she felt confident that it was also pale
blue shadowed with brown. The image was so detailed that Brenda could see
how the individual scales decreased in size as the tail narrowed toward its tip,
even though the image no more obstructed her vision than would a fingerprint
on the lens of her sunglasses. It was as if some previously dormant part of her
mind, rather than her eyes alone, was responsible for the seeing.

Odd as this was, perhaps the oddest thing was that although Brenda couldn't
see the entire dragon—only its tail, and only the part of the tail that crossed in front

of her—she could sense a bulk, a force, surrounding her, much the way the press of a crowd is felt even when no one in that crowd is making actual physical contact.

She shivered in her skin, simultaneously delighted and mildly claustrophobic.

Des trotted over to close with her. The dragon's tail reacted to his proximity with rippling undulations, but it wasn't until Des took a swing at Brenda's face that the coils rose and interposed themselves. Brenda jumped back, and found that the entire coil moved with her.

"Hold still!" Des commanded. "You need to learn to trust the protection."

Brenda did as ordered, but she flinched anyway as Des's balled right fist came toward her face. It stopped about six inches short of impact. He brought his left fist up in a sharp uppercut that she didn't even see until the dragon's tail stopped it.

Riprap had come over to join them.

"So she doesn't need to direct it," he said. "It intervenes on its own. Nice. How long will it last?"

Des shrugged and kicked out at Brenda's shin. "Depends on the strength of the caster, on the strength and type of blows being blocked. This one probably has at least another fifteen minutes in it. Take a swing. I want you to see how it feels."

Brenda felt a mixture of indignation and pleasure as Riprap obeyed orders with alacrity. He pulled his hand back, shaking the fingers slightly.

"Didn't exactly hurt, but I knew I was hitting something."

Taking advantage of his greater height, he aimed a blow from above. Brenda saw the tail snake across to block, but also saw that the coverage was less complete.

"Careful," she warned.

Des nodded. "This is a pretty basic protection. It works best for attacks from front, rear, and sides, less from above and below. It will work against fists or weapons, but a really skilled practitioner might be able to slip a blade through the coils. It works less well against missile attacks, and even less well against those that involve a scattered projectile of some sort—birdshot, flame, or liquid. It can't stop gases, but it might slow them long enough for you to do another spell."

"Basic," Brenda agreed, "but cool. What about if I trip and fall—like when I was trying to dodge you—will it catch me?"

"Maybe," Des said, "but don't count on it, especially if it's blocking an outside attack. Protecting from outside menace is its first order of business."

Des went back to the bench and returned with a pair of outlandish-looking things—sort of a cross between brass knuckles and garden cultivators, but a whole lot more menacing-looking. He slipped them over his hands with accustomed ease.

"My grandmother—the Exile Rooster—had these made. She called them the Rooster's Talons."

Again, without giving warning, he slashed out at Brenda's face. She managed to hold her ground, though her eyes squinched shut.

"What did you see when the Talon hit?" he asked.

"There was," Brenda said, "a sort of bluish light, a thin line of it where the Talon slashed the dragon's tail."

Des nodded in approval. "If you see that, watch out. That means whatever weapon that hit your spell has the ability to weaken its ch'i."

"So the spell will break faster?" Brenda asked.

"Right," Des said. "Then would be a good time to cast a follow-up or get out while you can."

Riprap had been about to take another swing, but now he let his hand drop, obviously not willing to risk breaking the weakened barrier.

"Can she do anything from inside there?" he asked. "I mean, anything to attack."

"Sure," Des said. "She could cast spells or even throw a punch."

"The dragon's tail won't get in the way?" Riprap asked.

"Somewhat," Des admitted, "but as you'll see when you're inside, the coverage isn't complete. You can work around it. But, to repeat myself, this is a very basic spell. Its greatest virtue is it is relatively easy to create, and reliable within its limits. If you get interested in combat armor spells, there are others that are more versatile."

"But harder to do," Riprap said.

"Exactly."

Brenda scooped up a few pebbles from the ground and experimented, imagining that a shrub was one of their enemies. She decided that if she practiced, she might even hit occasionally. Her own lack of skill, not the Dragon's Tail's blocking, was the greatest impediment to success.

But I doubt we'll get too much practice—at least with the spells, she thought. *These bracelets take too long to make for us to use them up—especially with real enemies out there.*

Brenda's spell didn't last much longer, and she gladly changed places with Riprap. She was interested to see that unless she concentrated hard, she couldn't see Riprap's dragon's tail at all.

"Is that because I'm not really the Rat?" she asked, dancing around and taking jabs at Riprap, feeling more than seeing the solid, flexible force that kept her blows from landing.

"No," Des said. "It's because you have very little training. There are spells that permit the caster to see magical energy. They're very useful, and you'll all be learning how to do at least a simple one."

"As a bracelet," Riprap said.

"At first," Des agreed. "In time, you should learn how to focus your ch'i on demand."

After the lesson was over, they went back inside. Des presented Riprap with a selection of amulet bracelets.

"My crafting," he said, "and somewhat generic. However, they will give you some protection as you're traveling. Pearl brought some along for Nissa. We don't expect either of you to have trouble in public areas, or even in private, but it never hurts to be careful."

"I will," Riprap promised, sliding the bracelets onto his wrists and practicing getting them off smoothly. "I assure you, I will."

The next morning, Brenda and Des drove Riprap to the airport in Albuquerque. The previous day hadn't been all work and lessons. Des had taken them for a walk through several historic areas, and later to dinner at a high-end restaurant called the Pink Adobe that was quite proud that its building had once been a brothel.

Almost everywhere they went, Des was greeted like an old friend by someone or other. Apparently what Pearl and her dad had said was true. Even in a city known for being a haven of movie stars, artists, and writers, Des was something of a celebrity.

As they went from gallery to shop to cathedral, Brenda couldn't help but notice that for all Des chattered away about the local sights in a relaxed and animated fashion, he also kept them to areas where they were always in the vicinity of other people. She also noticed how Riprap kept scanning their surroundings and fingering the bracelets on his wrist.

Brenda was surprised at how quickly she had started to feel naked without the one she'd made, but when on their way back from the airport she asked Des if she could have a couple, just for now, he assured her that for now he'd protect her.

"Besides," he said, grinning at her sidelong in a way that reminded Brenda that Desperate Lee was a father and teacher, as well as local celebrity, "wanting some amulets of your own is the best incentive I can think of for you to stop worrying and start doing something—even if it is something as demanding as making those bracelets."

Brenda, who knew she'd been hoping to get out of the routine drudgery, found herself laughing as she hadn't since a piece of paper thrown in a LoDo parking garage had transformed her father, and in the process changed her as well.

Pearl was glad when Nissa came over to the hotel bearing a bag packed with takeout sandwiches from a local shop. She had spent less than thirty-six hours with Foster by then, but the dual roles of jailer and host were proving unexpectedly wearing. She'd made the excuse of having picked up a touch of the flu during her flight from California to explain both her keeping to her room and her need to have meals left outside her door.

However, while the hotel did breakfasts well, their other food was indifferent, and the smoked-turkey club that Nissa had provided as proper invalid fare was very welcome.

Other than delivering food, Nissa could provide Pearl only a limited amount of help. She'd agreed to work her usual hours at the pharmacy for the next few days—the least she said she could do since Bob wasn't firing her.

"And since keeping my job, even if I'm not drawing a paycheck, lets me keep my medical insurance," Nissa said, "even if I do have to pay more, I'm eager to please."

"I'll take care of the premiums," Pearl assured her, "and send Bob something interesting in the collectibles line once I have time to rummage in my attic. After all, our goal is to remove disorder from our lives. What good would that do you if you ended up unemployed?"

"I'd be alive and have my memory," Nissa said softly, "and know that Lani is safe. That's plenty."

They were sharing sandwiches at the small table in Pearl's hotel room during Nissa's lunch break. Foster sat cross-legged on the floor watching educational television and eating his own sandwich and a salad with his fingers, licking off the honey-ginger dressing with an appreciation he had not shown for the two slices of provolone cheese that were set neatly to one side.

"You have a cell phone, right?" Nissa asked.

"Of course."

"How about a computer? Did you bring a laptop?"

Pearl shook her head. "No."

"Oh." Nissa frowned thoughtfully. "I know you told me that certain things are not to be discussed on the phone or e-mailed, but I think we should keep in touch. Brenda has her computer with her, and I've e-mailed her more pictures of Foster. I've also sent a bunch of me and Lani."

Pearl nodded. "That's fine, but remember, no discussion of anything arcane. Think of it as a matter of security."

"And you," Nissa said, rising and stuffing the trash into the bag, "consider that we'll be worrying about you and Riprap while you're on the road. You'll call me when he gets here?"

"Promise. And if anything else changes."

Riprap arrived that evening, about an hour earlier than Pearl had dared hope.

"Flight was on time, rental car was ready, and the lady at the counter gave me good directions. I slept on the plane, so whenever you want to leave, I'm ready."

Pearl reached for her cell phone. "Let me call Nissa. I've already handled late checkout, explaining that a friend was going to drive me to the airport, but I wasn't sure when."

"They were okay with that?" Riprap asked. "Most hotels charge extra for late checkout."

"I thought they would," Pearl said, "but instead they asked me to sign a few pictures for them. I think this room is going to get a 'Pearl Bright Slept Here' sign."

"Pearl Bright," Riprap said, glancing over to where Foster was huddled in a corner, watching him with dark eyes that seemed as much fascinated as afraid, "and someone else."

"But they don't know about the someone else," Pearl said firmly. "My hypothetical flu has been ample excuse for no one coming in here other than Nissa."

"How're we going to get your guest out without anyone seeing?" Riprap asked.

"There's a back stair," Pearl said, "that leads to the lot where guests can park. It's locked from the outside, and so doesn't see much traffic. In any case, if anyone sees him, we'll say he arrived with you."

"Okay," Riprap said.

"Now let me call Nissa," Pearl said. She got through, and Nissa said she could be over in a half hour.

"I want to meet this Riprap," she said. Unspoken was her need to be assured that Pearl was leaving of her own choice, and in her own right mind.

"I'll tell Bob I'm bringing you a care package. Can you use anything?"

"Shampoo," Pearl said. "My travel bottle is empty, and I don't care for the hotel's choice. I could also use some deodorant for my young friend."

They discussed brands for a moment, then Nissa rang off.

"Before Nissa gets here," Riprap said, glancing over at Foster, "there's something I want you to know. I've brought a handgun."

He opened the briefcase he'd carried up with him and allowed her a quick glimpse of a gun resting in a holster. Pearl knew only enough about guns to guess this one was an automatic. It was relatively small, but looked deadly efficient.

When Pearl nodded, Riprap snapped closed the briefcase and zipped open a side compartment.

"Here," he said, "is my paperwork. The gun is registered, and I have all the appropriate permits to carry it in most of the states we'll be passing through—my work with 'disadvantaged' kids takes me into some pretty rough areas, and my teams go outside of Colorado pretty regularly. I also want to tell you before you ask, no, I don't plan on shooting anyone, but there are a lot of people out there who can be dissuaded by the sight of a gun pointed at them."

Pearl nodded. "I can't blame you for wanting to have that edge, but I ask you to be very careful when you choose to use that thing."

"I will be," Riprap promised. He tapped his wrist where the white tiles of an assortment of amulet bracelets shone against his dark skin. "These first. Fists second. Gun only if that's my only choice. I've got a mini-safe to keep it in when we're at your house, so there'll be no need to worry about Lani or anyone else getting their hands on it and causing harm."

"You seem to have thought of everything," Pearl said, permitting mild amusement to color her voice.

"I'm trying, ma'am. I'm trying."

Nissa arrived inside the promised half hour, bearing not only shampoo and deodorant, but chocolate bars, bottled water, trail mix, and a separate bag containing a small packet of antidiarrheal pills and another of antacids.

"Bob's gift," Nissa said with a grin, handing the small bag to Pearl and setting the larger package on the table. She turned to Riprap and offered him a hand.

"Nissa Nita, apparently the Rabbit—or the Hare."

"Charles Adolphus," Riprap said, making her hand vanish in his own, "but call me Riprap. I'm just getting used to this Dog thing. Can you scout ahead and see if the stairs to the parking lot are clear? I moved out Pearl's luggage, and didn't meet anyone, but I'm just sure that when we move him . . ."

He gestured toward Foster. The young man was neatly clad in clean clothes. His alert expression showed that he was fully aware of the changes, and more than a little worried about what they implied.

"Right," Nissa said. She took up the bag of goodies, balanced it on one hip, and flipped open her phone. "I'll call from the stairwell and let you know if anyone's there."

There wasn't, and they got Foster out to the car with ease. Pearl settled him in the sedan's roomy backseat and, after hugging Nissa, got in beside Foster.

"We don't know how he'll react," she said, "so Riprap is going to have to play chauffeur to my grand lady."

"Driving Miss Pearl," Riprap said. He shook Nissa's hand again. "Pleased to meet you. See you in California."

Foster jumped when Riprap turned on the engine, bracing long fingers against the seat, but otherwise not expressing any fear.

He's brave, Pearl thought, as Riprap took them onto the road and Foster's fingers tightened their hold. *But that doesn't make him any less dangerous. It almost certainly makes him more.*

★

Brenda and Des caught a flight from Albuquerque to San Jose after Pearl and her guests were safely arrived in San Jose. The five days they had spent together in Santa Fe had alternated between intense focus and casual touring.

Each day, Brenda worked on making at least one amulet bracelet. She wasn't the only one doing so. While she settled in at Des's dining-room table, Des took his own equipment into an adjoining room. He never let her see the end results of his work, probably because he knew she'd try and compete with him. Focus, rather than speed, was what was important, as Brenda found to her chagrin on the day she proudly presented Des with two completed sets of tiles, only to be informed—and then shown via a spell of Des's casting—that the tiles were nothing more than beautifully carved polymer clay beads.

Every day, Des took her to see some of the museums, galleries, and natural wonders that made New Mexico a tourist destination. Noticing that Des continued to choose places where they would be in the company of other people, Brenda began keeping a nervous watch on her surroundings. A few times she thought people were following them, but as tourists tend to cross and recross each other's paths with a certain predictable regularity, she couldn't be sure.

Even though she felt positive he'd laugh at her, Brenda confided her suspicions to Des.

"I don't claim," she said, "to be any great detective, but I was in student government all through high school, and it sort of gives you an eye for remembering people."

"And I bet Gaheris has taught you," Des added, "the value of remembering a name and a face. I believe you when you say you've noticed the same people over and over again. Point a few out to me, especially if they seem really persistent."

Brenda did, but whether because of their watchfulness or because the people in question were really innocent tourists, no harm came.

And the worst thing, Brenda thought, *is that we can't even be sure what our enemies look like. It would be a mistake to think that they're Chinese because Foster looks Chinese. Even if they are Chinese, we know they must have local allies.*

Riprap and Pearl reported that they had learned little or nothing from Foster. His life before he had awakened in Pearl's hotel room was completely gone, and he clung to them as the familiar constants in a steadily changing world. He was, however, showing himself very adaptable and very intelligent.

"Television helped," Pearl admitted. "During our first several days of driving, I would frequently hear him say 'I saw that, on the picture box. I saw that.' He's also picked up a few words of English, but certainly not so much that we need to worry about him eavesdropping."

Despite the phone and e-mail contact, it had been a relief to get on the plane for San Jose, to know that soon their scattered forces would be joined. Brenda knew the reassurance she took in this was irrational, but didn't deny herself this slight comfort when everything else was so unsettled.

At the airport, Hastings, Pearl's driver, was waiting for them.

"Miss Bright sends her apologies for not meeting you herself," Hastings reported formally, "but she said she needed to remain with her other guests. She said I should ask you if there are any stops you need to make before we go to the house."

Des asked to stop by a craft/hobby shop, and took Brenda in to help him clear the shelves of white polymer clay, various etching tools, brushes, and paints. When Brenda protested mildly that surely Pearl had some of this stuff, Des said with a laugh, "Absolutely, but what makes you think she'll want a bunch of novices messing up her tools?"

San Jose proved to be a pleasant city. From the guidebook Des had given her, Brenda knew that the city had a population of nearly 900,000, but it didn't seem like a big city. The airport was pleasant, even intimate-seeming, and although there were clusters of tall buildings, the residential areas they glimpsed from the freeways were varied and attractive.

The area where Pearl lived was long-established, if the size of the trees and shrubs was any indication. Green lawns, flowering shrubs, and large but genteel houses seemed the rule. Brenda liked the area immediately.

Brenda didn't know what she had expected Pearl Bright's home to look like. All she knew was that the house the chauffeur drove them up to was not it. For one, although Pearl's house was located in a very nice neighborhood, there were no towering gates, no sweeping circular driveways, no sense of show. The tidy stone walkway that led to the steps up to the front porch began behind a waist-high wrought-iron gate that Brenda could have climbed over with ease.

The house itself was fairly narrow at the front—probably no wider than two large rooms and an entryway, Brenda guessed. It was painted a soft dove gray that held just a trace of lavender, the shutters painted a few shades darker. Although the overall impression was one of modesty, the house possessed at least three floors and seemed to extend a fair way back into the lot. Touches of stained glass over the front door and windows provided a little flourish.

Yes. Pearl's house was nicely kept, even elegant, but nothing Brenda hadn't seen before. The plants in the flower beds that bordered the small front porch seemed to be mostly roses, not the exotica Brenda had subconsciously expected from a movie star's home in California. The front yard was small, what might be described as "tidy," but there were hints that the backyard was much larger.

There was one odd thing about Pearl's neighborhood, and it made up for the relative mundanity of Pearl's house. Her next-door neighbor was not another house or even a shop. It was a museum, and not just any museum, but one set in ornate gardens that looked as if they had come directly from ancient Egypt. There were even sphinxes and gigantic statues of pharaohs.

Brenda stood in the street and gaped.

"That's the Rosicrucian Museum," Des said, his tone not quite hiding a ripple of laughter. "It's more than just a museum. It's an educational and philosophical center—and the gardens are fantastic. Pearl is associated with the museum somehow, although I'm not quite certain in what capacity."

Riprap had come out of the house, and now he had moved around to the back of the car and was helping Hastings unload the luggage. He voiced what Brenda had been thinking.

"Even with the museum, this doesn't seem much like a place a movie star would live, does it?"

Des reached to carry a couple of his bags. Since they'd been coming from his home, he had more luggage than either of the other two. Brenda grabbed her laptop, determined not to be useless. Des turned to the driver.

"Go ahead and take the car around, Hastings. We can manage this." Then he returned to their conversation. "It does and it doesn't. You'd be surprised how expensive the Rose Garden—that's the name of this area—is. Expensive and classy. It fits Pearl perfectly. She refuses to say just how she managed to get a house on the same block as the museum, just smiles and looks enigmatic. However, I do know that her mother invested a good bit of Pearl's early earnings in real estate. I wouldn't be surprised if that was the answer."

"So Ms. Bright didn't get shafted by her folks," Riprap said. "That's good to know. I was feeling a little uneasy about her hiring me for however long this lasts."

"Ms. Bright's parents," came that lady's voice from the top of the short flight of stone steps that led up to the front porch, "were alternately embarrassed and delighted by her success. And, unlike Americans, Chinese are very careful about money, and Jews even more so. My mother was a Hungarian Jew—a Jewess, as they used to say in the press releases that mentioned her at all, a very poetical word, I have always thought. Not only did my parents do well by me, they managed to have me do well by themselves and by my brothers as well. There were times I blamed them a little for that—being as egotistical as the next young thing, and wanting it all for myself. Now I am deeply grateful. Come in now, so you can meet Nissa and Lani."

Brenda noticed that Pearl had not mentioned her other guest—or captive. Was he asleep? Locked up?

The truth turned out to be more prosaic, and yet slightly sinister.

"We arrived after dark, and went to great trouble to get Foster into the house without him being seen," Pearl explained. "You should not mention him on the street, or even that there is another resident. Whoever Foster was working for certainly has missed him by now. When they start looking, our homes are among the logical places to check. I have warded my home and garden as best I can, but wards will do no good if we are careless."

Luggage was left in the front hall while Pearl led them toward the back of the house. She paused in a formal parlor to introduce them to her two pet cats. Bonaventure, a moderately long-haired grey, and Amala, a fuzzy, pale orange, marbled tabby, blinked politely at the guests, but made no effort to get up and greet them. Brenda guessed they must be fairly jaded.

From the parlor the group looked into a formal dining room, then to a more casually furnished family room that adjoined a nice kitchen. When taken as a whole, the decor of Pearl's house was nothing like what Brenda had subconsciously expected.

The formal rooms were done in antiques that Brenda vaguely thought were French or Italian. The family-room furnishings, which included a deep leather recliner, could have been bought at any of a dozen home decorating centers. There was nothing of the exotic as in Des's house, none of the elaborately Oriental as in Albert Yu's office. There was none of the flash Brenda had expected of a movie star—not even a wall adorned with signed photographs.

It was a nice home, a comfortable home, a home that—despite exquisite maintenance—showed signs of long occupancy. There were none of the little compromises that Brenda knew from her parents' home. All that was here was good, but very much the result of one person's taste.

What did I expect? Brenda thought ruefully. *A bunch of clichés I would have been furious to have applied to me.*

Brenda knew she was thinking about furniture to distract herself from the meeting she had been both dreading and anticipating for a week. She shook hands with Nissa, agreeing with the bright-eyed, fair-haired woman that they were already on their way to being friends through e-mail. She knelt and shook Lani's shyly proffered hand, and admired the little girl's toy cat. Through it all, she was aware of the young man who stood at the back of the room, a toy dog the match of Lani's cat dangling from his hand.

Foster was definitely the young man from the parking garage. The eyes were the same, the black hair, although swept back in a modern ponytail, framed a face with high cheekbones and absolutely perfect lines. He watched the introductions shyly, but with a trace of innocent eagerness.

He's been looking forward to more company, Brenda realized with a start. *It must have been lonely for him, with Auntie Pearl barely veiling her hostility, and Riprap and Nissa taking care not to annoy their hostess.*

"This is . . ." Pearl Bright began, her tones, previously so warm and conversational, now touched with ice.

"Foster!" Lani interrupted gleefully. "Say 'hello,' Foster."

"Hello," he said, and his voice was familiar, too, even to the slight note of indecision. Brenda remembered that same voice saying how she shouldn't be able to see him, and the panic that had underlain the notes. For a moment, she felt sorry for him.

"Hello," she said, and Des echoed her greeting.

They all stood staring at each other rather stupidly, a thousand questions that couldn't be asked echoing in the air.

Then Auntie Pearl said briskly, "Let me show you your rooms. This place is bigger than it looks. I had the plumbing redone just a year ago, so everyone should be quite comfortable."

The house was indeed bigger than it looked from the outside, but somewhat narrow. Brenda was given a room that shared a bath with the room in which Nissa and Lani were staying. Pearl's own suite was across the hall on the same floor, but the three men were staying on the next floor up, where there were more rooms and a sitting area, all fully furnished.

Brenda dropped her bags in her room and trailed after as the group moved upstairs, wanting to see more of the house.

"Wow, Auntie Pearl. You have a lot of bedrooms for one person."

Pearl laughed. "I actually do take on interns from time to time, and when I do I usually offer room and board as part of the package. I don't have any this summer because I was planning on traveling. I've contacted a few theatrical agents I know, because we're trying to line up a few auditions for Lani."

She glanced at Brenda and Des, who nodded to indicate they'd heard Nissa's cover story.

"However, other than that, I'm relatively free. I'd told most of the committees I serve on not to expect me to attend meetings in person for the next few months."

"But Auntie Pearl," Brenda said, "won't we be crowding you?"

"I grew up surrounded by people," Pearl replied, "my family, mobs of child actors, my parents' friends. Although I like my privacy, there are times when I flourish in a crowd."

Foster had been given a room that had its own adjoining bathroom. Des and Riprap would share a bathroom.

"I thought it made sense," Auntie Pearl said softly, "to put Foster in a room where, in a pinch, we could keep him without undue difficulty. I have a woman who drops in to clean three days a week, but I'm going to tell her to leave the guest rooms alone for now. It shouldn't be a problem, since she normally confines herself to the downstairs and my suite. My friends do not drop by unannounced."

Des set his bags down. "What about your driver? Does he live on the premises?"

"Hastings rents an apartment of his own," Pearl said, "but also has use of a sort of studio apartment in the garage. During the day, he's usually there, because he likes to memorize his lines aloud, and his recitation drives his roommate up the wall. In any case, Hastings doesn't have a key to the house. If we keep the back door locked . . ."

Everyone nodded, but Brenda wondered if she was the only one who felt uncomfortable. It just wasn't right to be keeping someone prisoner, even if he had been a sort of assassin—a memory assassin. Was that like a character assassin?

Brenda realized she was drifting off into nonsense. The last week had been tense. She almost wished she was having a normal summer: working at her dad's friend's business, swimming with her friends at one of the area pools, talking about how to change the universe, and all the mistakes they would have never made if they were in charge.

Change the universe, Brenda thought with a shiver. *That's what's happening. My universe is changing, and I'm changing with it—and being asked to take a part in the transformation.*

Auntie Pearl was saying, "I've already put towels up here, but Brenda's are in the dryer. I wasn't quite ready for a house party. Brenda, will you come and get those?"

"Yes, Auntie Pearl."

She followed the older woman down to a tidy laundry room tucked off the kitchen. It smelled of warm fabric softener.

"These machines used to be in the basement," Auntie Pearl said, "but when I had the plumbing redone, I had them moved up here. Stairs are fine for now, but the ones to the basement are particularly steep. Also, I don't know about how stairs and I will get along ten years from now, and I hate being dependent."

Brenda thought that Auntie Pearl had nothing to worry about. The older woman moved briskly, without the least trace of stiffness in her gait.

They went upstairs together, Brenda with her arms full of still-warm towels, Auntie Pearl with a basket of clean laundry.

"Can I help you fold those, Auntie Pearl?" Brenda asked.

"My unmentionables?" Auntie Pearl laughed. "I think not. Oh, something I have been meaning to ask. Would you mind just calling me 'Pearl'? I have never minded the other name—it's what Gaheris has always called me, and it seemed natural that his children would do the same—but if you're going to be posing as my summer intern, just my name would be easier. During the drive here, I almost succeeded in convincing Riprap to stop calling me Ms. Bright. That young man has excellent manners, but they're a bit much for California."

"I'll do my best . . . Pearl," Brenda said, then laughed self-consciously. "What's next?"

"Next we all rest until after dinner. Then I think Foster is going to be asked to go to his room for a while, and we will have a council. Lani should be asleep by then. Nissa usually puts her to bed no later than seven."

"Won't Foster be bored?"

"Possibly, but then again, he may want some time alone after being Lani's toy for most of the day. Not surprisingly, he reads Chinese, and I've given him a large selection of books."

Brenda wondered about that "not surprisingly." There had been something in the inflection that indicated Pearl had drawn some conclusions about Foster. She thought about asking what these might be, but decided to wait until after dinner. Right now a break and a chance to call some of her girlfriends sounded better than anything.

She thought of Foster, about getting to know him better, about doing something to solve the question of who he was, why he had come after them as he did, and amended her thought.

Than almost anything. It would be better than *almost* anything.

★

Pearl pushed her chair back from the dining-room table. Des and Riprap had collaborated in the kitchen, and the resulting dinner had been very good. Brenda had known how to make a chocolate mousse that measured quite favorably against those Pearl had eaten in some very expensive restaurants. It had been a fit end to a fine meal.

When Nissa had taken Lani up to bed, Foster had obediently gone to his own room. He and Pearl were developing an odd relationship, this despite Pearl's desire to have no relationship at all with him. Certainly, the fact that she had been the only one other than himself who spoke Chinese had something to do with it. However, she thought Foster might be developing some version of that syndrome she'd heard hostages went through—the one where they started identifying with their captors.

Now that Des had arrived, there would be someone else who could talk to the boy in his own language, a man at that. Pearl hoped this would give her some relief from interacting with Foster. She knew she was being unfair, but Foster reminded her so much of her father that she kept expecting to see Foster's slightly vague expression of fear and wonderment change into her father's scowl of disappointment, an expression that no achievement on Pearl's part—neither as an actress, nor as a sorceress—had ever erased from her father's face.

The five of them settled around the dining-room table, cleared now but for a pot of tea, a thermos carafe of coffee, and a cut-crystal pitcher of iced water.

"So," Pearl said. "Where shall we begin?"

Riprap was quick to respond, quicker than Pearl had expected, having grown accustomed to the Dog's place as faithful follower. Dogs were scouts, too, she reminded herself, their sharp senses compensating for their more impaired human associates. And Riprap was not the Dogs she had known. He was a coach, a former soldier, and a former baseball player—in short, a pack leader, not a follower.

"I want to know what's behind all of this," he said. "From the start there has been a larger history lurking in the background. Both you and Des have implied that the Thirteen Orphans came from China, perhaps from some outlying semi-independent kingdom, but that doesn't feel right."

Pearl glanced around the table. Des cocked an eyebrow at her. He'd already told her that he didn't think they could hold back the information for much longer. Nissa looked inquisitive, Brenda almost defiant. Des was right. They couldn't wait much longer, no matter how unlikely the explanation was that they had to give.

"Where to start?" Pearl said. She saw Riprap frown. "Put your hackles down, young man. I am going to explain. However, this is not an easy thing to explain, especially when the question of where to begin is factored in."

"How about geographic location?" Riprap said simply. "Longitude and latitude. Borders. Whatever."

Des answered, "East of the sun and west of the moon. The center of the universe. The heart of a word."

Riprap pulled his head back slightly, his expression guarded, but maybe because Des had been functioning as a teacher—a coach—he reacted as if he had been handed a puzzle, not insulted.

"I don't get what you're saying, man."

"Where our ancestors, the Thirteen Orphans, came from is not a place we can show you on any map," Des said.

Brenda said softly, "That's what Pearl told me, when she and Dad were trying to tell me about why the mah-jong tiles can be used for magic: 'A land not found on any map.' I thought they meant that it hadn't been located by modern explorers, or that it wasn't recognized by modern governments. I mean, China's always not recognizing places. They don't recognize Taiwan and Tibet, or do they now?"

Nissa broke in. Her expression had grown very still and very quiet, just as it did when Lani was being particularly trying. It was the expression of someone trying to keep control, no matter how challenged.

"That's not the point, Brenda. I mean, Taiwan and Tibet aren't the point. I know that phrase 'east of the sun, west of the moon.' It's from fairy tales. It means a place that doesn't exist—or at least not in the way we think of places existing. It's the type of place a hero finds when on a quest for three eggs the same size that can still fit inside each other. It's where a girl weaves a cloak from moonbeams and fog to protect her lover from a manticore."

Nissa had spoken quickly, all on an exhalation. Now she paused, looking back and forth between Pearl and Des.

"So what you're trying to tell us is that our ancestors came out of a fairy tale. Is that it?"

"I wish is was that nice," Pearl said.

"Fairy tales," Nissa said, "aren't nice. Not the old ones. They're ugly, full of rape and abuse. In the old Sleeping Beauty, she isn't awakened by a kiss. She wakes up because she's having a baby. The prince had sex with her while she was asleep and then left. The wolf doesn't just swallow Little Red Riding Hood's grandma whole and then play head games with the girl. He does something much nastier. Even the cleaned-up stories aren't very nice."

Brenda and Riprap were staring at Nissa in disbelief. Apparently, this was all news to them, but Pearl knew the old stories, as did Des. It was true. Sometimes the only thing that made a fairy tale bearable was knowing it would come out all right in the end. And sometimes what the old storytellers defined as "all right" still wasn't very much of a victory by modern standards.

Riprap said, "Not on any map, but not a fairy tale, either. What are we talking about, an alternate dimension or something? Some alternate version of reality as we know it? Those come up all the time on television, especially when the budget is too tight for really great sets. Why not in reality?"

Pearl waggled an admonishing finger at him. "Now you're just being flip. No. Our ancestors were not exiled from an alternate dimension, not in the sense you mean—not one of those stories where Fidel Castro decided to play baseball not politics or where Alexander Hamilton survived being shot by Aaron Burr . . . Is Burr the right name? I always get that one confused. The land from which our ancestors were exiled, does, however, have a close tie to our world, most specifically to China, because certain events in China gave birth to this other land."

"The Lands Born from Smoke and Sacrifice," Brenda said softly.

"That's what it is called," Pearl agreed. "Pour me some tea, and I will tell you from what that smoke rose, and who was sacrificed."

Brenda poured pale green tea into Auntie Pearl's cup, her heart pounding unnaturally fast, as if some part of her, dormant until now, dormant even while Des taught her and Riprap how to make magical spells, was coming to life.

This is what Dad wanted me to learn when he took me to meet Albert Yu. In a moment I'll know what both of them have forgotten. That's too weird. It's like somehow now I'm more Dad than he is.

Pearl sipped her tea, and then spoke in a soft yet compelling voice. "Now, I'm sure all of you know that China has the longest continuous civilization of any now on Earth. Most estimates settle on five thousand years—three thousand if one only counts written history. During that time, China was not always united under one ruler, but there were peoples within what we shall consider China's borders who shared a great deal in common, including language, religion, philosophy, as well as artistic and cultural values.

"Thus, although China was not a unified nation in the political sense, it was, in many ways, already a nation before the Ch'in Dynasty came into power and made it unified in fact. The time that concerns us is the beginning of the Ch'in Dynasty, specifically the year 213 BC."

"Ah, relatively recent history," Riprap muttered.

Pearl raised her elegant eyebrows, but otherwise did not respond.

"Now, the period directly before this was known as the time of the Warring States. As the name implies, this was a time of great disorder, with various nations competing for primacy. In the end, Ch'in won.

"Times like that of the Warring States are not pleasant for anyone, soldier or civilian, noble or commoner. Therefore, it is not too surprising that when, about eight years after the Ch'in emperor had taken power and his rule began to suffer unrest, one of his advisors made a radical suggestion.

"The advisor was named Li Szu. What he suggested was no less than cultural genocide. The letter he wrote his emperor—of which the text (although not the actual document) still exists today—pointed out that the emperor's problems would be solved if all history, philosophy, theology, and the like were destroyed.

"In a twisted way, Li Szu's reasoning was very sound. The Ch'in government had established an entirely new world order. For the first time ever, all the Middle Kingdom was united under one ruler—and under one set of rules. Scholars alone, with their annoying habit of consulting the past for precedents, were the ones who complained. For example, the Ch'in government would pass a law or edict, and the scholars would immediately start harping on all the reasons the law or edict was unwise or unjust.

"When speaking in court the scholars were prudent and polite, but away from court, they had an annoying habit of engaging in public debate. They couldn't even agree with each other as to what the correct course of action would be, except that the emperor's course was wrong.

"According to Li Szu, the only thing scholars were good for was creating unrest. Get rid of the scholarly works, and you get rid of what the scholars used to prove how much better some past ruler or law was.

"A few things could be preserved. The history of Ch'in could be preserved, because Ch'in's ways were now to be the ways of all the Middle Kingdom. Technical manuals and handbooks of medicine, divination, agriculture, and arboriculture could be kept, because those were simple and useful, but all the rest should go.

"If the scholars protested, well, that would be unwise and they would be warned. If they persisted in their unwise acts, then they would be executed. Those officials who aided or abetted renegade scholars would be enslaved and sent to work on the Great Wall. When the scholars and the contesting works were eliminated, one way of thought would dominate. Then peace and unity would be preserved and all China would live in contentment."

Nissa leaned forward, her elbows on the table, reminding Brenda of a larger version of Lani.

"And I'm sure the emperor agreed that this policy should be promoted, didn't he? He would have thought that was a great idea."

"The emperor agreed," Pearl replied. "Li Szu's edict was duly published, and the scholars were given thirty days to burn their books."

"But I bet," Riprap said, "that there were some scholars who refused, weren't there?"

"There were many," Pearl said. "Four hundred and sixty scholars are on record as having concealed their books. They were executed as a result."

"Four hundred and sixty?" Brenda said softly. "That many?"

"That many and more," Des replied. "History records the scholars, but there were many family members and retainers who died as well, rather than betray the principles of their head of household. These scholars died, but some did not. They succeeded in concealing their texts. Later they reproduced and recirculated them. Many of the scholars who managed to succeed in saving some of their documents were Confucian. This means that a majority of what survived were Confucian texts, which is why that philosophical point of view remained dominant in China right up to . . ."

Pearl interrupted. "Des, please. What happened in China after Li Szu's edict is fascinating, I agree, but we're telling them about what else happened because of this edict."

"Sorry," Des said, and looked as if he meant it. "I get carried away."

"Four hundred and sixty," Brenda repeated, imagining four hundred and sixty men who looked like Des. "And those were the ones who tried to conceal their books. Hundreds, probably even thousands of libraries would have been destroyed. Hundreds, perhaps thousands of scholars committed intellectual suicide."

"That's right," Pearl said. "As you have learned, the written word held—still holds—a very special place in Chinese lore. The written word itself is special, sacred, even magical."

"The written word," Nissa said, "not just what is written, like the Bible or the Koran or some other holy text. The word itself. All those words burned."

"And all those people who were masters of writing," Riprap added. "All those scholars executed."

"The Lands Born from Smoke and Sacrifice," Brenda said, and felt her voice rising with excitement. "That's what you've been talking about. Are you saying that our ancestors came from a land that was somehow created when those books were burned and those scholars murdered?"

"That is what I am saying," Pearl agreed. "That land is where my father was born. From what he told me and my brothers, it was a very strange place. Unlike histories in this world, where one event evolves from another, where events follow a somewhat logical progression, in the Lands Born from Smoke and Sacrifice, things are jumbled together. Mythological creatures are as real as dogs and cats. Magic is as viable a science as any technique evolved from the scientific method. Remember, a few types of books were spared from destruction, and these were all the more practical texts."

"Agriculture," Riprap recited, "arboriculture, medicine, and something else . . ."

"Divination," Nissa added. "Which seems impractical to me, but I guess they considered divination a science. And the histories of Ch'in were spared, too, so I guess Ch'in isn't present there."

"I am not sure what is or isn't there," Pearl said. "My father hinted that once smoke and sacrifice created the land, then a conduit existed. I don't think every book ever burned ends up there, but he gave me the impression that it was no more a closed system than our own Earth is. Just as falling meteors add material to our planet, so the occasional burning of treasured words brings more material to the Lands.

"I wish I knew more, but I fear I was not always the best student. Once I realized all my lessons were—from my father's point of view—meant only to make me a fitter conduit through which the Tiger's abilities could be passed to some future male, I fear I grew less than attentive."

Brenda felt uncomfortable whenever Auntie Pearl talked about her father. It brought home how great her own dad had been, that he had been happy to have his daughter as his heir, even though he had two sons. But she had to face Pearl's reaction. That anger was a real part of Pearl Bright. Brenda bet old anger had a lot to do with how Pearl treated Foster: Foster, whom Pearl had known was a Tiger because he looked like her father.

Pearl smiled, perhaps aware how her anger made the others uneasy, and tried to be reassuring. She tapped her chin lightly with two elegantly manicured fingers.

"I am surprised," Pearl said, "how calmly all three of you are taking this. I have participated in the initiations of several heir apparents, and I can assure you, your reaction is hardly typical."

Brenda knew her own smile was tight and humorless. "Remember me, oh, two weeks ago, Auntie Pearl? Back in those dark ages when we were in Albert Yu's office, looking at a messed-up mah-jong set you said he'd been using to tell fortunes? A lot has happened since then. I watched my dad have part of his memory stolen away. I've learned to make a few simple amulets. Des has shown us some interesting effects he can pull off, and no matter how hard I try to come up with other explanations for magic, I can't. I've just about used up my ability to disbelieve."

Riprap fingered the bulky bracelet containing the Dragon's Tail spell he wore around one broad, dark-brown wrist. "Like Brenda says, Pearl. We've seen a lot. What you've told us isn't a whole lot harder to believe than that if I invoke the spell in these tiles a dragon is going to wrap its tail around me."

Nissa nodded. "I haven't seen as much as these two. In fact, I think I've got some classes to catch up on, but I saw Foster come at you, and I saw what happened when you threw that Tiger paper at him. It's easier to believe than disbelieve. I think I was already partway there, although I'll admit, I figured we were talking about some outlying province in China, not Somewhere Else entirely."

Des nodded his approval. "I came out of a tradition that made a lot of this history easier to accept—and a whole lot harder, too. I asked my father if a new land got born every time a book was burned in China and got whacked. It doesn't, of course. What happened during Li Szu's purge was the combined effect of an attempt to wipe out almost all conflicting knowledge, whether it was contained in written form or in teachers. Even those scholars who obeyed the edict and let their books be burned were denied permission to teach.

"There was a small handful of scholars, those who had achieved the rank of Scholar of Great Learning, who were permitted to keep otherwise forbidden books, but you can bet that after watching their friends and associates be executed they were very careful about what they said.

"According to later histories, one of the elements that led to the downfall of the Ch'in Dynasty was that no one felt safe any longer. Demotions became common, not just in scholarly rankings, but in administration and the military. No one was immune to execution, even on trumped-up charges. So, in a strange way, Li Szu's edict, which was meant to make Ch'in safe forever, was the beginning of the end of that dynasty's prestige."

"But it was the beginning of a new world," Pearl said. "A strange world, a world without order as we know it, but a world that my father and the other Orphans treasured so greatly that they went into exile rather than see their battles contribute to its destruction. When I was a little girl, I would listen to the survivors reminisce. Even though I cannot remember details, those tales color my dreams. I think that land must have been a beautiful place, although far from a safe one."

"Must *be*," Des said with emphasis on the second word. "Must be, not 'have been.' Pearl, where else can our attacker have come from? I have had time to talk with Foster, and he speaks what I was taught is the peculiar dialect of that place."

"Dialect?" Riprap said. "You mean like accent?"

"Not only accent," Des said. "Word use. My father told me that in the Lands Born from Smoke and Sacrifice they spoke Chinese, but a very strange Chinese. Words from different time periods are mixed up—even from different versions of Chinese."

Brenda said, "I know that there's more than just Mandarin Chinese. There's Cantonese and other versions, too, right?"

"Right," Des said. "Mandarin—or northern Chinese—was the language of scholars, but that doesn't mean it was the only one spoken by scholars or in which texts were written. The dialect of Foster's homeland is primary Mandarin, but with other words mixed in. What's really strange is the mixture of expressions from various time periods and classes."

Des paused, obviously hunting around for a comparison.

"Imagine if you were listening to the evening news, and all of a sudden the reporter started mixing in phrases right out of Shakespeare and Milton and a bit of street slang. That's Foster, but it's clear he's not speaking an affected pattern. He's just talking normally. He thinks Mandarin is odd. Limited. A bit lacking in nuance and color."

Brenda had a thought. "What does my dad talk when he talks Chinese? Mandarin or what Foster talks?"

Pearl said, "I initially taught him Mandarin, but he learned some of the other form later. That's what he used when he called me on the phone. Even if someone had tapped the call, they would have needed to be a linguistic historian to understand him."

"Back up," Nissa said. "You're saying that since Foster talks this other form of Chinese, that must mean he's from this other land. What if he was tutored by someone who knew the language, like Gaheris Morris was? Then he could be from here."

"Possible," Des said, "but Gaheris talks other languages. English. Mandarin. Foster talks only this. Seems to limit the options."

"I have been thinking something similar," Pearl said. "During our drive, I tried to catch Foster out, but either he is a superlative actor, or his ignorance is real."

"But he talked English in the parking garage," Brenda said. "I heard him."

"Obviously," Pearl said, "we cannot yet resolve where Foster is from, and I think that Nissa is right that we should not be too quick to dismiss the possibility that his origin is local. However, this question of language also brings us around to the question of why Foster has amnesia. I believe I have a somewhat better understanding of why the others have amnesia as well."

She reached into her pocket and drew out a small silk-covered box, opened it, and displayed something Brenda had seen in the photos Nissa forwarded to her phone, but not in person: a crystal sphere, a bit larger than a large marble. Imprisoned in the sphere was an amazingly lifelike three-dimensional image of a tiger—lifelike, except that it was green.

"This," Pearl said, "is Foster's memory, or rather, the memory of the Tiger."

★

Pearl watched the expression on each of the three young people's faces as she displayed the crystal sphere. Riprap looked respectful, even apprehensive. Nissa looked fascinated, as if she'd just learned that what she'd taken for a bit of dime-store jewelry was a priceless heirloom.

Brenda's reaction was the strangest. She looked a little sick, but when she leaned forward to examine the sphere her expression flickered through a gamut of emotions: apprehension, loathing, interest, and what Pearl would have sworn was something like wistfulness. Maybe she was simply wishing that her father's memory was so close to hand, but Pearl wasn't sure. She'd seen how Brenda looked at Foster, and it was clear the young woman was fascinated by him—an unhealthy fascination, like that a bird feels for the serpent.

"Foster's memory, the Tiger's memory," Riprap said. He reached for his coffee mug, found it empty, and refilled it. His spoon clanked against the sides as he stirred in sugar. "You're talking like they're one and the same. In Mr. Morris's case, they were pretty separate."

Des glanced at Pearl, and at her nod took it upon himself to answer the question.

"Pearl and I have discussed this a little," he said. "The theory we've come up with is that the spell in question—the one that we saw written on that piece of paper you gave us, Riprap, the same one Pearl used on Foster—is meant to separate all memories of Dogness or Tigerness or Roosterness from the current member of the Thirteen. In Mr. Morris's case, being the Rat was important, but it did not touch many other aspects of his life. Moreover, because of the kind of man he is, outgoing, social, a bit—sorry, Brenda—opportunistic . . ."

"That's Dad," Brenda agreed. "Go on."

"Because of that, Gaheris tended to make connections outside of their shared roles with those heirs of the Thirteen he knew. He did business with them, befriended them, whatever seemed most appropriate. That means, when his Ratness was taken, he didn't forget these people, his mind simply bridged the gap. If he was really pressed for how he happened to know someone, he might get uncomfortable, but he's facile. He'd come up with something."

Pearl took up the thread. "In Albert's case, though, well, Brenda, even you who didn't know him well saw that something was not right. We suspect that this was because so much of who and what Albert is . . . was . . . is linked with being the Cat. Unlike Riprap or Nissa, who knew they had an interesting heritage, but not much more, or you, who would have gotten something of a formal initiation, Albert grew up knowing he was the grandson of the exiled emperor of a fairy-tale land. It colored everything he did. When his Catness was taken from him, his personality changed."

"But Albert didn't forget people," Des added, "because he had manufactured excuses for him to know about the Thirteen and their families, to seek information about them. Are you with us?"

"With," Nissa said, "and maybe a bit ahead. You're saying that Foster was reared to be the Tiger. He probably started training for his role when he was just a boy. Maybe he had an ambitious family, maybe the person he was to succeed was old and there was no time to waste. Whatever, he's the Tiger and has always been the Tiger, and when you take that away, he can't even remember his name. We're probably lucky he can talk at an adult level."

"Just so," Pearl said. "Moreover, like Albert, Foster may have suffered something of an alteration of personality. The man you and I met, Nissa, was willing to attack an old woman and a young mother with a sword. It is likely that the real Tiger is as vicious and ruthless as his namesake beast can be. We must not forget that, not for a moment."

Pearl tried not to look too pointedly at Brenda as she spoke these words, but she saw the younger woman color and look down at the table, avoiding anyone's gaze. Fine. Brenda had been warned. Hopefully, that would be enough.

Riprap was looking thoughtful. "I think I'm following why Foster would also forget how to speak English and details like who we are—although he must have known, in order to stalk us. Those things would have been tied very tightly to being the Tiger."

"Precisely," Des said. "It might even be more than that. It is possible that Foster never really spoke English."

"We heard him," Brenda protested.

"I know. Hear me out. He may have learned English through a spell. That spell would have been on the Tiger, not on Foster—or whatever his real name is. If he was given information about us, our appearances, habits, et cetera, through a spell, that also would have been the Tiger who was ensorcelled. It's completely possible that if Foster regains his memory, he still will be unable to speak English or remember us. The spells will have been broken."

"Regain his memory," Nissa said. Pearl watched as she extended a finger as if to touch the crystal sphere. "Can we help him to regain it? Do we want him to regain it?"

"That," Pearl said, "is precisely what we need to discuss next. Before we discuss whether or not we should break the spell, I need to confess that neither Des or I are certain if we can even do so."

Pearl saw that while Nissa and Riprap accepted her words at face value, Brenda was less certain. Brenda didn't go as far as protesting, but doubt flickered across her features, doubt mingled with concern.

Des must have seen this as well, because he hastened to clarify.

"Although both Pearl and I received some magical training, there is a difference between knowing a skill, and being able to adapt those skills creatively."

Riprap nodded. "I've seen the same problem over and over again with the kids I coach. Most can learn the rules for whatever game we're playing. Almost all of them can memorize plays. Fewer can evolve and adapt those plays when the circumstances change. The real geniuses are those who not only come up with their own plays, but see how their changes are going to affect the game—even the entire team."

"That's it," Des agreed. "Pearl and I are equivalent of your beginning players. We've memorized plays. We're even good within those limitations, but we've never really had need to adapt what we know."

Nissa grinned mischievously. "I'd think that would be what you'd want to do right off . . . Spread your wings. Find your own way to do things."

"You'll think differently once you've done some work with spells yourself," Des said, glancing over at Riprap and Brenda, who nodded agreement.

Brenda tried to explain. "One of the first things Des did with us was show us how working with magic attracts—attention is the only word I can think of. You can set up shields against anybody interfering . . ."

"Anybody weaker than your shield, that is," Des cut in. "Sorry. Go on. Pearl's glaring at me for going off on another tangent."

Brenda went on. "But even those shields are noticeable, like if you erected a wall up around your house. Your neighbors wouldn't be able to see in, but they'd sure wonder what you were doing behind that wall that you didn't want them to see."

Nissa fingered her teacup, spinning it around and around on her saucer.

"I understand," she said. "Working in the pharmacy isn't much different, really. You don't mix pills and powders at random, just because you think they'd work well together, maybe even beneficially. You think about drug interactions, even with something as basic as calcium or iron supplements. I had a client who gave herself stomach problems taking aspirin with orange juice. Too much acid. Okay. I'll admit that maybe experimentation isn't as great a temptation as I thought it would be. What you're saying is the spell to release imprisoned memory isn't in your pharmacopoeia?"

"At least not thus far," Des agreed. "We're both still working through our lists, seeing if anything seems promising, but an immediate solution hasn't presented itself."

"There isn't an 'open sesame' spell?" Brenda asked. "I'd think something like that would be very useful, even routine."

"'Say friend and enter,'" Des quoted. "Oh, there is, but that's for opening simple closures, like basic locks. There's another one that will throw back a bolt, but that's a summoning, rather like the Dragon's Tail. Neither of those would work in this case, partially because of the medium in which the memory is being held."

He looked over at Pearl, who slid the silk-lined box containing the crystal sphere over to him. He took the sphere out, and held it up for their inspection.

"This isn't glass. It's natural rock crystal. Quartz, I'd guess, although we haven't had it tested. Now, in Chinese mythology, natural rock crystal is anything but natural. There are two theories as to its origin. One is that it is formed from ice that has remained frozen for so long that it has turned to stone."

"Like petrified wood," Riprap said, "only this would be petrified water. Makes sense, really, especially since Des told us that wood and water were two of the five elements, right? I mean, if wood can turn to stone, why not water?"

Des all but beamed. Pearl thought that Riprap probably had been a good player—one of those who learned the plays and adapted them.

"The other source for rock crystal," Des went on, "is even more arcane. You find it written up in more detail in Japanese sources, but there is little doubt that the belief was originally Chinese. Rock crystal is thought to have formed from either the congealed breath or the saliva of dragons."

"Dragons," Brenda said. "That was mentioned in the spell Riprap showed us, something about giving into the dragon's hold."

Des quoted, " 'Silence the Dog's mind. Send it forth into the Dragon's care.' Exactly. So it's likely that not only is rock crystal the medium, but that at least one dragon—maybe more—has been ensorcelled into the task of guarding what is within the crystal. Any attempt to release what the crystal holds, without getting the procedure perfectly right, would bring the guardian."

Brenda touched the plaques in her Dragon's Tail bracelet.

"And I'm willing to bet," she said, "that it wouldn't be a relatively mild dragon like we contacted for these."

"That," Des replied, "would be a very fair assumption."

Silence fell as everyone considered this. Riprap started the coffeepot around the table. Pearl did the same for the tea. When everyone was settled in, Brenda broke the silence.

"But we need to figure out how to break the sphere, don't we? I mean, we'll need to know if we're going to get my dad's memory back. I know Dad probably isn't the most important one for you guys. Albert Yu probably is, since the Twelve are his guardians and keepers. But for me it's Dad."

"I've known your father since he was a boy," Pearl said. "Believe me, setting him right is important to me as well."

Brenda looked apologetic, but Pearl waved a hand.

"You've raised a crucial point. Whether or not we choose to return Foster's memory, we will almost certainly need to know how to safely open the crystals if we are to help his victims."

"I'm with you," Riprap said, "but would it be right to leave Foster without his memories? Don't get mad at me, Brenda, but Mr. Morris is doing all right without his. Sounds like this Albert Yu might even be doing better. From what I've heard, he's acting a lot less uptight, a lot less full of himself. But Foster, he's got nothing. He can't even remember his name."

"How can you miss what you don't know you don't have?" Pearl said, but knew she was being callous and immediately amended the statement. "No. I don't seriously agree with that. Foster may not know his name, but he knows he should have one. The same goes for all the other victims."

Nissa added, "Sometimes it's the things you can't remember that drive you nuts. I've not been able to get to sleep at night, knowing there's something I should remember. Then I realize it's something stupid, like putting ketchup on the grocery list, and I feel dumb. Dumb but relieved. It's got to be worse for Foster. I know you said we should be careful around him, but he seems nice. Not having his memory isn't going to make him nicer."

Pearl thought, *Depending on how he was before, lacking his memory could make him a lot nicer. Nuttier maybe, but nicer. Still, Brenda is already looking at me sideways. I'm not going to press the point.*

Aloud Pearl said, "Then are we agreed that we should at least put serious effort into researching how to undo the spell?"

Nods went around the table.

Nissa said, "I'd like to help. I'm actually pretty good with formulas, but I'll need to learn the basics first."

Des nodded. "I'll start you with what Riprap and Brenda already know while I move them ahead."

"I guess being able to share a classroom is an advantage to us all being in one place," Nissa agreed. "But I've been worried about that, too."

"About being in one place?" Pearl said.

"Yeah. Someone's out to get us, and we've put the last four Orphans under one roof. That makes it easier for us to work together, but it's sure going to make it easier for someone to work against us as well."

Brenda didn't intend to eavesdrop on the argument between Pearl and Des that occurred a few days after their all taking up residence in Pearl's house in San Jose. Des had made something spicy and Chinese for dinner. The difference between what Brenda's South Carolina upbringing and Des's New Mexico conditioning considered "mild" had resulted in an upset stomach that wouldn't let her settle into sleep.

Brenda hadn't heard Pearl come up to bed, so she'd padded down the carpeted front stairs in her bare feet, planning to ask if Pearl had any antacids. She'd been about to knock on Pearl's office door when a murmur from behind the door caught her ear. The voice she heard was definitely her hostess's.

Pearl's probably on the phone, Brenda thought, cupping her free hand over her lower abdomen. *She won't mind if I bother her for something like this.*

Brenda held her hand from knocking when she realized that there were two people speaking, both at once, and neither of them sounded happy.

Pearl was saying, ". . . realize you consider me unreasonable, but that young man is . . ."

Des was saying, "I realize what you think, but is that any reason to keep him unable to communicate?"

Brenda let her hand drop, her stomach ache forgotten. They had to be talking about Foster. Proximity had not dimmed Brenda's unwilling attraction to the young man, and she held her breath so she could hear better. Happily for Brenda, although the old door between the office and the hallway was thick and heavy, it had long ago ceased to maintain a perfect fit. The voices came through, faint but clear.

Pearl said, "His inability to communicate was what made it possible for Riprap and me to get him across country without difficulty. It keeps him dependent."

"His inability to communicate," Des responded, "is beginning to drive Foster a little crazy. He's isolated. The only people he can talk to are the two of us. You make it quite clear that you don't want to talk to him. That leaves me, and since I'm teaching the other three, there are hours on end that Foster can't exchange a single word with anyone. Lani chatters, but even the most talented two-and-a-half-year-old is hardly a great conversationalist. Then you insist on Foster being locked up at night, and those are more hours when he can't talk to anyone. Damn it, Pearl! Solitary confinement has been known to drive people insane."

"Foster is not solitary," Pearl said, ice in her tone. "Against my better judgment, a young man who we know to have twice made attacks on members of the Thirteen—who we *know* to have succeeded in the case of Gaheris Morris, who we suspect to have succeeded in other circumstances—is being treated like a house guest rather than the prisoner of war that he is."

"Prisoner of war," Des repeated. "Is that how you see him?"

"I do. What other way is there to see him?"

"How about as a potential source of information?" Des said. "Right now Foster remembers nothing, but if we work out how to break that spell, his memory should return. Do we want him to remember us as having been cruel or kind? If he remembers that we were kind to him despite the circumstances, we might have made an ally."

"I've been considering the question of his memory," Pearl said. "I wonder if we need to return his memory at all? Perhaps we can find a way to read or view what is contained in the sphere, to learn what is there without returning the young man's memory to him. Such must be possible. Why would our enemy be stealing memories if there is not some way to use them?"

"That would be cruel!" Des protested. "Foster knows he can't remember. What if we damaged his memory in viewing it? Foster might be condemned to never remember."

"That might be for the best," Pearl said. "You might feel differently about 'Foster' if you had been the one to find him in your room, armed with spells and sword. He was no gentle babysitter then, but a Tiger with fangs and claws."

"I've looked at his weapons and clothing," Des said, and Brenda thought she heard a note of resignation in his voice. "He certainly was armed for bear. . . ."

"For Tiger," Pearl said. "For Tiger and for Rabbit, as he would have come later armed for Rooster and Dog. I admit, the current version of Foster is somewhat appealing: kind to children, possessed of very nice table manners and a certain courtliness of bearing. However, I cannot forget that he has successfully attacked nine of my associates—some of whom, like Gaheris, like Albert, like Shen Kung, are also my friends."

"You cannot forget," Des retorted, "that Foster looks rather too much like your father did as a young man."

"What of that?" Pearl said. "My father was from the Lands Born from Smoke and Sacrifice. He may have been a very apt representation of the type of person who lives there. All the tales we have heard report that the Lands suffered frequent war. Our ancestors were exiled because they were on the losing side of one such conflict. Even after they were exiled, they were still pursued—and not from a desire for reconciliation. Judging from the evidence, the tendency toward violence persists. Foster is a young warrior born in that land, of that tradition, and you want me to treat him like a house cat? Perhaps I might, but only if you find a way to declaw him."

There was a sound, as of one of the heavy armchairs being pushed back. Brenda darted to the foot of the stair, but continued to listen.

Des sounded tired, and she wondered if he and Pearl had gone through some version of this argument before.

"Pearl, I'm going to bed. Much as I want to figure out how to unlock the crystal, I can't concentrate now. I'm going to ask if Foster wants me to move into the room that connects with his. I know it's a risk, but I can't be part of this isolation policy of yours. I think I'd rather lose my memory—and it means a great deal to me, I assure you—than behave as you would have me do."

Brenda saw the doorknob start to turn and fled up the stairs, but Pearl's voice carried clearly through the opening door.

"Your memory? Des, I would take care that you don't lose your life."

Back in her own room, Brenda rushed into the bathroom. Eavesdropping had not cured her of her upset stomach, but agitation had definitely moved the problem along. She wondered if she had disturbed Nissa and Lani, but there wasn't a sound from the other side of the door.

Brenda almost wished there had been. She would have liked to talk about what she had overheard with Nissa. Although Nissa was only a couple of years older than Brenda, early motherhood and the peculiar semicommunal lifestyle she shared with her sisters had given her an interesting perspective, even something like wisdom.

Brenda went as far as turning off the bathroom light and opening the connecting door a crack. Soft breathing and the smell of baby powder and grape juice were her only greetings. She shut the door carefully, and retreated into her own room.

She tried lying down and going to sleep, but although her stomach was better, she could not settle. She reviewed what she had overheard again and again. Pearl's callousness troubled her, but even with Brenda's interest in Foster, she had to admit the older woman had a point. So did Des, though, especially that bit about considering how Foster's attitude toward them in the future would be influenced by his current treatment.

Surely treating Foster like a prisoner at first had made sense, especially with having to get him across country and all, but now? Didn't prisoners get privileges for good behavior? How long before Foster started considering another tactic? If good behavior got him nothing, then he might start acting bad.

Pearl and Des both seemed to have overlooked that even disarmed and without his memory, Foster had a lot going for him. Brenda ran a mental finger over those assets. Foster was strong, muscular, and very graceful.

Foster was observant, quick to offer a hand, especially with Lani, but also with things like setting the table. He was also obviously intelligent, judging from how he had picked up a bit of English with no one but Lani and children's television as a tutor. At first he didn't have much more than "hello" and "good-bye," but he'd started picking up nouns from the television. He'd also gotten "please" and "thank you" down pat, probably because Nissa frequently reminded Lani to use the "magic words."

Good thing Foster didn't know they weren't really magic, especially given what Brenda was learning about the magic of words. What if that triggered some latent memory? Would removing his memory have also removed his ability to use magic?

So if Foster decided that good behavior was getting him nowhere, and he stopped feeling quite so out of place, then he could be a real danger. He could take one of them as a hostage, or decide to run away.

No. Both Pearl and Des were right, but Des was more right. Pearl was acting as if the situation could be held static, but Foster was anything but static. The situation would change, and Des was right. They needed to make sure that when it did, Foster thought of them with as much fondness as possible.

Having reached this conclusion, Brenda immediately felt like a traitor. She was thinking about treating the man who had attacked her father—and Riprap and Pearl and Nissa—with kindness, with accommodation. But she was only going to treat him that way so that they could learn what they needed to return her father to normal. That was all.

Wasn't it? It was. Brenda's own perfectly natural attraction to an almost too perfectly handsome man was not an element, especially as she was all too aware of that attraction—and he, equally apparently, was unaware of her.

Brenda forced those thoughts from her head, and found herself again tracking through the argument she'd overheard. What was it that Des had been saying at the beginning? He'd been implying that it would be possible to give Foster the ability to communicate. Obviously, Des meant something other than the fragmented English Foster was already acquiring. That meant magic: either magic to let Foster understand English or to let them understand Chinese.

Brenda rose from her bed and turned on the desk lamp. She got out her lesson notes and spread them out on the desk. One of the things Des had insisted they copy out was a long list of limit hands, since each of these contained in their patterns the concealed form of a spell. Now which ones might work to give someone the ability to speak another language?

At first glance, nothing suggested itself, but Brenda knew she was probably thinking too literally. Would she have thought of Dragon's Tail as a form of protection? Would she have considered Winding Snakes as a form of noninjurious attack? She needed to stretch, think less literally.

Reviewing the list, Brenda saw that there were several limit hands that involved pairs. That made sense, since getting pairs was, while not easy, one of the more obvious ways various tiles could be grouped. She turned to a blank sheet in her notebook, and started a list.

There was a hand called Four Friends, although Des had noted it was also called Four Blessings. Still, what was a greater blessing than for friends to be able to talk? Brenda noted it down and moved on.

"Knitting" might be a possibility. Knitting involved interlocking patterns. What else?

There were several "twin" hands. They might have the same association as pairs. There were also five or six limit hands involving winds. Breath was wind. Speech was wind. Those might work. She added them to her list.

Too many possibilities, but at least she had somewhere to start. Des had been giving lessons daily. She'd start asking questions about what different limit hands could do. This list would at least give her a starting point for her questions.

Suddenly tired, Brenda folded up her notes and got back into bed. She was asleep almost before her head sank into the pillow, but one stray thought mingled with her dreams.

Des wanted Foster to learn to talk to them. Maybe, just maybe, he'd let something slip—especially if Brenda gave him an opening. She needed to give him an opening . . . An opening . . .

Open.

★

The morning following her latest argument with Des, Pearl sat beneath the ramada in her backyard, stroking Amala and watching Lani play some elaborate game with herself. The yard invited such imaginings. Although not overly large, it featured numerous twisting paths paved in brick. These split and crossed, intersecting and separating, creating the illusion that the tangled growth went on nearly forever. Where a path ended, there was usually some surprise: a small fountain, a statue, an inscribed plaque, a dwarf tree, this often heavy with fruit or flower.

The ramada under which Pearl sat was overgrown with grapevines, their fruit sweet and dark, good for the table. This year's crop wasn't yet ripe, but it looked promising. She'd need to speak with Wong the gardener, when next he came by, about some judicious pruning.

Pearl went over arrangements that needed to be made for the continued smooth functioning of her household. Like the chauffeur, the gardener rarely came into the house. One of the paths ended in a charming little potting shed with its own running water. Still, she'd need to make certain that Foster was under wraps when next Wong was due. And she'd need to do something to make sure she didn't lose her maid service. They took the occasional cancellation well, especially if you let them know in advance, but although all her guests—even Riprap, which had rather surprised her—had proven willing to keep the house neat, still Pearl liked to have the antiques dusted and polished.

"An' Pearl?"

Pearl felt a tug on the edge of her skirt. Lani was standing there, looking up at her.

"When's Mama going to be home from school?"

Nissa was actually in the house, but to Lani school was something that happened elsewhere.

"After lunch."

"Oh." There was a pause while Lani contemplated this. "Is she gon have lunch with us?"

"That depends on what her teacher says."

"Des. Des is teacher."

"That's right."

"Des is funny. He has a funny face." Lani made a motion to indicate that what she meant was Des's long mustache.

"It is funny," Pearl agreed.

"Can I have juice?"

The word was pronounced more like "deuce," but Pearl had been with Lani long enough to have had some practice with her version of English. Really, for two and a half, the child spoke very well, but only Nissa understood her all the time. Brenda had a worse time understanding Lani than did either Riprap or Pearl, but then Dylan and Tom were both a long way from the years of childish prattle.

Des managed fine. And Foster, well, he didn't speak English at all, so Lani's version wasn't a problem.

Pearl put Foster from her mind. After her argument with Des, she didn't want to think about him.

"An' Pearl," Lani said, her tone one of long suffering, "can I *please* have some juice."

There was a slight emphasis on "please," and Pearl realized that the child had taken her lack of attention as a reprimand for not using the "magic word."

"Of course, Lani," Pearl said, getting to her feet. "Is your cup inside or out here?"

"By the ch'i-lin," Lani said, and ran down the twisting path to retrieve the plastic cup from where it rested on the pedestal next to the horse-dragon creature sinologists usually referred to as the "Chinese unicorn." She returned quickly. "I like the ch'i-lin."

"So do I. I did when I was your age, too. That statue is from before I was born."

"Wow!"

They went into the kitchen, and Lani was supplied with apple juice and a small container of unsweetened dry cereal. Nissa had filled everyone in on acceptable and unacceptable snacks, but overall she had a very reasonable attitude toward her daughter's eating. As long as she ate something healthy, Lani could graze all day.

Pearl, remembering times when the demands of her profession had meant she went without eating anything for hours, thought this very reasonable.

"Where's Foster?" Lani asked.

"In his room."

"Has he been bad?"

Pearl considered this. "He needs to rest. Would you like a nap?"

Pearl's question diverted Lani as she had hoped it would. The girl's eyes widened with horror.

"Not now! Naps aren't until after lunch."

"Would you like to go out to the garden again?"

"I can feed the ch'i-lin and the phoenix cereal," Lani said.

Probably because she thought Pearl might try and settle her down for an un-scheduled nap, Lani vanished down one of the paths almost immediately. Pearl moved her chair to where she could keep an eye on the child without invading her sense of privacy. She was a firm believer in letting the imagination grow un-hindered.

Lani's voice, prattling—the word was all too appropriate—to the statues was as Proust's madeleine to Pearl's memory. Her own childhood had been filled with the sound of children, for, although she had later become a star, and taken part in movies where she was the only child player, her early roles had been in shows where there was a children's chorus of some sort—often on the slimmest excuse.

Pearl had stood out from the start because of her attention to detail. She would remember her marks. If given a line or a bit of a solo, she didn't forget it. Then, too, she had provided a fine contrast to the curly-haired, blue-eyed blond child who had frequently been her opposite.

Sometimes Pearl played the good child, while Shirley was the wild, mischie-vous one. Other times Shirley was the little angel, and Pearl the bad girl. Neither had minded, although there had been a bit of good-natured tussling over who got the better part. The thing that had made them both stand out was that they loved the profession. The other children were there because their parents wanted them to be. Shirley and Pearl were among the handful who had been seriously bitten by the acting bug.

Neither of them had done much acting as adults, although each had won adult roles. Shirley had finally taken another direction entirely, and Pearl didn't blame her. Not only had her earnings not been well-managed, she must have gotten tired of always being cast as "Dimples," even when she had ample talent to be more.

In contrast to the financial mess that awaited the grown Shirley Temple, Pearl's parents had managed Pearl's earnings very well. The Chinese were frugal people, on the whole, and both Pearl's parents were immigrants. Her father's early training had not prepared him to manage money, but he had learned the necessity during those early years in China, before the exodus to Japan, and then into the U.S.

Pearl remembered the stories. Her father hadn't told her directly, but although the Thirteen had scattered after their arrival in the U.S., the Tiger, the Rooster, the Cat, and several others had remained in California. Even those who had moved elsewhere came out to visit. Traditional foods were easier to get in California, and were much more affordable, enough to make the journey and the expense worthwhile.

Then, too, when there were just over a dozen people in all the world who shared your heritage, the very natural desire to talk to people who sounded of home, who knew what you meant when you referred to the scent of the moonflowers that grew over the Pavilion of Milky Jade, was a tremendous lure.

Pearl let her mind drift back to those gatherings. Her father had been among the youngest of the Thirteen—only the young emperor had been younger—and had taken some time to marry. His reasons for the delay had not been romantic, but because of how seriously he took his role as Tiger. Tiger is among the most martial of the signs, and in those early decades when the exiles were still hunted by the wizards from their homeland, a warrior was needed.

Finally, Pearl's father had given in to pressure to assure there would be someone to inherit his role and married. His first wife had been a Chinese immigrant. Based on stray comments Pearl had overheard, the marriage had been, if not happy, at least stable. However, in the ten years of its duration, it produced no children. Pearl had never been clear if the marriage had ended in divorce, that first wife's death, or some less formal separation.

The Thundering Heaven's second marriage had been to Pearl's mother, and had been fruitful. Pearl had preceded her younger brothers by some years, enough time for her to realize that having an heir apparent to train was essential for each of the Thirteen, enough time to also realize that although she was her father's heir apparent, he was not happy to have her as such.

By the time Pearl was born, the first anxiety over how to direct the passage of the Earthly Branch powers the Twelve controlled had been addressed. Of the Thirteen Orphans, six were women, and not all of those six were of an age that they could hope to conceive and bear a child. Ox had faced this first. She was a woman of some sixty years when exile was forced upon them, already into menopause. However, she was also a steady and resourceful person.

"So," she had said, "what if I cannot bear a child? In our homeland the talent often is not passed within families. Very often the one who is best suited comes from another line entirely. I will find my heir among these people in this new place."

The second Ox had been realized in a Chinese foundling, one of those unlucky little girls whose parents did not want her, but who were not quite cruel enough to either kill her or sell her into direct slavery. She had been working as a bond servant, paying off her parents' debts to a landlord with her labor, when Ox's divinations had located her.

Ox promptly bought the girl, ignoring the protest of some of her associates, who thought that the talents should be kept within the family, so to speak. After all, some of them might have more than one child, and how nice if the Ox's powers could be passed to one of them.

Ox had ignored them. The new girl was named Hua, which can mean "flower," although the girl was far from flowerlike by the standards of the time and place. The same character can also mean "China," and thus was a tribute to her birthplace. Hua's brown, flat peasant face was sun-browned, and she had big hands and even bigger feet. But under Ox's loving care, the flower that was Hua had blossomed. After some training, the child had shown such a gift for magical working that from being criticized for her impulsiveness, Ox had been highly praised for her sagacity.

Pearl's first memories of Hua were as a kind young goddess of supreme elegance and adulthood, although she probably had not been much older than Nissa was now. Hua had tended to her adoptive mother, now well into her eighties, with a loving devotion that held no trace of servility. This had been Pearl's ideal model of how the relationship between senior and junior representatives of the Earthly Branches should be. Pearl had tried to treat her father as Hua had treated the Ox, only to realize with burning shame that not only didn't he want her attentions, he didn't want her.

That had hurt, for Pearl was a child quite accustomed to being wanted. Her mother was very proud of her, driving her to auditions and rehearsals with endless patience. Pearl didn't win all her auditions for lead roles, but if she didn't get the lead, she usually got a bit part, sometimes even an understudy. When Mrs. Bright entertained, her lady friends were delighted to hear Pearl sing and dance. Her Hungarian Jewish grandparents, formerly less than happy with their daughter's marriage to a Chinese, softened as they grew to dote on their talented granddaughter.

At first, Pearl had thought that if she worked as hard to learn what her father valued as she did her lines, she could win his approval. She had seen Thundering Heaven brooding over the Tiger mah-jong set, so she memorized all the tiles. She learned to speak Chinese flawlessly, not only Mandarin and Cantonese, but the strange dialect her father spoke only with his friends.

Thundering Heaven practiced with various weapons, so Pearl would stand in the background, out of his direct line of sight, miming his moves with sword or spear as she had learned to mime complex dance steps at the various studios. He never seemed to notice.

Later, when her father had begun to teach Pearl the lore he had brought from his homeland—a place she had gathered was not quite the same as the China of which the people she met in Chinatown spoke—Pearl was thrilled. She memorized dynasties—which were not, after a point, anything like the dynasties she encountered in history books. She learned the contents of heavy bestiaries, always with an emphasis on what made a certain beast dangerous, and what made even the most dangerous beast vulnerable.

Finding that Pearl had the talent, her father also taught her how to work magic. The early lessons were not unlike those Des was giving to the three now inside her house, but for Pearl there had been no polymer clay to make shaping tiles easy. She had to learn to etch in ivory and bone, and if she spoiled a piece, her allowance would be cut—a thing she thought dreadfully unfair, because even then she had begun to realize that she was the one who earned most of the money that came into the house.

Mrs. Bright was paid something for acting as Pearl's handler and dresser, but as far as Pearl could tell, her father earned nothing, and seemed to think that his endless sword practice and research into Chinese history and legend were far more important than making sure the family had rice to eat and a roof over their heads.

Pearl's training as an actress had made her quick in body and mind, and had given her both stamina and attentiveness far beyond that usual in a child of her age. She learned her lessons quickly and well, and by the time she was eleven or twelve, she knew enough that she imagined her father approved of her. This was good, because she was beginning to find winning movie roles harder.

By this time, Pearl had been prominent long enough that even the studio's judicious editing of her age couldn't represent her as a little girl anymore. She'd remained petite, and that helped, but the gangly years are rarely kind to a girl, and her half-Hungarian, half-Oriental looks were not what the studios wanted for "cute kid" roles. She was several years from where she'd have a chance to try for roles as a romantic lead.

Waiting for auditions, for callbacks that didn't come, Pearl concentrated on her father's lessons, as well as on the schoolwork her mother gave her. She practiced shaping summonings in her mind, learning the elemental tang that accompanied contact with various creatures that almost everyone she knew thought were imaginary.

One day, out shopping for groceries, Pearl saw an old woman step out in front of an oncoming bus. She summoned an invisible Dragon's Tail to protect her. When the bus stopped short of hitting her, the woman claimed her guardian angel must have stepped between herself and the vehicle. Everyone cried out that this was a miracle. No one but Pearl's father, who had been walking with his daughter, his arms full of library books as hers were filled with bags of groceries, knew that the source of the miracle was Pearl.

Pearl had hoped her father was impressed. When a few days later his martial associate, the Horse, had come to visit, Pearl had brought in the tea, then lurked outside the door, hoping to hear something said about her performance.

The Horse had begun promisingly. "Pearl is shaping up into a fine woman. I quizzed her a little, while your son was running to bring you from your studio, and she seems to know her lessons perfectly."

"The girl is attentive."

"Perhaps you are reconciled to having her inherit the Tiger's place?"

"A female Tiger is an abomination. Never has one held the post. I thought the ritual Dragon sent might release the power and pass it to one of my sons, or to any of a dozen promising young men I have found. It remains firmly rooted in that chit."

Pearl had felt tears well in her eyes. She remembered the ritual. She had thought it was meant to make her stronger, not to strip her abilities from her.

"I firmly believe," Thundering Heaven went on, "that this perversity is a direct result of some curse laid by our enemies."

"Other heirs apparent have not matched the traditional genders," Horse protested. "That has not mattered."

"They are not Tigers," her father said. "Gender matters for Tigers. We are the essence of yang. A yang female is a perversion. Since all of Dragon's wisdom cannot break this curse, nor Rat's cleverness, I have applied myself to teaching the girl what I can. My path is one filled with danger. I may die before she bears my proper heir. Therefore, she must be prepared to pass on the lore. Still, it irks me. . . ."

Pearl slunk away before she could hear any more, and from that day forth she never hoped again for her father's favor or blessing. However, she leapt upon even the least teaching he offered her, learning it, hoarding it, but not to pass it on. The Tiger's lore was hers. She would never pass it on—at least not to someone of her father's choosing.

Foster's image floated unbidden into her mind.

Never.

15

Breaks, as Brenda had learned the hard way, were as important to her doing a good job with her new lessons as the time she spent memorizing lists or working in polymer clay. Even so, determined to keep up with Riprap—and even with Nissa, who'd started out behind but was rapidly catching up—Brenda often tried to combine the two.

Although they had been told never to go out in groups smaller than two, Pearl had made an exception for the Rosicrucian Museum and its grounds next door.

"You can go there alone," she'd said. "I've arranged for memberships. You'll be safe both in the buildings and in the gardens."

None of them—not even Riprap, who loved asking questions—asked why. Brenda thought that this was because no one wanted to risk a repeal of this little bit of freedom.

So with freedom uppermost in her mind, when Des told them they could have a half-hour break while the latest batch of tiles baked, Brenda headed to the museum gardens. As she grabbed a bunch of grapes and a bottle of water from the fridge, Brenda heard Nissa calling for Lani, saying it was time to call "Aunt

Nancy and the cousins," and Riprap thumping down the steps to the basement where he'd set up a makeshift weight room.

That man works too hard . . . Brenda thought with an affectionate grin, and trotted down the front steps of Pearl's house, along the sidewalk and up the stairs that would take her into the museum grounds.

The gardens were not precisely crowded, but there were several groups out enjoying the mid-June weather, the brilliance of the roses, and, above all, the neo-Egyptian architecture. Most seemed so busy taking pictures of their friends in front of this sphinx or that obelisk that Brenda felt almost invisible. Probably that was why she noticed the strange motion from one edge of the garden.

It was a man's hand, moving back and forth over the top of the neatly trimmed flowering hedge. At first, Brenda thought the man was picking flowers from the hedge, but the gesture was too swooping, too feathery, as if the hand was writing in the air.

Brenda moved a few steps closer, intrigued and curious. She caught a glimpse of a not overly tall, powerfully built, round-faced Asian man, dressed in khaki trousers and a tan sports shirt, moving briskly down the sidewalk away from the museum grounds.

Brenda considered following him, but Des and Pearl had been adamant about their not going anywhere alone. In any case, what would she do? Accuse him of picking the flowers? The man was out of sight almost before Brenda finished shaping her thoughts.

"Too late," she murmured to herself, and realized she felt relieved. She was tempted to dismiss the entire thing, but a sense of responsibility made her confide in Des.

"Had you seen that man before?" he asked.

"I don't think so. He could have been one of those people I saw in Santa Fe, but then again . . ." She shrugged.

Des nodded. "Better not to jump to conclusions. In any case, even if the man you saw was one of our enemies, he couldn't have harmed you there. The Rosicrucian Gardens are well protected."

"I thought they must be," Brenda said, "since we're allowed to go there alone."

"So relax," Des said. "But not too much. We're going to do fake combats. Test how fast you can get bracelets off and into action."

"Good," Brenda said. "I could use some exercise."

That evening, edgy despite herself, Brenda tried to distract herself with a mystery novel. Instead, she found herself peeking over the edge, her attention drawn to where Lani and Foster were playing a strange version of Go Fish. The little girl chattered almost constantly, but her version of English was quite difficult to understand. Foster's English consisted mostly of nouns, occasional verbs, and very few modifiers. Despite this, the pair were managing to communicate.

Lani held up a card that depicted three blue fish along with a large number three. Foster made a great show of carefully inspecting his hand. Then, with feigned reluctance, he handed over a matching card. In this version of the game, you needed four of a kind to make a set, and when Lani triumphantly set down three cards, Foster shook his head and counted off "One, two, three . . . No four. Go fish!"

"Aw!!!"

But Lani picked up her hand and drew another card.

The game went on until Foster went out with a quartet of Two Green Fish. Nissa, who had been watching from the doorway, now stepped forward.

"Time for your bath, then to bed, Lani."

Lani knew better than to argue. Nissa was a gentle mother, on the whole, but certain events—bed and nap times among them—were not negotiable.

"The schedule is as much for my sanity as for her health," Nissa had admitted. "I need to know that after about seven-thirty, my evening is my own, even if all I do with it is stare at the tube."

When mother and daughter left, Brenda was suddenly very aware that she was alone with Foster. Des and Riprap had gone to run errands. Then they were going to some sports event. Pearl was sequestered in her office, researching the spell that would let them release the memories trapped in the dragon crystals.

Foster was making himself very busy tidying up the cards, but Brenda sensed that he, too, was aware that they were alone. Over the days that they had shared a house, this had not happened very often. Lani made an excellent, if unintentional, chaperone. Foster was not welcome at the daily lessons that occupied so much of Brenda's day, nor at the practice sessions that were "lab" to Des's "lecture."

The rest of the time, either Nissa or Riprap was around, but now, for at least the next half hour . . .

Brenda put her book down, and motioned to the deck of cards in Foster's hand.

"Want to play?"

Foster looked at the cards and grinned, a spontaneous expression that not only welcomed her overture, but showed he was fully aware of how ridiculous it was for two adults to play this game.

They ripped through a few hands of Go Fish in very little time. Foster proved to have a good memory, and after he poached from Brenda's hand a couple of times, Brenda found herself taking care not to ask for a card unless she was almost ready to complete a set.

She wanted to teach him a more complex game, but wasn't sure that the different suits on a standard set of cards would be as obvious as these brightly colored fish. Then there were the face cards. Brenda was trying to figure out how to explain that kings outranked queens, but that they didn't outrank the almost identical jacks, and that the non-face-card ace outranked everything else, when a wonderful, if somewhat terrifying inspiration hit her.

What about teaching Foster mah-jong? He might even already know the game. Des had explained that although the primary knowledge that had created Foster's homeland had occurred in something like 213 B.C., there was ample evidence that other information had leaked through since.

Mah-jong shouldn't be particularly magical for Foster. That association belonged to the Thirteen Orphans alone, their private mnemonic. For millions of people around the world—this world at least—mah-jong was just a game. Why should it be anything different for Foster?

Brenda held up her hand in the gesture that had come to mean "wait a second" or "hold on." Foster paused in the middle of shuffling the deck of Go Fish cards and looked at her quizzically.

"I have an idea," Brenda said, although she knew he wouldn't understand.

She was very conscious of Foster watching her as she unfolded herself from where she'd been sitting across from him on the floor. His gaze followed her as she crossed to a cabinet in which she'd noticed that some board games were stored, among them a completely modern, utterly unremarkable mah-jong set.

"Do you know this game?" she asked, bringing the plastic case over and opening it to show the tiles.

Foster looked momentarily puzzled; then his gaze brightened.

"Yes. *Ma que. Ma jiang.*" The names were Chinese, but Brenda could hear the familiar echo of the English name, especially in the latter term.

"Come on," she said, and gestured to the table set to one end of the room. After all, the tiles couldn't be scattered on the rug as the cards could.

Suddenly, Brenda felt shy. What if Foster didn't want to play? Why was she giving him orders? Why was she assuming he'd want to play?

But Foster was on his feet, pausing only to stow the Go Fish cards in the basket that held Lani's toys. When they were sitting across from each other at the table, Brenda felt the language gap more than ever. Did they even know the same rules?

She took three matching tiles from the case and set them in a line. "Pung." Then, quickly, before Foster could wonder, she added a fourth. "Kong."

Three in sequence—one, two and three of bamboo: "Chow."

Foster was nodding now, obviously comparing his own knowledge with her words. He took fourteen tiles from the box and laid them out. They made four sets of three—four chows—and a pair.

"Mah-jong," he said, and his pronunciation was fairly close to her own.

Brenda grinned. They could do this! She took out more tiles and constructed another hand that would also qualify for mah-jong, although not as highly scoring since this one included runs or chows, not sets.

Within about ten minutes, she and Foster had worked out their basic rules, establishing that both of them knew that kongs gave bonus points, and that a concealed set scored higher than the same set unconcealed. Winds and dragons, the two honors suits, were familiar to Foster—far more so than the European kings, queens, and jacks would have been.

Foster's *Sesame Street* English worked surprisingly well for this. He had a grasp of "big," "bigger," "biggest," and related these back to scoring points. Other elements of the game were harder to get across, and by the time Brenda took various tiles and used them to mark out one of the simplest limit hands, All Pair, Foster fully understood why she waved her hand over it and said, "No. Not now."

"Too much," he agreed. This was one of Lani's favorite phrases, usually used to explain why she wouldn't finish a meal. In this case, it adapted very well.

They turned the tiles over, and began the rhythmic shuffling that guaranteed that the playing pieces would be well and completely mixed. The plastic tiles clattered against each other in a fashion that was like but unlike the traditional bone and bamboo.

Nissa came in at that point, wearing a different T-shirt. Apparently, bathing Lani had been an active event.

"Mah-jong!" she said, and her inflection held in it all of Brenda's own rationalization for why this game couldn't be dangerous, not in and of itself. "But how are you going to play it with only two people?"

Foster clearly didn't understand most of this, but he caught the word "two." His eyes widened and then he began to laugh.

"One fish," he said, pointing to himself. Then, pointing to Brenda: "Two fish." He indicated Nissa last: "Three fish?"

Nissa laughed and pulled out a chair.

"Three *people*," she said in her best "mom correcting child" voice, but the grin on her face kept this from being a true reprimand.

"People," Foster agreed. "Mah-jong. Four, biggest. Three big."

"Poor guy needs more than children's television comparatives," she said to Brenda.

Brenda nodded agreement, feeling a twinge of embarrassment that in her eagerness to find a game Foster might know, she'd forgotten that mah-jong really needed at least three players. Nissa didn't tease her though.

"My mom taught my sisters and I to play ages ago," she said. "We haven't played much lately—too many kids running around—but I love this game."

Brenda admitted to herself that there was another reason that her cheeks felt hot and her heart was thumping along uncomfortably. She'd been momentarily angry when Nissa came butting in. She'd wanted to be alone with Foster, although in this household that would be pretty much impossible.

Brenda wondered what Foster thought of Nissa. Nissa was pretty in her way, all fair and fluffy, but she was a mom. . . . Did that make her more or less appealing? Did it make her seem old and settled, or interesting and experienced?

None of them—not even Foster—seemed to know how old he was, but Brenda had thought of him as about her age, maybe a little older. That would make him Nissa's age. Brenda felt a surge of competitiveness. She'd seen Foster first, there in the parking garage in Denver.

When he'd been stealing her dad's memory.

Brenda felt suddenly cold, wondering what madness had made her seek to befriend this strange man. They drew tiles for who would have what chair, then shuffled the tiles and built the wall. Brenda was east, so it was up to her to roll for the first break in the wall.

Brenda rolled and counted, and the wall was Foster's. He held out his hand for the dice, and she dropped them into his hand, noticing the calluses. They must be from where he held his sword, and even the week and a half that had passed hadn't been enough for them to grow softer in the least. Did he practice up there, in the privacy of his room, going through the motions without a sword?

Soon after their arrival in San Jose, Brenda had come down early one morning and seen Pearl out on the patio, alone except for her cats, going through some moves Brenda had thought were tai chi. Brenda had asked about the routine. Pearl had explained that actually they were sword drills, and that when she'd warmed up she'd repeat them with her sword. Brenda hadn't asked more, but now she wondered whether Foster—another Tiger—practiced with equal devotion, or his daily routines had been taken from him along with his memory.

Foster counted, one through ten in English, then switching over to Chinese as the count took itself around the bend in the wall in front of Nissa. He reached awkwardly in front of the fair-haired woman and lifted out the appropriate tiles, setting them aside where they would be used to make up for bonus tiles, or for the fourth tile in a kong. No matter what, the hand must contain a minimum of fourteen tiles at the end.

Just like there must be the Thirteen Orphans, drifted a stray thought through Brenda's jumbled mind. *What happens when there are only four Orphans left, four and one confused junior Rat?*

The game progressed haltingly. Brenda and Nissa both played with a polite convention that the name of a tile should be spoken aloud when discarded, then discarded faceup, so that the other players would have an opportunity to claim it. Foster had clearly learned his game in a more competitive school. His discards were spoken, then flashed down, blank side up in the center of the square. Nissa kept reaching out and turning them faceup, and Foster seemed to think this was a comment on his ability to pronounce the English equivalents of the tiles.

Brenda wanted to explain that this was just a game among friends, no need to be so competitive, but she didn't have the words and her impulse failed her. Was this a glimpse at Foster's true soul, the soul of the Tiger, the soul of the swordsman?

No, she chided herself, watching as Nissa called out "mah-jong" and turned out the part of her hand that had remained concealed to prove her claim. Foster laughed and patted his palms together in polite approval. *He's just playing the game as he has been taught. That's all.*

Brenda's own hand was a mess, hardly any more organized than the mix of tiles she'd drawn at the beginning. Nissa had appointed herself scorekeeper, and snorted as she counted up the minimal points Brenda had managed. Foster was already knocking over the old wall, turning over the tiles, getting ready to shuffle for a new hand. Brenda forced herself to pay attention. She was enough her father's daughter that she didn't like making such a poor showing.

The hands went around the table. They weren't really keeping score for an overall game, just one hand at a time, seeing if they could all manage to play out each hand without needing to pause and explain some rule or other. Foster's version of the game was a little different from the one Brenda knew, but then so was the version Nissa had been taught. The variants mattered little in this simplified version, although the scoring could be tricky.

The four-person version of the game often ended in a stalemate, each player holding on to honors tiles in the hope of getting a higher score. A three-person game, such as the one they were playing, almost always went to mah-jong because the lack of one player created surplus tiles.

Something like six games in, Brenda had her hand almost ready to go out before the last of the four walls was even breached. All she needed was a one dot to complete the "pillow," or pair, that would complete her set of fourteen.

She'd managed to clear her hand of all suits but dots and honors. She had a nice concealed kong of green dragons and a exposed kong of the round's wind—west in this case. It was a good scoring hand, but would go for nothing unless someone mah-jonged and the hand was scored.

All Brenda needed was the one of dots, and only one had been discarded. She hoped no one else already had them set in their hand as a concealed pung.

"Brenda's fishing," Nissa said. "She hasn't changed a single tile in her hand for a while now."

Foster grinned. "Go fish!"

Brenda drew a tile from the wall and glanced at it. "Red dragon! I could have used that earlier."

She discarded it in the center, but no one claimed it. Brenda really hadn't expected anyone to do so. There were two red dragons out there already, and unlike the suit tiles, which could be used in chows, honors were useful only in sets of three or four—or as a pair to complete the hand.

The lone, unmatched tile in Brenda's hand stared up at her like a single eye. She had an exposed pong of four dots, a concealed pong of eight dots, her four lovely west winds, and that fine concealed kong of green dragons. All she needed was that last one dot, and she was beginning to believe it was sitting in someone else's hand, part of a chow, perhaps, or, with a certain amount of irony, as someone else's pillow.

They drew more rapidly now, each player knowing what tiles he or she could use. Nissa claimed one of Foster's discards, and Brenda held her breath, waiting for Nissa to call mah-jong and go out. That was one of the things that made mah-jong fascinating. The person to go out got a bonus, but didn't necessarily gain the most points.

Brenda counted tiles in the wall. Four draws left for each of them. Foster's lips were pressed together, his gaze darted over the tiles in the discard area. She thought she saw them narrow, as if he'd noticed a discard he hadn't seen before, and realized he couldn't make some play good.

Three draws. Two draws. They went into the final round. Nissa drew a three bamboo and slapped it down in the discard heap.

"I'm dead," she proclaimed.

Foster drew a five characters and said something in Chinese that sounded rude as he put it down next to Nissa's tile.

"Five character," he said, almost as an afterthought.

Brenda reached for the last tile, noting that Nissa was already starting to spill her tiles out of the rack, because a round in which no one went mah-jong wasn't scored.

"Wait," Brenda said. "I've got a tile yet, and I want to see which one of you has my . . ."

She stopped in midphrase. The tile she'd turned over was one dot, the tile she needed to complete her hand. She snapped it into place, turning her rack so the other two could see.

"Mah-jong!" she cried, but even as she said the words, even as she went through the familiar motions, she was aware of a roaring in her ears.

Brenda pressed the heels of her hands against her ears. The roaring sounded like ocean waves beating hard against a cliffside, pummeling the rock into minute grains of sand. There was a sense of pressure, as if something was pushing against the walls of her mind.

Nissa also had her hands to her ears. Foster's expression was shifting from mock anger that Brenda had managed to go mah-jong with that final tile, to confusion at their odd behavior. He was rising to his feet, reaching out toward Nissa, who sat in the seat closet to him, saying something, probably in Chinese.

At the other side of the house, there came a muffled crashing sound as the door to Pearl Bright's study was flung open. The older woman was coming down that hallway, stalking like the tiger she was, shouting something that Brenda couldn't quite make out.

Brenda lowered her hands from her ears, since with Pearl's appearance the roaring sound seemed to have moved back a little. She wanted to quest after the sound, try to figure out its source, but she forced herself to concentrate on what Pearl was saying.

"What have you been doing? Have you been showing anything to this boy?"

Pearl snarled the last two words at Foster, who stepped back as if she'd slapped him.

"No," Nissa said. "We were just playing mah-jong."

"With Foster."

"With Foster," Brenda said, moving around the table to put herself between Foster and Pearl. "It was my idea. I thought he might be able to play, and that it would be nice for him to play something other than Lani's baby games. We've been playing for hours now, ever since Nissa came down from putting Lani to bed."

Pearl glanced at the discard tiles, at the pad of paper that they'd been using to score the hands, at the plate of cookies and the carafes of tea and coffee.

She also turned a long, hard look at Foster, and must not have found anything to fear there, for something of the tightness around her mouth went away.

"I must have fallen asleep," she said, and her tone was no longer angry, although it was far from apologetic. "Or I would have heard the tiles. I came around when something tripped my wards."

"Is that what I feel?" Brenda asked. "The crashing sound?"

"The crashing sound," Pearl said, "is something trying to break through the wards. You say you weren't trying to do spells?"

"No!" Brenda said firmly.

Nissa shook her head and added. "We weren't even playing with limit hands. I mean, that would be dumb. Anyhow, how could we have explained those to Foster?"

Pearl moved over to the table, assessing the tiles before each player's seat with a quick, experienced gaze. Foster's hand elicited a mild "He would never have gone out. Nissa has his last wind."

Nissa said almost inconsequentially, "I have so much trouble making myself discard honors."

Pearl didn't seem to hear. She was staring at Brenda's hand. "Brenda, you went mah-jong. Did you do it by drawing the last tile, and, by chance, was that tile one dot?"

Brenda felt confused. "It was, but how did you know?"

"I know what's outside my wards," Pearl replied. "You inadvertently completed a limit hand when you drew that last tile. It's a very, very rare hand, so rare it's probably not even on the list Des made up for you. If you complete a cleared hand with one dot and draw it as the last tile of the wall, that is called Picking the Moon from the Bottom of the Sea."

"You're kidding," Brenda said. "That's so . . . obscure."

"Most limit hands are," Pearl agreed. "It's hard to believe you did this accidentally, but in a three-person game, it's not as unlikely." She sounded like she was trying to convince herself.

"Pearl," Nissa said, "you said you knew what was outside your walls. Is it dangerous? Should I get Lani out of bed?"

Pearl shook herself from her meditation on the tiles.

"Why? So the child can distract us further?" Then she softened. "No. Lani will be fine as long as my wards hold, and they should hold long enough for us to banish what Brenda has unwittingly summoned."

Pearl turned to Foster, but the young man seemed to have already gathered that he was less than welcome.

"Foster go to bed," he said. "I go. Good night."

Pearl hesitated, obviously uncertain whether Foster might be more dangerous here where he could see them do incomprehensible things, or alone in his room. Foster waited for her to accept his offer to leave.

"Yes," Pearl said, then added a few sentences in Chinese.

Foster replied in the same language, and then he bowed formally to her. He waved more casually to Nissa and Brenda.

"Thank you," he said. "Good night."

Brenda looked at Pearl. "What did you say to him?"

"I told him that he was to go to his room, but that I didn't blame him for the commotion. He replied that he thought your play so incredible that he was glad to stop while he had some luck left."

"That's it?" Brenda said. "He didn't think we'd all gone nuts?"

"I don't know what he thought," Pearl said, "but if he had any doubts about our sanity, he was too polite to voice them. Now, as to dealing with your inadvertent summoning . . . I promise I'll give you the lecture on the moon and all its potentials another time. Right now, what you need to know is that the moon is a powerful symbol to have invoked. Another problem is that this summoning is going to be creating emanations that will attract the attention of others—both creatures and practitioners of magic. Are you with me?"

As Des had repeatedly drummed into his students the need to set protective spells there were no questions.

"Very good. What I want is your support while I do three spells. One will banish the summoning. One will misdirect any attention that it has brought. The last will reinforce the wards. Have you learned either Knitting or Triple Knitting?"

"Knitting only," Brenda said for both of them. "Des said we didn't have enough control for the other."

"Fine," Pearl said. "What that means is that each of you is going to need to feed me ch'i individually, rather than our being able to unite as a team. No matter. Do you need to get your notes?"

Both women shook their heads.

"Fine. Come down to my office. I'll feel more secure there."

Brenda didn't feel the need to ask "Secure from what?" Pearl was going to try something very complex, especially for someone who had already been tired enough that she'd fallen asleep over her books. This was not the time for a casual interruption, and, although Pearl was very good at what she did, comfortable surroundings would bolster her abilities.

Before she left the kitchen, Brenda reached out and knocked over the rack holding her tiles, breaking up the accidental limit hand.

"The power isn't in that," Pearl said, but her tone said she understood the impulse.

"I know," Brenda agreed, "But I feel better without it staring at me."

In the office, Pearl went to a closet and took out what Brenda recognized as her sword case. Then Pearl settled herself into a high-backed chair upholstered in red leather, opened the case, and settled the sword across her knees. As she did so, she waved Brenda and Nissa to chairs facing her own.

"I'm going to start," Pearl said, placing her hands on the sheathed sword, "with All Winds and Dragons for the banishing."

"That's a powerful spell!" Nissa protested. "I asked Des about it just the other day."

"You don't think the moon is powerful?" Pearl countered. "After that, I'm going to work Confused Gates. Then I'll do Sparrow's Sanctuary. Got that?"

"And we just feed you ch'i?" Brenda said.

"That's right," Pearl said. "Take time to focus, and I'll let you know when to start the Knitting. Oh . . . Avoid dots in your mental imaging. They're evoking the moon right now, and we don't need that."

Brenda nodded. She thought she should have realized that without being reminded, but, in the corner of her heart where she was completely truthful with herself, she admitted that Pearl's advice had saved her from what could have been a dangerous mistake.

Brenda closed her eyes, and pressed the upper parts of her fingers to her temples, forcing herself to concentrate. Knitting really wasn't a hard pattern. You simply paired a tile from one suit with its match from another suit, and repeated for seven sets. Des had said you could even use the same pair repeatedly—as long as you didn't exceed four such pairs, since there were only four tiles of each type in a suit.

Also, Brenda thought, *then you'd have created kongs, and that would possibly create a different spell. Pongs would, too. Better not exceed one of each set.*

Since Pearl had ruled out dots, Brenda's choice of suits was already made: bamboo and characters. Characters were the hardest for Brenda to visualize, since they showed actual Chinese words.

Oh, well, she thought. *If I forget one, I can move to the next. This spell doesn't require sequencing the numbers. At least the bamboo will be easy. Except for one bamboo, they're just sequences of canes.*

One bamboo was always represented as a bird, so Brenda envisioned a tile printed with a peacock, then set a tile with the character for "one"—a simple, horizontal line—next to it. Two was even easier: two bamboo canes, one above the other, and two horizontal lines, the higher somewhat shorter than the one beneath. Three was three bamboo canes, and three horizontal lines. Four characters wasn't hard to remember, because it was a simple pictogram, almost like a face. Four bamboo, stacked two and two, went next to it.

Brenda couldn't remember five characters, and quickly skipped to six. Seven characters reminded her of an arrow set in a drawn bow, and came quickly to mind. When she finished setting seven bamboo next to it, Brenda wondered why she didn't feel the little tingle that usually told her a spell was ready to be released.

Of course! she thought, mentally counting through her row of tiles. *I am a first-class moron. I skipped five, so I need one more set.*

Eight was one of the simpler numerical characters. Des had shown his students how it had been reduced from a much more complex design to end up rather like an abstract depiction of two legs, running independent of a body. Eight bamboo, by contrast, was the second most complex of the bamboo tiles, showing the eight canes arranged in two mirror image "gates."

When Brenda finished imagining the last cane on the lower gate and ran through her sequence again, she felt the now-expected tingle. She also felt her ch'i damming up behind the pattern. Des had warned them not to hold the flow back for too long, as it could cause injury to the physical body, but Brenda didn't think that caution applied to that moment.

She opened her eyes and assessed the situation.

Pearl had risen to her feet and was standing a few paces in front of Brenda and Nissa, her sword stuck in the belt of her bathrobe. Her hands were shaping what Brenda knew was a Buddhist mudra, a hand form used to focus the attention in meditation. Brenda didn't know this particular mudra, but it was pretty complicated, and she bet Pearl had built it as she had created her spell.

Pearl might even have already invoked it. Brenda didn't have the sophistication to tell without casting a spell of her own, and she knew all her ch'i must be reserved to assist Pearl.

All Winds and Dragons didn't mean that Pearl would be summoning all four winds and all three dragons, but that she would make up her pattern from a selection of those honors.

Choose one menu item from Column A and one from Column B, Brenda thought, and stifled a giggle. She felt her control on the prepared Knitting spell waver, and forced herself to concentrate.

There was no danger involved in losing control of this spell—not like with a summons—but if she lost concentration Brenda would lose all the ch'i she had prepared to transfer, as well as losing time as she set the spell a second time. From experience, Brenda knew that she always found it harder to shape a spell a second time in close succession. Her attention kept going back to the prior attempt, muddling the clarity of the images.

Once she had her focus back, Brenda allowed herself to speculate as to which winds and which dragons Pearl would summon. There would be a mixture, or Pearl would have chosen Four Wind or perhaps Three Great Scholars, but what was the advantage to a mixture?

Brenda's attention was in danger of wavering again when Pearl unwrapped her fingers from their complicated pattern. Without looking directly at the two younger women, she said in a stern voice, "I am ready. Knit."

16

Pearl didn't want her two young partners to realize just how dangerous a creature lurked outside her house, especially since it was still held—if only barely—by her wards. If Brenda and Nissa realized just how great the danger was, they might panic and fail to feed her the ch'i Pearl would certainly need before this was over. Then, truly, they would be doomed.

The moon had many occupants, but only one was likely to be attracted by the bright coin that Brenda's unintentional spell would have flashed when she drew that final tile.

The Three-Legged Toad.

The Three-Legged Toad was always attracted by things that were bright and shiny. There were tales told about the Immortal Liu Hai who had ridden the Toad, luring it to unwilling servitude by dangling a string of shiny gold coins. Pearl had no desire to control the Toad. All she wanted was to make it retreat to its home in the moon.

The Toad pawed with its one front paw against the wards and Pearl could feel them bending. The Toad was enormous, not simply by toad standards, but by any standards at all. After all, it could be seen up there on the moon by those who dwelt upon the Earth, so it must be enormous. And then Liu Hai had used it as a steed, so it must be at least the size of a horse.

Immortals were shaped by myth and legend. That was part of what made them so powerful.

"Pretty, pretty, pretty . . ." the Toad croaked, or something very like that. Pearl's ward was one that granted unnoticeability along with protection from intrusion, but the toes on the Toad's three legs had suction-cup pads and stuck to her ward as if it were a crystal globe and they the memories held within.

"Want the pretty, pretty, pretty . . ." the Toad clarified. His mouth was very wide, and the warts on his bumpy skin oozed little droplets that Pearl knew were a poison that caused heart palpitations and paralysis.

Pearl fed a little more ch'i to strengthen the wards, retaining sufficient to sustain her control over the winds and dragons when she summoned them. Then she ran her thoughts over the shape of her spell and found it ready.

She planned to summon the red dragon of the center, since its symbol was the walls around the world. She would then augment it with all four winds. The fourth wind would be the weakest, since it would only be represented by a pair, but that couldn't be helped. She chose east for this weak wind, because east was the gentlest of the winds, and because she had plans for the others.

Pearl imagined her spell with the red dragon in the middle, an extra wall coiled around her wards, surrounded by the four winds. At her command, the spell came to life, and the Toad found itself buffeted. The cold of the north wind blew from above, making the Toad sluggish. The heat of the south wind dried the Toad's damp flesh without warming, for the east and west winds dove between, creating a barrier between the extremes, rocking the Three-Legged Toad back and forth on its now unsteady footing.

With the casting of her spell, Pearl also brought herself out of awareness of the office room where her body stood and into a place where she could direct what she envisioned. This was not something she did often, for it was easy to become quite lost, forgetting the connection to one's own body until one lacked the ch'i to return. This time Pearl felt she must take the risk. This was not a battle to be directed from the rear.

She steered her winds, causing the north to nip harder, the south to burn hotter, but the Toad did not give up and permit itself to be driven away. Banishment was all Pearl dared hope to achieve. The Three-Legged Toad was an immortal creature, and as such had remarkable tenacity, even against banishment.

Destroying an immortal was not only beyond Pearl's powers, but also would

probably have repercussions so horrible that she'd wish that the Toad had de-
voured them all in the first place.

The winds were doing their best, but the Toad was not about to give up on
its prize. Pearl stirred the red dragon from its passive role as protector of the
house. It glowered at the Toad and breathed scalding steam, but the Toad only
pawed more fiercely against the wards.

"Home! Home! Home!" it wailed, its croaking voice full of fear and longing.
So potent was its despair that Pearl's wards began to buckle.

Pearl had feared this very problem might occur as soon as she had realized
what Brenda had inadvertently summoned. The Three-Legged Toad was only
one of the denizens of the moon. Perhaps of the most powerful of all the moon's
inhabitants was the Hare who pounded out the Elixir of Immortality with a gigantic mortar and pestle. The Hare's skills were so great that almost everything
that came from the moon ended up immortal, a fact that had caused considerable
trouble to gods and heroes throughout the ages.

Prolonged existence did not guarantee great intelligence, however, and the
Three-Legged Toad was far from the most brilliant of creatures. Its early attacks
had sufficiently weakened Pearl's wards so that now it could sense Nissa within. It
mistook her Rabbit aura for that of its familiar friend and neighbor. Why should it
travel through the fearful void when the moon was so close? The moon must be
close, the Toad's logic went, otherwise the Toad would not scent the Hare.

Bitterly, Pearl realized that far from driving the Toad away, so far all she had
succeeded in achieving was to make the Toad all the more desirous of getting
through her wards to where, in addition to something fascinating and shiny, it
would find itself safely at home.

Pearl did not dare drop the All Winds and Dragons spell and try another, for
the Toad had perforated her wards in countless places. As of now, the only thing
that was keeping the Toad out was the entwined coils and snapping jaws of the
red dragon.

Up to this point, Pearl had used only her own ch'i, planning to save Brenda's
and Nissa's for the other two spells that must be worked. However, there was no
helping it. If she did not succeed here, there would be little need for the other
two spells. Not only would her wards fail and let the Toad through, but before
long the mystic disturbance was certain to bring others. Some would be kept
away because they would not wish to challenge the Toad, but others would lurk
around the fringes, ready to pick at whatever was left.

"I am ready. Knit!" Pearl said, keeping her tones level with tremendous
effort. She felt the young women's ch'i race into her, each following its own

strand. By great good fortune, the two had chosen almost identical patterns for their spells, so that Pearl could absorb the energy without any confusion.

Brenda apparently had problems remembering the character for five, while Nissa had a perfect sequence, but other than the elimination of five in one spell and the inclusion of eight, they matched seamlessly.

As the twinned ch'i flooded to augment her own, Pearl felt her faltering control restored. Very well, since she could not drive the Toad away, she must take a lesson from Liu Hai and lure it.

Tiger occupies a nearly unique place among the creatures of the Chinese zodiac, for it is also assigned a role as guardian of one of the four directions—Guardian of the West. Only Dragon is also sign and guardian—in its case of East. This is why one is the greatest of warriors, the other the greatest of wizards.

Pearl called west wind to come away from teasing the Three-Legged Toad. It lopped over to her, taking the form of a great white tiger with eyes of shining blue. It rubbed against her, and she spared a moment to scratch it behind one elegant ear.

"We're going to lead that Toad on a chase," she said, and shaped in her mind an unplanned spell. "Carry me away from my house, but make sure Toad sees us. The other winds will encourage him to follow, and the red dragon will protect the house."

The White Tiger who was the west wind purred agreement with this plan, and Pearl threw her leg over his flank. She had forgotten she was a woman closer to eighty than seventy, and that she stood on a carpeted floor in a house in San Jose, California. Here she felt the White Tiger's fur against her hands and brushing her feet, felt the plushness of it, even through her clothing.

Pearl's heart raced with exhilaration. When the Toad noticed the motion of her departure, she quickly worked another spell. This one was called White Opal, and was somewhat kin to the spell Brenda had done, although not nearly as complex. This one relied on a tiny white dragon to add flash and sparkle to an array of dots. As Pearl had hoped, the already befuddled Toad was attracted to the White Opal as it had been attracted to Liu Hai's gold coin.

"Pretty, pretty, pretty," the Toad croaked, hopping after Pearl and her White Tiger. "Moon, moon, moon. Home!"

The pursuit went on, long and harrowing. The Toad was as large as a horse, large as a mountain. Their road took them up an uneven spiral stair, each tread of shimmering stars, and although they must flee or be swallowed, they must also keep the Toad close lest he be drawn back along the trace and resume his battering of the wards that protected Pearl's house.

They were climbing the stars of the Sieve when the Toad gained upon them, coming so close that its long tongue lashed out and grasped the trailing length of the White Tiger's tail, wrapping around it as it might have around a worm. The White Tiger slowed, and slashed out with a hind foot, but a tiger does not kick as effectively as a horse does. All his attempt to free himself did was cause the tiger to stumble, so that the Toad reeled more of the tiger and his passenger closer to that gaping maw.

Pearl felt for her sword and found it in her sash, just as it should be. She had no desire to slay the immortal Toad, for she knew that the ramifications of such an act would reverberate down the generations. Even more, however, she had no desire to be swallowed. Unsheathing the blade, she kept her hand steady—not an easy task while clinging to the still striving White Tiger with only her knees—and pricked the Toad several short, sharp jabs along its extended tongue.

Shedding drops of blood that glimmered and broke, rubies with hearts of poison, the tongue lashed back into the Toad's mouth. The White Tiger of the West sprang forward so fast that Pearl had to beg it to slow.

"Honored One, it would not do to lose the Toad now, not after we have come so far."

And the White Tiger slowed in reply, although she could feel its grumbling through her clasped knees.

Pearl made certain that the Toad was well away from her house before she threw the White Opal in the direction of the real moon that glimmered in the sky.

The White Opal soared, the eager trio of winds buoying it up. The Three-legged Toad hopped after the ersatz moon, using star formations as ladders. Pearl could feel when it moved safely out of range, forgetting the "pretty" that had drawn it down from the moon.

Pearl also could sense that the White Tiger wanted to join the chase, as cats will chase a rolling ball of yarn, but she could not spare it to join the fun.

"Back to my house," she said, scratching it between the ears. "I must reestablish the wards."

The White Tiger carried Pearl, not quite obediently, but with a certain friendliness that came from family feeling between Tigers.

As Pearl sought to keep her balance on the racing White Tiger, she realized that she was weaker than she had imagined. Nissa and Brenda continued to feed her ch'i, but ch'i was only energy—it could not substitute for concentration, and Pearl had already stretched her own tissue thin. White Opal and All Winds and Dragons were not like the little spells she had done when Foster had attacked her in her room in Virginia. Both were major summonings, and her immortal opponent had demanded all her attention.

Pearl realized that she wasn't going to be able to work the final spells, that if she tried, she might even leave the household in a worse situation than before. She must release her summonings properly, then, maybe, just maybe, she could direct Nissa and Brenda to finish the job.

Pearl kept her focus as she slid off the White Tiger's back and went through the ritual that politely and correctly terminated the summons that kept the winds and dragons in her thrall. With her last iota of control, she slid back into her body, only to feel it collapse onto the thick carpet on her study floor.

☆

"Pearl!" Brenda heard herself scream, and at the same moment she became aware that the ch'i she had been feeding through her Knitting was damming up.

Only then, as if coming out of a dream, did Brenda see that Pearl Bright had collapsed. Nissa was already down on her knees, her hand at Pearl's wrist.

"She's alive. Get me some water. Then run upstairs to Pearl's medicine cabinet and see if you can figure out what medication she's on. Look especially for any sign that she has heart trouble."

When Brenda came back with the water, Pearl was conscious and whispering to Nissa who cradled the older woman semi-upright in her arms. Actually, Pearl wasn't whispering. Those rasping tones were as much as the normally resonant voice could manage.

". . . in excellent shape for my age. I take something for my blood pressure, and something for cholesterol, but stress tests show my heart is just fine."

Pearl stopped to sip from the water Brenda held out to her.

"More important to get the other spells in place than to get me to bed. My wards are a mess. They need to be strengthened, even before we work Confused Gates. Can you do Sparrow's Sanctuary?"

"The sequence is in my notes," Nissa said, "but I haven't actually worked it. Have you, Brenda?"

"I haven't," Brenda said, "but I've looked at it. It's pretty. All bamboo. No honors."

"Green bamboo," Pearl rasped. "Important. Green growth."

Brenda recalled that some of the bamboo tiles were multicolored, probably originally to facilitate counting how many bamboo were depicted on the relatively small surfaces.

"I'll get my notes," Brenda said, "and my tiles."

She ran up the stairs and into her room. Through the connecting door into the bathroom came soft sounds, one of which sounded remarkably like "Go fish!" She wondered if Lani was alone in there, and decided to be glad the little girl was so content.

If Foster had broken the rules of his parole and gone in to sit with the little girl . . . well . . . Brenda personally thought that was the right thing for him to have done, and if she didn't look, she wouldn't know, and what she didn't know, she couldn't tell.

When Brenda returned to the office, Nissa had settled Pearl onto a long divan of the style that was rather appropriately, given its current use, called a "fainting couch." Judging from the ornately carved wood, the piece was old, but the plush red velvet was rich and dark. Obviously, Pearl valued the coach enough to have it reupholstered, even at current, ruinous rates.

"Envision the sequence," Pearl was saying. "You'll find the existing strands of my own spell there."

Brenda didn't interrupt, but went over to a nice ebony table and set down both her notes and the Rat's mah-jong set.

"I should have had you get mine," Nissa said, "but probably better we don't wake Lani. Did she seem okay?"

"I didn't hear her screaming or crying or anything," Brenda evaded.

Nissa seemed satisfied. "Can you set out the tiles for the spell? Pearl thinks that because I'm the Rabbit, I'd better be the lead and you stand by to support."

Brenda felt a competitive flare. After all, Brenda had been in formal training before Nissa. Still, Brenda decided that this was a stupid time to argue their relative merits as lead. She hadn't exactly seen what was out beyond Pearl's wards, but she'd sensed enough to be sure that whatever was out there had been very big and very . . . "nasty" really wasn't the right word. Persistent. What she had sensed had reminded Brenda of Lani when Lani wanted to hear the same book read to her " 'Gan!' " even though the child had it so well memorized that she would detect the smallest deviation from the text.

"You settle Pearl," Brenda said. "I'll get the tiles out."

The tiles were set on individual trays within the box, and Brenda had stacked them in order by suit. Glancing over to her notes, she pulled out the tiles they would need: all four one bamboo, then a pair each of two, three, four, six, and eight bamboo. Other than the ones, which showed a strutting peacock, these tiles were all green. The resulting sequence was rather pretty.

Nissa came over as Brenda set the last pair in the line.

"Want me to prepare a Knitting?" Brenda said.

"Please," Nissa said. She looked drawn but determined. "I'm going to need your help for this. I want to make sure those wards are strong enough that everything is kept out."

Away from my baby went unspoken, but Brenda didn't miss the way Nissa glanced up in the direction of Lani's room. She wondered if real rabbits were such fierce mothers.

They prepared as before, and then Nissa said, "Okay. I'm starting. Feed me a trickle right off. That way I'll know where to find it when I need it."

Brenda obeyed. She no longer wanted to be in charge. She just wanted this done right. Concentrating hard on the Knitting pattern, she created the desired trickle.

Probably because Nissa was so much less experienced than Pearl, Brenda found that the channel gave her a clear conduit into how Nissa was working the spell.

First, Nissa released the four peacocks. These promptly flew into a tangle of bamboo and became four tattered, brown sparrows. At first glance, the grove that surrounded these sparrows was so dense that anything larger than a sparrow should have had trouble getting through.

At second inspection, the tangle showed signs that something very large had been stomping on portions of it. Some bamboo canes were bent over. Others had completely snapped, their fibrous ends poking up like fine hairs. Leaves had been stripped off and littered the ground.

"This wouldn't protect a sparrow," Nissa thought. A plump brown cottontail rabbit with anomalous turquoise eyes hopped forward to inspect the damage. *"Let's make it grow."*

Brenda felt Nissa begin to draw on her ch'i. Immediately the grove sharpened and became brighter. Bent bamboo canes straightened, and broken ones sprouted strong new tops. Where the broken ends lay upon the ground, they became the basis for even more bamboo. Long leaves, pointed at end and base, unfolded from the tips of twigs, creating a green veil that sealed every hole, every perforation. Even the sparrows rounded out. Their tattered feathers became sleek. They began to fuss and chatter, as contented birds will do.

Denser and denser, greener and greener the bamboo forest grew until Brenda knew with certainty that it was becoming not a sanctuary but a prison. She was also aware that Nissa was draining too much ch'i, that if she continued there would be none left for the next spell, perhaps nothing left at all.

With a flash of insight, Brenda realized how dangerous Knitting could be if the partners did not keep faith with each other—or if the one taking the energy grew too absorbed in her casting.

Brenda tried to break the Knitting from her end, but she had envisioned the conduit as a thick knitted band, rather like a nice winter scarf. It would neither pull free, nor break. She tried to scream or shout, but her throat wouldn't work. She could read Nissa's thoughts as the turquoise-eyed rabbit glimpsed a tiny bare spot here, a broken branchlet there and hastened to mend it. For her part, Nissa was completely lost in the spell and could not hear.

Panic surged in Brenda's breast, making her heart beat fast and hard. She realized she was growing weaker. New bamboo leaves sprouted, new canes grew. If she didn't break the bond, she would soon be in as bad shape as Pearl. Worse, maybe. Pearl had known when to stop.

The rabbit didn't seem to realize that it had trapped itself inside the bamboo grove. Seeing Nissa as the rabbit, Brenda impulsively shaped the image of her own inner Rat. It was a very small rat, hardly larger than a mouse, but it was sleek and grey, with nice rounded ears and a very active pink nose surrounded by long, silky whiskers.

Brenda sent the little rat out onto the length of knitting and began gnawing away at the thick knitted scarf. Rats' teeth are very sharp. They can even gnaw through metal. Mere yarn was nothing to them.

As the last strands frayed, Brenda saw Nissa looking out through the plump brown cottontail's eyes, for the first time recognizing that she was trapped within a cage of tightly grown bamboo. Brenda felt a momentary mean impulse, a desire to leave Nissa there, not forever, just until Des got back. Then Pearl would think twice before saying that simply being the Rabbit was enough to make Nissa superior.

But Nissa had been nothing but kindness and gentle support to Brenda. She hadn't even teased Brenda for thinking she could play at mah-jong two-handed with Foster. She hadn't said a single unkind thing when Brenda inadvertently brought all this trouble down on them. Brenda might be a Rat, but she wasn't going to act like one.

She stopped the little rat from chewing through the last strand of yarn, and instead tugged at it.

"Grab hold," she squeaked. "I can pull you out. Bamboo is gracious. Bamboo will bend."

Nissa grabbed hold, and Brenda pulled. She concentrated on touching the tightly grown bamboo with a reminder that her ch'i flowed in their sap. The bamboo canes parted, maybe a little reluctantly, but with something of the thought that they were to keep things out, not in.

There was no transitional moment. One second Brenda was a tiny rat pulling on a strand of yarn to rescue a cottontail bunny, the next minute she was sitting on the carpet in Pearl's study, a soreness in her butt telling her that she had landed suddenly and hard. Nissa sat in front of her, one hand raised to her forehead.

"You okay?" Brenda said. Squeaked, almost. Her throat felt very tight.

"I bumped my head on the table when I fell back into my body," Nissa said, "but no great harm done. Thanks, Breni."

No one had called Brenda that nickname since her dad went away. Brenda reached out and hugged Nissa tightly. Pearl watched them, her gaze warm and compassionate, rather than critical as Brenda had expected.

"I should have warned you," the Tiger said, "of the danger of getting carried away. I can sense the wards and they are—remarkable. Good job. Are you willing to try Confused Gates? That's what's going to keep away any snoopers who might have been attracted by all this sorcery."

Nissa gave Brenda's arm a squeeze, then released her and pulled herself upward. She leafed through Brenda's study book until she came upon the pattern for the spell.

"Three different suits," she murmured, "and a really long sequence. I don't think I could keep it straight in my mind. Are you sure that Brenda couldn't . . ."

She let the question trail off, not really wanting to challenge the Tiger.

"We have a very interesting Ratling there," Pearl said, her tone both affectionate and puzzled. "I had enough energy to watch what you were doing . . ."

"Pearl!" Nissa protested. "You shouldn't."

"I had to," Pearl said. "Don't fuss. The ward you were repairing was originally mine. I used one of the sparrow's eyes to see through. I saw what Brenda did. It's very strange. Heirs apparent usually cannot manifest their other self, but she did. I wonder if that explains why she could see Foster there in the . . ."

Pearl halted her speculation, and looked at Brenda. "Do you want to try taking lead, Brenda? It's a hard spell, and you've already given of your ch'i repeatedly tonight. Des shouldn't be too late, and he and Riprap should be able to manage."

"But what if something comes before they do?" Brenda said.

"The Sparrow's Sanctuary you two wove would keep even a dragon out," Pearl said with a dry chuckle. "If you'd kept going, the problem would have been *our* getting out."

Brenda rose and studied the sequence for Confused Gates. Nissa was right. It was a hard one. Still, she'd gotten them into this. She'd like to do more to fix the damage than act as a sort of human battery.

"I can try," she said. "What could go wrong?"

"Other than your expending ch'i to no use," Pearl said sternly, "the reverse of Confused Gates would be open ones. You don't want to do that, especially since this is not a kind, gentle opening, but rather like using a battering ram to open a glass jar."

"Oh." Brenda considered, reached into herself and found that the little rat was feeling quite fat and sassy. "I'd still like to try. I promise that if I feel myself losing control, I'll let the spell drop, just like Des has coached us."

"Very well."

"I'll be behind you," Nissa promised. "I have ch'i. I'm just a little afraid that I'll lose focus."

Brenda squeezed Nissa's hand. "I completely understand."

She started laying out tiles. "Auntie Pearl, this one calls for all three suits, no honors, so I can't leave out dots. I was thinking about just one pung, and that of nines since they're small—more like stars than moons."

"Good," Pearl said. "I noticed you have a problem with remembering characters. However, if you use them for the long sequence and the pair, they'll serve better than either dots or bamboo. Bamboo would be like hiding a forest with trees."

"I've got you," Brenda said. "I'm okay with characters when they're in front of me. I'll lay them out here."

She wondered briefly how Pearl had known about her "handicap," then realized she must have read it in the Knitting. Clearly, Pearl was so far ahead of Brenda in ability and flexibility that she could do things on reflex for which Brenda would need an entire ritual.

Brenda laid out the tiles: a pung of nine dots, a pung of five bamboo (chosen because they had mingled red and green canes, so had not been part of the Sparrow's Sanctuary), a sequence of characters running two through eight, and a final pair of nine characters.

She recited her selection to Pearl, and the old Tiger seemed to purr—although that could have just been her still raspy voice.

"Whenever you're ready," Pearl said. "Nissa? Are you rested enough?"

Nissa nodded. "There's something out there, isn't there? I feel the bamboo bending, just a little."

"Something small," Pearl agreed. "Something we can easily confuse."

Brenda wondered if Pearl was only being reassuring. Her sense of the ward was much less acute, but it seemed to her that anything that could bend Nissa's mighty canes couldn't be insignificant.

Brenda nodded to Nissa. "I'll start now. Knit in when you're ready."

With assumed confidence, Brenda ran her gaze over the neat line of characters. She felt a tinge and a click as the pattern locked into place. Good. Now to make it stronger. She wanted to make her spell a fitting complement for Nissa's.

Nissa's ch'i was channeling in nicely, and Brenda used it to etch a line of fire into the incised patterns of the tiles. She closed her eyes, and set herself to concentrating.

It should have been easy to keep the shape of the spell steady in her mind; she'd already gone over the sequence several times. Even so, Brenda found her own fears dreadfully distracting. What if she got drawn into the spell as Nissa had done? What if she really didn't have the skill to pull off something so complex? Pearl was right. Brenda hadn't trained very long. She wasn't the real Rat, just an heir apparent, and with her father's memories stolen was there anything for her to be heir apparent to?

Concentrate! Brenda ordered herself sternly. *Don't let your insecurities stop you from even trying to get this just right.*

But did she really need to try to make the spell particularly strong? Des should be home soon. True, he and Riprap had sort of indicated that they were going to make a night of it, stop out for something to eat or whatever after the game. But surely if anything got through Brenda's gates, Nissa's wards would hold. They were so strong that they'd nearly trapped Nissa inside them.

Concentrate! Come on. Pung. Pung. Run. Pair. You've even got the suits chosen. Characters are tough, but like you told Pearl, you've got them set out in front of you. It's not like you need to do this from memory.

Brenda realized she'd done something silly when she'd closed her eyes in order to concentrate. She needed to concentrate on those tiles.

Brenda tried to open her eyes, and with horror realized that she could not. Her hands were pressed to her temples. Her eyes were squeezed shut. Her feet were planted firmly on the floor, but other than those sensations, she could feel nothing. She reached for where Nissa's Knitting should anchor, and found nothing there. Her ears brought her only the buzz of her own pulse. The inside of her mouth was dry.

Has something grabbed me? Brenda thought. *That big thing I sensed outside the ward. Has it swallowed me?*

The now all too familiar sensation of panic set Brenda's heart beating wildly. The sound was a wild drumming in her ears that made concentration difficult. She felt herself fraying, being pushed away. Confusion flooded her mind, making thought difficult, but oddly that confusion brought her insight.

I've done just like Nissa, Brenda realized. *I've wandered into my own spell. Nissa nearly trapped herself. I've confused myself, almost to the point of incoherence. Confused Gates. Right. If I can just squeeze back to the other side of the gate . . .*

Once more, Brenda tried to open her eyes, but they wouldn't open.

"Okay, little rat," she thought, and wasn't at all sure who she was addressing. *"What do you see?"*

An image came into her mind from somewhere around ankle level. Indeed, Brenda saw her ankle in the vision, grotesque and angular, the little scrapes and scratches she had gotten running around Pearl's house and garden in her bare feet augmented to ripples and ridges the color of dried blood.

"I'm not interested in my ankle, little rat. Where are we, and more importantly, how do we get back?"

The image shifted. Brenda saw herself standing on a roughly spherical form shaped from twisted bamboo canes. Leaves poked out here and there, tickling her feet. A thick haze rose from the bamboo, twisting and curling like smoke from the tip of a freshly lit cigarette. It made interesting shapes—medieval castles, sailing ships, craggy mountain peaks, a Swiss chalet, pagodas, a cairn of rocks, something rather like Stonehenge. Any of these were more interesting than the bamboo sphere, and Brenda felt herself drawn to explore.

She felt something sharp bite the side of her foot. The little rat, her own last shred of common sense, was reminding her that she'd not asked to see the confusion she'd created, but a way to get back into Pearl's house.

Rat's-eye view wasn't the best for elevated perspective.

"Climb up my leg," Brenda suggested. *"Onto my shoulder, even. I should be able to see better from there."*

Tiny claws prickled against Brenda's bare leg, and she felt weight hanging off the fabric of her shorts, then on her T-shirt. The tactile sensations were fascinating, but Brenda knew they could become their own lead into confusion and forced herself to remember her goal.

At last the little rat settled on Brenda's shoulder. She felt its long whiskers brush the side of her neck as it turned its gaze upon the one true gate that would take her home. The true gate was very hard to see, more like a hatch down into the bamboo sphere than what Brenda thought of as a gate. The smoke castles were really much more substantial-looking. . . .

A raucous sound drew Brenda's gaze back to the hatchway. It sounded familiar, bringing with it a memory of the scent of sawdust and feathers. A rooster crowing!

That was interesting enough to merit another look. On the other side of the hatchway stood a very cocky, very colorful rooster. He was of an exotic type, a breed that Brenda knew was probably Chinese, even as she knew that this rooster had to be Des.

He crowed again, and Brenda turned her feet toward the hatchway. It was hard navigating through the little rat's eyes. The perspective was too low and skewed to one side. She instructed the rat to climb onto her head, and it did, hanging down so that its head rested on her forehead. The perspective offered by its eyes was too narrow, but otherwise almost right.

Brenda moved toward the gate with greater confidence. When she reached it, the rooster unhooked the latch with its beak. Brenda sat and lowered herself over the edge, and with every foot she dropped she began to feel connected to her own body again, until as her head dipped below the level of the bamboo sphere, she could see again with her own vision.

She reached up, but the little rat was no longer there.

Brenda had no idea why, but without warning, she started to sob.

Pearl had not protested too much when Riprap offered to carry her from the fainting couch into the family room. Des had insisted on making tea, and she hadn't bothered to argue. She knew he was right. She needed a stimulant of some sort. In any case, her office was not a comfortable place to hold the conference she knew must follow.

Nissa had gone upstairs to check on Lani. Brenda, still looking a little wild around the eyes, had gone with her.

Pearl filled Des and Riprap in on the details, her voice now strong enough that she could easily make herself heard in the adjoining kitchen. Des asked a few questions, but Riprap listened in silence, only pausing once as he went about putting away the plastic tiles from the game that had ended in near disaster.

"Now," Pearl concluded, "what I want to know is what brought you home so fortuitously. Brenda might well have wandered much further if you hadn't gotten here to crow her back."

"Foster called me," Des said. "He knew something was wrong."

"You taught him how to summon you?" Pearl snapped. She'd been half reclining in her favorite chair, but now she struggled upright. "Of all the injudicious, criminally incautious . . ."

"Pearl!" Des's tone was as sharp as her own. He stalked into the room, looking no less angry or dangerous for the large tray of nacho chips covered in ground meat, cheese, black olives, and jalapeños he carried in one hand. "That is uncalledfor! You're becoming paranoid about Foster. Moreover, I am not an idiot nor injudicious."

"Then how did he reach you?"

"I gave him my cell phone," Des said, his tone dropping to conversational ranges, "and preprogrammed it with Riprap's cell phone number."

Pearl flopped back in her chair and covered her face with her hands. Even so, she could feel the blush creeping out around the edges.

"Oh, dear lord," she said. "Des, I am sorry. After what we've been through tonight, I honestly forgot that there were simple, ordinary ways of doing things. You gave him your cell phone. Of course. . . ."

"Of course," Des said. "At your insistence, Foster is hugely isolated here. He's scared to talk to you, and he can't really talk to the others. If he has a simple question like where we keep the spare toilet paper or whatever, he's not going to ask a girl in any case. He has no memory of his past, but judging from his actions, I wouldn't be at all surprised to find he was raised in some sort of monastery. He likes the girls—but he talks about them like they're some sort of aliens."

"I'm sorry, Des," Pearl repeated. "I have no excuse. A desire to transfer some of the guilt I'm feeling may explain my reaction, but it doesn't excuse it. I beg your forgiveness."

Des was still glowering, but after a moment he gave a curt nod, then let a smile creep through the curtain of his mustache.

"All right, but you're going to owe me. You can start by getting some of this nice greasy cheese into you."

Pearl accepted the plate he handed her. Her father had possessed the usual Chinese distaste for cheese, but her mother had no such dislike. Pearl ate cheese with great enthusiasm, and felt that the extra calcium had done its part in saving her from the usual weakening bones of old age.

As she ate, Pearl heard Nissa and Brenda coming down the stairs. She felt fairly certain that they had heard at least some of her exchange with Des and was not pleased. She preferred that the senior members keep a united front, and Des already had the edge on her in influencing the younger three, since he was their teacher.

And who do you have to blame for that, Tiger Bright? Pearl asked herself. *You could have made yourself teacher, but it was just too much trouble.*

Nissa looked severely shaken, but could at least walk under her own power. Pearl felt a trace of envy, then reminded herself that youth was not the only reason for Nissa's and Brenda's resilience. Each of them had done much less than she had that night. They had worked only two spells apiece, and that had nearly broken them.

"Pearl," Nissa said, taking a seat on one end of the sofa and accepting the plate of nachos and glass of sweetened iced tea Des handed her, "I've got to agree with Des. You're paranoid about Foster—at least about the Foster we have here and now. I'm not saying you don't have reason to worry about who he might be when he gets his memories back, but the young man we have with us in this house deserves better than you've been giving him."

Pearl tried to think of something icy and cutting to say, but Nissa anticipated her and waved her down with a soggy chip.

"Pearl, do you know what I found when I went up to check on Lani? Foster. He was in there, singing to her, keeping her calm. There were cards all over the floor from where they'd been playing Go Fish.

"If it wasn't for Foster, we might have failed tonight, because if my baby had been screaming I couldn't have done even what I managed to do—and I know I didn't do my part all that well. Foster didn't get in the way, didn't interfere or snoop, but when he had to face punishment for breaking out of that jail you've made for him or letting my baby be scared, he took the risk.

"You should have seen his face when I went in there. His eyes went all wide and he scrabbled back a little from where he'd been sitting on the floor with Lani on his lap. He can't talk English very well, but he tried, begging me not to tell you he'd not stayed in his room. As far as I am concerned, this has gone far enough. You want my help on this Thirteen Orphans business, well, then, we treat Foster better. Otherwise, Lani and I will go right on home, and if I lose my memory, well then, I lose the memory of being party to abuse of a perfectly nice young man!"

Pearl had known Nissa all her life, had been entertained by her in the role of an honored family friend. But never before had she heard such a flow of words from her. Brenda was staring at Nissa with shock and admiration, but she managed to pull her gaze away and look over at Pearl.

"Me, too, Auntie Pearl. I'm sorry."

Des looked at her. "You already know my feelings about this matter, Pearl. Riprap?"

The big black man shrugged. "I can see it both ways. I don't much like the idea of losing my memory. That probably means I'd lose some of my best memories of my father, and I don't like that. That said, I'm not really happy about our slowly driving Foster up the wall. I've played a bit of catch with him, and deep down where memory doesn't matter, he's sharp—fast on his feet, and as calculating as you are. I agree with you that Foster would make a bad enemy, but I do think he'd make a good friend."

Pearl nodded. "I see. If this were a democracy, I'd definitely be outvoted, but we can't take risks on something as untrustworthy as a majority vote. Will it be enough for you all if I promise to give this serious consideration—more serious and more sincere than I can the way I'm feeling now?"

Nissa, who did not look in the least ashamed of her outburst, nodded. "I don't feel too well myself, and you have to feel worse. I can wait, but I'm not going to forget, and I'm not going to be put off."

"Same here," Brenda said. "There's Dad and all that's happened to him, but I'm not sure treating Foster badly is going to help me help Dad."

The two men nodded agreement. Des had brought in a tray of seasoned potato wedges and another of fried cheese sticks.

"I didn't know we had this stuff in the house," Pearl said, looking for the first time at the plate of nachos in her lap as something other than much needed fuel.

"We didn't," Riprap said. "Des and I had just gotten our order when Foster's call came. Des settled the tab, and I grabbed boxes and stuffed the food in. We were too worried to think about eating while Des ran red lights to get us back here."

Brenda grinned. "I didn't realize you were into such healthy eating, sports star."

"We burned enough jumping up and down during the game," Riprap said with an answering grin. He scooped up a couple of cheese sticks and dipped them into sauce, then looked over at Pearl. "I want to know why you said to Des that you might have gotten so angry because you're trying to transfer guilt. What do you have to be guilty about?"

Pearl frowned. "Not about Foster, if that's what you're leading up to. Hand me a couple of those potato wedges." He did, and she considered, "Because I was not paying attention to what was going on. Because I was focusing so hard on research that I fell asleep at my desk. Because in doing so . . . Well, I might have created the circumstance that led to Brenda drawing that hand."

That last got all eyes turned on her. Pearl ate the potato wedges and daintily wiped her fingers before explaining.

"The moon is the realm of transformation, so I have been doing a great deal of research into spells related to the moon. I may have unintentionally infected the—call it the 'ether'—within my wards, making it more likely that spells in-volving the moon would, well, happen."

"And it could just be coincidence," Brenda said. "I was looking for a cleared hand, and getting bamboo like crazy because both Nissa and Foster wanted other suits. My mom is no sorceress, but she's a smart lady where it counts and she says that guilt doesn't do any good. Knowing where you've been wrong and trying to fix it, that's good. Grabbing onto guilt and using it as an excuse for trying to find excuses or justification or just to feel bad, that doesn't make sense."

"I've always liked Keely," Pearl said. "And now I have another reason to do so. I know you and Nissa are feeling pretty guilty yourselves, and I want you to consider this—we had a near disaster tonight, but we pulled though. We learned something vital as well."

"Oh?" This came from both young women in chorus. They looked at each other and giggled, the high, slightly shrill giggles of the overtired.

"I've been underestimating what you're capable of," Pearl said.

"*Under*estimating?" Nissa said. "I'm not sure about that. I managed to pull off Sparrow's Sanctuary, and then got myself trapped."

"But you pulled the spell off," Des said, "after a relatively short period of training. This shows a considerable amount of potential. Brenda . . . Well, Brenda just keeps getting more interesting."

"Interesting?" Brenda said. "Des, you say that like it's a curse. I like being interesting."

Pearl thought, *I bet you do, my dear, and since I'm currently on your black list for how I have treated handsome Foster, I'm going to leave explaining this to Des.*

"May you live in interesting times . . ." Des said. "Some say that's a curse—although not necessarily ancient Chinese, no matter what you've heard—because interesting means out of the ordinary."

The expression Brenda turned on Des was guarded without being hostile.

"Why don't you tell me why I'm 'interesting' when Nissa is merely loaded with potential. I don't see that I did anything she didn't do—and I certainly didn't make any worse mistakes."

"That's just it," Des said. "You did what Nissa did—and you shouldn't have been able to do so."

"I don't get it," Brenda admitted. "Why shouldn't I be able to do what she can? Why shouldn't I be able to do more? I've had more training, and you told us from the start that magical ability isn't limited to the Thirteen."

"Right on all counts," Des said, "but you did one thing that you should not have been able to do until you are a member of the Thirteen—you manifested a

rat. A little rat, true, but a completely useful rat, one whose senses you could em-
ploy. As far as I know, this has never happened before."

"Oh," Brenda looked thoughtful. "I saw Nissa's rabbit, and so I thought
about rats. I didn't really try to do it. I mean, later, I realized I'd trapped myself,
and I wanted to figure out a way out of my own trap, but I didn't think 'Well,
let's summon up a rat.' It just happened."

"And that is what's interesting," Des said. "I can think of no reason why it
should have 'just happened.' "

"But it was a good thing," Brenda said. "Right? I mean, it made it possible
for me to get back when you called."

"I wish I knew" was Des's cryptic reply. From the way he said it, it was also
clear that he wasn't going to offer more in the way of encouragement. Brenda
obviously knew her teacher well enough to read his mood, and stopped pressing
for his approval.

Riprap had been listening intently, quietly working his way through enough
potato wedges that Pearl felt a little queasy. Now he interrupted.

"I think I need to know a little more about what happened there. I mean, I
heard what Pearl told Des, but I don't understand it. What's this about getting
trapped? How could that happen? And turning into hares and rats? Am I likely to
turn into a dog?"

"It's entirely possible," Des said, "but not in the way you're thinking—at
least not unless you work on it. It's late. I'm tired. You're tired. So I'm going to
just touch the basics."

Riprap nodded, but there was a stubborn set to his shoulders that said that
while he'd take the short version now, he wasn't going to stop there. Pearl wasn't
surprised. Dogs were persistent. Like so many qualities, it was both a strength and
a weakness.

"Okay, Des," Riprap said. "Start with this. If I turn into a dog, do I, like,
have any choice about it? I mean, I really couldn't handle being a Pekingese or
one of those little fluff dogs. I just couldn't."

Des chuckled. "No worries. I'm not saying there haven't been Dogs who
manifested as Pekes, but you do have some say in what happens—a lot more than
you realize, and a lot less."

"This is not helping," Riprap said.

Des nodded. "Let me back up a bit. None of you have really asked where the
dragons you've learned to summon live."

Nissa said, "I thought that they came from the same place that our ancestors did, that we were tapping the homeland of the Thirteen Orphans. You did say that creatures that we think of as mythological were common there."

Brenda nodded. "Me, too. Especially since those dragons were all so, well, Chinese. I mean, I'm part Irish, part German, too. Shouldn't I get a dragon like the one in Wagner sometimes?"

Des rubbed his forehead with the side of one hand as if massaging away a headache.

"Brenda, I'm not even going to get into that right now. Nissa, you're right and you're wrong. The spells existed before the Lands Born from Smoke and Sacrifice existed—although perhaps not in precisely these forms. So you're not summoning from there—you're summoning from a third place, accessible from both, that touches both here and there."

"But what about what you told us?" Riprap said. "About dragons being associated with water—and with wind and rain? That makes it sound like they're here."

"They are," Des said. "Do you believe in an afterlife? Or a soul?"

Riprap blinked at him. "I guess. Sure. Maybe not like my mama's church does, but I know there's something that's me that you might call my soul."

"Can you find it? Weigh it? Measure it?"

"No," Riprap said, nodding as he did so. "And you're saying that's the way it is with these dragons?"

"And with other creatures as well," Des said. "They don't need to be material any more than what you might call your soul would show up on an X-ray. Dragons are in the oceans, but no fisherman is going to catch one in his nets—although they did so often enough in legend."

"Are we losing the point here?" Riprap said. "I asked about how Brenda or Nissa could get trapped while crafting a spell, about why they turned into animals. What does this have to do with souls?"

"That's the part of them that got trapped," Des said simply. "Brenda and Nissa got so involved in their spells that their souls leaked out into the crafting. Sorcerers often do so intentionally. It's a technique that makes for very solid creations, but it has some dangerous side effects, even for a skilled spellcaster."

Pearl saw Nissa glance over at her, and nodded confirmation.

"And rats and hares?" Riprap asked. "And dogs?"

"What shape does a soul have?" Des replied. "Explaining more would take hours and probably only raise more questions for you. Nissa was spellcasting in her role as the Rabbit, so it's not surprising that her soul took that form. Brenda . . . I suppose she could simply have thought of herself as a little rat, but there was something there. . . ."

Des shrugged. "I'm too tired to work it out now. Is that enough to hold you?"

Riprap nodded. "For now, coach. For now."

★

Brenda woke the next morning to sunlight streaming between the slats of the blinds that covered her bedroom window and pain racking the inside of her skull that made the worst hangover she'd ever experienced seem like a gentle love tap. With tremendous effort, she managed to get her pillow over her face, blocking out the worst of the light.

From the bathroom she heard the unmistakable sound of someone throwing up, repeatedly and violently. The sound alone was bad enough, but when a trickle of sour vomit stench drifted her way, Brenda pressed the pillow more tightly over her face, stuffing her head with the light floral scent of the fabric softener.

She heard the door between her bedroom and the hallway open, then close. Someone was moving around, and in a moment she was aware that the room had gotten darker. She relaxed slightly, heard the toilet flush, and then a spray can being plied. In a moment, a different floral scent blended with that of the fabric softener.

Funny, Brenda thought, *all those novels where you read about kings and queens and exotic perfumes. I bet the corner drugstore has more perfumes than all the caravans of the fabled Indies.*

Brenda knew her geography was muddled, but forming even a partially coherent thought made her feel better. She decided to try another one.

"Whoos der?" she muttered indistinctly into the pillow. Then she moved the part of the pillow that wasn't over her eyes and tried again. "Who's there?"

"Riprap," came the deep voice. "And don't worry. You're decent. Poor Nissa. She didn't care if she was decent or not. All she cared about was getting cleaned up."

"Whass wrong?" Brenda managed through lips that felt swollen and stiff. "Did yer takeow give us food poisn'?"

"My understanding," Riprap said, "is that both of you ladies are suffering from ch'i depletion. Last night, by the time Des intervened, you were running on adrenaline and nothing more. Des hoped all the fatty stuff last night would have given your bodies something to convert to energy. Guess you didn't eat enough."

Brenda thought about it. "Thin' I was queasy then, already."

"Quite possibly," Riprap replied.

She could hear him moving about her room, and she guessed he was assuring himself that the sunlight at her window was well and fully blocked. Brenda appreciated his efforts. Right now the least bit of light felt like red-hot daggers being pressed into her eyes.

"Why din Des warn us?" Brenda asked. "Wooda eaten more."

"He says he didn't want to stress you further. Bad enough what you'd been through without telling you how you might pay for it in a few hours. He says that sometimes the suggestion can trigger the response. He hoped ignorance would be bliss, but no such luck."

"Pearl?"

"She's still in bed, so tired she looks transparent, but otherwise she's fine. She says she has you and Nissa to thank for that."

"Urggh."

"Think you can keep some water down? Des says we can't risk you getting dehydrated."

"Thin' so.'

"I'm going to move the pillow, put my arm around you and hold you up just a little. The water's in one of Lani's sippie cups."

"Urggh."

"Don't worry. It's clean. No stale fruit juice."

"Please, don't. Jus' thinkin' gonna make me sick."

"Gotcha, girl. Now, ready?"

Brenda felt a broad, strong arm effortlessly prop her up. Then the sheltering pillow was removed, and she squished her eyelids tightly shut. Riprap had done a good job, though, and the darkness was as complete as she could wish.

She felt the plastic edge of the cup against her lips and sucked eagerly. The water was chilled but not cold, and went down well. The cup was removed far too quickly.

"Hey!" The sound was almost like a baby's whimper.

"Let's see if you keep that much down before giving you more, Brenda. I've mopped up enough messes for one morning."

"Oh . . ."

But Brenda kept both that water down, and what Riprap let her have later. She sank back into sleep, and when she woke this time there was no light glimmering around the edges of the window. From the reduced hum of street noise, Brenda guessed it was night.

She felt better now, although very thirsty. She propped herself cautiously upright, then swung her feet onto the floor. There was a faint buzz of pain behind her eyes, negligible after what she had experienced earlier. Making her way into the bathroom, she drank several cups of water from the tap, then felt weirdly triumphant when they went down and stayed.

Brenda listened, and thought she heard a noise from downstairs. For the first time it occurred to her to look at a clock. Eight in the evening. Probably most of the household would still be awake.

She found clean clothes and padded barefoot down the stairs. Nissa wasn't present, but Lani was, busy building something elaborate out of wooden blocks, her expression serious. Brenda wondered whether Lani was so quiet because she was worried about her mother, or because she was hoping no one had noticed she was up past her bedtime.

Riprap was seated at the long table near the kitchen—the same table where the disastrous game of mah-jong had been played the night before. Tonight, however, the tiles were nowhere to be seen. Instead there was a scattering of six-sided dice and a score pad.

"I'm teaching Foster to play Yahtzee," Riprap explained. "Seemed safer than mah-jong. How're you feeling?"

Brenda considered. "Transparent, like I'm not all here. Otherwise, not bad. Where are the others?"

"Nissa's still in bed. Pearl, too. Des brought her a tray, and they're talking. Foster went into the kitchen for some coffee."

As if his name had been a signal, Foster walked in, a big pottery coffee mug in one hand. He gave Brenda a shy smile that made her heart flip-flop.

"Feel better?" he asked.

"Feel better," she repeated. She looked at Riprap. "What are doctor's orders in regards to eating?"

"Des and Pearl say anything dairy is fine. Fresh fruit or veggies are fine. We got about a case of yogurt today. There's ice cream. You're to avoid meat. Something to do with the ch'i from dead things."

"Yogurt actually sounds good," Brenda said. "Though why it should, I don't know."

"Guess ch'i depletion isn't like having the flu," Riprap said. "Maybe you need all those active little cultures."

Foster had been listening, and Brenda thought he perked a little when Riprap mentioned ch'i. Then again, it might have been nothing—or at most a familiar sound in the midst of a babble of the unfamiliar.

Brenda went and got herself a carton of blueberry yogurt, considered, then stacked one of raspberry on top. She poured herself cold water from a pitcher in the fridge, and carried her meal out to the table. She took a seat a couple down from Riprap and watched the game as she slowly spooned yogurt into her mouth.

Once again she couldn't help but notice that Foster was an aggressive player. He took risks, too, more than once going for a five-of-a-kind when he should have tried for a combination that would get him fewer but more certain points. Riprap wasn't exactly passive, and the two of them played with a great deal of laughing and groaning.

Eventually, Lani came over to watch, clambering up into the chair between Riprap and Brenda. Not long after, she leaned against Brenda, then drifted into sleep, sliding down so that her head was in Brenda's lap.

"Good," Riprap said. "She had a tough day, poor thing, what with her mom so sick. Moms aren't supposed to get that sick. Still, Lani was pretty good. Played with me and Foster and let Nissa rest."

"Nissa is going to be all right, isn't she?" Brenda asked anxiously. She'd been so busy concentrating on her own small triumphs in handling the artificial light, and keeping food and water down, that she hadn't really had much thought to spare for anyone else.

"Des says so. He says that you both ran yourselves dry and that your bodies rebelled."

"Stupid bodies," Brenda said. "Stopping us from refueling."

"As I understand it," Riprap explained, "it's more like they stopped you from doing anything that might be more draining. Makes sense in a weird way."

Foster had been listening, but as their conversation was in English, he probably didn't catch much.

Brenda looked at Riprap. "Any word from Pearl about . . . y'know, what we asked?"

Riprap shook his head. "Nothing. Des might push her for an answer, but I didn't dare. Even worn transparent she's scary."

"I think Pearl counts on that," Brenda said. "She is an actress, after all. She'd know how to scare even you."

"I hadn't considered that," Riprap said. "Interesting. One thing I'm sure of, though. She really is worn out. Bonaventure and Amala are stretched out next to her, each to one side of her legs. She doesn't even have the energy to shoo them away."

"I'll give you that Pearl would be really tired, not just acting," Brenda said. "I know how I feel."

Riprap nodded. "Honestly, I'm a little scared to try a working on that scale now that I've seen what the penalties are for playing too rough."

He looked embarrassed, and glanced over at sleeping Lani.

"She looks like she's out enough that I can carry her upstairs without waking her," he said. "I need to check on Nissa anyhow, and someone should tell Des and Pearl you're back on your feet."

"Mostly," Brenda agreed. "I think I want more yogurt. If you take Lani, I can get it before my leg goes to sleep. She's got a heavy head."

Riprap nodded. "Babies do."

He slid Lani up easily, and she only stirred to cuddle up against his chest. "I'll be down in a little."

Brenda went and got some more yogurt, peach this time. Riprap hadn't been joking when he said they'd bought a case. She noticed it was all fruit flavors, though. No chocolate custard or other of the flavors that were meant to make people think they were eating dessert.

Foster was sitting at the table, sipping his coffee, studying his score sheet. He looked at her when she came in and motioned to the dice.

"You play? You know?"

For answer, Brenda slid into the chair across from him and took hold of a dice cup and set of dice. She shook them for emphasis, and then spilled them out onto the table.

"Who goes first?"

"Avon calling!"

Pearl opened her front door to find Gaheris Morris standing on the stoop, his eyes bright and his expression—there was no other word for it—cheeky. He held a briefcase in one hand, and was dressed in a sports shirt and neat trousers, what she knew was his work uniform for casual California.

"Gaheris!" Pearl stepped forward and embraced her visitor, her mind spinning as she tried to remember where Foster was. Possibly in the family room, possibly out in the garden with Lani. Des had insisted on extending the young man's parole that far, saying that there was no way the little girl should be expected to stay inside all the time, and with Nissa still weak, they really needed Foster as an extra sitter.

Pearl had given in with what grace she could. She was still dodging the language question, and this gave Des a small victory. Besides, they did need another sitter. The gardener and the chauffeur had been introduced to Foster as a young cousin from China. She guessed that if Des didn't get Foster under cover before Gaheris saw him, the same excuse could be used on Gaheris.

Releasing her embrace, Pearl asked, "Not that I'm not thrilled, but what brings you here?"

"Brenda's mother," Gaheris said, "has been talking to her daughter, and says Brenda has some sort of flu. I juggled my travel schedule, and here I am, ready to soothe an anxious mother's heart."

Pearl motioned for him to follow her inside. "Didn't Brenda ever get sick when she was away at college?"

Gaheris gave an embarrassed grin and spread his hands. "I think Keely is having a little trouble loosening the apron strings. It was one thing when Breni was away at school—that's usual—but Keely wasn't ready for her one and only daughter to be gone all summer. She's threatening to adopt a cat or dog or bird—species doesn't matter as long as the creature isn't male."

Pearl chuckled. "Well, you'll find your daughter doing much better, I think. She's upstairs taking care of some paperwork for me. I'll go get her."

"Let me run up and surprise her," Gaheris suggested, hand on the banister.

Pearl stopped him with a regal hand on one arm. Actually, Brenda was practicing drawing the nine characters, as these remained her weakest area for forming spells, and Brenda wasn't far enough recovered that she could actually cast anything.

Riprap was with her, not precisely keeping her company, but making spell bracelets in polymer clay. The young man had been thoroughly spooked by the damage using freely flowing ch'i could cause. With Gaheris's memory gone, this "craft activity" would be quite hard to explain.

"Let me go up," Pearl insisted. "Brenda is doing better, but she's still not well. She might be working in her robe or pajamas."

Gaheris nodded. "I keep forgetting. Brenda's not the baby whose diapers I changed. I'll go wait in the family room."

Pearl, who had been listening, and was fairly certain that Gaheris would find the family room empty of anything but Lani's scattered toys, nodded. She hurried up the stairs.

Neither Riprap nor Brenda greeted Pearl as she came through the door. Brenda was holding the bamboo handle of the traditional ink brush with greater ease than she had initially, but little flecks of ink on the newspaper she was using to practice on showed that she had yet to master the technique. Riprap was inking in the character for a green dragon in the white clay, his focus intent. Pearl let him finish before speaking, not wanting his ch'i to be wasted.

"We have a visitor," Pearl said when two pairs of dark eyes looked up at her inquiringly. "Brenda's father is here. Brenda, what does Gaheris know about those who constitute our household?"

"I told him and Mom you'd taken on other summer interns, and that Des Lee was out this way also working with you. I didn't get too specific about what Des was doing, but I think they figured it has something to do either with your charitable foundation or with acting."

"Good," Pearl said. "Well, come on down and see Gaheris. He arrived just a few minutes ago."

Brenda, ink-splatters and all, was already halfway out the door before Pearl finished speaking.

"But do take it easy," Pearl said to her retreating back. "You're still not exactly well."

Riprap paused long enough to cover his completed tile with a bit of plastic wrap. The polymer clay would not dry out from exposure to air, but it did accumulate dust.

"I guess I would seem bad mannered if I didn't go down to see Mr. Morris," he said. "But I still feel weird seeing him, knowing what he should know and doesn't remember."

"So do I," Pearl said, waiting for him to pass her, then closing and locking the schoolroom door behind them. "More than you can imagine."

"I'm sure, ma'am," Riprap said as he followed her down the stairs. "You've known him a long time. Where're Foster and Des?"

"Out in the yard, I think," Pearl said. "I'm going to step outside and see."

Foster and Des were outside. Des was lounging on the veranda under the grape arbor, and Foster was just visible at the end of one of the curving paths. Lani was invisible except for her giggles.

Pearl told Des about Gaheris's arrival.

"What do we do about Foster?"

"Out of sight, out of mind?" Pearl suggested. "If Gaheris happens to see Foster, we'll explain him as a cousin of mine from China."

"But doesn't Gaheris speak Chinese—in his own right, I mean," Des said, "not just through enchantment?"

Pearl slapped the tips of her fingers smartly against her forehead. "I'd forgotten. Knowing Gaheris, he won't be able to resist showing off his fluency. Damn!"

"Does it matter?" Des asked. "Neither Foster nor Gaheris seem to remember anything important."

"Foster's amnesia is distinctly odd—as is his dialect."

"Both could be explained away as a result of a head injury, and the head injury could be the reason for Foster's coming to visit you."

Pearl considered. "Still . . . I don't feel comfortable about their meeting. What if whoever is behind this not only stole memories, but planted some sort of ability to use them to spy?"

Des ran a finger along one edge of his long mustache. "I think that unlikely, but you're right. This is not the time to be less than cautious. I'll take Foster inside via the basement. When the coast is clear, invite Gaheris to have his reunion with Brenda here on the veranda. Nissa's being asleep upstairs is a good reason. Foster can go up to his room."

"Good," Pearl agreed. She headed inside as Des rose and went swiftly down the pathway toward Foster and Lani. She heard Chinese being spoken as she went in and closed the kitchen door behind her. Once in, she took a post by the window, and saw Des escorting Foster toward the basement door. Des held Lani, who was protesting the loss of her playmate.

"Gaheris," Pearl said when the coast was clear, "why don't you all come outside and sit on the veranda. I'm sure Brenda has told you that one of my other interns, Nissa, is still recovering from whatever flu or food poisoning it was that hit Brenda. Des is minding Nissa's little girl, Lani, outside. Lani's getting just a little cranky because she thinks she's missing the fun. Better we don't bring her in where she'll disturb her mother."

Pearl knew she was talking a little too much, but she had to give Riprap and Brenda some idea of the shape of her plan.

Riprap said, "Is there anything you need me to get, Pearl?"

"I wouldn't mind if you went down to the basement and brought up some of the beer. I'm sure Gaheris wouldn't mind something stronger than iced tea."

"I wouldn't say no," Gaheris admitted, "but Riprap doesn't need to run errands for me. I know where the spare fridge is."

"I wouldn't hear of it," Riprap said firmly. "I'm on staff. You're a guest. Why not help your daughter outside? Brenda's a little more fragile than she likes to admit."

Brenda looked cooperatively frail, leaning just a little against the wall. Gaheris gave in with grace.

"Hard to find myself a guest in a place I once thought of as my second home. Breni, need to lean on the old man's arm?"

Brenda grinned at him. "Why not? You were telling me what the boys are up to this summer. Is it true that Dylan broke Mr. Anderson's window?"

"With a baseball," Gaheris admitted with a sigh. "Such a classic summer accident should be celebrated, but Mr. Anderson wasn't celebrating anything but my signing a check. . . ."

Pearl listened with half her attention as she ushered Gaheris and Brenda outside. The story of Dylan and the baseball faded into greetings, and Gaheris saying, "Now, Des, what's brought you to San Jose? Brenda's been cagey about it. Something to do with films?"

"Costuming . . ." Des was saying as Pearl heard the basement door, which opened into the kitchen, squeak.

"Coast's clear," Pearl called softly, shutting the door to the outside. "Bring Foster on through."

When Riprap emerged, Foster right behind him, Pearl said politely in Chinese, "Foster, we have an unexpected guest. Would you mind going to your room? I will make sure you are sent refreshments."

Foster gave her a deep bow, very appropriate from youth to age, student to scholar, captive to captor, but he said nothing. Pearl had noticed that lately Foster rarely addressed her even in Chinese. She wasn't sure whether this expressed respect, fear, or his own small rebellion.

Right now, that didn't matter. She should get outside and make sure everything was under control.

Under her control.

Toothless Tiger.

★

Brenda was thrilled to see her dad, even if the situation was a little awkward, what with Foster being hidden away upstairs, and her not being able to talk about what she had really been doing since she joined Pearl.

She almost tripped herself up by mentioning how Pearl had gone to Virginia to pick up Nissa, but caught herself in time. Dad would have wondered why she hadn't mentioned it earlier, and he would have *really* wondered what Brenda had been doing in Santa Fe that she hadn't wanted to mention.

It was also odd that Mom would have worried so much about Brenda's being ill. Mom had what Brenda had learned was a pretty typical parental reaction to an oldest child being ill—as long as Brenda was up and moving, Brenda didn't come in for a lot of smothering attention. The younger kids had needed that, and Brenda had never minded. If she was really sick, then she had all the attention she could use, and that was what was important.

So why was Mom suddenly having a fit about Brenda catching a summer flu? Mom hadn't worried that much when another girl on Brenda's floor in the dorm came down with mono—and mono was a lot more severe and really contagious. But that time, once Mom had made sure Brenda was taking intelligent precautions, that had been the end of fussing. Mom had been more concerned about the trouble Brenda was having with getting a decent grade in advanced German.

Still, who could understand what motivated a parent?

Sitting in the shade of the grape arbor, a glass of iced tea in one hand, an almond wafer in the other, Brenda listened to her dad try to convince Des that the theater company Des was advising really needed to buy a selection of bobble-headed mandarins for their gift shop, and felt content. Dad pitching some tacky item was utterly and completely Dad.

Eventually, Gaheris Morris gave in. "Well, that makes my second 'no sale' of this trip. I stopped by Albert Yu's shop. I've gotten a line on the cutest set of containers shaped like Chinese takeout boxes—but in really bright fluorescent colors. The smallest size would be just perfect for one or two of those expensive truffles Albert sells, but he wasn't having it."

"How was Albert?" Pearl asked. She was coming down the short flight of stairs that led from the kitchen door, a glass of iced tea in one hand, a tray of beer glasses balanced on the other. Riprap was behind her holding a cardboard six-pack of long-necked beer bottles, and a bowl of chips and salsa.

"Albert seemed in a very good mood," Gaheris replied. "He invited me into his office, and treated me to tea. When he heard Brenda was ill, he sent her a little gift."

He bent down and opened his briefcase, extracting a small lozenge box painted with pink peonies. The blossoms spilled over the top and onto the sides.

"This is some sort of exotic and high-priced mint," Gaheris explained, "blended with concentrated extract of green tea. It's supposed to be good for both the blood and digestion."

He pulled another box out of his briefcase and handed that to Pearl. "This is apparently a selection of your favorite chocolates."

Gaheris looked momentarily puzzled. "I don't recall Albert being so generous before. He was in a good mood, too. I wonder if he has fallen in love."

"Anything is possible," Pearl said mildly, setting the box to one side. "I think I'll put the chocolates by for when the girls are better. In any case, they'd be wasted with beer."

Brenda felt a little wistful. Her own Yu chocolates were but a delicious memory now, but she had to admit that her stomach roiled a little at the thought of trying to deal with something so rich and so dense. She had no problem turning down a beer when offered one. Instead, she nibbled an almond wafer and tried to be glad that her system would let her eat something other than yogurt.

"Maybe business is just good," Des suggested. "Albert's shop is quite trendy these days. I saw it mentioned in a couple of high-end magazines as *the* place to get good chocolate. There were rumors he's branching out into teas as well."

"He is," Gaheris said. "He mentioned something about how tea is going to be the new coffee. I'm not sure that Albert isn't right. Maybe I should offer him the bobblehead mandarins. He might be able to use them in a holiday promotion. Wasn't one of the villains in the *Nutcracker* a mandarin doll that nodded?"

"I think that was in 'The Steadfast Tin Soldier,'" Brenda said, "and the mandarin wasn't really a villain there. I think the villain was the jack-in-the-box."

"Oh." Gaheris looked momentarily disappointed, but Riprap offered him a beer, and the question of selling Albert Yu mandarin bobble heads was forgotten in the pleasure of discussing local micro breweries.

Albert Yu's not the only one who has mellowed, Brenda thought. *Dad seems to have lost that . . . bitterness? Sense of rivalry? Whatever it was that made him so uncomfortable with Albert. Pearl said they'd been rivals as boys. I guess Dad didn't like how Albert assumed that being the emperor's heir made him more important. Now that the emperor has been forgotten with the rest, I wonder if they're both not happier.*

It was an uncomfortable thought. Up until now, Brenda had been focused on getting back for her father what had been stolen from him, but what if Gaheris Morris was happier without his memories of the Rat? Brenda wasn't certain that *she* wouldn't be happier without what she'd learned. Since she'd inadvertently drawn down the Three-Legged Toad, the universe had seemed fragile, as if made of cheesecloth or tissue or something else that gave the illusion of solidity but was too easily poked full of holes.

Dad stayed for dinner, which was served out on the patio out of deference to Nissa's need for quiet.

He succeeded in charming Lani, whom he claimed to have met when she was an infant, when he was out in Virginia doing a deal on key chains printed with the UVA logo as an alumni athletic club tie-in promotion. Of course, Dad had forgotten that he'd ever had a more personal reason for wanting to know Nissa's family.

"But you've got the wrong sort of name," Dad insisted, as an enchanted Lani sat on his knee, snapping her finger under the chin of a bobble-headed penguin figurine he'd given her. "You can't be Nissa's daughter. All the girls in her family have 'N' names—or are you a little boy?"

Lani was appalled. "I'm a girl! An I do have a 'n.'"

"Lani doesn't begin with 'n,'" Dad insisted, being deliberately obtuse.

"Noelani!" Lani insisted. "My name is Noelani."

"No-lani. I got that," Dad said. "Your name is not Lani. All right, what is it?"

Brenda thought Dad was pushing the kid a bit hard, but evidently Lani had heard similar teasing before.

"My name is Noelani," Lani repeated, not only showing excellent patience with this stupid adult, but also demonstrating the best diction Brenda had seen from her so far. "Noelani begins with 'n.' It's Hawaiian for something . . ."

She looked inquiringly at Brenda. "I can't say it."

"Beautiful one from the sea," Brenda said, who had asked Nissa about the odd name. "It's a pretty name, and my dad is being difficult."

"Am I?" Gaheris grinned. "Then maybe Noelani, who does have an 'n' in her name after all, needs someone to keep Mr. Penguin company. Would you like a Mrs. Penguin?"

Lani was delighted with the set, and settled in to feeding them bits of hotdog and loose grapes. Brenda and Riprap took turns making sure that Lani herself got a few bites.

Later, as Brenda took Lani up for her bath and bed, she heard Pearl apologize that she didn't have a spare room. Dad didn't try and press for a space on the sofa. Brenda would have worried that in losing his memories of the Rat he'd lost his legendary sense of economy—or cheapness, as her mother had been known to call it—but then Dad mentioned he had a meeting at his hotel early the next morning with a manufacturer from China.

"It's great you taught me how to speak the language, Auntie Pearl," he said, kissing her cheek in parting. "With China entering the world economy in a big way, I have a huge advantage. You really ought to see about getting your movies released there. I bet you'd outsell your old rival."

"Never a rival," Pearl said, her smile audible. "Shirley had me beat all the way—and I liked working with her. Still, I'll talk to my agent and see if anything can be done."

With Mr. and Mrs. Penguin nodding approval from the dresser top, Lani was the soul of cooperation when it came time for her to go to bed. Brenda came down in time to visit a bit more with her dad before he had to leave.

"You get some sleep, Breni," Dad said, hugging her. "I'll tell your mom she worries too much, but don't let her know I said that, okay? She's so proud of how well you two get along, she'd be annoyed that I let on that she still worries about her little girl."

"Promise," Brenda said, hugging him back, but as she went up to bed shortly thereafter she found herself wondering. Had Mom really been the one who was worried, or had it maybe been Dad?

Dad. It made a lot more sense if it was Dad.

She wondered why the realization made her so nervous, and pulled the sheet right up to her chin, then, on impulse, up and over her head.

★

The day after Gaheris's visit, Pearl waited until Des was busy with Brenda and Rip-rap, and Nissa and Lani were napping. Then she climbed the stairs to the third floor, where the men had their rooms. The time had come for her to talk to Foster—and to address the questions of his freedom and his ability to communicate.

After a great deal of meditation, Pearl had arrived at a solution that she thought would satisfy her allies, reward her unwelcome guest for his good behavior, and provide her with an edge for the future. She had confided her thoughts on the first two points to Des, and he had agreed to be satisfied. The third point, however, Pearl had kept to herself.

As Des had threatened to do after one of their earlier arguments regarding Foster's treatment, he had rearranged the sleeping arrangements so that he and Foster now shared a bathroom.

The area at the top of the stairs opened into a broad, comfortable foyer. Long ago, Pearl had furnished this as a informal sitting area, where her boarders might visit without needing to invade each other's rooms—or her own living areas. That was where she found Foster, seated cross-legged in a wide, high-backed chair, a book in his lap, his elbows resting lightly on the arms of the chair.

His posture was perfect, loose-limbed, yet not in the least bit sloppy. Pearl envied him that young, graceful body, that hair that shone as dark and glossy as her own once had, that youthful skin, clear and golden brown, without the faintest of lines or wrinkles.

Foster rose when he saw it was her upon the stairs, a graceful movement, lithe as that of a young animal. When Pearl topped the stairs, all too aware of the dozens of tiny protests age had set as a symphony in her limbs, he bowed deeply and stood with his hands folded before him, a gesture that recalled how he should have worn embroidered robes into whose wide, deep sleeves those strong, long-fingered hands would have vanished.

Pearl gave him a polite bow in return, and was pleased to see Foster's eyes widen slightly in surprise at her courtesy. That was all that gave him away though. He stood, still and straight, a young tree, a young tiger, and waited to see what new storm the old woman in front of him would bring into his life.

Pearl spoke to him in Chinese, deliberately using the strange dialect which mixed up times and histories and that was the native tongue of those from the Lands Born from Smoke and Sacrifice.

"Foster, please, I pray, be seated. I have come to speak with you about some matters of great import."

Foster moved a step closer to the chair in which he had been seated, but did not sit until Pearl herself had taken a seat in the matching chair. Then he lowered himself in, drawing up his legs and crossing them with automatic grace and ease. The chair had been upholstered in red, but over time the color had faded to the dusty hue of dried and faded rose petals saved from a Valentine's bouquet. The color went very well with Foster's coloring, and again Pearl felt the dangerous shifting of envy.

However, she had not come here to attack this young man, no matter that everything about him set her teeth on edge and made her want to growl.

"The other night," Pearl said, "the night when you, Nissa, and Brenda played at mah-jong, I have been told you did us a great service. I am grateful."

"I played with the babe, Honorable One," Foster replied. "That is all I am good for, and if I did this well, then I accept your gratitude."

There was bitterness in his tones, and in the cast of his eyes. Pearl could sense that Foster sought to hide that bitterness, but her ears were too schooled in the nuances of language and expression not to catch the hints. She didn't doubt she knew the reason for Foster's bitterness. Even if he remembered nothing about himself, he must feel certain he had been more than a nanny. The T-shirt he wore exposed his arms, and she could see the thin silver lines of scars. When she and Nissa had undressed Foster back in Virginia, they had seen other scars, including one that crossed his chest, as if a sword or spear might have cut quite deeply.

No. Foster only need look at himself in a mirror to know that once he had been more than a nanny.

"Let us not play games with each other," Pearl said, adopting the tone of general to soldier. "We both know you are good for far more than playing with the babe. We do not know what other talents you have. Perhaps in time we will learn."

"Desperate Lee says that you and he study upon the matter," Foster said. "Have you learned something?"

"Some things," Pearl countered, "but nothing that would mean anything to you. Foster, I have come to tell you that in reward for your patience and valor—in reward for your tending Lani with such gentle strength and so freeing her mother to enter into a battle from which she is still healing—in reward for these things, I have decided to grant you a gift."

Foster's face settled into neutrality, and no wonder. Pearl had shown him very few kindnesses. She recalled how she had learned to suspect her father's gifts, to look for what Thundering Heaven hid behind apparent kindness. The recollection made her feel uneasy. She had seen her father in Foster's face and form. She had never thought that she herself might have become a more genuine representation of Thundering Heaven's self.

"A true gift," Pearl hastened to clarify. "You have been barred from ease of communication with any in this house but myself and Des. I have it in my power to grant the others the means of understanding your tongue."

Foster did not ask her how she could do this. If he had any trace memories, they would include sorcery. Words for spells and amulets were part of his vocabulary, those words untainted by any sense that "magic" was in the least a matter for doubt.

"I would like this," Foster said politely. "I will admit to frustration that I can talk less easily than does young Lani."

"I have another gift for you," Pearl said. "Would you like to be able to leave this house and see something of the places without?"

This time Foster's control failed him. He gaped at her, then collected himself and gave a seated bow.

"I would be very grateful, Honorable One. Your palace is lovely, filled with miracles, and with items of great beauty, but I will admit that the walls do close upon me."

"Then you will have your freedom, but with one condition." Pearl went on quickly, lest Foster think this reward no reward. "For now, I ask that when you leave the house, one of our number accompany you. You will not be able to speak to the majority of those you meet. There should be someone present who can translate. Also, there are many strange and dangerous things out there, and I would not have you go free only to have you harmed."

Foster grinned, for a moment a young man, not a warrior/courtier. Then he resumed his more formal manner.

"Honorable One, I remember the journey I made with you and Riprap. I saw the many dangers, even though we traveled mostly within the car. Then, too, Nissa showed me the dangers in things as innocent-seeming as electrical cords and outlets. I can understand only too well how many other dangers there may be. I will abide by your ruling with honor and faith."

"Nissa still rests," Pearl said. "And the others are at their studies. Will you permit me to be your first escort? I fear my old limbs may have some difficulty keeping up with your young ones, but perhaps for a first venture, you will not need speed so much as care."

Foster leapt to his feet and bowed.

"Shoes. I will need to put on shoes as I have not since coming to your palace, Honored One. If you would wait?"

Pearl smiled. "By all means. I will await you down by the front door. I think you will find this neighborhood quite interesting. I look forward to showing some of its wonders to you."

There were several interesting developments in the days following Gaheris Morris's visit.

Brenda talked to her mom just about every day, and managed to confirm her own suspicion that Dad had come to check on Brenda on his own initiative. Nissa was up and mostly recovered in less than a week after the encounter with the Three-Legged Toad. Perhaps mostly importantly, at least for how it changed the dynamic of the household, Foster could talk—or rather, they could understand what he was saying.

The spell Pearl and Des had worked had been pretty complicated, a series of spells rather than a single one. The final spell in the sequence had been the only one Brenda had come close to understanding, and that was because she'd helped work it out, since it was the spell that let the others link with her mind. The formula had involved her element, wind, time of birth, direction, color, and other things, but the end result was worth the effort.

Unlike the Dragon's Tail or the other spells Brenda had learned so far, the sequence that let them understand Foster was relatively permanent. Until the spell was undone, Brenda's brain had effectively been reprogrammed to believe that it had always known the peculiar form of Chinese Foster spoke.

Brenda even dreamed in that language now—not always, but enough that she was beginning to stop feeling startled by her new ability.

Foster hadn't given up his desire to learn English, and he was learning a lot faster now that his teachers could explain complicated parts of grammar. Lani had been included in the spell, but there was no childlike innocence and ease in her acceptance of her new ability. She nearly drove them to distraction asking "why," and Brenda privately believed that Nissa had gotten out of bed a day or two earlier than she really should have just to escape the little girl's unceasing questions.

But chatting with Foster proved not to be as easy as merely bridging the language gap. His lack of memory made the kind of shared anecdotes that were the foundation of most friendships impossible. From him there was no "I get you. I remember when I first . . ." He listened with almost ferocious eagerness to their conversations, but unless they were discussing small household matters or the weather, he had little to contribute.

Now that Foster was off "house arrest," Riprap decided to teach him basketball. Nissa wasn't up to all the jumping about, but Brenda and Des took up the invitation to join. Brenda had played a little, both in school and with her brothers—although, honestly, she preferred soccer. As the hoop outside his house testified, Des liked shooting baskets.

There was a nice little park not overly far from Pearl's house. Especially during the week, the half-sized court was usually empty.

Brenda was much smaller than the three guys, but she was quick and lithe—and tough enough that her episode of ch'i depletion had left her without any scars. She became adept at stealing the ball, although she didn't make many baskets. Despite this, she enjoyed the games, enjoyed the time away from the excruciating memorization that went into learning how to create spell sequences.

Riprap and Nissa were both more attentive students than Brenda was, and Brenda knew this was because in her heart of hearts she felt like a fake. They were the Rabbit and the Dog. She was not the Rat. Whatever it was that might make her the Rat was gone, stolen away, perhaps forever.

During the basketball games, Brenda could forget this, forget how she didn't quite fit in. It helped that Foster didn't fit in even more than she did—or didn't—or whatever. It helped that Foster seemed to like walking beside her when they went over to the park. It helped how her heart would beat harder when his hand brushed hers—always by accident, ever by accident, although sometimes, lying in bed at night, Brenda would replay the moments in her mind, wondering if there might be just a little bit of "on purpose" involved.

Maybe Foster liked her. That was impossible, of course. He was gorgeous. She was just her. He was someone remarkable, even if he didn't remember right now who that was. But sometimes, when he smiled at her, or when he paused to let her go through a door in front of him, or when he seemed to wait for her to walk with him when surely one of the guys would be more interesting, then Brenda wondered.

Brenda knew she was behaving like an idiot, letting so much of her thoughts be occupied by something that was certainly all in her imagination—certainly, almost certainly, maybe not?

A bright-feathered, strangely colored bird flew overhead.

Foster, walking beside Brenda as they returned to Pearl's house after a particularly spirited game, grabbed Brenda's hand and pointed.

"Look!"

Brenda's heart beat and her breath caught, so that all words, any words, in any language fled. Her world shrunk to that warm, roughly callused hand that held hers in a warm, living clasp.

Oh, please, she breathed in silent, inarticulate prayer. *Oh, please. Almost certainly. Please, not maybe, not.*

★

Pearl was amused to see that a new development had evolved from Foster's increased freedom. Deprived of her playmate, Lani had cast about for others and had discovered Wong, Pearl's gardener.

In short order, Lani had charmed Wong and been charmed by him in turn, so on the days he was working they became an inseparable duo. That gave Nissa a much-needed opportunity not only to catch up on her studies, but also to be something other than a mother/student.

Everything within and without the little household was quiet and peaceful. Pearl wondered why. She hadn't expected it to be so. She had rather expected otherwise. She thought she had dangled bait so that surely the settled situation would unsettle. She wondered what she had missed.

She and Des continued to work on possible ways to break the spells that held Foster's memory in the crystal globe. They were handicapped in that they could not test their theories without risking that they would work—and Pearl was not certain she wanted them to work. Foster as he was now was a tiger declawed. Foster with his memory back might well be a challenge to rival the Three-Legged Toad.

A knock came on the door of her office one afternoon as Pearl was making a phone call, setting up a screen test for Lani, arranging for someone to escort the child so that Nissa's studies would not be interupted. Bonaventure was curled in her lap, a pot of tea near to hand, and for that moment she felt quietly content in a fashion she had not since Albert had been attacked.

"Come," she said, expecting Des. Instead, the tall, dark, muscular form of Riprap nearly filled the doorway. "Come in."

He did, treading lightly on the thick Oriental carpet. Big he was, but there was nothing cumbersome about his movements. Pearl remembered how Riprap had expressed apprehension that he would manifest as one of those little yap dogs that were what most people thought of when they thought of Chinese dogs at all: a Pekingese or a Shih Tzu or a Lhasa Apso. His aunt had manifested as a Lhasa Apso, although Riprap didn't know that.

Pearl herself thought Riprap would be one of the hunting dogs, guarding dogs—a Chow Chow, maybe, or a Tibetan mastiff. Of the latter it was said that one alone could kill three wolves or two together a tiger.

Looking up and meeting soft dark eyes behind velvet lashes, Pearl felt suddenly glad that there were not two of Riprap, and wondered at her sudden chill of apprehension. To this point, she had found Riprap the easiest to deal with of the three apprentices, but today there was something undefinably different about him.

"Have a seat," Pearl said. "Would you like tea?"

"I'm fine," Riprap said, taking the chair she indicated. "I wanted to talk to you about what we're doing, why we're not doing more."

Pearl looked at him, tilted her head to one side, projecting a willingness to listen, wanting him to explain himself. To her surprise, Riprap waited her out, silence matching silence, not in a duel of wills—or at least not overtly so—but of courtesy to courtesy.

Pearl remembered the account Brenda had given of her first meeting with Riprap, of watching the big man working as a bouncer in that noisy Denver club. Brenda had marveled at how Riprap had been able to control drunken tourists and cowboys on holiday without throwing a punch, only by speaking a few words. For the first time, Pearl wondered if she'd misunderstood Riprap, underestimating his complexity because he'd been the only one who seemed to be more on "her side" during the whole tension over Foster. Maybe he hadn't been on her side, but on his own.

Time she learned what that side was.

"What we're doing," Pearl said. "Educating you, Nissa, and Brenda. Trying to find out what we can about the spell Foster would have used on me, but that I turned back on him. What more should we be doing?"

"That's what I want to ask you," Riprap said. "I made copies of the Brave Dog stories before I left home. I've been reading them when I have time—at night, mostly, before I go to bed. What keeps getting to me is how the emperor is at the heart of these stories. Brave Dog protects him, leads his enemies astray, hunts out those who would harm him. There's no emperor in our story. Heck, Nissa and I haven't even met him."

"That's because he's gone," Pearl said gently. "Whoever is after us already captured Albert Yu. He has no memory of who he was. He's just a man who sells expensive chocolate."

"And tea and mints," Riprap added without a trace of a smile. "I tell you, it doesn't seem right."

"What would you suggest?"

"Oh, no, ma'am. I already know you don't take suggestions very well. I'm just asking some questions."

Pearl raised her eyebrows and permitted herself a small smile. "That bossy, am I? Very well. Ask away."

"All right. I'm good at this amulet-making stuff. I know it. Nissa's good, too. I mean, as far as I can tell, both you and Des have let the Sparrow's Sanctuary she put up stand unaltered, and you wouldn't have done that if her spell wasn't as good as you could do. So why aren't we doing more?"

Pearl pursed her lips. "Nissa spent four days flat on her back after building that barrier. Do you call that good?"

"Nissa built that barrier after feeding you ch'i for your own spell. Then she got carried away. As I see it, the problem wasn't that Nissa couldn't handle the spell, it was that she wasn't taught enough about the complications that could arise when doing something that complex."

Pearl sighed and slid a finger under the tea cozy to see if her teapot was still warm. It was, and she poured herself a cup, then raised the pot in invitation to Riprap. He shook his head, and sat watchful, waiting.

"Riprap, you and your 'classmates,' for lack of a better term, had to learn to walk before you could run. To be more accurate, you had to learn the alphabet and the sounds the various letters make before you could learn to read. I suppose Des and I could have given you long lectures about potential dangers, but I'm not sure they would have made an impression."

Riprap allowed her a brief smile. "Yeah. I've seen that. We start kids on a sport, and we're required to tell them why they need protective equipment or helmets or whatever, but there's nothing like a knee in the wrong place to teach a boy why he needs to wear a cup."

"Brenda's summoning of the Three-Legged Toad shows how much worse than a knee in the wrong place," Pearl said a touch primly, "mistakes in magic can be. I know Des put up wards before permitting you and Brenda to start your first spells. I'm sure he warned you that if something went wrong, the consequences might be far worse than a mere loss of ch'i."

"He did," Riprap leaned forward, laced his fingers over one broad kneecap. "Pearl, you said we had to learn the alphabet before we learned to read. That's what we're doing now: learning the basic forms and combinations, how they can be shaped and reshaped to summon, to build barriers. I've a feeling there's more to it. That spell you worked so we could talk to Foster, that was no simple 'sentence.' What you and Des have been working on, trying to create a spell that would release memories from the dragon crystals, that's something again. Are we going to learn that, too?"

"In time. To stretch the analogy, what we've been teaching you is less to read than to memorize and recite. The memorization and recitation serves two purposes. One, it gives you tools you can use to defend yourselves, or in a limited fashion, to attack. We're also using those recitations to teach you about the elements that go into spells."

Riprap nodded. "Right at the start, Des showed us how we could use a basic limit hand and it would work, but he also showed us how if we tailored our choice of tiles to our own directions, winds, whatever, we'd create a stronger spell."

Pearl smiled approval. "And learning to calculate those elements—suit, direction, wind, dragon, later on variations represented by the flower and season tiles—will give you what you need to work complex spells like the one we used to permit you to talk with Foster. Later still, you may learn what you need to create unique spells, but that is something not everyone learned—even back in the days when the Twelve were not exiles and were the protectors of an emperor. By the way, do you know why we chose to work the spell so that you could talk Foster's language, rather than having him learn English?"

Riprap met her gaze unflinchingly. "I figured it was because you are better able to control Foster if he still is suffering under a language barrier."

Pearl rewarded him with a marginal inclination of her head. "That is part of it, but the other part is that we know nothing about Foster other than his gender. We can guess he is a Tiger, or more accurately, that he *was* a Tiger. We do not know what type of Tiger he is. He does not know his date or time of birth. We cannot calculate his Heavenly or Earthly Branches. In other words, we lack what we would need to tailor a spell to him."

"Interesting," Riprap said. "I can see that. So you might have tried to work the spell to let him comprehend English, but it might not have taken."

"More likely, it would have taken for a short period of time, but gradually it would have unraveled."

"I see." Riprap sat considering for a while, while Pearl sipped her tea. "Pearl, are we going to need to wait until we're all-star players before we do something more than practice routines? We've been in California for ten days now. Albert Yu was attacked three and a half weeks ago. I know we're not even to the end of June, but eventually, Brenda's going to need to go back to college or face missing a term. Both Nissa and I have jobs that will wait for us, and you're helping us meet the bills, but I can't help but feel we should be doing more."

"What would you have us do?"

"Brave Dog would search for his master, not hide away learning tricks."

"Brave Dog was a character in children's bedtime stories, not a real person." Pearl held up her hand to interrupt Riprap's protest. "Brave Dog may have been based on a real person, but that doesn't mean he's real, any more than the George Washington who chopped down cherry trees was a real person. He was an ideal, even a role model, but that doesn't mean he was a real person."

"I still think we should do something," Riprap said stubbornly.

"You are. You're learning the alphabet. You're learning to read."

Riprap held up a broad wrist encircled by several polymer tile bracelets. "Can't these 'sentences' help? Can't we use spells for searching?"

"We can," Pearl said. "Des and I have tried, but whoever our enemy is, he has hidden himself much as we have hidden ourselves."

"So we're stuck here, waiting until our enemy—or enemies—finds us and make a move. Seems to me, he's being pretty slow. I mean, it's not like we're hiding out in the Batcave or something. You may have an unlisted number, but it's not like people can't find out where Pearl Bright lives. We suspect we're being watched, but that's not enough."

"But here we are guarded," Pearl said. "I assure you, I have already laid in place various plans that should draw our enemies into revealing themselves."

"I've noticed we're dangling Foster as bait," Riprap said. "But no one's biting."

"Not that we know of," Pearl corrected.

A knock sounded on the office door, and Des stuck his head in. He had his hair braided tightly back and a pink satin mandarin cap Brenda had bought for Lani was perched jauntily atop his head.

"Dinner will be ready in less than ten minutes."

"Thank you," Pearl said. "Des, do you have any plans for after dinner?"

Des shook his head. The pink cap wobbled but kept its precarious balance. "Nothing that will take too long."

Pearl went on. "Riprap has been asking me some questions. I'd like to have a group meeting after Lani is in bed. Would that work for you?"

"Fine," Des said. "I was going to call my older daughter tonight—it's her birthday—but I can do that while Nissa is putting Lani down."

"Give Julie my best," Pearl said, rising to her feet and gently pushing Bonaventure to the floor. When Des had gone upstair to tell Nissa and Brenda that dinner was nearly ready, Pearl returned her attention to Riprap. "Satisfied?"

"Sure," the big man said. "Especially if we figure out how to do more than just talk."

★

Brenda was reading her e-mail when Nissa entered her room through their connecting bathroom. Brenda waved the other woman to a seat.

"I'll be off in a minute. Just checking in with some of my friends."

"How do you explain your summer internship?" Nissa asked. She sounded genuinely curious. "I mean, my sisters don't really ask for details. We're all used to each other taking off and doing strange things. My boss is the one who wants to know every detail. He's already imagining Lani starring in a film."

"What have you been telling him?" Brenda asked, logging off and shutting down her laptop.

"That auditions take a while. That San Jose isn't exactly the heart of the California film industry. I sent him copies of the pictures we had taken last week for Lani's portfolio."

"So you're safe," Brenda said.

"You sound relieved."

Brenda shrugged. "I guess I'm getting tired of not being able to talk openly to my friends. When I first came out here, I told them I had gotten a good internship working for a friend of my dad's. That's true enough. I didn't mention just who that friend is, not that I think most of them would be impressed by my working for a long-ago movie star. The details of what I'm doing here have been pretty easy to avoid since most of what my friends want to talk about is mutual friends or what we're going to do when school starts. It's me who wants to talk about more."

"Are your friends mostly from college?"

"Some. Some from high school have stayed in touch, but we've got less in common now. One of my best friends from high school—we were in student government together—still keeps in touch. We have this strange story we're writing together, and she's been doing more with it now that it's summer and her job—she's got something in a state senator's office—is boring her to tears. I try to keep up with my part, but . . ."

Brenda shrugged again.

"I didn't know you wrote. What kind of story is it?"

"Sort of a fantasy thing. It seemed weird and really original when we started it, all about the two of us being transported to this kind of King Arthur world, getting separated, and what happened afterwards. We sort of tried to one-up each other on outrageous encounters with monsters and knights of the Round Table, but after the last few weeks, well, imaginary knights and ogres just don't have the same appeal."

"No kidding!"

"Yeah." Brenda grinned.

The grin they'd shared faded from Nissa's face. "Look, Brenda. I had something serious I wanted to talk to you about. You've got it bad for Foster, don't you?"

"Oh, god . . . Is it that obvious?"

"Probably to everyone but Foster . . . and maybe Lani, and I wouldn't be too sure about Lani."

Brenda felt both crestfallen and relieved all at once. "You mean, I haven't acted like too much of an idiot?"

"I mean that men—the good ones, at least—are usually the last to figure out when someone likes them. The ones who walk around assuming that every girl has fallen for them aren't worth knowing. Trust me on this."

Brenda thought about Lani, and how Nissa wouldn't tell anyone who the girl's father was, and thought she understood. She hesitated, then decided to plunge in. Talking about her crush was a relief after so long.

"So, Nissa, you think Foster is one of the good ones?"

"This version of him is," Nissa said promptly. "I mean, he's kind to Lani, and that takes some doing. I'm her mom, and I adore her, but a toddler is a demanding creature. Foster seems intelligent, and he's very patient. And let's not forget he's drop-dead gorgeous. That wouldn't matter if he were a creep, but it sure makes him easy on the eyes."

Brenda didn't know whether to blush or feel territorial. She had tried hard not to consider Nissa as a potential rival, but for all Nissa had a kid, she was still young and pretty and single—and easy, too, apparently.

Nissa gave Brenda one of those all too knowing looks, and Brenda felt her ears get hot.

"Okay, Brenda," Nissa said. "Your mom isn't here, and you don't have any sisters. Your girlfriends don't know you have a crush on Mr. Gorgeous, because you can't really explain about him with having to explain a whole lot more. So I'm going to stick my nose in. Guard yourself. One of these days, Foster's going to notice your interest, and he's man enough that he might decide to take advantage of it."

Brenda blinked, and suddenly got really interested in her fingernails.

"Brenda . . ." Nissa sounded exasperated, but not angry. "Look. He's a guy. You're a girl. I've noticed how you keep looking for a few minutes alone with him. I don't think you're trying to jump his bones, not consciously maybe, but depending on what Foster's social programming is he might decide that's just what you want. And that might lead to more than what you want. Got me?"

"Foster hardly ever talks to me," Brenda said, trying not to let her sudden defensiveness surface. She *had* been finding reasons to seek Foster out when no one else was around. She didn't know what she expected, but there was a high that came from being with him, waiting to see what he'd do. "I mean, not about anything other than the weather or basketball. I don't think we're exactly heading for bed."

"What else does Foster have to talk about?" Nissa said practically. "He has no memory. No past. He's got to feel like he has very little future, too. That's not exactly going to make a man feel chatty—if he was chatty to begin with, and I have a feeling that Foster wasn't."

"Why?"

"A hunch."

A knock came on the door and Des called, "Ten minutes to dinner. Nissa, I think Wong's been helping Lani make mud pies."

Nissa jumped to her feet and called, "Thanks, Des!"

She turned back to Brenda and said in a softer tone of voice. "Think about it? At least be careful?"

Brenda smiled, suddenly feeling a whole lot less alone. "Promise. And thanks."

After dinner, Brenda took her turn doing the dishes while Nissa put Lani down. She wondered a little at the tension she'd sensed between Pearl and Riprap over dinner. It hadn't been exactly unfriendly, but it had been there.

She looked around for Foster, telling herself that she just wanted someone to help dry the pots, feeling her cheeks get hot when she remembered her earlier conversation with Nissa. But Foster had gone upstairs after dinner, and there really weren't that many pots to be dried.

The tea and coffee, and the plate of brownies along the length of the long table between the family room and the kitchen, kept the meeting from seeming quite like a council of war, but as soon as Riprap opened his mouth any illusion that they were just meeting for dessert vanished.

Almost by reflex, Brenda opened her notebook.

"Earlier today," Riprap said, "I asked Pearl why we're not doing more to take the initiative."

"Initiative?" Nissa said. "You mean other than preparing to defend ourselves?"

"Right," Riprap said. "We've focused on that. Maybe we're even too good at defense, since we haven't glimpsed our enemies since Foster charged in after Pearl and Nissa."

"I saw someone," Brenda reminded him.

"You *might* have seen someone," Riprap countered. "That's not the same."

Pearl said almost reluctantly. "Riprap is correct. Our enemies are being very careful. I have even tried to prompt them to take some action by letting Foster leave the house. I'd thought that maybe they didn't know where he was, and if they did, they'd come for him."

Brenda didn't feel as shocked as she wanted to. She'd already guessed that Pearl hadn't softened toward Foster because she liked him any better.

"However, I have had no confirmed sightings of our enemies."

"Maybe we're going at this all wrong," Brenda said. "Maybe if we could figure out what 'they' want, we could figure out who 'they' are. What could be so important that they'd be willing to renew old conflicts generations later?"

"On that point," Pearl said, "my guesses might be slightly better than yours, but still guesses."

"I'd still like to hear them," Riprap said.

"Go ahead, Pearl," Des prompted. "It's probably beyond time for us to share some of what we've discussed with these three."

"Very well," Pearl said. "Now, remember, this is just speculation, some mine, some Des's. We have done some auguries trying to test our theories, but augury is far from conclusive as a test. If we were absolutely right, we might get some indication that we were right, but the augury cannot tell us where we are off track."

"Answer cloudy. Try again," Brenda murmured. "The old Magic Eight Ball."

"Rather more like that than you would imagine," Pearl said. "One of the most obvious reasons someone from the Lands might come after us all these years later is something to do with the Cat. For example, they might need a new puppet, someone with a legitimate claim to the throne."

Brenda noted this theory down, but even as she scribbled could think of all the reasons this wasn't the best explanation for someone to come after the descendants of the Thirteen Orphans.

"Surely," Nissa objected, "in a hundred years the people who usurped the throne would have fathered or mothered bastards or minor family branches or whatever. Why would they need to come into another world for a candidate—especially one who is the grandson of the original Cat?"

Brenda doodled next to the words "claim to the throne" a round-headed caricature of a Chinese boy surrounded by twelve rather ferocious-looking animals. The rendition was cartoonish, but she filled it out as Pearl went on to her next theory.

"Another option is that there is some old rivalry that has flared up—and not necessarily a rivalry of the personal kind. It might have something to do with property or some inheritance. Remember, one of the conditions that the Twelve insisted upon before they would agree to go peacefully into exile was that their families would neither be attacked or beggared."

After the number two, Brenda wrote: "Old Rivalry. Contested Inheritance."

Pearl went on, "The third option is harder to explain, but it has to do with the threat—however passive—the Thirteen offer the Lands as long as we continue to exist."

She glanced at Des, and Des took over.

"My theory is that as long as descendants of the Thirteen continue to exist, they provide something like a breach in the integrity of the Lands, a weak spot in its dimensional walls."

Brenda scribbled this down. If you bought into the idea that there were other worlds or universes or whatever, and that natives of those universes could more easily go between them, then this sort of made sense. Riprap seemed to think so, too.

"This works for me, more than the rest," he said. "That would explain why what they're stealing is memories connected to being one of the Thirteen. Maybe if they can take those away, the physical inheritance—which in any of us but you,

Pearl, is no better than a quarter and in most of us is a whole lot less—wouldn't be enough."

"Enough for what, though?" Nissa protested. "I'm beginning to see why you didn't try and explain this sooner, Pearl. If I hadn't sensed that Three-Legged Toad myself, seen the destruction it had done to your wards, I wouldn't be able to believe this at all—I'm having enough trouble as it is."

Brenda looked up from writing and saw that Pearl was staring at the Tiger's mah-jong set, which sat in its box on the corner of her desk. A fleeting expression that Brenda couldn't quite follow went across those elegant features.

"We can only speculate. There is one person in this house who knows for certain why we are being attacked, and he is not able to tell us."

"Foster," Nissa said softly.

"So," Brenda said, "we have a reason to want Foster to get his memory back. He can end speculation for us, give us the information we need to plan our own attack."

"Yes," Pearl said, "but Des and I have been unable to break the dragon's crystal, and until we figure out how to do so, we must manage as we can."

"Or," Riprap said, his voice hard, but the expression in his dark eyes full of worry, "risk breaking the crystal, and hope that the damage to Foster is not so great that he will be unable to tell us what we need."

The man's gestures said it all. *I've got the door open. Come in, but be quick and, for god's sake, be quiet!*

The entry foyer was mostly dark, lit indirectly by two lights. The first was a small one in the kitchen that sent just enough of a glow down the passage to make it possible for someone to navigate. The second was the diffuse and scattered offering from a streetlight near the curb outside. When the exterior door was shut, this second light source was almost eliminated, darkening some shadows, melding others into the general gloom.

With such poor lighting, it was very hard to make out the two who had just entered the locked and warded house. The first, the man who had opened the door, moved with the confidence of familiarity. The second was slender. Something in the grace of its movements hinted at exquisite femininity.

The watcher, sleepy, nearly unconscious, felt a trace of embarrassment. Perhaps one of the men had brought someone home to warm his bed. The matter hadn't been expressly forbidden, but the watcher doubted Pearl would approve.

The watcher stirred and felt uneasy, tossed and kicked off the cotton sheet that covered her, all without quite waking.

There was something very familiar about the man who was now leading the way up the flight of stairs that connected the ground floor to the second. Something in his very familiarity made the watcher uncomfortable: made her simultaneously angry, desirous of hiding her head under her pillow, and refusing to look any more.

At the same time, she realized this was all a dream, probably something a Freudian psychologist would have a great time with. The thought made her realize there was something very strange about this dream. It was just a little too much like being awake.

The pair who had entered so stealthily were now halfway up the staircase. They were moving with care, but with confidence as well. The watcher—Brenda shook herself, but the dream seemed to have a very tight hold on her—wondered at that confidence. In this strange household, night did not guarantee that no one would be up and about.

Lani slept with the restless unpredictability of the very young, and Pearl had the sleepless nights that plagued the increasingly aged. Riprap's tendency to decide he needed a snack at the strangest hours was becoming a running joke, and Des often came downstairs to conduct business via phone at peculiar times. He had friends and clients throughout the Orient. Sometimes the best time for a call was when saner folks were sleeping.

Why then were those two moving with such certainty? Yes, they were keeping fairly quiet, but neither had so much as cast a glance down the hallway or back over a shoulder. It was as if they knew the household's occupants were asleep, and that if they took care, the sleepers would continue to sleep.

Brenda watched. The somehow familiar man and the strange woman—girl— had reached the landing on the second floor. Again, they did not waste time looking around. Hardly a flicker of a glance was spared for the closed doors of the three bedrooms. The door to the room the household used as a classroom stood ajar, but the dark line at its opening gave testimony that none of the three apprentice scholars of the arcane were indulging in a little late night work.

Light from the large fan window at the far end of the landing fell clearly on the man's face as he continued forward. Brenda felt her earlier impression confirmed. The features were more familiar to her than her own: Gaheris Morris, her dad, supersalesman, husband of Keely, father of Dylan and Thomas, formerly the Rat, and now . . .

What was he doing leading that strange woman, still little more than a figure in the darkness, toward the closed door that led to the stairway to the third floor where the three male tenants had their rooms? Brenda strove for a clearer look at her father's features, saw them intent, but curiously vague. Was that merely an effect of attempting to navigate in near darkness or something else?

The woman who followed Gaheris was adept at keeping to shadows. She seemed to do it by instinct, rather than with conscious purpose. Brenda sought to see more of this strange invader, her father's shadow, caught only glints of green and silver, of a shining darkness that was long hair caught up in a series of bands, of a long-fingered hand holding what seemed to be a long knife, or perhaps a short sword.

That last caught the light for a moment, the edge so brilliantly honed that it seemed to slice the light and once again hide the weapon in shadow.

Terror, pure and absolute, as clean and horrid as an icicle touched Brenda when she saw that blade clearly. It was not crafted of metal, but of something organic, a fang, long and curving. Brenda had been born heir to the Rat, and she knew a Rat's instinctual horror when confronted with the hunting reptile. There was venom in that curving blade, venom and death.

Brenda sat bolt upright in bed, sheets tangled around her feet, her pillow still in motion where she had thrown it from her, a useless missile against an imaginary enemy.

God, she thought, swinging her feet to the floor and feeling reality seep back at the touch of the rag rug set as a barrier against the coolness of the boards. *That was one hell of a nightmare. Dad and some woman, a woman with a knife, sneaking into the house. I've spent too much time these last couple of days concentrating on enemies we can't put name or face to. No wonder I'm getting nightmares.*

She rose and stretched, reaching deliberately for the ceiling with her outspread fingers, taking deep breaths and trying to calm herself. Tonight's meeting had gotten sort of heated at the end, with Riprap offering himself as sacrificial Dog if that would just end the waiting.

They'd talked him down after a bit, and he'd apologized, but it had been tense. Who'd have thought the argument would give her such nightmares? Even now the sensation of dread was so intense that Brenda could imagine the pair in the hallway. Dad's hand would be turning the knob to the third-floor stairway, pulling the door back, making certain the hinges didn't squeak.

Brenda's imaginings were so acute that she thought she heard the characteristic squeak that door always made. Riprap had already oiled the hinges twice, but the squeak kept coming back.

Brenda let her arms drop, wrapped them around herself, shivering despite the relative warmth of the summer night. No one was out there. If she'd heard the door squeak, then it was just Riprap coming down for one of his interminable snacks. He was going to get fat if he wasn't careful.

She'd open the door, banish the nightmare. If Riprap was going down to the kitchen, maybe she'd join him. She didn't want anything to eat, but there was chamomile tea in the cabinet. She could make a cup. Maybe she'd even tell Riprap the dream. He was a really good listener.

Brenda glanced down at her nightwear, an old T-shirt worn to perfect softness and a pair of old shorts. Not sexy, but perfectly respectable. The weather was too warm to need slippers, and if her hair was a mess—as she was certain it was—Riprap had probably seen worse when he was doing nursemaid duty with her and Nissa.

Anticipating the comfort of a bit of friendly conversation, Brenda opened the door of her room and stepped out into the corridor, directly into her nightmare.

Gaheris Morris stood at the foot of the stairs leading up to the third floor, obviously about to begin the ascent. A dark shadow next to him resolved into a young woman Brenda's own age or maybe a little older. She was obviously Chinese, exquisitely beautiful, clad in one of those long, close-fitting, cap-sleeved gowns that Chinese beauties always wore in old movies. This gown was the color of pale green jade and worked with sinuous figures in gold and silver embroidery. Even in the faint light Brenda could tell the embroideries were of snakes.

"You should not have wakened," the young woman hissed.

The language she spoke was not English, but the variant of Chinese they had learned in order to communicate with Foster.

Brenda felt both annoyed and a strange sense that she'd heard something very like this another time. However, this was not the time to search after memories. The young woman was moving toward her with amazing swiftness, especially considering how tight her dress was. That remarkable dagger was raised, and Brenda did not doubt that this slim, exquisite woman was quite prepared to use it.

Brenda did the only sensible thing she could. She screamed. Not an inarticulate scream of terror, but a yell, a holler, a sound meant to raise the roof and bring the troops.

"Pearl! Nissa! Riprap! Des! Anybody!"

No one stirred, not even Nissa, who usually slept lightly because of Lani.

"I took care of that," the woman hissed. "I only wonder why you failed to remain asleep."

Brenda didn't feel like telling this woman about her dreams, her nightmares. She stole a glance over at her dad, but Gaheris Morris stood much as before, turned toward the stairway as if about to mount the stairs. His expression was not so much vacant as abstracted, as if he was caught in the middle of a thought.

"Do not look to him for help," the woman said. "He thinks he is somewhere in a memory, a memory of a time when he stayed in this house as a guest, and was not above sneaking outside at night, when he thought his hostess would not notice. A few times he brought back a 'guest.' Do you like knowing such things about your father, knowing that he has been less than trustworthy?"

Brenda didn't, but she wasn't about to give this woman the satisfaction of knowing. Besides, she hadn't forgotten that strange dagger, and how close it was to the bare skin of her arm.

Almost bare. She'd forgotten. She still wore one of the first tile bracelets she'd made, one that held the Dragon's Tail. Des had insisted that his students get used to wearing at least one of the bracelets at all times. At first the bracelet had felt clunky and awkward, but after several weeks Brenda would have felt naked without it.

Dragon's Tail. Protection. Protection enough against that poised and poisoned viper's fang?

"Now," the woman hissed—a mannerism that was really beginning to bother Brenda, not because it was affected, but because like everything else about the woman it was so polished, so sexy. "I want you to tell me where you have imprisoned the Tiger. Not the old woman. The young man. We lost him when he went hunting the old woman. We have seen him coming from this house and returning here. Tell me or else I shall bite you with this!"

She feinted with the curved dagger. Brenda flinched back, swinging her arms behind her as she did so. She caught at the edge of the bracelet with two fingers, pulling it over her hand, talking all the while as she did so. The sound of her voice covered the slight clatter as the tiles hit against each other.

"The young Tiger? You mean Foster?" Brenda dropped her hands in front of her, concealing the bracelet in the curve of one palm. "I mean, he looks like you, sort of. Pearl brought him back with her from Virginia."

"Don't play the fool with me!" The melodramatic words seemed quite fitting coming in that sensuous hiss. "Your father is the Rat. You dwell beneath the Tiger's roof and have been taught by the Rooster. The Dog and the Rabbit are your companions. You cannot be so ignorant."

"How did you get through Pearl's wards?" Brenda asked.

"Your father invited me. The house is not warded against him. Now, where is the young Tiger, this one you call Foster?"

"Upstairs," Brenda said. "His room is right next to Des's—the Rooster's. And he isn't a prisoner. Not really."

For the first time, the woman in the jade-green gown looked unsettled. "He must be, else he would return to us—to me!"

Her inflection on those last two words was possessive, intimate. Brenda's heart gave a strange twist of pain.

The young woman's smile was cruel. "This one you call Foster is my beloved. I have come to him. Now I will set him free."

Brenda's pain made her own words harsh. "He doesn't even remember you exist. Pearl stole his memory with his own spell. Even if you were to take him away, he'd still be hers."

"That explains much. Did our Tiger have his memory, nothing could have kept him from my side. Still, his body in our possession is better than leaving him to you. I will have him!"

She said the word "body" with such a caressing inflection that Brenda saw red. She smashed the Dragon's Tail bracelet against the floor and felt the spell rising around her.

"Not if I have anything to do with it," she said, and lunged toward the other woman, grabbing for the wrist that held the knife, seeking to twist, to break the other's hold.

Des kept reminding them that the Dragon's Tail was a relatively minor protection, that it worked best against someone hitting out at you, whether with a hand or a weapon. It worked less well against missiles, because those might have the momentum to push through the barrier. It worked least well against those things that were diffuse: fire, liquids, and the like.

So Brenda was pleased but not entirely surprised when the other woman struck out at her with her free hand and something translucent and scaled stopped the blow about six inches out from Brenda's head. She was less pleased to find that the same barrier made it hard for her to grasp at the other woman's wrist. She did, however, succeed in knocking the woman's hand back, and the blade with it.

"Little magics," the other woman sneered. "I learned such in the cradle."

She began muttering what Brenda thought might be a banishment. That wouldn't do. Brenda punched forward, aiming for the other woman's mouth. The Dragon's Tail cushioned her hand, rather as a boxing glove would have done. It stopped some of the force of the blow as well, but enough went through that the muttering stopped.

Brenda was beginning to like this. She'd never been a brawler, but there had been a time or two when one of her rivals in high-school politics had escalated their disagreements beyond intellectual debate. Brenda remembered a few of the tricks and reached for the other woman's long, silver-banded braid. The Dragon's Tail made her grip clumsy, but she managed a tug that sent her opponent off balance. The intruder stumbled backward, out of Brenda's immediate reach, cursing at the sudden pain.

But Brenda could feel that her luck wouldn't last. There was something deadly and dangerous about this woman, and although the Dragon's Tail had given Brenda a momentary edge, her true advantage had been that of surprise, and surprise was now gone.

"Bitch!" the other hissed, and sheathed her momentarily useless dagger, drawing out in the same motion a slip of red paper on which characters had been drawn with brushstrokes that Brenda—a novice at the same art—recognized as the work of a true artist.

Artistic appreciation or not, Brenda wasn't waiting around to see what that slip of paper could do to her, or to her surroundings. Des had warned them that the Dragon's Tail could not protect them from a fall or from a rain of fire or from a magical attack. Brenda could feel that the Dragon's Tail wasn't as firmly wrapped as it had been, and didn't think it was going to hold much longer.

There were other bracelets in her room, right on top of her dresser, so Brenda broke and ran, darting back into that darkened haven. As she did so, she was all too aware that Gaheris Morris still stood where he had all this time, waiting to ascend a quiet stairway.

The other woman—the Snake, as she must be—threw the red slip of paper. It struck the doorway and Brenda smelled the acrid scent of acid, even as she heard it sizzle against the paint. Brenda fumbled in the semidarkness for the shallow box in which she kept her bracelets, cursed herself for an idiot, and spared a moment to turn on the reading lamp.

Light made finding the box easy, but more importantly, it made it possible for Brenda to read the English letters penciled lightly on the back of the tiles, identifying the spells. Des had suggested the crib, saying that since none of his students read Chinese, and so many of the same characters were combined and recombined for each spell, it was a good idea.

"After all," he'd said, "what use will they be if you need them in a hurry? You can't go looking them up."

Brenda blessed her tutor's forethought, and kicked herself for not seeing that this—just like the wards around the house, and a dozen other small precautions—had been a warning and a reminder that those they were up against were truly dangerous.

First to hand was another Dragon's Tail—not surprising, since Des had insisted that they get this protective spell down cold. Brenda cracked it against the floor, felt a second tail coil around the first, sustaining and enhancing. Then she dug after a Dragon's Breath. The Snake had tried to throw acid on her. Maybe she'd like a touch of dragon's fire in return!

Brenda heard the Snake coming through the bedroom door and wheeled, smashing the Dragon's Fire bracelet onto the floor and holding out her right hand, palm raised as Des had made them practice. In practice, the gesture had felt rather silly, like something out of one of those chop-socky flicks her folks loved, but now it felt entirely natural.

Flames, orangey-red into white-hot, flared from Brenda's hand, directly at the Snake, but they wrapped around her almost caressingly, leaving her unburnt.

"My father is the Dragon," the Snake hissed, "did you think he would leave his daughter unguarded?"

She flung out another of her bits of red paper. It flew with the speed and accuracy of something far more solid, as if it had momentarily been transformed into metal or wood. Brenda dodged, but felt a searing pain as acid fizzled and sizzled through her Dragon's Tail barrier, tracing lines through her sleep shirt and blistering the skin below.

Brenda heard her own inadvertent cry of pain, but she was too scared to back down. For the first time, she really understood why a trapped rat is dangerous. Deep down inside, knowing they have nowhere to go, they become vicious.

She had a cluster of bracelets hanging from her fingers. Dragon's Breath was apparently useless, and she didn't think Winding Snake would work against this woman as it had done against Foster. What did that leave her? What didn't snakes like? Cold. Mongooses . . .

There had been a spell Des had taught them for summoning a specific wind. Windy Nines. She hadn't made that one, but she had done another. . . . Frantically, she searched through the tiles, all too aware that the Snake was readying another of her pieces of paper.

The paper was flying toward her as Brenda threw down the bracelet for Windfall. It blasted forth with a swirling tornado that ripped the red paper into confetti in midair and then swirled as a barrier between Brenda and the Snake. The pages of the novel Brenda had been reading before bed fluttered and began to shred, and the lace curtains at the window flapped wildly, but for the moment Brenda was safe.

Stalemate! she thought in relief.

The Snake's long hair was tossing in the wind, tendrils coming loose from the braid that had restrained it, but the young woman's tight-fitting dress hardly moved, except to show the heaving of the Snake's rounded breasts as she snarled at Brenda.

"I'll rip your head from your shoulders and swallow you whole, Ratling," she snarled, moving closer, raising hands empty of all but long, polished nails. "I told you the Dragon is my father. I know ways to pry apart those tails that you have wrapped around you."

Brenda didn't doubt that the Snake meant what she said. The bracelets Brenda held might contain another trick or two, but tricks were all she had. Brenda fumbled behind her and found the ladder-back chair that stood in front of her little writing desk. It wasn't much, but it might hold, and maybe Dad would break whatever hold this woman had over him and come to her rescue.

It was a slim hope, but a trapped rat doesn't back down.

Then Brenda heard a sound from the hallway outside her bedroom and felt a reverberation of ch'i that felt like a growl.

Pearl Bright stood in the doorway, a long sword in one hand and an expression of uncompromising ferocity on her face. Up until this moment, Brenda had always thought "old" with a degree of pity. Now she saw age for the magnificent thing it could be: the power of knowledge, the strength of certainty.

Pearl moved her sword so that the shining length of the silver-bright blade rested point against the carpet and took a step into the room.

"You made a mistake, Snakeling," she said, her tone conversational, but holding menace nonetheless. "You found a guide to invite you within my wards, but didn't you bother to consider that I would have other wards active—and that certainly I would notice alien sorcery within these walls?"

The green-gowned Snake was no less exquisitely lovely than before; her glossy black hair had lost none of its shine. Her strong, young body lacked none of its supple strength, but suddenly she looked overdressed, awkward, immature, even, Brenda sought for the vaguely old-fashioned word: callow. That was it. She looked callow.

By contrast, Pearl, standing there in a lightweight summer bathrobe printed with peonies, was the incarnation of power.

I mean, Brenda thought, *Pearl took the time to put on her robe. She was aware a magical battle was going on, and she took the time to put on her robe!*

Momentarily, Brenda felt indignant that Pearl had not raced to her rescue. Then a realization brightened her soul, and she gripped the ladder-back chair with new determination. Pearl had believed Brenda could hold her ground or she would not have delayed. Brenda was sure of that.

That Pearl had believed in her was something to be proud of—if Brenda lived long enough to feel pride, for although the Snake had given Pearl most of her attention, she had not forgotten Brenda. The cool, mocking glance she gave the hands holding on to the ladder-back chair made Brenda alternately hot with embarrassment and chill with visceral fear.

But the Snake spared no words for Brenda, and what she said certainly gave away more than she had intended.

"I am no snakeling," she hissed, "but the Snake, sole and true. My father is the Dragon and our family is old in power and in wisdom and in cunning."

Pearl lifted the point of her sword from the carpet and with motions so quick and light that Brenda could hardly follow them traced patterns in the air. They left a glowing trail behind them in a deep forest green, Chinese ideograms, but not one of the handful Brenda had learned.

"I charge you to hold your attack," Pearl said, and flecks of golden fire sparked from the ideograms, "and answer my questions truthfully."

The Snake raised her dagger, and moved as if to cut Pearl's ideograms. Brenda watched in astonishment as the Snake's hand was held fast by the ideograms, which traced out ropelike extensions to wrap the arm that held the dagger. It began to squeeze, forest-green light pressing against the ivory of the Snake's arm, pushing into the flesh with such force that Brenda did not doubt that had the Snake not given way and let her arm fall uselessly to her side, blood would have welled forth.

"This blade is called Treaty," Pearl said, her tiger's growl more pronounced. "My father had it forged in China when it became apparent that a certain treaty of which I am certain you are aware was being honored more in the breach than otherwise. Spells cast through Treaty are especially potent against those who are in violation of that old bond—like you, Snake."

The disdain in the old Tiger's voice as she spoke the title made it more of an insult than "Snakeling" had ever been. Brenda saw the Snake's eyes narrow to angry slits, but the intruder said nothing.

"Now, I have questions for you," Pearl said, "and think of the consequences before you answer them less than truthfully. How many of you came from the Lands Born from Smoke and Sacrifice to this place?"

"Three."

"And they are?"

"I, who am the Snake, my father, who is the Dragon, and my beloved, who is the Tiger."

Brenda felt her hands tighten over the back of the chair. Of course Foster had to have had a lover. He was too gorgeous not to have had. He might have dozens, and this slinky bitch was just the latest. What a fool she had been!

But still, it made her angry to hear this woman boast of Foster in that way. Everything was defined in relation to her: her father, her beloved. Self-centered, egotistical, spoiled, arrogant . . . had she included self-centered in the list?

Brenda made herself focus, knowing that her anger was born from fear, and fear was not a sign of strength, but the reverse.

Pearl cut the air with her sword. "Why did you come here?"

The Snake might be bound by Pearl's spell, but she wasn't going to cooperate any more than necessary.

"To get something."

"What?"

"Something that was taken from our land that should not have been."

"What?"

"Something you have and know you have, although unknowing that you should not have it."

Pearl raised the sword blade again. Brenda held her breath, wondering whether Pearl was going to trace another ideogram—perhaps one compelling more full cooperation—in the air. Could Treaty's shining blade cut through whatever protective spells the Snake still had up?

A loud, thunderous knocking sounded against the front door of Pearl's house. Pearl tilted her head slightly, and Brenda felt certain she was reading the input from one or the other of her many wards.

"Brenda," Pearl said, "go downstairs and open the front door, but leave the chain in place. Ask whoever is knocking what his business is, then close the door and call up to me."

Brenda reluctantly let go of the chair, but kept a firm grasp on her remaining bracelets as she strode past the now smirking Snake and around Pearl into the hallway. Brenda wasn't sure what she could do with the handful of spells those bracelets represented, but they were the best weapon she had.

As she ran down the stairs, Brenda found herself wondering if the Rat had owned some sort of sword like the one Pearl had. Maybe she'd even seen it, tucked in a trunk at home with the delicate heirlooms and ornaments her parents had put away until the boys got past the age that they seemed to break things just by walking into a room.

Owning a sword would be cool, not that Brenda had the least idea how to use one. Still, she could learn. Des had those weird Rooster's Talons. She'd seen him practice both alone and with Pearl. Maybe she could get in on a session.

Aware that her mental blathering was because she didn't want to think too hard about who might be on the other side of the door, Brenda went down and turned open the locks—all but the chain, which she left on as Pearl had instructed. She glanced at the brass-colored links and saw they were etched with tiny characters. Doubtless they held a spell or so in their length.

A Chinese man, probably in his fifties, stood on the doorstep. He was square-bodied and round-faced, dressed in an old-fashioned Chinese scholar's robe, complete to a cap with wing flaps on the sides. He was clean-shaven, his black hair cut in a modern style. His posture managed to be both erect and formal, and yet to suggest that he spent a great amount of time stoop-shouldered, peering at closely written texts. Brenda did not need to look at the ornate dragons embroidered on his robes to know that this was the third of their enemies: the Dragon.

"I am Righteous Drum, and I have come for my daughter," the Dragon said with a bow. "I believe she is here."

"She is," Brenda said, not bothering to bow, as she figured the motion would look really silly with her wearing a sleep shirt and shorts—and an acid-burned sleep shirt at that. Well, he probably couldn't see more of her than her face peering around the edge of the door.

"Please permit my daughter to come out to me," the Dragon said. "Otherwise, given that breaking the very interesting and quite intricate wards about this house would be an unwarranted expenditure of energy, and doubtless attract unwanted attention, I would need to find ways to convince you that my daughter does not belong in your custody."

Brenda listened to the flow of words with mild astonishment. The Dragon's tone was courtly and so polite she felt embarrassed about keeping him outside.

"Uh, just a moment." Brenda closed the door as Pearl had instructed and called up the stairs. "It's the Dragon, at least, I think it has to be, even though he introduced himself as Righteous Drum, since he's asking for us to return his daughter."

"That is all he wants?"

"That's all he has said so far," Brenda said.

"Ask him what assurances I have that he won't attempt to breach my defenses if I open the door to let his daughter out."

Brenda opened the door the amount the chain permitted and repeated Pearl's words.

"My daughter is a pride and joy to me," the Dragon said, "but if an old man's desire to see his child free is not sufficient, then tell your Tiger that I have inspected the wards and am not certain I would care to attempt to break them without more preparation."

Brenda closed the door again. Feeling a swell of pride for the work Nissa had done with her help, she repeated what the Dragon had said word for word.

"Interesting. Tell Righteous Drum I have a mind to trade his daughter for something else. . . . He has stolen the memories from several of my friends and allies. Ask him how many of those he is willing to return to have the Snake returned safely."

Brenda heard a cry of indignation from above, and swallowed a smile as she opened the door and relayed Pearl's message.

The Dragon did not look surprised.

"None," he said, and the very stiffness of his reply showed his agitation. "There can be other Snakes, but what I have reclaimed from those this Tiger calls her friends and allies is irreplaceable. Tell the Tiger that if she does not release my daughter, I will go forth and do physical damage to those from whom thus far I have held my hand. Moreover, not a one of your friends or kin will be safe from my rage. If my daughter is returned to me, then I will withhold my hand from all of them."

Brenda felt certain the Dragon meant exactly what he was saying, but tried to keep her voice level as she relayed the words. Her thoughts were far from calm, though, imagining Mom or the boys killed by some weird assassin.

"Interesting," Pearl said in almost conversational tones. "Ask the Dragon if he would swear to withhold his hand from my friends and kin on my blade, which is called Treaty, and grows impossibly ferocious if oaths are broken. Ask him, too, if he would make the Snake swear to this as well, and if he would stand bond in life and afterlife for any of his allies who might be tempted to violate the spirit as well as the word of his vow."

Brenda repeated this, and watched Righteous Drum's face anxiously as he listened.

"I will so swear," he said, "but only when my daughter is at my side, free of constraints against her leaving."

"Tell him," Pearl said, "we'll be right down, just as soon as I put on some slippers."

21

Pearl didn't really need her slippers, but rather liked that parting line, so, herding the Snake in front of her with the dual prods of Treaty's edge and a quickly etched ideogram of coercion, she made her way first to her bedroom, then down the stairs into the front foyer.

Brenda stood there, holding the door open to the width of the chain, alternating fascinated glances out at the waiting Dragon with checking on Pearl's decorous progress. Her expression stiffened whenever she glanced toward the Snake.

Pearl didn't need to ask why. Certainly the Snake had attacked Brenda, but Brenda had held her own quite well, especially for a complete novice. No, what rankled was the claim that Foster was the Snake's "beloved"—a claim that forced Brenda, once again, to confront how very little about that young man she really knew.

But it was quite likely that Foster would soon no longer be a problem for them. Certainly, the Dragon would want the Tiger returned along with his daughter.

However, when they entered into their negotiations, Foster was not mentioned. The Dragon wanted his daughter returned, and made quite clear that if Pearl did not return her, then those members of the Twelve who were not already under Pearl's protection would suffer, as would friends and family of the protected four. Pearl noted that when negotiating for the young woman's life and freedom, he referred to her not by her title, but simply as "my daughter." She knew from this that she negotiated not with the Dragon, as such, but with a father.

Pearl didn't know whether she felt sad or envious that here was a father who could value a mere girl child.

Pearl knew she would need to return the Snake to her father, but she wanted assurance that once the Dragon had his daughter returned to him, he would not break his word and start taking hostages or otherwise attacking the friends, families, or allies of the remaining Twelve.

After all, the very fact that Pearl was willing to return the Snake to assure those people's safety proved their value.

Refining the wording of their complex agreement was torturous, but Pearl noted with approval that Brenda did not fidget. The young woman took notes of the discussion as Pearl requested, but never forgot to keep a watchful eye on the Snake.

Brenda's notes were written in English, but whether through magic or learning, both Dragon and Snake could read that language. A written text permitted no deviations, no "Oh, did I say that?" afterthoughts, and Pearl thought the Dragon approved of her care rather than otherwise—but then while dragons were known for their pedantry, tigers were not. However, Pearl was a Tiger who had been a Hollywood movie star, and she fully understood the importance of reading the fine print.

The person who grew increasingly restless as the negotiations went on was the Snake. Her father consulted her as to various points, but as captive her ability to influence the terms was limited. Still, Pearl was lenient and let the Dragon address his daughter through the chain-guarded opening of the door. After all, the Snake was going to need to swear to this agreement before Pearl let her go, and better the Snake did so with no reservations.

At last a text was arrived at that Pearl felt protected their friends and allies as thoroughly as she could manage. The Dragon reviewed it, politely asking Brenda to clarify a word or two, for the young woman's handwriting showed that she was more accustomed to composing on a computer than by hand. Then he glanced at his daughter.

"Do the provisions of this document suit you, Honey Dream?" Righteous Drum's tone made quite clear that he thought they should.

"But, Father," the Snake exclaimed. For once there was no trace of a hiss in her voice. "You have negotiated no provision for the Tiger's freedom!"

"There can be other Tigers," the Dragon said sternly. "Indeed, there will be those who will think there could have been other Snakes as well, especially after learning of your behavior this night. However, you are my daughter, and I permit myself a father's indulgence."

Pearl had a sudden insight as to the Dragon's willingness to make terms. *I bet he didn't want to involve any "civilians" from the start. His tactics show great care to avoid injury to anything but his victims' memories. I wonder if the other members of his Twelve made this a constraint before he was permitted to come here and attempt whatever it is he is attempting.*

The Snake was furious at her father's cavalier attitude toward Foster—and quite possibly toward herself as a member of the Twelve. "But, Father, our Tiger. Surely we owe him . . ."

The Dragon cut her protests off without apology. "The Tiger failed. He let a woman many times his age turn his own magic against him. He is not a Tiger we need to preserve. There were other candidates for the post, and if the auguries had been different . . ."

He stopped, perhaps recalling that what he was saying should not be heard by those who, despite the very civilized manner in which they had been negotiating, were his enemies.

Pearl decided to save face for him. The Japanese were not the only ones who valued that insubstantial quality.

"I will send out tea to you," she said, "while I brush copies of our agreement. Will you bide?"

"As long as my daughter is safe, I will treat our agreement as if already sworn to."

Pearl let the door remain open, but left the chain in place. She looked at the Snake.

"If you want to be out of here quickly, then do not distract me. I will let you have a chair, and you can converse with your father through the opening. Violate my hospitality and find out whether a Snake is strong enough to resist the wrath of a Tiger in her den."

The Snake looked distinctly unhappy, but when Brenda brought a straight-backed chair from the front parlor, she slid into it with sulky grace. Perhaps she hoped that she could convince her father that it was not too late to make an amendment to the treaty.

Brenda glanced over at Pearl. "Want me to make tea? Des has been teaching me how to make it right, and I know where the good oolong is. That seems rather appropriate."

Pearl nodded. Oolong was black dragon tea, and indeed, very appropriate.

"Thank you," she said. "That would be extremely helpful. While the water boils, take a moment to treat those acid burns. There's a first-aid kit in the kitchen."

Brenda nodded, winced as she touched a sore spot with a fingertip.

"I think I left some clean shirts in the laundry room. I'll change, too."

"Good."

Pearl went to her office, leaving the door open so she could see into the foyer. Pulling out inkstone, brushes, and appropriate paper, she quickly translated the treaty from English to Chinese, but for good measure included the English text beneath, just in case there should be any questions as to her choice of terms in Chinese.

As she was working, Pearl smelled a whiff of fragrant tea and looked up to see that Brenda had left Pearl her own small pot of oolong, along with a few almond wafers. Pearl smiled slightly, but her hand did not slow until she had finished the character she was writing. Blotting ink at this point would be a waste of good paper and time, especially since she wanted the two copies to be as close to identical as possible.

Pearl noticed with approval that Brenda had not asked why Pearl was going to all this trouble when she had both a computer that could produce texts in Chinese fonts, and a copier. By now, Des had drummed into his three students that for the Chinese the written word held its own magic, especially when lovingly created by hand.

Thus Pearl brushed elaborate patterns in ink, while Brenda played the contradictory roles of hostess and guard. When Pearl was done, she made photocopies of the treaty, and handed one of these, rather than an original, over the chain. The Dragon reviewed it.

"I see no reason for changes. This is as we discussed. Will you sign?"

Pearl nodded and handed ink and brush through the door.

"I have made two identical originals. I suggest that the Snake sign both first, since she is sitting here, then I will sign one copy while you sign the other. Then we will trade."

"I agree," the Dragon said, and there was that in his voice that dared his daughter to disagree.

The Snake didn't, and was graceful with brush and ink in signing both copies.

The other signatures were exchanged without prevarication or evasion, and as she brushed the final "Ming" on the page, Pearl felt a little click in her mind that meant she was bound by the agreement, and a fainter echo that told her when the Dragon was bound as well.

"Hold these, Brenda," she said, "and I will release the Snake to her father."

Pearl had thought about referring to the young woman by her personal name, but decided this would be gratuitously rude. Although she could not imagine such a situation, there might be a time when she would need the Snake's goodwill.

Brenda spoke as she moved to obey. "Pearl, what about Dad? What about the others? Will Dad come back to the present? Will the others wake up?"

Pearl looked at the Snake who was rising to her feet, smoothing out her elegantly embroidered gown, clearly seeking to regain some portion of her dignity.

"Can you answer Brenda's question?" she said. "The spells were yours."

Pearl managed to inflect this last to imply that she thought the spells had been cast by the Snake, but perhaps she had relied on someone else to create them. The Snake responded much as Pearl had expected.

"I created them," she said. "They will lose their hold shortly before dawn, and all will be as before. Gaheris Morris will be disoriented. He will have no memory of how he arrived here. I planned to return him to his hotel before my spell broke."

Brenda looked confused, and Pearl thought she knew why. The Snake's words implied that Gaheris was staying in the area. If he was, why hadn't he told his daughter?

"Where is Gaheris's hotel?" Pearl asked. "Perhaps we can return him and so avoid confusion."

The Snake told them, the routine designations and directions sounding very strange coming from someone as exotic as she.

"Thank you," Pearl said politely. "And, good night."

The last was a dismissal, and the Dragon took it as such. Gripping his daughter firmly above her elbow, he half marched, half escorted her down the stairs and off into the night. Pearl wondered if they had a car, but didn't leave the door open to listen. She had other things to do.

As Pearl turned from locking the door, Brenda was waiting, every line in her body showing her readiness to take orders, a certain tightness around her lips showing that she was bursting with questions, but knew this wasn't the time to ask them.

"Your father is safer than we are," Pearl said without pausing for preamble or praise. "The treaty we just made protects him as it does not protect us. I will go up and look to him. Go into my office and check the Rolodex for the number of Star Reliables. They're a chauffeuring service I use when my car is unavailable. Tell them I have someone I wish driven to his hotel and escorted to his room. Imply that he is a bit inebriated, and they will understand that they are not to ask questions."

"And Dad," Brenda said, "are you sure he's really going to be all right?"

"The Snake would not have dared lie, not after signing that treaty."

Pearl spoke with more certainty than she felt. Technically, the Snake had not been bound by the treaty when she first ensorcelled Gaheris, but Pearl had a feeling in her gut that the Snake would not have lied to her. Or rather, that she would not have dared evade, not with her father already unhappy with her.

We always make the mistake of thinking of "the enemy" as some sort of monolith, but over and over again we see how many different goals and opinions may govern their actions.

While Brenda made the call, Pearl went upstairs and checked on Gaheris. He had moved to a seat by the stairway to the third floor. His body language was very similar to someone who was so drunk that he could no longer think clearly. He met Pearl's gaze with his own dull eyes, but said nothing, not even when she checked through his pockets and wallet, finally locating the key to his hotel room. The folder that held the key also had the room number lightly penciled on it, so that was fine.

Pearl guided Gaheris downstairs, finding him willing but disoriented. The driver from Star Reliables was well-paid to do his job and notice nothing. Pearl knew Gaheris would be in his room well before dawn.

"Now," Pearl said to Brenda when the limo had pulled away, "if you and I were sensible, we would get some sleep. The others will wake at the usual hour and we will have a great deal to tell them. Do you think you could manage to drop off?"

Brenda shook her head. "But if you want to try, I could go do e-mail or read or something."

"I don't think I could sleep either," Pearl admitted. "Let's make more tea—or coffee if you'd prefer—and go into my office. We might as well note down everything that happened while it's fresh. Who knows what little detail might be important later?"

Brenda nodded. "Okay." She started down the hall to the kitchen, then stopped in midstride. "Pearl, you don't think I'm an idiot for suddenly feeling really scared, do you? I mean, we won, but it's going to be a long time before I can forget what it was like to wake up from a nightmare and find it real just on the other side of the wall."

Pearl stared at her. "What do you mean? What nightmare?"

Brenda blinked, then dragged the tips of her fingers across her face in exhausted anguish. "That's right. You don't know."

She told Pearl about her nightmare as they made both coffee and tea, then retired into Pearl's office. Pearl stroked Bonaventure and listened, a dozen speculations rising into her mind, but she kept quiet until Brenda had finished.

"You asked me if I thought you were an idiot for feeling scared," Pearl smiled. "Not in the least, my dear. In fact, I think being scared may be a very sensible reaction indeed."

★

Brenda thought she'd be tired by the time the others woke up, but her nerves were still singing with the experiences of the night before. This wasn't like the struggle against the Three-Legged Toad. After that she'd been physically and magically exhausted—as well as overwhelmed by having her worldview revamped to include monsters.

This time none of those things applied. The magic she had used had been stored in advance, and she'd pulled more than one all-nighter in school. Sitting up as dark grew into day, talking and drinking seemingly infinite cups of coffee, wasn't at all unfamiliar.

Riprap was the first member of the household downstairs, although the sounds of Nissa and Lani moving around had started earlier. Pearl did not stop the Dog when he headed outside for his usual morning run.

"Riprap should be safe," she said. "And better he fall into his usual routine since I don't want to start telling the others about last night until after Wong has arrived and we can ask him to babysit Lani."

"You're not going to ask Foster to watch her?" Brenda asked hesitantly.

"I think not," Pearl replied. "He may still be a target, and I would not put Lani in danger."

Brenda remembered the Snake's arrogant claims on "her beloved," and gritted her teeth together. When Foster came down, she found it hard to look at him, to meet his friendly smile, to answer his cheerful "Good morning, Brenda," spoken proudly in not too heavily accented English. She kept seeing him holding the Snake's sinuous body, perhaps running his hands over the curves that dress had shown off so effectively. She wondered if he had kissed the Snake, if he had done more.

Fortunately for Brenda's peace of mind, Nissa and Lani came down soon after, the two-and-a-half-year-old holding the bobble-headed penguins, one in each hand. Brenda forced herself to think about something even more unpleasant than Foster entwined with the Snake.

What had her father been doing in San Jose? California was on his beat, sure, but he usually restricted his visits to a few a year. Had their enemies used some magical influence to draw him back? What other influences might they be able to exert? Pearl had extracted an oath that their enemies would not harm those she defined as "friends and allies," but did "harm" extend to manipulation?

Was that why Dad hadn't called to tell her he was in town?

Her cell phone rang almost as soon as Brenda shaped that thought.

"Hi, Breni. Guess who's back in San Jose?"

"Hi, Dad." Brenda tried to sound enthusiastic, but she couldn't. "Back so soon?"

"You don't sound thrilled." He chuckled. "Yeah. I've got a deal ready to go for some of those bobble-headed mandarin dolls that Des didn't like. Turns out one shop with branches both here and in San Francisco . . ."

Brenda listened as Dad babbled about suppliers and sales. It sounded good, plausible, even. Still, she wondered if it had all been planted in his mind to make his coming to San Jose work for him. Was it a rationalization like those she'd heard both Dad and Albert Yu make to cover gaps in their memories?

"Want to come out for breakfast?"

Brenda started. "Oh, Dad. I can't. Pearl has something she needs me to do early."

"Will you be free by lunch?"

Brenda relayed the question to Pearl, who nodded.

"Auntie Pearl says I should be. Want me to meet you?"

"I'll swing by and get you. I want to show you some wonderful gardens a client took me to last time. I'll be by at or around noon."

Brenda rang off, wondering if she could learn anything from Dad while they were out—wondering if they'd be safe. She'd get Riprap to loan her a couple of his protective bracelets. They wouldn't be quite as good as the ones tailored to her personal elements, but they'd be better than the dusty scraps of polymer clay she'd swept up from her bedroom floor that morning.

Such thoughts kept Brenda well distracted as she took her turn with getting breakfast on the table, turning bacon, frying or scrambling eggs to order. Des came to help, although he probably would have preferred something like rice congee. Riprap reappeared, smelling freshly showered, and in time to do damage to something like half a pound of bacon and four or five eggs.

Then breakfast was over and cleared away. Lani was sent out to join Wong the gardener. Foster politely went to watch educational television up on the third floor, and Pearl convened a meeting around the long table between the kitchen and family room.

Pearl asked Brenda to begin, and so Brenda told about her dream that wasn't quite a dream, and what she encountered in the hallway. She carried the tale to where Pearl entered, then Pearl took over, providing a good many vivid details, but doing an admirable job of avoiding inserting anything in the way of interpretation. She finished by passing around copies of the treaty she had made with the Dragon and the Snake. When everyone had been given time to review them, she opened the floor to questions or comments.

The others had listened in nearly complete silence, Nissa and Riprap both taking notes in the spiral binders they used for their lessons with Des. Des sat with his hands folded in front of him, his eyelids drooping, but Brenda didn't doubt that he heard and comprehended far more than did the other two.

"Des and I seem to keep missing all the fun," Riprap complained. "First, we're out at a ball game when the Three-Legged Toad is summoned, then we sleep through an actual attempt to invade."

Brenda wasn't completely certain that he was joking.

"It wasn't much fun at all," she said, turning her gaze on Riprap.

"I've been in enough rumbles," Riprap said, his tone reassuring, "to know that they're no fun."

"As have I," Des added. "Try being a man who wears a dress." He kicked out against the hem of his long Chinese robe. "Or a Western historical re-creationist who reminds people that those golden days of old weren't all six-guns and some sort of chivalric code of honor. I've been in fights, and while I don't look for them, I wish I'd had Pearl's forethought and set up wards to alert me if magic other than our own was used."

"What could you have done that I did not?" Pearl said, not as a challenge, but in comfort. "The threat the Dragon used to neutralize my hold on the Snake was such that I would have ordered an army to retreat rather than have others harmed."

"Ever since we realized our enemies were from the Lands," Nissa said, "I've wondered at, well, how gentle they were being. They weren't the other times they came after members of the Twelve, or did I misunderstand?"

"You did not," Pearl said. "They physically attacked, took hostages, even, in a few ugly circumstances, resorted to murder. This stealing of memories is so unsettling that I had not thought to term it gentle, but you're right. By contrast, it is gentle."

"Gentle, but effective," Des said, "if their goal is to neutralize us as a unit."

Silence fell and Brenda knew they were all considering how little they still knew about their opponents' goals.

"I don't think," Brenda said, trying to keep her tone level and reasonable, "that whatever the Snake was doing was meant to advance, well, the memory stealing. She came for Foster. Once she had Foster, maybe she planned to start gathering the last four memories, but she wanted Foster first."

"I agree," Pearl said. "The Dragon had clearly decided that their Tiger— Foster—was a failure, and they did not need to retrieve him."

There was a note in her voice that told Brenda that, for the first time, perhaps, Pearl actually pitied Foster.

Nissa glanced down at her notes. "Pearl said that while the Snake wasn't exactly forthcoming about why they had come here, she did admit that it was 'to get something.' Then Pearl asked, what, and the Snake said, 'Something that was taken from our land that should not have been.' Then Pearl asked her to clarify, and what the Snake said wasn't a lot of help, but is still interesting: 'Something you have and know you have, but have unknowing that you should not have it.'"

Pearl's gesture acknowledged the accuracy of Nissa's transcription, then she sighed. "The Dragon's arrival was untimely. A few more questions, and I would have learned more."

"Perhaps we know enough," Des said. His eyes were shining, and Brenda remembered that this was a man who did crossword puzzles with an ink brush. "Something we know we have, but have unknowing that we should not have it. Okay. The mah-jong sets and various tools like Treaty were made after our arrival here. What else did our ancestors take with them?"

Pearl shut her eyes, her expression composed for thought. "They took a variety of things. Magical artifacts were forbidden, but a wide variety of personal items were brought with them. The Twelve were willing to accept exile rather than resist to the point of devastation. That meant they were permitted to take the means to assure they would be comfortable while they made the transition."

"Did they take anything living?" Brenda asked.

"Other than the young emperor," Pearl said, "not that I know. They were not permitted servants or acolytes, if that's what you're thinking."

"That," Brenda admitted, "or some—I don't know, magical animal or something?"

"Could they have gotten away with some part of the royal regalia?" Nissa asked. "I don't know . . . some crown or scepter or sacred jewel?"

"I doubt it," Pearl said, "but it is possible. What is maddening, is that whatever this thing is, we have it, we know we have it, but we don't know that we shouldn't have it. I can't imagine that if someone walked off with a sanctified item they wouldn't know it was something they shouldn't have."

Des had been drumming on the table with the tips of his fingers, "But the thing is, *we* don't know. Does that mean that one of the Thirteen Orphans might know, but can't tell us because of the loss of memory? Or did that 'we' apply to all of the Thirteen, and one of us has whatever it is sitting up in the attic, and these invaders are rummaging through memories looking for clues? That would explain why they're not killing us off. They need something we can only give while alive."

"And it may be something," Nissa said, bouncing in her chair, "that one of the four of us possess, since if they'd found it, they would certainly have packed up and gone home."

"Possibly," Pearl said. "Now, I recall that when I was a child . . ."

"Whoa!" Riprap said, holding up one broad hand, the pinkish tan of the palm a vivid contrast to the darker skin that covered the rest of him. "Pearl, are you just speculating, or do you have something specific in mind?"

Pearl looked a little surprised at being interrupted, but said courteously, "Just speculating, I suppose."

"We can speculate," Riprap went on, "about things we can't know—like what they're looking for and why they want our memories all encased in crystal—for a long time, and even if we touch on the right answer, we won't know. Before we get too far off the events of last night, I'd like to note one thing that really puzzles me."

"Go ahead," Pearl prompted. "You're right. Even speculation would be more productive if we have time to think through possibilities."

Riprap looked at each of them before going on, as if he could somehow read the answer in their eyes.

"I guess it's two questions, really. Why did Brenda dream what she did? And why, having dreamed what she did, could she wake up? The rest of us, even Lani, were dead to the world."

"Let's start with the dreaming," Des said, content to shift from one puzzle to another. "Does anyone other than Brenda remember dreaming anything that could be even remotely connected to what happened? Stretch. I'll accept dreams about real snakes, or dreams about burglars."

One by one, he looked at the others, and three heads shook "no."

"Me neither," Des said, "so Riprap is right to focus in on this. Why did Brenda dream so accurately that she walked right out into the scene she'd dreamed, but none of the rest of us even dreamed a shadow of it?"

"I didn't know I was dreaming true," Brenda hastened to clarify. "When I heard someone moving in the hall, I just thought it was Riprap going down for a snack."

"So you said," Pearl agreed, her tone comforting, but slightly absent. "I wonder if this is connected to the little rat Brenda manifested when the Three-Legged Toad appeared. She is the first heir apparent I have known ever to do such a thing."

Nissa nodded. "I was thinking the same thing. I've been wondering, could it be something Gaheris Morris did before his memory was taken from him?"

Everyone looked at Nissa, and as no one interrupted, Nissa went on, her words almost stammered as she thought aloud.

"I mean . . . What I'm trying to say is, if someone came after me, and Lani was anywhere near, I wouldn't be thinking so much about me as about keeping Lani safe. Right? And, well, what if that's what happened with Gaheris? He saw this warrior type, sword and all, coming at him, and he thinks, 'I'm done for, but they're not going to get my Breni,' and so he . . . I don't know, tries to give her the Rat, pass on her inheritance, do something so that she'll be protected. I know that's what I'd try and do. I mean, not that specifically, but maybe I would, since I'd want to do what I could to keep Lani safe."

Nissa heaved out a great sigh. "I didn't put that very well, but what do you think?"

"I think," Pearl said in what Brenda thought of as her "approving director" voice, "that you may have hit on something. The first Ox sought and chose her heir, and since her inner Ox agreed that Hua would be suitable, the power passed. Gaheris has never minded that his daughter, not one of his sons, was his heir apparent. He had come here to have Brenda initiated. Perhaps all that intention did something. He may have meant to cast some sort of protection on her, but when his memory—his Ratness—was torn from him, what happened instead was that a fragment lodged in Brenda and held. Very, very interesting indeed."

A slightly awkward silence followed as everyone studied Brenda, as if they should be able to see some sign of this transference. Who knew? Maybe Des or

Pearl could. For herself, Brenda had to resist an urge to reach up and feel if she suddenly had rat's ears on top of her head or whiskers under her nose.

Riprap was the first to break the silence. "That connection would explain Brenda dreaming true, and her ability to resist the spell that made the rest of us sleep. The Snake had to have some sort of magical hold on Gaheris, because he was guiding her into the house. She probably imposed that through his captured memories, since she was making him believe he was back in the days when he'd sneak in and out of this house. Since Gaheris wasn't included in the spell that made us all sleep, once Brenda got scared enough to wake up, neither was she."

"So," Des said, and he sounded very pleased, "to this point we've assumed that we only had the Tiger, Rabbit, Rooster, and Dog—now it seems we have at least a little of the Rat as well. I feel strangely encouraged by this."

"I," Brenda said, "only feel very, very strange about it. Very strange indeed."

"And so you should, my dear," Pearl assured her, leaning over the table and patting her hand. "When you are even a fragment of the Thirteen Orphans, feeling strange is the most natural thing in the world."

Soon after Brenda returned from lunch with Gaheris, Pearl called another meeting. This time when they settled around the long table, Riprap was restless.

"I'd hoped," he grumbled, "to make some amulets to replace those Brenda used last night."

"I understand," Pearl agreed. "We are all so much more aware of how vulnerable we are. Earlier we assessed the situation and what we had learned from it. Now we must plan how to take advantage of this new situation. The Dragon and the Snake are firmly bound, but if one of their allies chooses to defy them rather than honor our treaty, then we are all newly vulnerable once more."

"Nice trick," Des commented, "making the Dragon and the Snake responsible for the behavior of their own people."

"Thank you. It was necessary. Otherwise, all they needed to do was bring another of their number here."

Riprap was frowning at her. "But now that I think about it, Pearl, you took great pains to protect our friends and allies. Although you negotiated with the

Dragon to assure that our friends and allies would be safe, you overlooked our-selves."

Nissa cut in, "And Foster doesn't quite fall into 'friends and allies' category, does he? Or rather 'Foster' does, but not the person they think of as their Tiger. The Snake wants that Tiger very badly."

Pearl shook her head. "Overlooked? I did not. I knew without asking that our safety was a point on which the Dragon would not negotiate. He had already refused to return the stolen memories of the other nine of the Thirteen Orphans—even in order to free his daughter. How could I expect him to give up the op-portunity to complete the set? I rather suspect that if I had exhibited the temerity to suggest such a thing, the Dragon would have repeated that sad comment about there being other Snakes."

"True," Riprap said, "But I'm wondering . . . Did you have something else in mind? Did you mean to leave the Dragon wondering if, in your anxiety to protect friends and allies, you had overlooked something? He won't be sure, but he'll wonder."

"And so will the Snake," Nissa said. "And she's shown herself willing to act where her father would not. She's the one who has shown herself willing to chal-lenge our defenses—not her father."

Riprap leaned back and gave a gusty sigh, half admiration, half exasperation. "So that's why Pearl didn't write her treaty to include our personal immunity from attack. If she had done so, then the Dragon would have the right to request the same immunity for himself and the Snake. That would not suit your plan at all."

Pearl nodded. "And I do have a plan. We have now neutralized the threat that the Dragon held over those we love. That means the Snake is once again vulnerable—and, for all the Dragon spoke so lightly about there being other Snakes, there would be no replacing his daughter. We have bait to lure that Snake—a rather nice young man we call Foster. Moreover, Foster should be per-fectly safe in the role of snake bait, as he would be little good to her dead."

Des tugged at his mustache with the hand that was not resting on Bonaven-ture's back. "I wish I was so certain. I keep thinking of the story 'The Lady or the Tiger.'"

"Appropriate, I suppose. She is a lady, he a tiger. I recall Stockton's story as well. It is built around an ethical conundrum. The lady in question loves a man, but must choose between his being killed or being given in marriage to another woman. Yes. The story rather emphasizes that the lady in question might have a nasty enough temper to prefer him dead."

"So if the Snake can't recapture Foster," Des said with heavy patience, "she might try to harm him so that no one else—particularly our young Ratling, the same young woman who scotched the Snake's plans the last time—can have him."

Pearl glanced over at Brenda, but although a touch of color had risen to the young woman's ivory cheeks, her expression remained very neutral.

"So there is a risk to Foster," Pearl said. "But no greater than to any of us—less so, in fact. We will protect him and Brenda, if she will agree to partici-pate."

Brenda inclined her head slightly, and Riprap frowned, tapping one broad fingertip on the table.

"As I see your plan, when the Snake comes for Foster, we capture her. Then we offer her to her father in trade for the stolen memories."

"For them," Pearl agreed, "and, if at all possible, the means of restoring them to their owners. Des and I have not yet figured out how to break the spell with-out risking damage to the memories. Even if he would make a partial trade, we would be far ahead of where we are now."

"Your plan is interesting," Riprap admitted, "but it relies a great deal on the Snake acting as you predict. And the Dragon didn't make the trade when the Snake put herself into our hands. . . ."

"That time he had a means to threaten us," Pearl said. "As I said, our treaty has taken that from him—and I do not believe he will abandon his daughter. He might abandon 'the Snake,' perhaps, but not his daughter, Honey Dream."

"Perhaps," Riprap said, "but can we place so much on your guess as to how she will react?"

"If the Snake does not act of her own accord," Pearl said, glancing again at Brenda, "I believe we can prompt her. Young women in love are not rational."

There was a moment of awkward silence, and then Des laughed.

"Young men, either," Des said. "Young anythings. Actually, I'm not sure love is rational no matter what the age of those involved. Very well, we can try to lure the Snake."

★

Brenda listened as Pearl outlined her plan. She knew everyone expected her to be the one to protest, but she didn't intend to do so.

She hadn't liked Miss Honey Dream the Snake one bit. Not only had the Snake bragged about Foster being her "beloved," like that made him her prop-erty or something, but she'd used Dad like some sort of creepy puppet, and had tried to disable—maybe even kill—Brenda herself.

The idea of having the Snake's arrogance turned into the means of undoing their enemy's carefully worked out plans made Brenda quite happy. Anyhow, Brenda had something else to worry about, but she kept her peace until Des and Pearl were done.

After the plan had been outlined, Des and Pearl invited questions. Brenda didn't ask any, just listened intently, drawing elaborate curved designs of snakes on the pages of her notebook. She made them cross-eyed and rather stupid-looking, all twisted together after the fashion of Celtic knotwork.

Riprap had a few good questions about logistics. Nissa added her concerns that they might be overreaching themselves. Nissa also made quite clear she wasn't interested in taking part in any scheme that might remove the protections that had been placed around her daughter, sisters, and extended group of friends and family.

Brenda could feel when all gazes came to rest on her. She dotted in the eyes on her latest snake and looked up.

"What?"

"You've been very quiet, Brenda," Des said. "Do you have any questions?"

"No. Not really questions, at least. I have been wondering how we'll keep the Snake from getting suspicious that this is a trap. She's not only got us to worry about, she's got her dad, too. I met him, remember, and he's not going all hormonal over a cute guy. He's going to be suspicious, and even if he can't convince the Snake to stay clear, he's going to have made her more careful. I mean, I know I'd be more careful if for no other reason than I wouldn't want to screw up twice. If the Snake falls for this at all, it's going to be because she thinks she can pull it off, not because she can't keep her hands off Foster. I mean, she didn't come charging to the rescue until she came up with a plan she thought would work."

"Good point," Pearl said, "and something we should remember. Snakes are not as magical as dragons, but they are very, very cunning. So you have no problem with our using Foster—and possibly you—to draw the Snake out?"

"Nope, not as long as you and Des aren't automatically thinking the Snake is going to come running the moment Foster is outside the wards."

Pearl pressed, and Brenda didn't know whether to be amused or annoyed. "You understand that it puts not only each of us, but also Foster in jeopardy? Des and I will create amulets that will enable someone to watch you from a distance, and for help to arrive swiftly, but there will be a period of time when you must manage on your own."

"I followed that," Brenda said, deciding that she was amused, not annoyed.

Pearl studied her. "Then why do I have a feeling you're holding something back?"

Brenda met the older woman's gaze straight on. "Because I am, but it's not about this plan. I can live with it, even if I'm not sure it will work. What I want to talk about is something you and Des seem to have overlooked in your analysis of what happened last night."

Pearl looked momentarily offended, so much so that Brenda would not have been surprised to hear her snarl.

"Overlooked?"

"Yeah. My dad . . . and what the Snake was able to make him do. And what she or her dad might be able to make the others do—the other ones whose memories they have. They swore not to cause harm to them, but I think the treaty gives them a loophole of their own on that point. Would it be 'harm' to make one of the Twelve do something dangerous? I don't mean something like putting a gun to their own heads, just something not quite right—breaking into a house, for example. What about wandering out in traffic? I think that our families are pretty safe, but those nine whose memories the Dragon and the Snake still hold, they could be pretty vulnerable."

Pearl had pulled out a copy of the treaty, not one of the handwritten ones, but one of those run through the duplicating machine. Her eyes narrowed, and Brenda watched as they darted back and forth, reviewing certain lines.

"I hate to admit it," Pearl said, "but I may have made an error. If the Dragon and the Snake can manipulate the other nine through their captured memories—and we have good reason to believe they can—then our associates are indeed more vulnerable than I had imagined. How could I have overlooked that!"

Nissa bent a worried frown into a smile of reassurance. "Because you were snapped out of a solid night's sleep and into a fight? Because thinking about what had been done to Gaheris, who, after all, was safe upstairs, didn't seem as important as protecting those who were outside your wards?"

Pearl still looked annoyed at herself, but she nodded at Nissa. "I appreciate your kind words. Still . . ."

Brenda cut in. "Pearl. I didn't think of it either, then. It was only this afternoon that I started getting worried. Dad and I were out eating and chatting, and I was jumping at shadows, even though I knew it was unlikely anything would happen. But I got to thinking about how our friends and allies—especially those whose memories have been stolen—could be manipulated in ways that couldn't precisely be defined as harm."

Brenda took a deep breath and went on. "Look. I think your plan to use Foster as bait is a good one. In fact, I think we need to go with it more than ever, because if we just sit in this house protected by the strength of your and Nissa's wards, then the Snake and the Dragon are going to have no choice but to try and draw us out. The easiest way to do that would be to harm someone we care about."

Riprap cleared his throat. "I agree with Brenda. We're left with either attack or defense. Brenda has just shown us that our defense isn't as good as we thought. Let's attack—or rather, make them attack us directly, rather than through the others."

"I'm for it," Nissa said. "If they want to manipulate at least one of us and can touch those whose memories they don't hold, then Lani is an obvious target. I would never forgive myself if she was harmed or even frightened just to get at me."

Pearl's smile held both warmth and gratitude "Thank you, my young friends. I do appreciate your support—even when my shortcomings as a tactician have been made evident."

Riprap straightened in his chair. "Now that we're considering going on the attack, it occurs to me that there are options that weren't available to us until we knew who our adversaries were. Maybe I'm all wrong, and what I'm thinking about won't work."

Des said mildly, "We won't know until you tell us."

"I'm thinking about a more direct attack," Riprap said, "than drawing the Snake into our reach. Can't we find them? Find where they're staying? Go after them? Or is this useless? Are they commuting from their homeland to here magically?"

"Interesting," Des said, stroking his beard. "I doubt they are 'commuting,' as you put it, because passage between universes is not easy. That's why exile was a viable punishment. That means they are staying here, and possibly somewhere close."

"Chinatown?" Nissa asked. "San Francisco isn't that far away, and they could use public transport."

"That is one possibility," Des said, "and I can put some feelers out in the Chinese community there. I have a lot of friends there—as does Pearl."

Brenda leaned forward, elbows on the table. "You sound like you doubt they'd be there, though."

"Well, it's easy for us to talk about public transport," Des said, "but judging from how Foster initially reacted to cars and television, those haven't bled over into the Lands Born from Smoke and Sacrifice. Magic can give our enemies the ability to speak English, perhaps even some coping skills, but it's hard for me to imagine them hopping the BART or the intercity rail."

"Another reason," Des went on, "that I suspect they're staying closer to us, is that they would actually have more trouble blending into the Chinese community than elsewhere."

"Because," Nissa said, "their dialect of Chinese is strange. I bet their mannerisms are, too."

"Their clothing certainly was," Brenda added, "although maybe those were their working clothes, because they were doing magical stuff. They could have gone to a mall and gotten jeans or whatever."

Riprap barred his teeth in a smile that wasn't at all friendly. "And that raises the really interesting question of money. Can they make it magically, like fairy gold? Would their money last any better? In just about every fairy tale I remember, magical money turns back to leaves or dust."

"There's hell money," Des said. "Paper money that's burned at funerals, so the dead will not be poor. I wonder if what is burnt goes to the Lands?"

"I doubt it," Pearl said crisply. "If it did, then the people of the Lands Born from Smoke and Sacrifice would not only be hip-deep in paper currency, they would also have cars, computers, houses, stereo systems, cameras. I think you're letting your imagination go wild."

Des nodded, but didn't look in the least apologetic.

Riprap went back to his earlier point. "Money. Unless they're doing everything magically, the Dragon and the Snake will need some form of money. If they are doing everything magically, then isn't there some way you two can follow the signature? The first lesson Des gave me and Brenda was to ward ourselves before we worked on making those bracelets because things would come sniffing around. If the Snake and the Dragon are using magic for shelter, food, transportation, even clothing, then they're going to have left a magical signature—possibly a big one."

Pearl looked both interested and dubious. "There are ways of covering one's trail."

Des shook his head. "Most of those leave a mark of their own. It's like wiping out a physical trail with a pine branch. There's still the trail the branch left. Or wiping away fingerprints. The absence of prints is a sign all its own."

"You have always been more interested in theoretical magics than I," Pearl admitted. "I wish we had our Dragon. Shen Kung would be very useful now."

"Or the Monkey," Des said, "or the Ram. Both of those love trickery, but we lost them long ago."

Listening to them, Brenda was reminded of an earlier conversation.

"Back in Santa Fe," she said, "we talked about the possibility that our enemy could be one of us. Remember? I suspected the Dragon."

Everyone nodded, and Brenda went on.

"Well, we now know more about our enemies, and we also know that they can influence those whose memories they have taken. What if they're using their money, or their credit cards?"

Nissa grinned. "Brilliant! I hate to say this, Brenda, but your dad is an obvious choice. Is there any way you can get your mom to check his credit records? We might find charges for hotels or restaurants."

Brenda felt nervous about the very idea, but Nissa was right. Dad was an obvious target. He traveled so much that charges from weird places could show on his bill and the credit card companies wouldn't ask questions.

"I can ask about his cards," she said, "both business and personal. I can make some sort of excuse to Mom."

Pearl's expression mingled both interest and concern. "I can probably manage to get a few of the others to check their past charges and withdrawals. Given all the concern about identity theft and such, I'm sure I can come up with an excuse."

"We can split the list," Des said. "I do business with several of the Twelve. The problem is, what if one or more of them is a willing ally of our enemies? We can't overlook that."

"But we can't not check," Riprap argued. "Making them wonder if we're onto them might work for the good. They might get nervous, slip up, say something about something they shouldn't know anything about."

"I agree we need to check," Pearl said, "but who of the Twelve would turn traitor to the rest of us? What could the Snake and the Dragon offer? It's not like any of us think of that place as 'home' and want to return."

"Pearl, I know how you feel," Des said. "It's easy for Brenda and Riprap to talk about traitors in our own ranks. They don't know the people involved. However, I also agree that we can't overlook any means of finding out where our enemies might be based. Tracking the Snake and the Dragon to their lair must be our first priority."

Pearl cleared her throat. "When you put it that way, I must agree. However, I would like to keep all our options open and continue with efforts to lure the Snake."

No one protested, and Brenda felt her heart start racing. When Des and Pearl had presented their plan, implicit in it was that the Snake would be much more likely to come after Foster if she thought she was in danger of losing him to another woman. Brenda—who had already thwarted the Snake—was the obvious candidate for the role of romantic rival.

"Brenda?" Pearl said, turning to her.

"Yes?"

"Have you ever taken Foster walking in the Rosicrucian Museum's gardens?"

★

Pearl could feel that the mood within her household had changed. Even though similar tasks were being done, the sense of waiting, of preparing, had vanished.

In the upstairs "schoolroom," Riprap, Nissa, and Brenda still crafted their amulet bracelets and listened to Des's lectures, but this was no longer a theoretical exercise.

Brenda was crafting replacements for the Dragon's Tails and other spells that had kept her alive. Riprap was making not only pieces tailored to his personal needs, but more generic items that might be used by Foster. Nissa insisted that Lani needed amulets of her own. Since the mah-jong tiles the adults wore were too long to stay around Lani's tiny arms—even if pushed up over the elbow—Nissa had made much smaller molds and was carefully etching child-sized bracelets.

Pearl had practiced with Treaty just about every day of her life, but her fencing practice now held a new intensity. Brenda and Riprap demanded lessons, but Pearl forestalled them.

"Right now, you are better off with what Des is teaching you. Swordplay takes years to learn. You would be more of a danger to yourself than to anyone else. Do you have skill with another weapon?"

Riprap shrugged. "Sure. When I was in the army I learned to use firearms and fight hand-to-hand, but sword was not in the curriculum."

Brenda shook her head. "Nothing, unless a volleyball or soccer ball counts. But, Pearl, I didn't want to learn to use the sword to hurt anyone. I wanted to be able to defend myself if the Snake came at me with that knife of hers."

"Stick to spells," Pearl said. "They'll do a better job. It's only in the movies that a panicked novice pulls off brilliant parries against an expert."

"Pearl's right," Riprap said. "At this point, we might get mentally tangled in too many options."

Brenda didn't argue, but later, as Pearl was walking through the hallway from her office toward the kitchen, Brenda's voice came drifting from the upstairs classroom, asking Des if he could teach her a defensive spell stronger than the Dragon's Tail.

"The Snake's going to be ready for that one," Brenda said, "and probably will have something in hand to counter it. As she kept reminding me, her father's the Dragon."

"Then you're going to need spells that aren't based on dragons," came Des's reply. Although Pearl couldn't see him, she could imagine his long fingers tugging at his beard. "Perhaps we should avoid winds as well, since dragons can be winds, but that may limit our options too severely."

Pearl heard pages turning, Brenda's voice. "Winds and dragons are the two honors suits. Are there any powerful spells that don't use them?"

"Plenty," Des assured her. "Well, at least a few. I think you have made a good suggestion, but some of the ones I am considering cannot be worked by a beginner. I'll need to do them myself, or put Pearl to work."

"Seems like our ancestors could have arrived at a system with a little more variety," Brenda said. She sounded miffed, and Pearl didn't blame her.

"There is plenty of variety," Des said. "A skilled adept can work completely outside of the system represented by the mah-jong tiles."

"Like those sheets of paper that keep getting thrown at us?" Brenda asked.

"Precisely, but I don't think you're ready for those until your calligraphy is much better."

Pearl could hear the beginning of a lecture on the refinements of Chinese ideograms, and continued on toward the kitchen. In her imagination, Des's voice turned into her father's, lecturing her as she sat practicing her own calligraphy lessons.

"A stray line may change the meaning, girl! You write English so prettily. Your teachers always tell your mother this when she goes to the school. In English, a line can change an O into a Q, and F into an E. Why are you so stupid that you cannot see the same would be true in Chinese—the same and more so, because an ideogram is not just a sound, but an entire word."

Why? Pearl answered in thought as she never would never have dared in person. *Because I was already suspecting that you had little use for me, that you were training me because you had no choice.*

She distracted herself by pouring cold tea over ice. Her father had found that disgusting. Tea was meant to be drunk hot, not cold, certainly not diluted. As Pearl stood, listening to the ice cubes crack and settle, the door from outside opened. Foster came in, Lani clinging to his hand and chattering something about grapes, penguins, and very small rocks.

Foster gave Pearl a nod that was almost a short bow, his lips curving in a smile that was more friendly than it had been. Pearl smiled in reply, knowing the expression was stiff, but unable to relax. Except for that smile, Foster looked very much like pictures she had seen of her father when he was young.

A thought that had haunted the fringes of Pearl's mind since she had first seen Foster returned in that instant.

He looks like my father. . . . Are we kin then, perhaps close kin? My father was very young when he became the Tiger and was exiled soon thereafter, but he was not so young that he couldn't have fathered children. Foster could be his grandson or great-grandson, perhaps only a great-nephew or cousin. Even so, that would make him my nephew, great-nephew, cousin?

She shivered slightly, feeling the touch of a Tiger's paw passing over her grave.

Beneath the quiet yet increasingly intense activity of Pearl's household, Brenda was aware of another rumbling—this one within her own soul. She was beginning to suspect that she had fallen in love with Foster.

Oh, she'd been attracted to him from the first time she'd seen him—a figure in ornate green robes, incongruous against the dull grey metal and concrete of that LoDo parking garage. This was something else, a very fragile flower growing out of a soil made from little things Foster had done, not all—not even most—having to do with how he treated her.

This was Foster, sipping his first cup of black coffee, his face twisting in lines of dismay that started Lani hooting with laughter. This was Foster, features serene as he read one of the Chinese-language books from Pearl's library. This was Foster, washing dishes with a soapy rag, something in his motions saying that although he'd had to be shown how the liquid soap dispenser worked, these were far from the first dishes he had washed.

This was Foster, stretched out on his stomach on the bricks of the back patio, watching the ants carry off crumbs from his sandwich. This was Foster, playing

Yahtzee with Riprap, pounding the table in triumph as he rolled the double sixes he needed to complete five of a kind.

This was Foster, walking with her through the Rosicrucian gardens, enchanted equally by the statues of pharaohs and hybrid tea roses. This was Foster, taking her hand to help her jump a puddle after a sudden rain shower. This was Foster, walking away politely, unquestioningly every time Pearl or Des made clear that something must be discussed that he should not hear. There was honor in every line of that straight back, honor and loneliness, loneliness that shadowed his dark eyes, even when they filled with laughter.

Foster loved hearing stories of Brenda's life before this insane summer. The way he prompted her for anecdotes about her mother and brothers, Brenda knew that Foster was looking for some echo in his own soul that there was someone, somewhere to whom he belonged. In the Rosicrucian Museum they had looked at some terra-cotta statuettes, apparently solid, but one or two broken ones showing that they were actually hollow. Foster stared at one for a long time, and Brenda had heard him mutter in Chinese—a language he still occasionally forgot she understood—"I am like them, the shape of a man without, empty within."

So Brenda treasured Foster's smiles, the times she could make him laugh, the patience that echoed in his every motion as he learned new tasks. She hoped that the smiles, the shared laughter, the little triumphs might serve to fill his hollowness with new memories.

Their outings two, three, more times a day, alone or accompanied, were the rain that nourished the flower of Brenda's love for Foster. Mostly those outings were aimless walks where they looked at things, or practiced his English, or her Chinese. Brenda had found she could separate her brain from the spell, and commit words and phrases to her true memory. Foster enjoyed teaching her—or Nissa or Riprap. His command of the language was one of the few things that had not been taken from him by the spell that had robbed him of his memory.

I wonder how young Foster was when he became the Tiger—or began the training that would make him the Tiger. He must have been a child.

They went other places together. Sometimes Brenda borrowed a car and drove them to the grocery store or to one of the shopping malls. Contrary to common depictions of the amnesiac or the transported yokel, Foster did not gape at the strangeness of modern American life. To him everything was equally strange, and television had prepared him to accept the world outside the walls of Pearl's house as brightly colored, noisy, and always a little artificial.

Brenda felt safer when they were shopping than when they were on one of their walks. No one expected the Snake to make her play for Foster when there were other people around. Brenda had accepted this, without question, but Rip-rap, who was always asking questions, asked Des during one of their lessons if they weren't putting what Riprap had termed "civilians" at risk by letting Foster go out in public.

Des laughed, not mockingly, just as one does who realizes he's forgotten to pass on some basic piece of information.

"I think I've mentioned that the Thirteen Orphans are not the only people in the world who can do magic?"

Riprap shrugged. "You have, but I haven't much thought about it. Until I met you folks, I didn't know that anyone really could work magic."

Des turned serious. "Almost every culture has its traditions, but some are stronger than others. These days there is one constant in each tradition, however. You might call it a rule. 'Don't get caught.' "

"Why?" Brenda and Nissa asked simultaneously, then giggled.

"Think about it," Des said. "Think about the response most people would give to magic. It's not that long ago that people burned witches in this country. There's a veneer of tolerance now, but the fact is the only reason that psychics and fortune tellers and New Age witches are permitted to live and let live is no one really believes they can do anything. That dam of disbelief is all of our best pro-tection. If someone starts acting wild, enforcers, I guess you'd call them, start by warning and finish by, well, finishing."

Nissa and Riprap asked a lot of questions, but other than gathering that prac-titioners of any functional magical tradition were pretty rare, Brenda didn't dwell on too many of the details. It was enough to know that as long as they didn't do anything too outrageous, they'd be left to go about their business.

It also gave yet another reason why the Snake and the Dragon had been as subtle as they had been. Des figured they knew about the "Don't get caught" rule.

But none of this, fascinating as it was, intellectually, changed how Brenda felt, was starting to feel, no, *felt* about Foster. She loved him, and she thought he might be coming to care about her, too.

And so she was very vulnerable when near the end of June the Snake made her move.

Brenda and Foster had driven to a park that was nowhere in particular, one of those urban open spaces with paths enough for walking. They'd discovered this one completely by accident when running an errand for Des. The car's front tire had gone flat, and they'd pulled into the park's small lot to fix it.

It had seemed a pleasant place, with oversized flowerpots spilling multicolored petunias down their sides, and winding paths that went nowhere in particular.

There was a children's play area, and a neatly mowed field just perfect for throwing something for a dog to chase. On weekends the park was pretty busy, but midday in the middle of the week, even in summer, it was usually fairly empty.

Brenda and Foster were sitting on a couple of swings, resting after a fierce competition as to who could get higher—a competition that had been decided as a draw when the chains from which the seats were suspended had started bucking in protest at the demands being put on them.

Brenda was about to suggest that they go across the street to a little strip mall where there was an ice cream shop that made—so she'd discovered on an earlier visit—really good milkshakes. She was trying to figure out whether she had enough pocket money to cover them both, or if she should hit an ATM first, when she saw the Snake sauntering across the mowed field in their direction.

The Snake wasn't dressed at all like the last time Brenda had seen her. Her long, midnight-black hair was loose, spilling in a silken cascade over her shoulders, down past the middle of her back. Gone were the ornate robes, gone the embroidery. Instead, the Snake wore a pair of very low-waisted, very short shorts, and a middie top that displayed the up-thrusting curves of her breasts and the indented curve of her waist to equal advantage. The only emblems of her identity were a snake tattooed around her belly button, and another one tattooed around her right ankle. Neither ornament was large, but the sinuous outline was so exquisitely worked that Brenda had no doubt what the lines depicted, even from a distance.

Brenda had dressed with some care for her outing with Foster, figuring that even if he did sometimes glimpse her frumping around Pearl's house in her bathrobe or in the less than elegant T-shirt and jeans she wore to spare her better clothes from ink stains when practicing calligraphy, it didn't hurt to remind him she was a girl. The tank top she'd picked out was in a ribbed knit that showed off what breasts she had to good advantage. Her shorts were a practical khaki, but the tank top was a shade of lavender that made the golden-brown of her skin glow. Brenda had put on lavender jade teardrop earrings, and even a touch of perfume—in addition to, of course, a selection of amulet bracelets.

Compared with the elegant sensuality coming across the lawn, Brenda felt gawky. It didn't help that Foster's attention immediately shifted to the newcomer, or that he kept staring. Brenda glanced over at him. Puzzlement had drawn a line between his brows, as if some memory had been touched. Somehow, the thought that memories of the Snake could penetrate where nothing else had managed to do so hurt Brenda even more.

The only good thing Brenda could see was that the Snake's outfit was so skimpy there was no way she could even hide a slip of paper in it. Then the Snake moved her right hand, and Brenda saw what looked like an envelope concealed in the curve of her palm.

Quick as thought, Brenda slipped one of the amulet bracelets off her wrist and held it ready in her hand. It contained an expanded version of the Dragon's Tail spell, worked so that it would shield both her and Foster—as long as he stayed within a few paces of her, something Brenda was not at all certain he was going to do.

Foster had risen to his feet, and was studying the Snake with such intensity that he didn't seem to notice the swing seat gently tapping the back of his legs. Brenda also rose, wondering if anyone at Pearl's was alert to the changed situation. She hoped so—or did she? Might it be better to know what the Snake wanted before the cavalry arrived?

The Snake practically caressed Foster with her gaze. "Hello, Fei Chao. Do you remember me?"

Brenda's ears heard the Chinese, but her magically augmented vocabulary provided an automatic translation: Flying Claw. Was that Foster's real name?

Foster looked confused. "I . . . I almost think I do. Are you a movie star? Did I perhaps see you on the television?"

Brenda saw a mixture of pleasure and disappointment flicker across the Snake's face. No wonder. Even if Foster hadn't known her right off, he'd still thought she was a movie star.

"Foster," the Snake said softly. "That's what they call you, right? Foster. I want to talk to Brenda for a moment. Girl talk. Can you step back?"

Foster glanced at Brenda. Brenda shifted the bracelet in her hand. If Foster moved too far, she couldn't protect him, but hearing what the Snake didn't want him to hear might endanger them both.

Brenda nodded. "Go ahead. We won't be long."

Foster moved a few paces away, where he would be out of earshot, but not, Brenda noticed, so far that he had to abandon his intense scrutiny of the Snake.

The Snake's gaze took a moment to shift back to Brenda, then the Snake said, "You're right. We won't be long. I know you probably sent some sort of alarm to your allies when you realized who I was. Despite this, I have made certain that we should have time enough for me to tell you something—to make you an offer. An offer between you and me, me and you."

"An offer I can't refuse?" Brenda said caustically. "Go on."

"The Chinese are great bargainers," the Snake said, "as you would know, if you were something other than a mongrel. Here is my offer, very plain and simple.

An offer from me, to you. I want Foster and I want the crystal that holds his memory. I could take his body here and now, but without his memory, he might be of some use . . ."

Her smile was slow and lascivious. She ran the tip of her tongue over her lips while Brenda burned with a mixture of anger and embarrassment.

"But," the Snake went on, meeting Brenda's gaze and holding it so that nothing in the universe seemed to exist but the two of them, "Flying Claw would not be himself, and I want him all—mind and body. If you bring both Foster and his memory to me, then in return I will give you the crystal holding your father's memory. I will also give you an amulet holding the spell that would permit you to free Gaheris's memory and return it to him."

Brenda felt her jaw drop. She'd expected a fight. She'd expected threats. She'd never expected this. Her head felt light, and clear thought was difficult, but she managed to ask a coherent question.

"Your father refused to trade the crystals to Pearl to gain your safety. Why should he let you do this now?"

"This is not a bargain between your Tiger and my Dragon. You are not talking to my father. You are talking to the Snake." There was bitterness in Honey Dream's voice. "This is between me and you, you and me, remember? Perhaps I want Flying Claw more than my father wanted me."

Brenda remembered the Dragon's cool voice saying, "There can be other Snakes," and understood that bitterness. She also noticed something interesting. The Snake was assuming that Brenda would not talk to the others about this. Perhaps her anger at her father blinded her to Brenda's different position. Considering this, Brenda pressed for details, wondering if her allies would show up, despite the Snake's precautions.

"How do I know you wouldn't trick me? Give me a false Rat crystal or an incomplete spell?"

"How do I know you wouldn't trick me?" the Snake countered. Her gaze had fixed on Brenda with such intensity that Brenda felt her head swim. "How do I know if you love your father enough to want him whole again? Perhaps you like him this way more. You and I would need to trust each other."

"I would need time," Brenda said. "Pearl keeps Foster's memory locked up in her keeping. I don't even know where, except that it's probably in either her bedroom or her office."

"Time." The Snake shrugged one shoulder. "Perhaps you have plenty. Perhaps not. My father is not precisely confiding these days. However, he will not be dissuaded from his goal for long."

"And that is?"

"He wants a set of twelve memories," the Snake hissed. "And once he has them, I can use them to find where Flying Claw's memory is hidden. This Pearl's memory would be at my disposal. But I would prefer not to wait."

Because she's not sure her father will let her rescue Foster, Brenda thought. *Once Righteous Drum has what he wants, he may just drag her off home.*

"I'll think about it," Brenda said.

"Don't think too long," the Snake said. "When you have the crystal, put something red in your hair when you next walk out with Foster. I will then make arrangements for when and where you should meet me. And don't think you can trick me. This is between me and you, you and me. I'll be able to tell if you have the crystal."

Brenda didn't know if the other woman was bluffing, but she nodded, trying to look appropriately intimidated. That last wasn't hard—she *was* intimidated.

The Snake had been talking very fast, so the exchange had taken only a few minutes.

"Think about it," the Snake said, "but like I said, don't think too long."

She turned and waved to Foster. "Bye-bye, Flying Claw. I'll see you again, soon. . . ."

Foster hurried over, but the Snake was already retreating, her undulating walk slow, but somehow covering a great deal of distance. Brenda suspected magic was involved.

"Wait!" Foster called after the Snake. "Why do you call me that name? Who are you? Do I know you?"

But the Snake neither turned nor looked back.

Brenda saw the hope on Foster's face fade, his expression changing to one of hurt and frustration.

"Who was she?" he asked no one in particular, but Brenda decided to answer.

"Just a snake in the grass . . . a real snake in the grass."

When they got back to Pearl's house, Brenda asked a few questions, and managed to ascertain without giving anything away that no one knew anything about her encounter with the Snake.

Pearl was at a committee meeting, so she'd been out of the loop, but Des, who had been at the house, seemed unaware that anything had happened. He was wearing the amulet bracelet that should have alerted him, so Brenda was forced to assume that the Snake had been successful in temporarily blocking the snooping spells. It shouldn't have been too hard. It wasn't like whoever was on watch sat and stared at a TV screen, watching whatever Brenda and Foster were doing. Their small group was stretched too thin to manage that kind of surveillance, especially when Brenda and Foster's outings lasted for hours at a time.

Spell jamming made sense in a weird way, but when Brenda found herself thinking how ugly things could have gotten if the Snake had wanted to do more than talk and no backup had shown, she got cold inside. Then again, maybe if the Snake had tried to do anything other than talk, that would have broken through whatever jamming device—might as well think of it that way—the Snake had set up. The lack of backup was worrisome, but not nearly as worrisome as the decisions Brenda needed to make.

On the drive back to Pearl's house, Brenda had convinced Foster not to mention the Snake to the others. It hadn't been hard. Foster was smart, and he was all too aware that his freedom to leave Pearl's house was based on his behaving in a trustworthy fashion.

If the three adults who were at home noticed that both Foster and Brenda were distracted and a bit tense when they came in, and that the pair avoided each other afterward no one commented.

Brenda wondered if they put it down to a lover's spat. That thought annoyed Brenda almost as much as the Snake had. It was bad enough that her friends thought she and Foster were closer than they were without having to deal with their quiet sniggering.

Damn it! she thought. *Foster hasn't even really held my hand, and he certainly hasn't kissed me. I'm not sure he even likes me as much as I'd hoped. I mean, the way he looked at the Snake . . .*

Brenda shook herself. A man who wouldn't look at the Snake was probably either dead or neuter, and neither interested her in the least. She'd just need to do her best to prove to Foster that she was worth looking at. . . .

Looking, she thought. *Looking isn't what I want, but how do I know that this man I think I love is really the man I think he is? How do I know that he wouldn't be happier if I just let him go? And even if I decide to let him go, will the others agree?*

★

When the knock came on her office door, Pearl wasn't at all surprised. According to Des, Brenda had been tense and miserable since her return from the park earlier that afternoon. Now here was Brenda, looking like someone who had made a difficult decision.

"Pearl, can I talk with you, privately?"

"Sit," Pearl said, coming from around her desk and motioning toward the more comfortable sitting area. "I just brewed tea. May I pour you some?"

"No thanks. I got myself some lemonade before coming in."

Brenda set the glass on a table next to the chair Pearl had indicated. As they settled themselves, Amala and Bonaventure appeared, each cat claiming a lap.

"They must know we're going to have a long talk," Pearl said, encouraging confidences with her tone.

Brenda ran a hand down Amala's spine. "Pearl, the Snake came to the park today."

Quickly, and with a conciseness that told Pearl the girl must have been rehearsing what she was going to say for hours, Brenda gave an account of the Snake's visit.

"Foster's memory in exchange for Gaheris's," Pearl said. "Interesting. Are you willing to try it?"

Brenda looked sad. "I don't see that I have a choice. My dad is being used. He has been given a sort of lobotomy. And Foster . . . He was just starting to get used to this weird new life of his, but seeing the Snake tore him up."

"Did he recognize her?"

"No. But she knew him—or acted like she did. Hell! I know she recognized him, and he knew she did, too. It made him miserable, knowing she knew all those things he wants to know but can't remember."

Pearl saw the anguish in Brenda's eyes and deliberately shifted the discussion to practicalities. "If she trades Gaheris's memory to you, the Snake would be risking her father's anger. Or do you think she was only pretending to be working behind his back—that she has her father's approval after all?"

"I think the Snake's working on her own," Brenda said, "just like she assumed I would be doing. She kept saying the deal was between just the two of us. I'm guessing that whatever spell she worked that kept Des from knowing what was going on would also have kept her father from snooping. I've tried to work out what the Snake is planning. My guess is that she has some idea that when she has Foster back, she can recapture both the crystal with my dad's memory and the spell amulet. Then she would have gotten what she wanted without losing anything."

"Do you think she could pull it off?"

Brenda nodded, showing a lack of conceit that Pearl found endearing.

"Of course she could, Auntie Pearl. I'm a trainee. She's the Snake. Foster is their Tiger. My guess is that the Snake expects me to act pretty much in the same way she is—to behave like some idiot out of a girls' adventure novel, swipe the crystal containing Foster's memory from you, come out in the middle of the night, whatever. We'd rendezvous by midnight or some time where the Snake would have the edge. Once she had broken the spell on Foster, they'd both go for me and I'd need to surrender Dad's memory again—and maybe more."

"You sound very certain," Pearl said mildly.

Brenda tugged at the tip of one of Amala's ears. The cat twitched her tail in annoyance, and Brenda gave a sheepish grin.

"Maybe I'm so sure because I came pretty close to doing just that. I figured I could learn where you and Des have the crystal, and come up with some clever plan to get it. Then I realized how stupid I was being. If you have wards up against magic being used here without your permission, you must have the crystal protected. And how would I explain afterwards, when Dad's memory was suddenly intact and Foster was gone?"

"So you came to me instead—even though this was a deal between the two of you."

"The Snake said that, not me. Pearl, I don't want to give Foster up, but how could I leave Dad the way he is? He's like a caricature of himself—and he's vulnerable to their manipulations as well. We know that. And besides . . ."

Suddenly Brenda looked much older than her years.

"How can I talk about giving Foster up when I don't really have him? Nissa's been trying to get me to face reality, but I haven't wanted to listen. Today, though, today that Snake called him Flying Claw. She knows his name. She probably knows his mother's name. His father's name. If he has brothers and sisters. What his favorite food is. The more I thought about it, all that seemed a lot more intimate than if they're lovers or engaged or anything. She knows his past. All I know is a really handsome, kind, in-over-his-head guy who might not even think of me any more affectionately than he does Nissa—or Lani!"

Pearl was fairly certain that Foster felt differently about Brenda than he did about the other women in the household, but what good would come from her saying so? Brenda had made the decision to give up her lovely illusion. That was what she needed to do, what Pearl had been hoping she would do. Why then did Pearl feel so sad?

Pearl shook her head as if she could physically clear a thought, then sipped her tea to give herself time to consider.

"Brenda, you arranged a delay with the Snake?"

"I did. I mean, I had to, didn't I?"

"Then we must think how to use this to our advantage. When he has not been studying or making amulet bracelets, Riprap has been following through on his plan to see if he can find where the Dragon and the Snake are staying. If we could find where they are living, then I think we could use this."

"Is Riprap having any luck?"

"Only in the negative. We are fairly certain that our enemies do not have access to the type of electronic credit they would need for a major hotel. The current rash of fear regarding identity theft proved extremely useful in testing that. In some cases, where Des or I had a strong contact with one of the vulnerable nine, we simply called and told them to check for unexpected charges—especially coming out of this area. We spun a good yarn about a scam we'd learned about.

"In other cases, Riprap simply called and posed as an independent auditor for major credit holders. He was adamant about not wanting to know any details about any accounts, simply requesting that they review their accounts and let him call them back. Again, he used the story that someone was making the charges in northern California."

"And it worked?"

"Riprap can sound very convincing, and I helped him with his script. Since he told those he called that he did not want any identifying information, not even the type of card or cards they held, they were inclined to go along with it."

"I guess I would," Brenda admitted. "I mean, I'd worry."

"Exactly."

"So probably they're not staying at a major hotel—or even a minor one."

"That's right. Most will insist on a credit card in case you use the phone or do something that will run up charges. You can still pay in cash if you want, but they're going to protect their interests in advance."

"How are you handling the less fine establishments?" Brenda asked.

"Des and Riprap have done some drive-by snooping. Depending on the place and its tone, they ask questions. Des uses a touch of magic—nothing too powerful, just looking for signs that someone else is or has been using magic in the area. Again, we've come up with nothing. Nissa has been tracking down less formal rental options. She represents herself as a student, hoping to rent a room or a suite for a week or two."

Brenda nodded. "Seems hopeless. Maybe we should give in to the Snake, give her Foster's memory, and then do our best to learn from Dad—if we get him back—if he knows anything."

Pearl kept her tone gentle, hearing despair in Brenda's voice. "He probably wouldn't. I think the Snake would make sure of that."

"Yeah." Brenda rose and carefully set Amala on her chair. The cat curled into a ball, taking advantage of the warm spot. "I think we'd better fill the others in. Should I get them?"

Pearl nodded. "Nissa should be done putting Lani to bed, and I decreed a moratorium on any amulet crafting after dinner. Riprap in particular seems to have forgotten that absolute concentration is necessary to incorporate the spells correctly. The amulets cannot be churned out in a production line."

"He's scared, Pearl," Brenda said. "So am I."

"So am I, my dear," Pearl said softly. "More than you know, so am I."

"It seems to me," Des said after Brenda had finished her report and their small group had briefly discussed how they might take advantage of the situation, "that the Snake tried to hypnotize Brenda into keeping this matter to herself. Hypnotism is a traditional power of the snake, but the Snake would not have known that Brenda is at least a little bit the Rat, and so has the power to resist."

"Resist because she is a little the Rat," Riprap asked, "or because she's a little one of the Twelve?"

"The Rat specifically," Des said. "Although all the Twelve would have more ability to resist than would the average person, the Rat has even greater ability. Birds," he gave a deprecating little shrug, "are the most vulnerable, as are those who are ruled by emotion. The Rat is among the most intellectual and calculating of the Earthly Branches."

Brenda forced a grin. "If the Snake thinks I'm head over heels for Foster, not to mention a wreck because my dad is messed up, well, then she probably has every reason to think I'm ruled by my emotions."

And who's to say I'm not? I came close enough to giving in. I should have told someone right away about what happened, but instead I wanted Foster to keep quiet, and nearly didn't confide in anyone. If Pearl wasn't "Auntie," if I'd felt resentful of the others—maybe because they were "real" members of the group and me just a hanger-on—I could have fallen so easily.

Those thoughts were still vivid in Brenda's mind when she walked out the door four days later, Foster beside her, car keys dangling from one hand, a duffel bag that sagged heavily from the other. The garage was empty except for the little sedan Pearl had rented when relying on the chauffeur-driven town car was clearly not enough for her expanded household's needs.

If anyone had been watching earlier that morning, they would have seen Hastings drive Pearl, Nissa, and Lani off at about eight o'clock. They would have seen Riprap and Des, both dressed in running clothes, jog off a little later, heading in the direction of a small strip-mall gym.

We're the last, Brenda thought, glancing at her watch. It was approaching nine o'clock, the start of the Double Hour of the Snake. *Pearl predicted the Snake would pick this time. I hope she's as right in the rest of her suppositions.*

So many of their plans had needed to be based on guesswork. If even one of those guesses was incorrect, so much could go wrong. Brenda stashed the duffel in the backseat, then got into the driver's seat and slid the key in the ignition.

"Buckle up," she reminded Foster.

After all, she thought, uncomfortably aware of the hard, round crystal sphere that held his memory pressing against her hip where she'd stuffed it into her jean's pocket, *it would be a shame to lose you to a traffic accident when you're closer than you know to getting back everything you want.*

Foster snapped the belt into place.

"Sorry," he said. "I was thinking."

He spoke English, his accent on that particular phrase an unwitting mimicry of Des, who said it so often it had become a joke.

"Well," Brenda said. "You've had a lot to think about lately, haven't you?"

She backed the sedan out onto the side street, checking carefully for oncoming traffic. The Rosicrucian Museum didn't come close to having enough parking, given the popularity of its gardens, exhibits, and lectures. The already narrow side streets were further narrowed by parked cars, and in her few weeks' residence, Brenda had learned from a few terrifying encounters that any moment might bring a confused tourist barreling along far more rapidly than was wise.

Once they were out on the wider streets, Brenda reached up and touched the red ribbon in her hair. A tingle of déjà vu ran through her fingertips as she did so. This was the second time she had worn that unaccustomed ornament. Two days ago had been the first, when she'd gone out to signal to the Snake that she was ready to make a deal.

That time they hadn't seen the Snake. Instead, Brenda's cell phone had rung after they'd strolled a couple of blocks from Pearl's house.

Clipped and sounding, so Brenda thought, a touch nervous, the Snake had said, "Ready to deal, then."

"That's right," Brenda said, glancing over at Foster. He showed no interest in her call, having grown accustomed to the phone ringing at odd times, since Brenda's mom and friends regularly called to chat.

"Fine. Two days from now. Nine o'clock in the morning. Go to . . ." The Snake named a big shopping center Brenda was already familiar with. "Go to the shop that sells teaching toys: Bright Futures is its name."

"You'll be there?" Brenda asked. "Are they open that early?"

"They are. Go there. Come alone, except for Foster. Understand?"

The connection was cut off. Brenda sighed and slid the phone back into its holster. Foster continued walking, oblivious of the fact that Brenda was now "back." He'd been distracted since their encounter with the Snake, as if drawn into what fragmentary memory he possessed, trying to draw lines between the dots and come up with at least an outline of who he was.

Today, as then, Brenda longed to reach out and touch Foster, even if just to stroke his hair as she might have done with one of her brothers—before they'd reached they age when they'd get indignant about such "soft" stuff. But her feelings about Foster were too unruly, too uncertainly certain. She didn't dare.

Occupied as she was with her thoughts, Brenda almost missed the turn into the mall. Her head was hammering with the beat of her pulse and her palms were sweaty as she parked the car. Foster looked at their surroundings with some interest.

"I didn't know we were coming here," he said, and there was apology for his distraction in his voice.

Brenda had already thought of a reason. "Nissa and I thought Lani might need cheering up after today's screen test. Pearl has tried to explain that winning a screen role is not as certain as Lani seems to think. I guess she's been read too many stories where, despite the odds, the plucky little girl gets picked for the team or the club or whatever."

Foster understood about screen tests. They had been a major topic of conversation of late, ever since Pearl's agent had surprised them all by lining up several opportunities for Lani. Foster smiled now, his fondness for the little girl pushing away his moody abstraction. He spoke in Chinese, evidence that he was eager to communicate something more complex than his English could manage.

"Everyone is the hero of his own story, I think. Lani is small, but she is no different. So we will get her something, so she will not be too sad. That's a good idea."

"And maybe," Brenda said, forcing herself to sound cheerful, "Lani won't have reason to be sad."

But she will, Brenda thought, her heart giving an aching twist, *because even if everything goes perfectly right, the Foster who has been her friend, her playmate, will have vanished. Instead there will be a stranger, Flying Claw, the Tiger.*

Brenda forced herself not to think about that. The Snake was likely watching, whether in person or through some spell. Foster had brightened in anticipation of shopping for a treat for Lani, and he walked beside Brenda commenting on the weather, what their budget was for the gift, and similar trivialities. Brenda managed to keep up with his chatter, not wanting him to think she was being quiet because he'd annoyed her with his former withdrawn mood.

Only minutes left, Brenda thought. *Just a few more minutes. Then he'll be gone. . . .*

When they entered Bright Futures, Brenda glanced around for any sign of the Snake. There were two clerks: an older woman whom Brenda knew from past conversations was a retired grammar-school teacher, and a young man with "summer help" all but tattooed across his broad shoulders. He was helping a round-faced Hispanic woman with something at the register, while the former teacher assisted a tired-looking balding man who was looking with mild embarrassment at an array of dolls.

Brenda nodded to the former teacher, following Foster as he made a beeline to the section he already knew had toys appropriate for a child of Lani's age. Brenda was just passing the register when the phone at the checkout counter rang. The male clerk answered it, looked mildly confused, then glanced over at Brenda.

"Would your name be Brenda Morris?"

"Yes."

"I have a call for you."

Brenda took the phone, and heard the Snake's voice. "Go from that store to this park."

Honey Dream gave directions, and Brenda knew the place immediately. It was much like the park in which they'd first encountered the Snake, but more isolated, screened by trees that had grown thick with time and neglect. It was a perfect place not to be noticed.

"Bring Foster," the Snake continued, "but no one else. Be there by nine thirty."

Brenda glanced at her watch. She could manage, even if they stopped long enough to buy something for Lani.

"Right," she said, but the connection had already gone dead.

Brenda handed the phone back to the clerk. "Sorry to bother you. Someone wanted to reach me, and my cell phone wasn't picking up. They knew I was coming here. . . ."

She shrugged and the clerk grinned in understanding. "My phone was always doing that until I got some really good batteries. The ones they give you with the phones are crap."

Brenda nodded, thanked him again, and went after Foster. As she did so, she pulled out her phone and punched various buttons. It was working fine. The Snake must have wanted to confirm that Brenda was where she was, when she had said she would be there. Interesting. That might indicate that the Snake's resources were stretched, perhaps preparing something against Brenda and Foster's arrival. It might also indicate that the Snake didn't want to do anything magical that would attract her father's attention.

And it might mean nothing at all, Brenda reminded herself.

Foster was holding two different counting and alphabet games, one in each hand, trying to figure out what made one better than the other, handicapped by his inability to read the glowing reviews printed on the packaging.

"That was Nissa," Brenda half lied. "She reminded me that Lani had been particularly interested in this game . . ." She tapped one box. ". . . last time we were here."

Foster nodded, replying in Chinese. "I thought so. I could not be sure. I wish that Pearl could make me read English as she made you understand my speech."

"Soon you'll be so good," Brenda decided not to say at what, "that it won't matter. Shall we get this one?"

Foster put down the rejected game and led the way to the checkout counter. Brenda paid, and tried to sound casual as they walked back to the car.

"There's a nice park not too far from here. Want to go for a walk before we head back?"

Foster agreed readily. Brenda had thought he'd get tired of their walks, but he never seemed to do so.

Maybe he's making up for all that time he spent under "house arrest." Maybe his body remembers what his mind doesn't—that he had to have lived a pretty active life before we got ahold of him. Those muscles didn't come from sitting around and being fed chocolates by pretty girls. I wonder if he'll miss chocolate? Do they even have it in the Lands?

Brenda realized she had lagged behind when Foster reached out and caught her hand in his.

"Come on!" he said in English, then switched to Chinese. "Worrying won't help Lani on her screen test, and you're prettiest when you smile."

Brenda thought about pulling her hand away, but squeezed his in return.

Last chance. Why not enjoy it? And if the Snake's watching, I bet her cold heart is burning hot as fire!

✩

"Lani will be fine," Pearl promised Nissa, as they got back into the car after dropping the girl off with one of Pearl's professional contacts—a hairdresser and makeup artist who doubled as a sort of stage mother. "We couldn't leave Lani at the house, not even with the gardener. Besides, you need some films to show Bob the Pharmacist, right?"

"But . . ."

"Don't worry. Lani's a good girl, and quite capable. Joanne will watch out for her—and take it from me, sometimes it's easier to perform your best when your mama isn't watching."

Nissa bowed her head, her luminous turquoise eyes shut, her features composing into resignation. Pearl leaned forward and spoke to the driver.

"Take us to the edge of Japantown, Hastings." She gave him a street address, heard his acknowledging "Yes, madam," and slid the privacy panel shut.

"You're right, Pearl." Nissa straightened against the leather upholstery, squaring her shoulders. "Besides, if we don't deal with these distant relations of ours, whether or not Lani has her mother's hand to hold this morning won't matter much."

Pearl was startled. "Distant relations? Is that how you think of them?"

"Sure. Isn't that what they are?"

Pearl pursed her lips. "Rivals rather."

"But you said you knew who Foster must be because he looked like your father. That argues he's a relative."

"Or that I'm so twisted," Pearl said, not caring to admit she had thought the same thing, "that I see my father in every handsome young man of a certain type."

Nissa gave Pearl a sideways glance that said more eloquently than any words that she wasn't going to argue the point. Instead, she looked at the passing view through the tinted window.

"I'm impressed that Riprap tracked down where the Snake and the Dragon are staying. Do you think they will have gotten wind of us?"

"I don't think so," Pearl said. "We've told no one what we've learned, and I don't think their ability to spy extends to inside my house. We've arranged to meet as indirectly as possible, so that no curiosity should be aroused."

"And will Brenda be all right?"

"That is a good question," Pearl said. "She agreed to turn over Foster and his memory. She has agreed to let them 'take back' Gaheris's crystal if that is necessary. Thus far both the Snake and the Dragon have taken care not to do physical harm."

"Except when the Snake came after Brenda with that dagger," Nissa reminded her.

"She was panicked and trapped," Pearl said with more confidence than she felt. "In this situation, Brenda should be completely nonthreatening. And, in any case, we've loaded Brenda with enough protective amulets that she could probably walk across a highway at rush hour and not get hit."

"True," Nissa said, but she nibbled at the edge of one fingernail, a nervous gnawing that was really quite rabbitlike.

The intercom hummed to life. "We are nearly at our destination, madam."

"Very good. Pull over wherever you can manage, then go your way. I will call if I need to be picked up."

"Very good, madam."

"And, please, Hastings, stop with the Jeeves imitations."

"Yes, madam," he said, but he was chuckling.

Hastings parked and hopped out to help Pearl from the car, handing her the long, narrow leather sword case he had taken from the trunk. As Pearl slid the broad strap over her shoulder and adjusted the weight down her back, Nissa slipped out of the car and dropped a wrapped mint into Hastings's hand.

"Your tip, sir."

He grinned, and said in a deep, sonorous voice, "Madam is too kind."

As the car pulled away, Nissa looked around. "Japantown doesn't look like much. I expected, I don't know, something other than a few restaurants."

"The area was more flourishing some years ago," Pearl said, starting off down the sidewalk. "And actually there are some very nice curio shops, and, of course, our destination. However, time changes neighborhoods, and Japantown never was the tourist destination that Chinatown in San Francisco is. It was simply an area with a large immigrant population. It still is. The immigrants are what has changed."

Nissa sniffed appreciatively at the food smells coming from a Mexican restaurant that, although the "Closed" sign still hung in the window, was probably preparing for lunch.

"Not all change is bad," she said. "I just expected something else."

"Yes, but the very polyglot nature of this area is what made it perfect for our . . ." Pearl paused, then borrowed Nissa's phrase: ". . . distant relations. It is not unified either by culture or economic standing. They must have known they would be odd, so they chose to base themselves in an area where everyone would be at least a little odd."

Nissa chuckled. "At home in Virginia, that's pretty much the definition of California: the state where everyone is a little odd."

Pearl nodded, feeling a native Californian's pride in her home state. "That's why it's such a good place to be."

She turned the corner and took a few steps. Within a moment she heard Nissa's soft gasp. "Who would have thought!"

Pearl had to admit, the sight was all the more striking for its setting. There, in the middle of an otherwise perfectly ordinary semiresidential, semicommercial neighborhood, stood an elegant Buddhist temple, curving roof, sculptured pillars and all. A mediation garden, small but perfect, stood to one side, water spilling from a simple fountain.

"It's absolutely lovely!" Nissa gasped. "I thought that the Rosicrucians with their Egyptian statues had cured me of ever being startled, but this . . . It's like someplace from another world dropped in a very ordinary city block."

"And doubtless," Pearl said, "that is why our distant relatives chose to dwell nearby. An anomalous place will attract anomalous people."

"Is that why you live near the Rosicrucian temple?"

Pearl gave a slow cat's smile, narrowing her eyes. "Maybe so. Shall we go across and see if the gentlemen are here?"

They had hardly crossed the street when Riprap and Des emerged from the shelter of some of the abundant greenery.

"There's a service of some sort going on in the temple," Riprap explained. "Didn't want to bother anyone."

"We've stayed under cover," Des added. "And I have—with great difficulty—restrained the urge to snoop."

Both men were dressed in summer-weight slacks and polo shirts. The running clothes they had been wearing when they left were in the bag that dangled from Riprap's hand. He looked at the long case Pearl braced slightly with a thumb on the strap.

"Want me to carry that?"

"I'm fine," she said, and was. Treaty's weight was actually something of a comfort, familiar as they moved into the unknown.

Des gestured with a motion of his head. "That's the building we want. Can you see the stairway going up the back?"

Pearl nodded. It was rickety and made of wood, probably a holdover from the days when the building had held a small factory and the owners had not wanted their workers to enter and leave through the showroom.

"That's our best way in," Des went on. "The ground floor holds a shop, and the door leading into the apartment building above is locked on that side."

"But not in back?" Nissa said.

"If it is," Riprap said, "Des says he can get us through. If he can't, I can."

"I feel funny trying something like this in broad daylight," Nissa admitted as they left the vicinity of the Buddhist temple and walked to where an alley would give them access to the back of their target building.

"The Snake chose our time for us," Pearl reminded her. "Either her father is here alone, or their rooms will be empty. Whichever the situation, we have an advantage."

Nissa nodded, but she didn't look convinced.

The alley wasn't exactly cluttered. In fact, it was relatively clean, although there were the usual cigarette butts, soda cans, and bits of paper. A long fence topped with razor wire protected the narrow back yards—although "yard" glamorized the spaces beyond what they were, areas for storing empty boxes, trash cans, and bits of broken furnishings that no one had quite gotten around to hauling to the dump.

The back gate was latched, but Des slid his hand through and undid the simple spring fastening.

"Fire code. During business hours they can't leave it locked. Probably they chain it at night, and the tenants have keys to the lock. Riprap, you go over and test the stair. If it can't hold you, the rest of us shouldn't bother."

"Right."

Des held the gate open for them, and they made their way inside. Nissa's eyes were very wide, and Pearl could hear her breathing fast and frightened.

Like a rabbit, Pearl thought, *and that is just fine because Rabbits find courage in curious places. I, however, am the Tiger, and fear is not for me.*

She told herself this as she had once told herself mantras, and the strangest thing of all was that her body believed her. She was tense and alert as she followed Des, who had followed Riprap, but not in the least afraid.

At least she was not afraid until her feet touched the first landing. The old wooden staircase switchbacked in its progress up the side of the building, the changes in direction necessary both so that the stair would remain anchored to the brick wall, and so that there would be access to the stair on each level of the building.

When Pearl first felt her breath coming fast and her heart begin pounding, she thought she had overexerted herself.

Perhaps I should have taken the elevator, she thought. *I'm too old for this. I should stop here, work my way down more slowly. This staircase isn't safe. I shouldn't be on it, much less with three other people. Riprap alone must weigh as much as any two of us. I'll just pick my way back down. Level ground. That's what I want.*

She was halfway into a turn when she caught sight of Nissa, who had been behind her, already heading down the stair.

"Nissa!" Pearl said, her voice soft, but long practice putting the note of command in her voice. "Where are you going?"

"I'm getting off this deathtrap!" Nissa replied, her own voice soft, as if she feared that her raised voice would cause tremors. "Lani needs her mommy. She can't manage without me. If I end up a broken wreck in a pile of shattered timbers, she'll see it on the news and learn she's an orphan."

The words came in a rapid cascade, but otherwise Nissa's motions were so deliberate that if she had not clearly been terrified out of her wits, the sight would have been funny.

Pearl felt an urge to rush after Nissa, but Des's voice, cool and analytical, caught her up.

"I feel the same fear," he said. "Except it is my own children I was—am— worrying about. What are you afraid of, Pearl?"

"What every older person comes to fear," Pearl said, forcing herself to hold her ground, "that my body will betray my ambitions."

"And I," said Riprap, "saw myself a cripple in a wheelchair, a quadriplegic from a broken back. Pretty weird, us all getting scared like that."

"Weird in the old sense of the word," Des agreed. "As in someone has been working magic here, a magic meant to intensify our natural fears."

As he voiced his explanation, Pearl could feel her fear ebbing. Yes, her heart was pounding fast, but from terror, not because she had gone beyond her limits. Yes, she was breathing hard, but not because she had done more than she could.

She climbed the stairs in her own house many times a day, and the flights were at least this long, at least this steep.

Nissa looked confused, but continued to edge down the stairs. Pearl wasn't surprised. Nissa was both mother and father to her daughter, and while Des felt a father's love and protectiveness, his children were grown and had their mother besides. It said a great deal about how deeply he loved them that fear for them had been what the enchantment had touched.

"Nissa," Pearl said soothingly, "Lani is safe. This staircase is solid. If you turn back now, all you achieve is making yourself more vulnerable. How will that help Lani?"

"I know," Nissa whispered, "but my soul doesn't know. I want to run and hide."

Pearl took a step or two closer, feeling her own inclination to flee growing with each step downward. Some small corner of her brain admired whoever—the Dragon, surely—had crafted this element of the spell. She looked for the marks of the spell. At least some of them should be here, for both the fear and the urge to flee had begun at the first landing.

Pearl glanced down toward Nissa and saw that Nissa was holding her place a few steps away, up and saw Riprap forcing himself to climb one step at a time. Des, his wide forehead beaded with sweat, was holding on to the railing with one hand, but his eyes were alive, darting back and forth as if he, too, had reached the conclusion that the marks of the spell must be here.

"Found them!" he said, the words coming on an exhalation, as if he had been holding his breath. He reached into his pocket and came out with a clasp knife. With great care, as if the simple action was suddenly complex, he pushed out the blade and leaned over to scrape at one of the balustrades. Whatever he had seen was written on the up-slope side, so Pearl couldn't read what characters had been used to shape their compulsions, but she did not doubt they were there. Even as some small part of her brain continued to worry that she had triggered an impending heart attack, her intellect and training reminded her what she had learned about the art of such inscriptions.

Nissa had minimal training to balance her fear. She shrieked and turned to run. Pearl reached out and laid a firm hand on the trailing edge of her sleeve.

"He's cutting through the staircase!" Nissa whimpered, fear making her immune to the sheer impossibility that a wooden staircase, no matter how old and apparently rickety, could be cut down with a pocketknife.

"He is not!" Pearl snapped, praying that Nissa's shriek had been lost in the general babble of city traffic noises. Otherwise, they were going to need to come up with some fast explanations. "You're going to feel better in a moment."

Nissa stared at her, but even as Pearl felt a release in the pressure in her chest, a slowing in her breathing, sense returned to Nissa's gaze and the turquoise eyes lost their wildness. From above, Pearl heard a whoosh of relief from Riprap and a sharp, satisfied snap as Des closed his knife.

"Spelled to repel intruders," Des said. "Actually a fairly routine enchantment. Those who have a right to be in the building would have no reaction at all, but anyone else, whether conventional burglar or unconventional 'guest,' would feel some fear, probably centered around those admittedly untrustworthy stairs."

"Was there a ward to alert the occupants against intruders?" Pearl asked.

"Not within the characters I cut away," Des replied, "at least I didn't see anything. However, if the one who set the spell there is attuned to his casting, he's going to know it has been effaced."

"So we may have rung the doorbell," Riprap said. "We'd better get moving in case whoever answers the door doesn't do so politely."

But no one came to the door at the first landing, nor to any of the doors on the other lower landings. As Pearl climbed the stairs to the final landing, she realized that this lack of acknowledgment was making her more tense and edgy than any overt attack possibly could have done. She imagined eyes watching from behind the curtained windows although the curtains hung still and limp.

"Open the door," she said to Riprap, her own voice giving her confidence, "and let us in."

The park was empty except for a voluptuous yet slender figure seated on one of three swings that were the centerpiece of a playground, and a robin busy questing among the damp grasses under the trees.

The park's sole human occupant was dressed neither as exotically as the first time Brenda had seen her, nor as erotically as the second, but even in faded jeans and a crew-neck T-shirt that would have been nondescript but for the Chinese character painted splashily across the breast, Brenda had no difficulty in recognizing Honey Dream, the Snake. She even recognized the character written on the shirt. Unsurprisingly, it read "Snake."

Foster recognized Honey Dream at once as well.

"That's the woman who called me that name—Fei Chao—as if it was *my* name," he said. He was unbuckling his seat belt and moving to get out of the car even before Brenda had turned off the engine.

Brenda felt bittersweet pleasure that Foster was apparently attracted to the Snake solely because she held information he wanted. He was moving away so quickly. She'd wanted to say . . .

What could you say? Brenda chided herself, reaching into the backseat and lifting the duffel bag out. *I think I love you, but not for who you are, because you don't know who that is, but because of who you have chosen to be? Better shut up, Brenda. Foster is gone. Flying Claw, the Tiger, is all who remains.*

The Snake had risen when Foster got out of the car, her expression hungry. In one hand she held a small brocade bag, the bottom rounded by something small and heavy. Brenda thought she knew what that had to be, but she didn't rush forward to claim it. Instead, while the Snake was completely absorbed in watching Foster rush toward her, Brenda dropped an amulet bracelet to the pavement, and broke it under her heel with a stomp that owed more to her desire to wipe that greedy, longing look from the Snake's face than to the need to activate the stored spell.

The spell was called All Green. Des had crafted it so that Brenda would be able to confirm whether the crystal the Snake had brought to trade for Foster was counterfeit or not. It would also permit her to see the aura of magical workings for the next few hours—an ability that should give Brenda warning if the Snake tried anything less than kind.

As All Green took effect, Brenda felt her vision momentarily blur. When it cleared, the brocade bag dangling from the Snake's hand glowed with a faint black aura. That was good. Black was the Rat's color, a hue not nearly as ominous in its associations within Chinese culture as within Western society. Brenda had to remind herself of that as she followed Foster across the park to where Honey Dream waited.

Tense as a coiled snake, Brenda thought wryly. *Or is that a cliché? Is it a cliché to think an image that's true, even if sort of trite?*

Brenda forced herself to focus, remembering what Des had said about emotional upheaval being something that could be used against her, but it was almost impossible to keep calm. The rattle of her thoughts—inane as some of them might be—was preferable to the misery slowly seeping into her soul, a despair that grew almost palpably heavier as she advanced to where Foster now stood face-to-face with the Snake.

"Why did you call me that name?" Foster was saying. Brenda knew the tension in his shoulders. She'd seen it when they were playing Yahtzee or cards, and he had given up playing the conservative game and was going to put all his faith on one throw, one draw.

"Why shouldn't I call you by your name, beloved Flying Claw?" the Snake said. "You're all worked up, but don't worry. In just a moment, I will have given you everything you desire."

Her tone implied that his desire included a lot more than answers to a few questions. Brenda wanted to punch Honey Dream solidly in that smiling mouth, but she kept her attention focused on that black glow.

Think about Dad. Think about the time you're winning for the rest. Think, Brenda.

Foster was angry now. "What do you mean? What . . ."

"I mean," Honey Dream said, "I have the means of restoring your memory, unless Brenda there is going to try something clever. You're not going to try something clever, are you, Miss Morris?"

Brenda looked at her. "You talk a lot, you know that? My mom always said that when a person talks a lot that person is really nervous. I'm here to do business. What about you?"

Foster looked at Brenda, his brow furrowing. "Business?"

"This . . . lady," Brenda said, facing him, "tells me she can get your memory back."

"She can? How? What?"

Brenda reached out and put a hand on Foster's arm. "Foster, explaining would take longer than you want—especially since if this lady can do what she claims, you're going to understand everything much faster than I can talk."

"So you're doing it all for 'Foster'?" Honey Dream said with a sneer. "Not one bit for Daddy?"

Brenda let her hand drop from Foster's arm. The warmth of his skin lingered on her fingertips. She faced the Snake squarely.

"Believe it or not, I'm doing it for them both—and for me. You've put me through hell, Miss Honey Dream. I'll admit that, since I know that's what you're longing to hear. I've had a lot of sleepless nights lately, and I'm going to have more. But I'm doing the right thing. Now, will you keep your side of the deal?"

The Snake laughed. "Now who's talking too much? Fine. We'll get down to business. Where's the sphere that holds Flying Claw's memory?"

Brenda slid her hand into her pocket and took it out, cupping the solid heaviness of the crystal in the palm of her right hand so the Snake could see it. The green tiger frozen within was beautifully lifelike, right down to the shading of his stripes, darker green against the pale.

"My dad's?" Brenda countered. "And the spell you promised?"

The Snake opened the brocade bag and took out a crystal sphere, identical to the one Brenda held, except for the black rat within. The Rat sphere glowed in Brenda's enhanced vision, its authenticity assured.

"As for the spell," the Snake said, "come over to that table."

She motioned toward a concrete picnic table.

"Why?"

"Because I promised to give you the means to restore your father's memory, but I'm not going to reveal *my* father's secrets. I've already written the key elements, but after you see the paper isn't blank, I'm going to complete the spell, then seal it before you can read it. You'll still be able to use the spell to restore your father's memory, but not copy it."

Brenda thought this care to keep her from even glimpsing the written spell expressed a lot more faith in Brenda's ability to read Chinese than she deserved, but she wasn't about to tell her that.

Honey Dream had been walking over to the concrete table as she spoke. Now Brenda saw there was a daypack on the bench. Honey Dream removed a calligraphy set, the elements not dissimilar to the ones Brenda had neatly put away in the classroom at Pearl's house after her last study session.

Foster had trailed after Honey Dream, but now he looked over at Brenda. "Are you sure about doing this?"

"I am, Foster," she said, wrapping her fingers around the Tiger sphere as if she could touch the memories within.

"But Pearl . . ." he said. "She's not going to like this."

"Auntie Pearl," Brenda countered, "doesn't like a lot of things, but what I'm doing right now is something she's going to need to learn to live with. I'm not giving her a choice."

The Snake had taken a piece of red paper from a folder in her pack. It was partially covered with a long line of Chinese characters. Brenda recognized the one for the Rat at the top, but that was it, except for a vague recognition that the style of the characters was archaic. She wondered if using archaic characters was necessary, or an affectation on the part of the Snake—like a Goth using some archaic font on her e-mail.

"Listen carefully, Brenda," Honey Dream said. "I'm going to brush the final characters onto this, then roll it into a bamboo tube. The first time the paper is taken from the tube, the spell will manifest as ink dripping from the interior of the rolled piece of paper. Hold the sphere under the ink, and when the ink flow ceases, your father's memory will be restored."

"Does Dad need to be near when I do this?" Brenda asked.

"That would probably speed the process," the Snake said. "It will also keep Gaheris's memory from returning in disorderly fragments. Remember, though. You get one shot, so don't try and be cute and see if you can copy this off before the spell dissolves."

Brenda extended her hand in mute acceptance of both the terms and the spell. The Snake took her brush, wrote a few final characters, blew lightly on them, then rolled the paper into a tight spill that she dropped into a slim piece of hollow bamboo. The entire process took less time than Brenda would have needed to load her own brush with ink. She felt a familiar touch of envy.

"Here," the Snake said, putting the bamboo tube into Brenda's outstretched hand. Brenda pushed it into her pocket. "Now shall we trade the spheres?"

As neatly as if they'd practiced the exchange repeatedly, Brenda held out the Tiger crystal to Honey Dream and accepted the Rat crystal in return. Foster watched in silence, but the tension on his face was painful.

Brenda started to turn away, then felt the forgotten weight of the duffel in her hand. She held it out to Foster.

"Your things," she said. "The robes you were wearing, and your sword. I figured there might be more trouble if you remembered you should have them and then didn't, so I brought them along."

Foster accepted the duffel, but didn't look inside. "Thank you."

Brenda began to walk briskly in the direction of her car. The Snake called after her.

"Don't you want to see how the transformation works?" Her tone held bragging invitation and challenge. "Don't you want to see what the real Flying Claw is like?"

Brenda swallowed hard. She didn't want to see Foster as anyone but Foster, not really, but then again, she did. And she hadn't forgotten that the longer she had the Snake under her gaze, the longer the Snake wasn't charging off somewhere and maybe messing up what the others were doing. The trick was balancing the two obligations. She wouldn't do the other four any good if they had to rescue her.

"Sure. I'm game." Brenda didn't move back to the table, but leaned against a convenient tree a few paces from where her car was parked. She hoped she looked casual and relaxed. She'd hate for the Snake to know how wobbly her knees were.

The Snake's expression settled on Foster, proprietary and satisfied. Her next words were addressed to him.

"Black and red were easy enough to do," she said, somewhat confusingly, until Brenda recalled that red was Snake's color, as black was the Rat's. "But if I'd dug out green paper and green ink and started working with them, my father surely would have noticed. But those were the colors I needed. You, Flying Claw, wrote your own spell—the one that was turned against you—I wanted to balance the resonance."

She is nervous, Brenda thought. *Mom is right about people talking when they're nervous.*

"But one of the few good things about this horrible land into which the Exiles were sent," Honey Dream went on, "is how easy it is to get just about any material goods, so I bought appropriate ink and paper."

Foster studied her. "Why wouldn't your father approve?"

"He would approve of my getting you back," the Snake said, "but not about my trading the Rat sphere to Brenda. You'll understand in a minute. Just wait."

"I am getting very tired of waiting," Foster said. "Especially now that you and Brenda both have promised me that great revelations will come when that waiting is ended."

Honey Dream smiled at him, "I understand, my impatient beloved. Just a few moments more."

Foster seemed to flinch slightly at the caress in her tone, but Brenda wasn't sure.

Probably wishful thinking on my part, she thought.

Honey Dream poured green ink onto a new inkstone, and loaded a fresh brush. Now she dipped the neatly shaped tip into a pool of green ink and drew it across the paper with flowing, graceful motions. The first character was the one for tiger, but after that, Brenda's knowledge failed. Moreover, Brenda stood several feet away and the ink was darker only by virtue of its wetness than the paper upon which the Snake wrote, making discerning the fine lines impossible.

Ink-brush calligraphy takes years to master, but completing a piece can take only moments—something that frequently deceives the uninitiated into believing that such art would be easy to master. Brenda had learned enough to appreciate what the Snake's skill told her. They seemed to be within a few years of each other in age, but clearly the Snake had been to a much more demanding school than Brenda's. Yet the Dragon claimed there were "many Snakes," "many Tigers"? What a terrifying world they must come from.

Brenda found herself hoping that whatever had brought these strangers from their home would be easily resolved and that they would go away—and stay gone.

"There!" said Honey Dream in satisfaction, lifting her brush and holding it to one side lest a stray drop ruin her work. "Done. Now, 'Foster,' would you have your memory back? Would you know yourself again as Flying Claw, the Tiger?"

Foster stepped forward eagerly, not bothering with words, and without the slightest glance for Brenda.

"What must I do?"

Riprap tried the door at the top-floor landing.

"Locked, but that's no surprise. Is it warded?"

Des answered before Pearl could focus on the appropriate charm. "Yes, but the alarm will function on about the same level as a door buzzer. We can silence it easily."

He moved forward and began sketching characters on the doorframe with a ballpoint pen. Nissa moved close to Pearl, and spoke softly.

"I'm sorry about losing my head. I'm not usually such a—well—such a rabbit."

Pearl reached over and patted her. "That's quite all right, dear. I know you're not. One of the beauties of that spell is that it uses one's strengths—what one cares about the most—against one. It is the sort of spell a Snake or Dragon loves: twisted and clever. There is one problem with cleverness, though."

"Oh?" Nissa didn't sound convinced.

"Yes. The clever forget that there are more direct ways to achieve one's goals. Look!"

Des had finished his writing. Through spells Pearl had prepared in advance, she saw his spell had countered the other—not neutralized it, simply balanced it. The universe held many paired forces. The "buzzer" would sound, but the opposite of sound is silence, so Des had arranged for that sound to be silenced.

Riprap was dealing with the door's lock in a much more direct fashion. During his tour in the army, he had learned how to open locked doors for reasons he never quite got around to explaining. Pearl suspected that Riprap had done some work for what was romantically referred to as "covert ops."

Certainly, there was nothing of the thief about Riprap as he picked the lock. Anyone watching would have seen a man unlocking a door, his big, dark hand concealing the somewhat unorthodox form of his key.

"Directness can often undo the most clever," Pearl said. "Dogs are marvelous at being direct. So are Tigers. Shall we join the gentlemen?"

Nissa grinned at her, and Pearl could almost see the Rabbit's ears perk up with renewed confidence.

"I'm set."

The outside door led into a hallway that separated the two apartments that occupied this floor, as well as connecting to a stairwell going down. No sound drifted up the stairs, making Pearl feel certain that, except for the shop below, the building was likely empty. Even so, they kept their voices low.

"This one," Riprap said, indicating a door marked 5B. "Des?"

Des studied the door. "Give me a moment. There are more complicated wards here."

While Des scribbled on the wood of the doorframe, Riprap examined the array of locks set in a metal plate above the knob.

"The locks are a bit more complicated, too. At least one's a deadbolt, but even the best of those will open to the right master key, and this one isn't the best."

"So you have a master?" Nissa asked.

Riprap nodded. "There are things you don't leave for your roommate to find. Given I knew we were hunting trouble when I left Denver, I packed appropriately."

Pearl recalled that lock-picking tools were among the less dangerous items Riprap had brought with him. Riprap wasn't "packing" today. None of them were, although Pearl was a competent shot with a handgun, and Des was actually quite good—although his choice of weapons was often as eccentric as his lifestyle. However, today firearms would serve only to complicate a matter that was already far too complex.

Fleetingly, Pearl wondered how Brenda was doing. The young woman had been very brave, going off on her own like that. The protections they had given her would work only if Brenda remembered to activate them. Still, the risk had to be taken. They needed to draw the Snake off, and the Snake had insisted that Brenda come alone.

What if they had been wrong and the Dragon was working with his daughter on this, rather than the pair being at odds?

Too many guesses, Pearl thought, *but our other choice was to wait for our enemies to act—and I think we would have liked that less.*

The door snicked open, sound punctuation to Pearl's thoughts. Des checked, then nodded.

"We can go in."

"The place sounds empty," Nissa said. "Isn't it strange how an empty apartment sounds different than one where people are home?"

"Maybe to Rabbit ears," Riprap said. "Let me go first. For some reason, people tend to freeze when they catch sight of me without warning."

Nissa didn't protest, now seeming as confident as earlier she had been afraid. Perhaps her Rabbit nature was assisting her. More likely, she was simply attuned to her surroundings, and trusted what her senses told her.

For Nissa was correct. The apartment was empty, not only of residents, but almost entirely of furnishings as well. The area was fairly small, all but the kitchen visible from the front door. To the left side of what might be politely called an entry foyer were three doors, all standing open. To the right was a wall, and where it ended was an open, multipurpose area. Mismatched curtains hung in all the windows, filtering the copious light that seemed to be one of the apartment's few positive qualities.

The wall to the right of the entry proved to be one side of a galley-style kitchen, its walkway so narrow that two people would have had difficulty passing each other within. A battered Formica table and two chairs with corroded chrome-steel tube frames and vinyl seats—these liberally patched with duct tape—were the sole furnishings in a dining area that began in the multipurpose space off the kitchen.

A battered sofa covered by a clean but utilitarian sheet, and a coffee table made from an old hollow core door set on short stacks of cinder blocks, turned the rest of the room into something of a living room. There was no television, not even a transistor radio.

Since the doors to both bedrooms stood open, their contents were equally visible. Each was furnished with a narrow bed and a trunk that seemed to be doing double duty as nightstand and clothes chest. The bathroom that separated the two rooms was small. The white porcelain fixtures were of the cheapest make, old and chipped besides.

However, despite the poverty of the apartment, the rooms were scrupulously clean. The air smelled of good cooking after the Chinese fashion, underscored with lotus incense and strong soap. Small touches showed that at least one of the residents had an instinct for beauty. Wild flowers displayed in vases made from glass bottles had been carefully placed on the windowsills in both bedrooms, and on the center of the dining-room table.

"Furnished two-bedroom walk-up," Des said, disgust in his voice. "Private entrance. Rents by the week. Still, it's clean and dry. I suppose they could have done worse."

"I wonder," Pearl said, "why they did not do better. We know they would have wanted privacy, and proving good credit would have been a problem, but still . . ."

Des grinned sardonically. "Proving good credit would have been more of a problem than you could imagine, Pearl, at least in an establishment with any pretensions to honesty. I don't think the Dragon would have wished to bring his daughter—who is quite attractive from what you've said—to a crack house or a dive that doubled as a house of prostitution. Then, too, with San Francisco so close, San Jose can afford to pick and choose. There are fewer no-tell motels than you would imagine."

"I suppose," Pearl said.

She shook off an odd impulse to invite the Dragon and the Snake to come stay with her. After all, they were relatives of a sort, and both her Chinese and Jewish upbringing emphasized responsibility to family. Somehow, until she'd seen those sagging beds, that travesty of a coffee table, it had been easy to think of them as something other than people who would need to eat and drink—people who were exiles, far from home.

Nonsense! These are the people who exiled my father and his friends. They are the enemy. No feud is worse than a blood feud.

Nissa was looking around the living room, sniffing the air, picking up things and setting them down again. "I thought we'd have to spend hours searching, but there isn't much of anywhere to look. Des? I suppose going through the trunks makes the most sense. Do you see any wards on anything?"

"Not on the chests," Des said. "Not at a casual inspection, but that doesn't mean we shouldn't search them."

"The chest in the Snake's room isn't even locked," Nissa said, drifting that way.

Pearl didn't need to ask how Nissa knew that the rearmost bedroom was the Snake's or how Nissa knew the trunk wasn't locked. A bright pink sleeve of something, probably a T-shirt, hanging out the trunk's side explained both.

"Check out the Snake's room, Nissa," Des said. "I'll take a look at the Dragon's. Riprap, you have any thoughts about other hiding places?"

"Lots," Riprap said. "Unless you see some helpful aura that's going to guide us right where we need to go, I'm going to start in the bathroom. Toilet tanks are classic hiding places, so are dummy pipes. That medicine cabinet looks loose enough that something could be stashed behind it."

"I'll take the kitchen," Pearl said. She set Treaty, still in its carrying case, on the scratched and stained counter.

"Good," Des said. "Even as thin as I am, I think I'm too tall to bend over in that travesty of a kitchen to inspect the cabinets properly. I'm not sure that Riprap could even fit in there."

"Sure I could," Riprap said. "If I held my breath."

They moved to their various assignments. The apartment was small enough that conversation could continue without anyone needing to raise his or her voice.

"We're looking for the crystals," Nissa said, her voice slightly muffled. Probably she was kneeling over the trunk. "Anything else?"

"Any indication that the three we know of have other allies here," Pearl said, quickly checking the canisters on the counter to make sure they held nothing but rice, flour, and tea, "and who those allies might be. I'm still wondering how they have managed to adapt this well to our world. Spells can help with language, but the Snake called Brenda's cell phone. That means they understand phones. I'm wondering if they understand cars as well, or if all their travel has been magical. In their pursuit of the other members of the Thirteen, they must have been over a good part of the U.S."

Pearl opened a kitchen cabinet. Two plates. (Two others were drying in the dish rack along with some handleless teacups.) A few saucers and bowls. Two chipped mugs. A stack of plastic cups. Chopsticks, the cheap kind that splintered, were stuck into yet another plastic cup. She turned her attention to the refrigerator.

"Money," Riprap said a few moments later to the accompaniment of a clink as he put the top back on the toilet tank. "Credit cards. We still haven't figured out how they're paying for what they do buy. That didn't bother me at first because I thought they were like Foster was when we first saw him, sort of exotic, vanishing and all, wearing robes. Now we know otherwise. They're living like real people, not like genies. So where's the money coming from to pay for their food and rent, for their contemporary clothing?"

Pearl snapped open each of the opaque plastic containers arrayed on the wire rack shelves in the refrigerator. Hiding money in a butter tub was an old trick, but a good one. Few thieves wanted to take the time to check every container in a fridge. She found garlic, ginger, various sauces and seasonings. Cooked rice. A box of eggs with five left. Some leftover stir-fry that had lots of eggplant and garlic in it and smelled lightly of vinegar. The remains of a can of bamboo shoots.

"Diaries, journals, spell books," Des said. "Anything we can use to learn more about them."

The refrigerator was clean, not only of items of interest, but of mold or must. Wondering whether the Dragon or the Snake was the excellent housekeeper, Pearl moved her attention to a shelf holding dry goods, including several bags of various kinds of rice. These had all been opened, and part poured into canisters for easier use. Moving ten-pound bags every time one wanted to make a cup of rice would be a pain.

Although the rice bags were heavy, Pearl lifted each of these down. Amid the jasmine rice, her fingers encountered something hard and round. Before she could say anything or check further, there came the sound of the front door opening.

A new voice, unmistakable nonetheless, spoke.

"Do you wish to know more about us?" asked Righteous Drum, the Dragon. "Why not ask?"

Pearl lifted the bag of jasmine rice back onto the shelf, and moved to the kitchen doorway.

The Dragon stood in the doorway to the apartment, an apparently ordinary Chinese man, round-faced, somewhat squarely built. Clad in neat slacks of a tan verging on yellow and a button-down sports shirt the color of sunflowers, Righteous Drum looked much less exotic than the figure who had stood on Pearl's front porch that night some weeks ago, but he was no less commanding.

"During the Double-Dragon Hour," the Dragon went on, "I usually do tai chi and then meditate. It strengthens me for the rest of the day. Today, I came out of my meditation to discover that my daughter, Honey Dream, had gone away. She had left me a note, promising that she would return shortly. However, Honey Dream has been restless these past few days, a thing she has taken great pains to conceal from me—as if her own father would not notice. I decided I should go after her, and preserve her from whatever foolishness she intended. I was riding in a taxicab, greatly annoying the driver with my erratic directions, when I felt one of my wards very neatly defaced. I suspect that the cabdriver was relieved rather than otherwise when I asked him to take me back here."

During this speech, the Dragon finished entering the apartment and closed the door into the hallway behind him. Des, Riprap, and Nissa had come to the doorways of the rooms they had been searching, and stood in a more or less straight line. Pearl was weirdly reminded of one of those game shows where contestants wait by doors number one, two, and three.

"I should have taken more time disarming that ward," Des said quite conversationally when the Dragon stopped speaking, "but Nissa was frantic, and I fear I was not thinking too clearly myself. You have a fine sense for evoking personal terrors."

"Fear," the Dragon said, "is something any wise creature feels when approaching a dragon. We are sagacious, but we are also very powerful."

There was a threat in those polite words, but Pearl was a Tiger, and she had three good allies, while the Dragon was alone. She knew this, knew he knew it, and suspected that he was talking in the hope that his daughter—and perhaps even Foster—would arrive to help even the odds.

Keep him talking then, she thought. *It should not be too difficult. He seems to love the sound of his own voice. Or is it that to us, here, he can speak his own strange form of Chinese and be understood?*

But if that had been what motivated the Dragon's lengthy speech, it had not been his only reason. While he spoke, he had moved a few steps closer to Des, who was leaning against the doorframe of the Dragon's bedroom, the one closest to the outer door.

Swift as driving rain, with a movement of his right hand, the Dragon threw a piece of yellow paper at Des. It snapped as a kite does in the wind, but unlike a kite it moved with purpose and direction.

But Des Lee also had not been standing making idle chatter. They all knew something of their enemies and their tactics by now. That pose against the door-frame had concealed what Des had slid onto his left hand, probably as soon as he had heard the outer door begin to open. Long and wickedly curving, the unique martial-arts weapon created by the Exile Rooster rested with lethal effectiveness on the current Rooster's hand.

Des took full advantage of the surprise his left-handedness granted him. He slashed out, shivering the piece of yellow paper into strips, with a second slice reducing them to confetti.

The Dragon was only momentarily put off. He snapped forth another piece of yellow paper, but this time not at Des, nor at Riprap, who was charging at him from the bathroom door. This one filled the air with acrid smoke, setting every-one but the Dragon coughing and sneezing.

Through the noise, Pearl heard a faint beeping. She wondered if the Dragon had set off a smoke alarm, wondered, too, what would be her best course of action. She had discovered what they had come here for—she was sure of it. Should she get away with the crystals while she could?

She was one old woman. What could she add to a fight where there were younger people, male and female alike, to take the front lines? She had brought Treaty, but could she really cut into someone? No, better that she win the war by getting the crystals away, and leave her friends to the fight.

Turning, Pearl Bright moved back into the kitchen, reaching hurriedly to lift down the heavy bag of jasmine rice.

Honey Dream seemed to have forgotten Brenda's presence. Crystal in one hand, calligraphy in the other, she rose and glided over to Foster.

"Cup your hand like so to hold this," she said, setting the sphere in his hand. He held it as she directed, cupped close to his body, at the level of his solar plexus. "Now we will breathe on the paper as one."

She held the strip of green paper between them, positioning it so it dangled over the crystal.

"Now."

Foster bent his head to the paper, while Honey Dream slightly raised her lips to do the same. The motion was that of a strange kiss, especially as two sets of lips puckered to gently blow upon the green paper.

Brenda wanted to look away, but forced herself to focus. If in the next moment Foster would complete that kiss . . .

But he did not. The Snake was the one who rose onto her toes and pressed her lips upon his, the green paper dissolving as she did so, vanishing into a tightly focused shower that glittered as it fell down onto the crystal in Foster's cupped hand. The moment the first of the glitter touched the crystal, Foster—no, Flying Claw, Brenda must remember that was his name—reeled back half a pace, his head jerking back, his cupped hand clenching.

He gave a small cry that might have been pain, might simply have been shock, and stood frozen in that stance for what seemed like an eternity, but was only seconds as measured by the robin's triumphant song. Brenda thought she heard the peeping squeaks of young robins, but then again, the sounds might have come from Foster—from Flying Claw. His lips were pulled back now, slightly parted, his expression mingling ecstasy and pain.

There was a battle being fought in that lean, muscular form, one that contorted those handsome features into something grotesque, even ugly. Brenda noticed the Snake's expression had darkened from pleasant anticipation into concern, but other than taking a small step away from Foster, she did nothing.

At last the struggle ended, the long, strong fingers unclenched. The crystal sphere had vanished, and with it had vanished a certain questioning look that had never completely left Foster's eyes the entire time Brenda had known him. Without it, he would have looked enough of a stranger, even without the new stance he took, balanced lightly on both feet, even without the calculation that entered his gaze as he took in all his surroundings seemingly without conscious effort.

Before, even when throwing himself into a game of basketball or running after Lani, there had been something slightly awkward in Foster's bearing—something easily overlooked, because he was otherwise the embodiment of lithe grace. Now, though, his was the stance of a hunting tiger, poised to leap and rend.

"Flying Claw," the Snake breathed, raising one arm so that she could stroke Flying Claw's arm. "Your memory is returned to you?"

"It is," he said. "I thank you for your efforts, Honey Dream. I agree with you as I could not before. Righteous Drum, the Dragon, will not be pleased. You have taken much upon yourself."

"Risking my father's anger," Honey Dream said, "was fair price for regaining you as you were. Filial piety is a merit that can be abused."

"So you have broken filial piety," Flying Claw said, and his mouth moved in a strange frown, almost a snarl, a little bit of a sneer, "to return me to what I was. What I was, and maybe a bit else."

The Snake let her hand drop from his arm, stepping back as if that expression, those words, were a blow. She halted in midretreat and squared her shoulders—to great effect in how her T-shirt stretched over her breasts, Brenda noticed with a certain, sardonic humor.

"You are grateful," Honey Dream said, her tone soothing, "I think."

"I am," Flying Claw replied. "What man would not be for being made whole, after having been to himself what a shadow is to the rainbow?"

"Then you will approve that I have not been the fool you seem to think," Honey Dream went on, her tone caressing. "I have a plan to divert my father's wrath from you and from me."

Brenda recalled her conversations with Pearl, conversations in which Brenda herself had noted that the Snake was not likely to make a fair trade. The Rat crystal was in Brenda's possession, as was the spell to release her father's memory from its hold. She'd better get out of here.

Brenda started edging for her car, not wanting to run lest she attract attention to herself. For the moment Flying Claw—it was easy now to think of this hard-eyed stranger by that name—and Honey Dream seemed to have forgotten her.

But she was wrong. Honey Dream had not forgotten her.

"Don't go, Brenda Morris," she said. "I have a little something for you."

Brenda didn't hesitate, but moved to pull one of the protective spells from the array at her wrist. The motion began quickly, but as she looped her thumb beneath the band, she struggled, suddenly slowed. The All Green she had activated earlier now showed her that the black glow of the Rat crystal held something darker as well, a stain the deep red of congealing blood.

"You accepted an insignificant gift from me along with what I promised," Honey Dream laughed. "You checked for authenticity. Did you check for more?"

Brenda hadn't. She didn't know how to do so. Des's spell was not that sophisticated. Indeed, the fact that she was seeing anything other than the black surprised her. Was this that little bit of the Rat working in her favor again?

Brenda said nothing in reply. The slowness that had seized her limbs robbed her of speech as well. Honey Dream clearly expected this, for her next words were addressed to Flying Claw.

"There is a oddness about Brenda Morris," she said. "I want to find out what it is. While I am finding out her secret, I also will take back the Rat crystal and my spell. Thus, when I return to my father, he will have no reason to be angry with me. I will have regained our Tiger and lost nothing—and perhaps brought back the answer to why this Ratling is more than she should be."

Flying Claw raised his eyebrows. He looked interested in a cool, calculating fashion. He gave Honey Dream a small smile.

"Ambitious," he said. "But then the Snake loves intrigue as the Rat loves cleverness. You two are actually well-matched."

Honey Dream was clearly offended. "Matched? She is matched and beaten."

Flying Claw had moved over to the duffel as the Snake explained her plan. Now he knelt and unzipped it, removing his sword from within with an ease and confidence that demonstrated that what Foster had forgotten Flying Claw had recalled.

"Beaten?" He pulled the blade from its sheath, and the dappled sunlight caught against the shining steel. "By your trickery Brenda is indeed beaten, but by her kindness—and her filial piety—she is redeemed. You offered her a trade. I think that I will assure that trade is honored."

"What? I thought your memory was restored! You know that we need the Rat's memory. Why do you falter? Can you not see that she has been nothing but your jailer?"

Flying Claw did not sheathe the sword. "My memory is restored, dearest Honey Dream. I remember how Brenda treated me, although I think your spell was infused—purely by accident, I am sure—with the desire I not remember aught but blurred images of my days as Foster. I remember your love for me. I appreciate what tremendous risks you have taken in the name of that love. Consider it a sign of my love for you that I will not make you a liar. Brenda will go free, with the Rat's memory and your spell."

"But . . ."

Flying Claw turned the shining blade side-to-side. A trick of the light made it seem that the very shadows were cut by that honed steel.

"You will remove the binding from Brenda?" Flying Claw said. "In the name of honesty? Or shall I be forced to slice it clean away?"

Honey Dream's resistance melted all at once. She traced a few figures in the air, then made a throwing motion in Brenda's direction. The bloody hue vanished from the crystal's aura. In the same instant, Brenda felt the slowness leave her limbs.

"Drive safely," Flying Claw said in English. Then he switched to Chinese. "Thank the others for what kindnesses they showed me. However, from this moment, consider all debts paid between us. I have set not only you free, but set the Rat free as well. That is enough."

Brenda didn't hesitate. She wanted to say something, anything, be witty, intelligent, incisive, all those things Rats were supposed to be, but all she felt was scared.

When Brenda got into the rental car, the faint scent of Foster still lingered, tearing into her heart, a last trace of someone forever gone.

Then she backed up the car and pulled out onto the main road. She had to get to Japantown. The others needed to be warned that soon they would face not only a Dragon, but a Snake and a Tiger as well.

A young, strong Tiger with a great deal to prove.

✮

Eight small crystal spheres weighed a fair amount, but Pearl was less concerned about their weight than possible damage they might take whacking against each other if she were to drop them into her pockets or stuff them into one of the bags or containers that were available here in the kitchen.

Pearl was casting around for something to use to carry the crystals when she saw Treaty on the countertop. She couldn't very well leave her father's heirloom sword behind. Possibly the long case and some plastic wrap would solve her problem. She hurried over to retrieve the case.

Sounds from the other room were not encouraging, nor were a variety of strange odors. Pearl took a moment to activate one of the protective spells she had carried with her, choosing Winds over Dragons for obvious reasons.

Even with her protections in place, Pearl was glad that she would not need to cross the rest of the apartment to make her escape. The kitchen window was as large as any of the others—probably heritage from whatever the building had been before it was converted to apartments—and conveniently near the wooden exterior staircase. She should be able to go out the window and onto the staircase without stretching too far.

She heard a clash of metal against something solid, and hoped no one had gotten hurt.

Just give me time to get away, she thought, reaching for the sword case and sliding down the zipper. *I'm too old for this.*

"But not," asked a rough, growling voice within her head, *"for climbing out windows and leaping over to rickety wooden staircases? What is wrong with you, woman?"*

The voice was her father's—and was her own as well. Ever since she had been a small girl, Pearl had critiqued herself in her father's voice. If the voice seemed to be coming from where Treaty's blade shone, revealed in the flickering sunlight through the poorly curtained window, then so be it, but Pearl knew it for the voice of her own heart.

And with that reprimand in her father's voice, Pearl recognized the touch of the dragon's breath on her heart, the same fear that had nearly pushed her to retreat there on the stair. Was the Dragon causing it through one of the spells he had cast in the other room or had she triggered some ward when digging through the bag of jasmine rice? That hardly mattered. What did was that now that Pearl recognized the fear as not her own—or rather, as something she would not normally have surrendered to—she could fight it.

She did so, fighting down fear that made her limbs weak, pulling Treaty from its case, and putting the eight crystal spheres into the padded area where the blade had rested. Then she ventured into the combination living room and dining area, assessing the situation that had developed because of her cowardice.

Probably under the cover of the smoke that still lingered in high corners of the room, the Dragon had advanced past Des, but he had gotten only as far as the area that paralleled the bathroom door. There Riprap blocked him. Blood ran from Riprap's right knuckles, spotting the bare wooden floor; despite all the blood, the wound did not seem to have distracted the Dog.

Riprap had inserted himself bodily between Nissa and the Dragon, leaving Righteous Drum with several choices. He could retreat toward Des, hide in the bathroom, or back into the combination living and dining room.

Wisely, the Dragon had done this last. Des had moved forward to block his retreat from the apartment—and to intercept anyone else who might try to enter. He wore the Rooster's Talon on his left hand, but his right was free, the length of his long arm above his knobby wrist adorned with a choice array of amulet bracelets.

Pearl wondered if the Dragon had known she was in the kitchen when he chose to retreat in that direction. She wondered whether that knowledge would have altered his decision. After all, there was Nissa, cowering like—well, a rabbit—behind Riprap. Why should the Dragon think an old woman, one whose weapons in their prior encounter had been words and wards, should offer him much in the way of threat?

Time to show him otherwise.

Treaty came smoothly from its sheath, the steel blade glimmering with different hues of silver-grey in the filtered sunlight that penetrated the mismatched curtains. As always, its weight rested easily in Pearl's hands.

"Dragon," she said, challenge in her voice, "you are surrounded. Why not surrender and do what you should have from the first? Talk with us. Tell us what brought you from your own land into this."

"And why," Nissa said, moving forward to stand alongside Riprap, an amulet bracelet ready in her hand, "you're trying to steal our memories."

"I seek not to steal, but to retrieve," Righteous Drum said. "But rarely do thieves give back what they have taken willingly—and much less so when the stolen goods have become family heirlooms. I do not suppose that if I asked you to hand over what you so arrogantly call 'your memories,' then you would give them to me?"

"Certainly not!" Pearl snapped, and her defiance was echoed by the other three.

"Then I must take them!"

The Dragon had been standing loose-limbed but alert. With these words his stance changed. He held his arms bent at the elbows at an angle just shy of ninety degrees, and thrust slightly to the sides of his torso. His hands were held palms up, fingers curled and slightly clenched. It was an angry stance, filled with contained power.

Pearl concentrated on mentally sketching a series of characters learned long ago. Within a few breaths she could see the power shaping in Righteous Drum's hands. Glancing at her three companions, she could see that, like her, each of them had activated some form of protective spell. Like her, the choices had been Winds, for coming in they had known they would need to deal with someone who would have a special relationship with dragons.

The Dragon was also protected. Pearl could see the faint, wispy coils of spirit dragons tracing a protective pattern around his body. No wonder Riprap's knuckles were bloodied. He'd probably swung at the Dragon and his blow had met something far less yielding than the body of a slightly overweight, fifty-something scholar.

The wealth of protective spells also explained why Righteous Drum had not spread about more smoke or something even more deadly. At least for now, his opponents were shielded, but Pearl sensed this would not last. If this Dragon was anything like the Dragon of whom her father had told tales, if he was even anything like his exile descendant, then Righteous Drum would have long experience with the power of wind being used to counter that of dragons.

Pearl stood, knowing that Treaty would be useless for the moment, unless . . .

"Riprap, Nissa, Des . . . Toss out the strongest attack you have stored. Now!"

The two younger people responded blindly to the command in her voice. Des gave a thin smile, and threw the bracelet that was already in his hand. She and he had selected this spell together, for although it took a great deal of ch'i to work, it relied on neither dragons, nor winds, nor water—the last the element dragons are most likely to control.

There were triple crashes as carefully worked polymer clay became dust. Then three versions of the same dramatic sending rose: the Twins of Earth, the Twins of Sky, and the Twins of Hell.

Each pair stood armed and armored, magnificent male and deadly female versions of the same warrior principle. Each was dressed in the elaborate costumes of a China of old, but the details varied according to appropriate symbology. The Twins of Earth wore shades of brown and bronze, and their dark hair was bound with strands of rough gems. The Twins of Sky wore white and pale blue, their attire embroidered with signs of clouds and the sun. The Twins of Hell had dark red skin. Although they were as striking beautiful as the others, there was something of the demon about them. Their teeth verged upon being fangs. Their eyes were burning red.

The Twins of Earth carried long swords and shields. The Twins of Sky bore bows and daggers. The Twins of Hell held balanced in two hands long, forked spears that in some versions of the Chinese hell—as in the latecomer Christian— demons used both to herd and to torment their miserable charges.

The triple pairs of Twins occupied the same demi-plane as that in which surged and swam the dragons that wreathed Righteous Drum, otherwise the small apartment might have been so crowded that none could move. Pearl was glad of this, for her plan demanded that she, at least, be able to move swiftly and freely.

The Twins knew for what reason they had been summoned, and there was no need for them to be given commands. The Twins of Sky shot forth arrows at the dragons that wreathed the space above Righteous Drum, while the Twins of Earth and Hell attacked those that protected the man's lower reaches. Opaqued within the writhing spirit forms, Righteous Drum showed admirable poise as he continued to concentrate on whatever spell he had begun.

Pearl watched, a Tiger poised to spring. When a particularly well-aimed blow on the part of the female of the Twins of Hell left open a gap in Righteous Drum's protections, she leapt forward. Treaty's edge slipped through the gap in Righteous Drum's arcane shield, and Pearl brought the flat of the blade against Righteous Drum's arm and shoulder.

Her hope had been to disperse the contained ch'i he had been building before it could take whatever form he intended, but what her action actually did was send the spell forth before its time.

Four sharp-beaked firebirds with eyes and talons of wet ink sprang from their maker's hands. Their flames were red-hot, tinged with yellow. The heat from these proved sufficient to consume the lesser winds that protected Nissa and Riprap, but the winds protecting Des and Pearl retained some protective force, although they were much diminished.

As the firebirds swallowed the winds, they transformed, becoming darts of yellow paper scribbled over with elaborate characters in green, yellow, white, green, the colors appropriate to each of the four who stood there: Tiger, Dog, Rooster, and Rabbit.

Pearl brought Treaty around in a rapid cut that should have reduced the dart that was heading for her to shreds, but Righteous Drum had learned from his encounter with Des and his Rooster's Talon. This dart could dodge, and it did. Then it did something horribly clever, riding along the edge of Treaty's blade, using the sword itself to penetrate the final shreds of Pearl's failing defenses.

Once the dart was inside her winds, Pearl might as well have tried to parry falling rain. The yellow paper caught her across her face. There was a moment of silence, and then she felt herself being sucked outside of her body. Disembodied Pearl watched in horror as her body staggered back a few steps, then collapsed, a puppet doll with its strings cut, onto the sofa.

Oddly, though, Pearl could still see, although the perspective was weirdly distorted, as if she looked out through the sides of a soap bubble. The angle of vision seemed nearly omniscient. She could as easily focus in on the remaining Twins as they fought the remaining guardian dragons as she could the struggles of her three companions.

From this peculiar perspective, Pearl watched as Nissa staggered back, yellow paper sinking into her face, green ink rewriting the text of her mind. Nissa stood staring down with some slight curiosity at a crystal globe that rested on the wooden floor where she had been standing. Then, her expression blank, she backed from the room and took a seat upon the edge of the Snake's cot. There she folded her hands and waited.

These spells are more complex than the ones that took our allies before, Pearl thought. *The Dragon obviously did not want us wandering about, shouting protests, wondering where we were. He has sought to paralyze us, then to separate our bodies and minds, but not our memories from our minds. How very interesting.*

Des and Riprap had fared better than Pearl and Nissa. Riprap's spell appeared to not have "taken," for when the yellow dart came home to its target, he tore it from his face. For a moment he stood, confused, yellow ink running against his dark skin. Then the confusion passed and Pearl had the satisfaction of seeing the big man move, not to spring upon their enemy, but to draw a fresh protective amulet from his wrist and renew his defenses.

The one true combat veteran of the lot of us, Pearl thought. *I shouldn't be surprised that he reacts so intelligently.*

Des's protective shield of winds had been weakened, but not entirely broken. He quickly enhanced it with a second spell. This, chosen at random, was not very powerful, but it was enough to blow back the spell that sought his memory. The

Twins and guardian dragons had done for each other. They faded to wherever sendings reside, leaving a curious stillness behind them.

Into that stillness, Righteous Drum, the Dragon, spoke. "You have used your most powerful spells, and I still stand untouched. Two more of your number are in my crystals. Why not quietly surrender? You will not know that you have lost anything. I give you my sworn word that I will make certain that your bodies are returned to someplace safe—Pearl Bright's residence will do, I am sure—before you come out of my haze."

"Then," Des said bitterly, "we resume our lives, our brains scrabbling to create whatever bridges they can to justify our lost memories?"

"That is correct."

Riprap was staring down at the piece of yellow paper he'd ripped from his face, his brow furrowed with concentration.

"I'm not much at reading Chinese characters yet, but I spent a fair amount of time studying the first spell—the one Foster threw at me, the one that didn't hit. This spell isn't complete. Pearl didn't fail as entirely as you want us to believe, did she, Righteous Drum? She interrupted your spell. I'm betting we're not the only ones who have used our most powerful spells."

"Do you want to test that theory hand to hand, spell to spell?" Righteous Drum hissed, sounding rather like his daughter at that moment, for all that the timbre of his voice remained low and menacing.

"I think I must," Riprap said, his fingers running down the bracelets on his arm. Pearl knew he had marked their edges with different textures so he could read their class—if not precisely which spell was which—by touch. "Losing my memory of the Dog probably wouldn't change me much, but Pearl and Des? They've shaped their whole lives around living up to their heritage. Maybe they'll end up like that Albert Yu, a sort of weird parody of themselves, but maybe they'll end up like Foster, who's practically a zombie, for all he moves and thinks."

Riprap's fingers had come to rest on a bracelet while he talked, and now he stripped it off, flinging it to the floor at Righteous Drum's feet. Pearl saw the manifestation of Wriggling Snakes. The small spectral reptiles began twining up Righteous Drum's legs, both inside and outside his pants legs.

Riprap didn't wait to see how effective the distraction would be, but surged forward, almost roaring with bottled-up tension. He didn't have a weapon, but his big hands were weapons in themselves.

Righteous Drum responded by invoking another dragon spell, this one offensive, not defensive. A dragon with scales the color of iron ore and a rather grouchy look in its mud-brown eyes appeared. It launched itself at Riprap, stopping him in midstride with a slam of its body into his. Riprap's new protective spell was enough to save him from gross injury, but not sufficient to keep the summoned dragon from wrapping its coils around his body.

Pearl wondered if Riprap could see the fearsome monster that now coiled around him, breathing a sour miasma into his face, or if he was wrestling blind. She wondered, too, how long Riprap's protective spell could protect him from breathing the tainted air, and what effect the taint would have. She didn't think it would be mortally poisonous, but certainly the effect would not be pleasant.

Meanwhile, Des had not wasted the opening Riprap's attack had given him. He threw a bracelet directly at Righteous Drum, and Pearl saw the form of one of the least traditionally named spells—Gertie's Garter—wrapping its bindings around Righteous Drum's upper body, restricting his arms, as Riprap's snakes were doing his legs. Spell cast, Des moved forward, his Rooster's Talon poised to block any possible thrown spells, his right hand fumbling to slide another bracelet free for use.

Righteous Drum ignored the approaching Rooster, reciting a sequence of what had to have sounded like nonsense to Riprap, and probably to Des. Pearl, however, recognized the sequence as what she had been taught to call a Purity Hand, and groaned, knowing that in a moment both Wriggling Snakes and Gertie's Garter would have been consigned to oblivion. Then what would Righteous Drum do? To this point his desire to steal his victim's memories had made him take care not to harm their bodies, but how long would that constraint last?

He might decide that tracking down and assaulting Des's heir would be easier than dealing with Des himself. Would he have the means to know where the power passed?

Then Pearl caught a glimpse of something so interesting that she was distracted from these unhappy thoughts and even from the battle in front of her.

The kitchen window was sliding open. When it was open about eighteen inches, a slim hand gripped the sill. A moment later, Brenda Morris pulled herself in, carefully lowering herself onto the kitchen counter. Her face was drawn and an aura of bleak tragedy lit her dark brown eyes.

Brenda looked like someone who felt she had very little left to lose, and who was spoiling for a fight. Suddenly Pearl's soul, abstracted as it was, experienced a sensation curiously like hope.

Brenda's knees were shaking as she rested her weight on the counter of a narrow, poorly lit kitchen. Climbing across the open air that separated the window from the rickety wooden staircase was an experience she suspected would haunt her nightmares, but it had been necessary. She'd had a bad time, though, hoping the window wouldn't jam, hoping that if it did, she could get it open.

It had been both unlocked and slightly open, and she'd balanced over a nasty drop, while she forced the window far enough open that she could pull herself across and in.

Those gymnastics lessons weren't a complete waste of time, she thought. *But I don't think I can ever tell Mom just how useful they turned out to be.*

The air in the cramped kitchen smelled of sulfur and of something else that made Brenda want to cough and rub her eyes. She restrained the impulse. Given what she already knew about the situation, even a cough could be fatal.

From outside the kitchen she could hear Riprap grunting as if under some intense strain, and someone else chanting in Chinese. That was all she could hear, and the relative quiet bothered her more than any manner of commotion could have done. Was she too late? She saw Treaty's case lying on the kitchen counter, but the sword itself was gone. Then, as she lowered herself to the floor and ventured forward, Brenda saw Treaty itself fallen to the boards of the outer room, just behind a man dressed rather tastelessly in a yellow button-down shirt and khaki trousers.

Righteous Drum, the Dragon, she realized. *He came back or maybe even was here when they came in. Everything's gone to hell!*

Then Brenda saw what rested in Treaty's case in place of the long sword: eight crystal spheres, each containing the likeness of an animal. Eight of the Thirteen Orphans—or at least their memories. This was what Pearl and the others had come to find, and that at least they had succeeded in doing.

Maybe everything isn't quite gone to hell, Brenda amended, following what she was sure was a pack-rattish impulse, and stuffing the crystals into a variety of pockets.

They felt heavier than they should have, each one heavier than the one before.

I guess this is what they mean by the weight of responsibility, Brenda thought, and stepped out into the larger room.

Des and Righteous Drum were circling each other. Brenda could see by the faint glow that haloed them that each had at least one protective spell in place, and that they were trying to find ways to penetrate the other's defenses.

Riprap was tearing at open air that glowed pale yellow in the dying remnants of the All Green spell Brenda had cast in the park. He looked as if something was squeezing the breath out of him, and he was trying to pull it loose.

Pearl sat limply on the worn sofa. Nissa could be glimpsed seated in an almost identical attitude on the edge of a cot in the farther right of the two bedrooms. The absolute lack of interest they showed in the struggles going on before them told Brenda that the Dragon was ahead in this match. Two down, two to go, and both Riprap and Des were visibly fading.

Suddenly, everything she had been through in the last couple of days came to a head. Brenda privately thought of herself as a "firebrand"—one of the possible translations of her name—for far longer than she had thought of herself as a Rat. She didn't exactly have a temper, but she hated bullies. That hatred was one of the things that had drawn her into student government.

Slim, dark of hair and eye, with skin of golden ivory when the rest of her family was either German or Irish fair, Brenda had come in for a lot more unkind teasing than her parents had ever realized. She'd given as good as she got, and now a sense of incredible unfairness rose in her and gave her a courage that she hadn't known she possessed.

"God damn it all to hell!" she yelled. "I have just about had enough of you, Mr. Dragon, you and that pushy tart of a daughter of yours. You came into our lives and decided you could remove parts of them just like they were tumors or something. Well, I'm sick of your interfering. I'm sick of my dad acting like a weirdo. I'm sick of spending my summer taking a crash course in Chinese calligraphy. I'm sick of just about everything. Do you understand?"

Brenda knew she wasn't making a heck of a lot of sense, but that didn't matter. She was wearing the strongest of the defensive spells she had left—she hadn't been about to climb over those windowsills without something to cushion her fall if she lost her balance. She still had up the All Green. The weakening spell didn't offer a lot of detail, but what it did show her was that the bright ch'i that had emanated from the Dragon on their last visit was much depleted. Des and Riprap weren't the only ones reaching their limit.

Stooping, Brenda retrieved Treaty from where it lay on the bare boards of the floor and held it in front of her in one hand, using a stance borrowed from a movie. Then she fished into her pocket for one of the crystal globes. This one had a yellow Ox in it, and remembering the stories Pearl had told of First Ox and her adoptive daughter Hua, Brenda felt a protective connection to whoever it was locked in there.

She held the Ox crystal up in her free hand so that the Dragon couldn't miss what she had.

"I was there the night Pearl made her deal with you. You probably didn't notice me. I was the doorkeeper."

"I noticed you," Righteous Drum said mildly. "And I can see from how you grasp the hilt of that sword that you don't have the least idea how to use it. Put Treaty down. I offer you what your idiot friends were overconfident enough to reject: an end to this all. Give me the crystals and I will leave."

"Hah!" Brenda said. She marched over to where Riprap still struggled with the invisible whatever the hell it was. "I remember the pact you made with Pearl, the pact you made to rescue your daughter. Our allies were to be safe from further interference by you and yours. Very well. I think I'll try an experiment. I wonder if whatever is hurting Riprap can do so without harming the crystal as well?"

Worked up as she was, Brenda didn't stand around like some villain from a comic book making speeches. Instead, she suited action to words and stuffed the crystal into the open collar of Riprap's shirt. For a moment, nothing happened, but then Riprap relaxed slightly, and she guessed that whatever was squeezing him wasn't doing so quite as hard.

In her hand, Treaty seemed to pulse, and Brenda knew that the strange magics the Exile Tiger had put into his chosen weapon were alert to a potential violation of an oath sworn upon its blade and name.

I'm glad I remembered how vulnerable the Foster crystal was to magical manipulation. Now, before the Dragon thinks of some attack that won't harm the crystal . . .

Brenda grabbed a second crystal from another pocket—there was a white monkey in this one—and stuffed it down Riprap's collar to roll down after the Ox. She didn't wait to see whether Riprap was able to get free now. Instead, keeping Treaty raised, she pulled out a third crystal—this one holding a yellow sheep—and called to Des.

"Hey, Des. Basketball. Remember play four? Catch!"

Des grinned, and when she feinted right, he went left and neatly caught the crystal sphere as she passed it underhand. It wasn't a basketball, but it flew straight and true, like it wanted to go where it was heading.

Treaty's pulsing was visible now, a soft green light haloing the blade, becoming firmer, framing the metal with a sharpness that Brenda felt pretty certain would cut through even the dragons she could faintly glimpse circling Righteous Drum. Brenda found she was grinning from ear to ear. She suspected she looked a bit crazed.

"Treaty doesn't like whatever it is you're thinking, Mr. Dragon. I have absolutely no idea what it will do if you carry through, but I don't think you'll like it. And I figure that I'll just have to go along with whatever Treaty wants. I doubt a Ratling like me has the ability to control a sword of truce when it sees that truce broken."

"What are you?" Righteous Drum asked, his voice hoarse, with anger perhaps, perhaps with fear.

"I'm absolutely nothing at all," Brenda said. "I'm a college student who has had my summer really screwed up. I'm Gaheris Morris's daughter—although I think you knew that already. What am I? I don't know. Do you want to push harder and help me find out?"

She had dug out the crystal holding a magnificent red Horse, and tossed that to Des to back-up the first crystal. She still held four crystals, and now she moved to place one—a yellow Dragon, which she thought oddly appropriate—on Pearl's lap. Pearl's hand moved with something like determination, making Brenda think that Righteous Drum's hold was not as absolute as he might have thought. Within seconds those swollen-knuckled fingers were wrapped tightly around their prize.

There was no need to worry about protecting Nissa. As soon as whatever he'd been fighting had loosened up, Riprap had moved to the doorway of the room in which Nissa sat limp and uninterested. Brave Dog of Riprap's father's stories would have been very proud of his descendant. Brenda knew *she* wouldn't have cared to cross that ferocious watchfulness.

Des spoke into the tense silence that had risen in the wake of Brenda's hysterical harangue.

"Righteous Drum, why don't you give it up? I have no more idea than Brenda how Treaty might take oath-breaking, but I suspect you do. The man who enchanted that sword was one of the original Thirteen Orphans. That means his magical traditions were probably closer to what you know than to the bastard versions we use now. Exile Tiger's daughter has carried the sword since his death. Neither of them has ever been known to give an inch and if the legends are true that artifacts take after those with whom they associate then that's going to be one ornery sword."

The Dragon crumpled all at once. If Brenda hadn't been so strung-up, she might have pitied him, for the pure weariness and grief that washed over him made Righteous Drum's face suddenly look far older.

"All right! All right! I will honor the truce."

"Sorry," Brenda said. "That's not enough. I want Pearl and Nissa back like they should be."

The Dragon made a gesture and there was a sound of breaking stone and a ringing as of shattering glass.

"Done."

"And I want the other crystals broken and the Orphans' memories all returned to them. And I want you to promise you will leave us all alone from this day forth."

Brenda had been collecting the crystals as she spoke, using the bottom of her shirt as a makeshift basket. Now she spread out the fabric, displaying the spheres in a mute command for him to act.

Righteous Drum held up his hand. "Wait! Before we speak of these things, I beg you. Have you harmed my daughter?"

Brenda blinked. She hadn't realized that her sudden appearance might make Righteous Drum think that Brenda had somehow defeated Honey Dream, or at least severely disabled her. For a moment she was tempted to maintain a mysterious silence, but then she remembered that whatever else Righteous Drum was, this truly was a father who loved his daughter.

"No. Honey Dream is fine—but no thanks to you or to me. Foster stepped in when she was going to try something on me. I'd figured she would, and came prepared, and things might have gotten ugly."

"Foster?"

"Flying Claw," Brenda clarified unnecessarily. "Yeah. He stepped in. She gave him back his memory, but apparently he didn't forget everything we'd done for him and he wouldn't let her harm me."

"Ah. So she is well?"

"She was the last time I saw her, back at the park. Foster was with her. Now, about those other things I want. No dawdling while you wait for reinforcements. Get to them."

Righteous Drum stiffened, his face a mask of purest misery. "Wait. I am bound by conflicting loyalties. I wish to obey you, but it will not be easy."

"You broke the other two crystals easily enough," Brenda retorted. She'd glimpsed purposeful movement over behind Riprap and knew Nissa was safe.

"The spell was incomplete," the Dragon said. "The complete spell is harder to break."

Pearl spoke from beside Brenda, taking Treaty from the younger woman's hand.

"Thank you, Brenda. I appreciate all you have done." Then she turned to the Dragon. "My allies and I asked you to explain matters to us not long ago, and you weren't interested. Give me a good reason why I should care to listen to your excuses now?"

"Because," Righteous Drum said, "I beg you . . ."

Nissa had come to the doorway of the room in which she had been sitting, and now stood with her hand on Riprap's shoulder.

"Pearl, let Righteous Drum talk," she said. "We want to know what brought him here, don't we? But I don't think we should hold our coffee party here. For one, Lani's going to be back home and wondering where we are. For another, I suspect your house is a lot safer for us than any place this man has been living. Brenda is right to wonder if he's just stalling, waiting for reinforcements."

"Or for his ch'i to build up again," Des agreed. "Pearl, are your household wards up to letting this Dragon in the gates?"

"I would prefer not," Pearl said. "Why don't we hold our meeting in the Rosicrucian Museum's garden? It's right next door, so Nissa can check on Lani. Perhaps we will have a picnic lunch."

"Won't we have a lot of people bothering us?" Brenda asked. "I mean, it's a public garden."

"It is also," Pearl said, smiling mysteriously, "one of the most private places in all this city—perhaps on all this coastline—if you know the right charms, and it just happens that I do. The Rosicrucians will not interfere in my business, and they will assure that neutrality will be kept."

"Weather's not too hot," Riprap said, "and the gardens have shade. Sure. Why not?"

"My daughter," Righteous Drum said. "How will she find us?"

"Write her a note," Brenda said. "Unless she has a cell phone."

"I fear not," Righteous Drum said, "although acquiring such did have a certain appeal. However, we were not completely comfortable with such devices."

Brenda made a mental note to ask just how they had gotten as acclimated as they were, but this was neither the time nor place. Pearl seemed to be having similar thoughts, for she glanced around the apartment as if looking for signs of someone whose identity they did not yet know.

"Write the note," Pearl said, "and come along. We have a great deal to talk about. And don't try anything clever. We have had enough of cleverness."

"As have I," said Righteous Drum with what sounded like genuine emphasis. "As have I."

★

Long, long ago, even before her father's death, Pearl had taken it upon herself to study some of the other magical and philosophical traditions that coexisted with those her father and his friends had brought from the Lands Born from Smoke and Sacrifice.

Rosicrucianism had been only one of many. However, the friends she had made during that phase—although at first many had merely been fascinated at getting to know a still somewhat famous movie star—had remained her friends, even when Pearl's interests moved elsewhere. She was on several committees for the museum and periodically held a place on the board of directors.

These days her involvement was largely restricted to making donations and to drawing on her rather attenuated Hollywood connections when such might benefit the museum or its lecture program. Even so, Pearl was given full run of the establishment, including public gardens that possessed some rather specialized properties. Today, she led her little band to a corner of one of the gardens, a cozy alcove adorned with a statue of Isis, a long, dark pool in which the statue contemplated her own reflection, and a blazing array of pink and orange hybrid tea roses.

Before seating herself on one of the benches, Pearl respectfully inclined her head to the representation of Isis, among whose many names was "the Mistress of Magic," for it was under her aegis that this magically volatile conference would be held.

The benches were far more comfortable than they appeared to be at a casual glance. Although a few sparrows hopped over in quest of bread crumbs from the abundantly—if hastily—packed basket Nissa and Riprap had carried over from Pearl's house, the flies and other annoying insects (including tourists) simply drifted away from the area.

Nissa had taken the time to boil water. Now Pearl drank deeply from a restorative cup of tea. Righteous Drum and Des had accepted the same, but the young people had favored iced drinks.

They picnicked for a while as if they were any other group, allowing Lani to ask a million and one questions, and to report about her experiences at the morning's screen test. Pearl used the time to arrange her thoughts, and she suspected Righteous Drum was doing the same. He also could not refrain from looking around rather anxiously, and Pearl knew he remained concerned about his absent daughter.

Honey Dream is probably taking advantage of a little private time with her newly restored "beloved," Pearl thought. She could tell from the look of misery that drifted over Brenda's face whenever Righteous Drum looked about for Honey Dream that the younger woman was entertaining similar thoughts. *Very well. Let us get down to business and distract Brenda from her personal anguish by reminding her just how many others have suffered from this man's interfering.*

"You said you were bound by conflicting loyalties," Pearl said. "Would you care to explain yourself?"

"I would and will," Righteous Drum said with formal politeness, "but before I enter into those matters, I would like to remind you of something that, in your moment of what may feel like victory, you may have forgotten. You may hold the crystals, but I hold the means for opening them without damaging the memories stored within."

"I doubt either Pearl or I have forgotten it for a moment," Des said. "I, at least, am convinced that if given enough time we would figure out how to open them on our own. So stop posturing, and get on with your tale."

"May I ask one question first?" Righteous Drum said. "How was it that Brenda Morris arrived at my apartment in such an irregular manner? Why did she choose the window and not the door?"

Nissa giggled. "My fault. When you barged in and started breathing smoke on us, I was farthest away—other than Pearl, who was in the kitchen. I'd noticed the kitchen window was open about two fingers wide when we were coming up the stairs. And I knew that if Brenda came in through the apartment door, she wouldn't do any of us much good. So I grabbed my cell phone and left her a message when she didn't answer."

Pearl recalled the faint beeping she'd taken for a smoke alarm, and smiled. Seems she'd been a bit hard on the Rabbit. Nissa had acted quite wisely within the constraints imposed on her. And without Brenda arriving and then using the crystals so effectively . . .

And without my finding them in the first place, and without Des and Riprap holding back Righteous Drum for as long as they did. Success or failure, we're all equally to be praised or blamed.

Brenda spoke up. "When I got there, I really wasn't certain what good I would be. I thought maybe I'd just get away with the crystals, and try and negotiate with you later. Then I remembered the problem Des and Pearl kept having when they tried to dispel the crystals. Hard as they were physically, they were apparently magically fragile. Then there was Treaty, so I figured . . ."

She shrugged, and stopped. It was going to be a long time before any of those present forgot what Brenda had "figured" or that her gamble had paid off so well.

"Now," Pearl said. "Enough delays. Tell us, Righteous Drum, about these 'conflicting loyalties' of yours."

"It is a long story," Righteous Drum warned.

"That's fine," Nissa said, fixing a very no-nonsense gaze on Righteous Drum. Nissa patted the bench on which she sat and Lani climbed up onto it. "We like stories."

"Story, Mama?" Lani echoed.

"History," Nissa said. "You just sit here and play with Mr. and Mrs. Penguin, Lani-bunny, and let this man tell us about himself."

"Where's Foster?"

"He's visiting a friend. I suspect he'll be along any time now."

"Good. Foster likes stories."

"I think he already knows this one," Nissa replied. "Right, Mr. Righteous Drum?"

For answer, Righteous Drum began his tale. "From the skills you all have demonstrated, I believe that a tradition must have survived among you as to where your ancestors had their origin. Therefore, I will not go into details of that matter unless they are crucial to my account."

Pearl gave a thin-lipped smile. "I assure you, we are very good at asking questions if some point seems a bit vague."

"But," Riprap added, digging into one of the lunch hampers and finding a roast-beef sandwich that had been overlooked, "we'll keep a list and ask you all at once."

The Dragon looked mildly overwhelmed. Apparently, whatever background he came from did not include casual American chitchat. After a moment he regained his poise, and resumed.

"Since I have been in your land, I have tried to learn something of how China is perceived—and by China I do not necessarily mean the modern nation, but the historic being. One common conception that is both true and false is that China is a very old nation. The truth is that dynasty has succeeded dynasty, and that traditions often intermingled over time, without anyone finding this in the least contradictory.

"However, this perception of cultural continuity is false as well. Dynasty has succeeded dynasty, but not in the peaceful manner that one president follows another president in the United States, or even how modern European royal houses marry, and change their names while leaving essentially the same people in power."

Righteous Drum looked rather proud of himself as he made this statement, and Pearl didn't wonder that he did. If Righteous Drum had indeed learned all of this in a few months' time, then he was a scholar of note, even among Dragons, who were traditionally scholarly.

Once again Pearl wondered who might have helped Righteous Drum, Honey Dream, and Flying Claw after their arrival. She would not let Righteous Drum's eloquence make her forget to ask. But for now, she kept silent, and listened.

"War, civil and uncivil, was the common way for dynasties to change. Indeed, the emperor who ordered the burning of the books and slaughter of the scholars is still revered as the first ruler to unify China. One of the things he commanded be burned were histories of past rulers, past wars. His motivation, so he claimed, was peace, but there is a great difference between peace and pacification. Pacification is just another form of war. And because so many warlike histories were burned, my land is very unlike your China in two key elements. Not only is it not one nation, but it is also a land in which peace is difficult to attain."

Riprap nodded. "We knew that war occurred in the Lands Born from Smoke and Sacrifice, because 'our' emperor was defeated by your emperor, or at least his ancestor—grandfather, maybe? That wouldn't have happened if everything was peaceful—or stagnant."

"That is so." Righteous Drum looked a little sad. "Enough history. I will move now to the events that brought us here."

"About time," Brenda muttered, but she knew her grumpiness had little to do with the light brush strokes of history Righteous Drum was using to introduce his tale. It had to do with the same thing that caused Righteous Drum to periodically look around to survey their surroundings.

Where are Honey Dream and Flying Claw? she thought, and knew that her real question was *What are they doing?*

Brenda knew she was not beautiful, and there was no doubt that in her snaky way, Honey Dream definitely was not only beautiful, but sexy as well. How could Foster resist when she was coming on to him like that? Why would he even want to if they'd been lovers before?

Brenda bit into her lower lip to fight back tears, forcing herself to concentrate hard on what Righteous Drum was saying.

"I do not know whether you will feel pleased to learn that the emperor who succeeded the one your ancestors served did not hold the Jade Petal Throne for very long. Within ten years, he was assassinated, not by someone from the former emperor's faction, but from a faction led by a general who did not see why his former comrade-in-arms should suddenly acquire honors and divinity when this general—as well as many other former allies—knew how very human the new emperor could be."

Brenda noted that Des was surreptitiously counting something off on his fingertips. She thought she knew what he was considering. Could the various attacks that had driven the Thirteen Orphans first from China to Japan, then eventually to the United States have been influenced in any way by these political upheavals?

Righteous Drum continued, "The deposed emperor's advisors—the very ones who had offered exile to your ancestors—were not shown nearly so much mercy. They were executed. The new emperor had his own advisors in matters arcane, and these were the first to suspect that something had gone very wrong when exile, rather than execution, was offered to those you term the Orphans.

"You already know that although ability in the arcane arts is not limited to the Twelve Advisors of the Earthly Branches, special abilities accrue to those who take up the mantle of the Rat, the Ox, the Tiger, the Hare . . ."

"The Dragon, the Snake, the Horse, the Ram, the Monkey, the Rooster, the Dog, and the Pig," Lani recited in a singsong voice. "I know those. Mama is a Hare, which is a Rabbit, too, and I will be one someday."

Righteous Drum blinked in mild astonishment at the interruption, then inclined his head toward the child. "So it is, and I find myself rebuked for repeating a lesson even a child knows."

"Mama and I sing," Lani said, "songs about the animals. There's a Cat, too."

"Hush, Lani," Nissa said. "Mr. Righteous Drum needs to tell his story. Play with the penguins now."

"Okay." Lani allowed herself to be distracted, obviously pleased to have substantially contributed to such a serious discussion.

Righteous Drum smiled slightly, and Brenda found herself wondering if Honey Dream had been anywhere near as cute when she was the same age as Lani.

"As I was saying, special abilities accrue to those who take up the mantle of the Twelve Earthly Branches. What the advisors to the new emperor gradually realized after they were initiated into their posts was that the power they received seemed attenuated. At first they credited this to their own relative lack of training in such matters. The Twelve are normally chosen from those who have undergone extensive preparation, concluding with an apprenticeship under the one who they may, in time, succeed. I say 'may' rather than 'will' since the training is complex, and one who holds the title usually accumulates several apprentices, so that when the time comes for the title to be passed on there will be a suitable choice."

Riprap nodded. "Wouldn't do to have the whole mob be contemporaries.

After all, if the master chose to retain his—or her—title until he—or she—was of venerable years, a formerly young apprentice might be nearly retirement age him—or her—self."

"Precisely," Righteous Drum said. "Also, numerous apprentices provide some insurance against an accident in which both master and apprentice might be killed."

"Or," Pearl said dryly, "against the apprentice putting the master out of the way—especially if said master was reluctant to retire."

"You understand the complexities, then," Righteous Drum said, and Brenda thought his smile was uncomfortably sly. "Very well. Initially, these new Twelve thought they merely needed to study the appropriate rites and rituals, to school themselves in the appropriate branches of arcane lore. Former apprentices were located and convinced to become tutors. Many were very willing to do this, since having not been chosen themselves, they bore resentment at being rejected.

"Yet, despite extensive studies, despite examinations passed, thus proving that every theoretical point was perfectly understood, still the new advisors did not attain the strength they should have held. However, they were still very powerful, and possessed insights and abilities held by no others, and so they retained their posts. Moreover, the belief had come to be commonly held that when the mantle was passed to the next generation of apprentices, each of these duly trained and appropriately—rather than somewhat haphazardly—initiated into the rites, all would be well again."

Des grinned. "But the situation didn't improve, did it? How long did it take for someone to realize that in exiling the twelve duly appointed holders of the Earthly Branch titles, the full range of abilities had been exiled along with them?"

Righteous Drum drew himself up, and looked stiff and rather, Brenda thought, huffy. She swallowed a grin. It was pretty easy to see that Righteous Drum the Dragon was accustomed to being treated with the deference due to the person of high rank and prestige that he was in his own land.

But you're among equals now, Brenda thought, *sort of, kind of. That's the Rooster talking to you, not some underling. That's the Tiger looking at you through slitted eyes—and she's no young man you rather dislike because your daughter's in love with him. That Tiger may be old, but she's fierce. And that's the Rabbit with her daughter beside her, and the Dog on guard, just in case you think you can get away with something. Wake up to it, man. You're addressing your equals—and if I'm following what you're saying, your betters as well.*

Righteous Drum seemed to remember the need to mind his manners, and gradually the tightness in his shoulders eased and the air of affronted pride left him.

"The realization," Righteous Drum said, inclining his head toward Des, "as you term it, came slowly, and, even to this day is not universally accepted as the correct solution to the problem."

"After all," Pearl said softly, "to accept that as the answer would also be to accept one's own essential inferiority."

Righteous Drum inclined his head, and a trace of a smile pulled at one corner of his mouth. "That certainly was one source of resistance. There were others, and the disagreement among the various groups is one reason that your ancestors—and in some cases yourselves—experienced decades without interference from our universe."

Brenda cut in, her mind buzzing with the force of a sudden revelation. "But something has changed, hasn't it? Something recent—or relatively so. I'm betting there has been another coup, hasn't there? And that you represent those who helped overthrow the last government, right?"

Righteous Drum looked at her, and this time he made no effort to hide his astonishment. Then he looked suspicious.

"Did Flying Claw retain more of his memory than we were led to believe? Or has my daughter betrayed information that should be confidential?"

"Neither." Brenda fought an urge to roll her eyes in exasperation. She figured it would drive this man up the wall about as fast as it did her mother. "Look. It's obvious, right? Something is wrong in your homeland, something that drove you to the extremes of coming here. Now, maybe you represent a stable and well-established government, but there's a lot to indicate that you do not."

No one interrupted her, so Brenda started ticking things off on her fingers.

"One, there's Honey Dream and Flying Claw—your Snake and Tiger. They're both young. Pearl has told us about how although her father had spent his entire life training, he was still considered very young to take up the role as Tiger. I'm willing to bet that Honey Dream and Flying Claw are about the same age that Pearl's dad was.

"Pearl has also told us that the training for those who hoped to take up one of the named branches was extensive, and you've seconded that. So why, if everything was going well, would you and your associates select two young candidates from among the many apprentices? From what Des has been lecturing us about the talents associated with the various signs, in a crisis the Tiger is a war leader, the Snake a diplomat and spy. Well, I'd guess that Foster might be a pretty good warrior, but he's young enough that surely there should have been some apprentice Tiger who was older, someone with more experience in tactics and with actual experience in battle. And, I hate to tell you this, Mr. Righteous Drum, but whatever else your daughter is, a diplomat she is not."

Brenda waited for someone to tell her to be quiet, but only Des spoke, and he was encouraging, "Brenda, you said there were 'a lot' of reasons it was 'obvious' that Righteous Drum did not represent an established order. You've given just one."

"Well," Brenda said, "if Righteous Drum here is part of an established order, why is he undertaking this strange and dangerous mission with just two young assistants? There are twelve who bear the mantles, right? If things were peaceful, then I would think that everyone would want to be part of this. The job would go faster, too: one specialist per memory. But that's not how they went about it. That argues the others are needed elsewhere. One really likely reason they would be needed elsewhere would be because their emperor—and their own place—is endangered.

"Now, maybe the lack of participation is because not everyone likes the theory that they didn't get initiated into their full powers, but even so, there must be a few others who think this is a valid explanation. Moreover, if he—Righteous Drum—was making this move, and I were one of his associates, I'd not want him grabbing hold of something I'd want. Righteous Drum might not give the power over to me freely. He might trade favors for it. My best guess as to why the rest of their Twelve let Righteous Drum and his junior duo go after something so valuable is because they really, really need it—and that the need is so great that they figure he won't hesitate to turn over what's been retrieved to the proper owners, or rather to those they want to think of as the proper owners."

Brenda stopped talking, out of breath, and, momentarily, out of inspiration. This time Righteous Drum did cut in.

"You worked this out all on your own? 'Foster' did not remember fragments? Honey Dream did not trade information for Flying Claw's freedom?"

"I worked it out on my own," Brenda said. "Does your asking mean I am right?"

"You are very close," Righteous Drum admitted. "You are correct in that we—my associates in the Twelve and I—represent a new government. However, we prefer to think of ourselves as an older reign returned to power."

He stopped for a moment, and looked at them with an almost pleading expression. "You see, we are descended from those who served the emperor deposed by those who sent your ancestors into exile. In a sense, we are your kin."

★

Pearl stared at Righteous Drum in purest astonishment. This she had not expected, not even in her wildest speculations.

But you came close, she chided herself, *when you thought about how Foster might be related to you. You just didn't take it far enough. You thought Foster had simply entered some training hall, been taken under the tutelage of someone who was willing to overlook the sins of ancestors exiled for over a hundred years. Yet this is a better answer.*

She spoke aloud. "My father and his friends often wondered what had happened to the families they left behind. They had done their best to protect them, but once the Twelve found themselves attacked even here in the universe of their exile, they assumed that the treaty provisions meant to protect their families had been broken as well. Are you telling me that they were not?"

"They were, and they were not," Righteous Drum said. "Now that this rather astonishing young woman has deduced what would have taken me hours to explain, I need a moment to adjust my thoughts. There is still much to tell."

"Adjust," Pearl said, pouring tea from the thermos, "and then tell us how not only did our ancestral families survive, but how they came to rise to power once more."

"And why," Riprap added, his tone full of suspicion, "they are in trouble already, and why we should believe you anyhow. Seems to me, your tale is one crafted to undo the suspicions of a romantic soul."

He looked hard at Des when he said this, but Pearl smiled to herself as she filled Righteous Drum's teacup.

Romantic souls—like those who have modeled their own conduct after tales of a certain Brave Dog? Well, it takes a wise man to know his own vulnerabilities.

Righteous Drum nodded. "The families survived because the emperor who promised they would be left alone kept his word. He did not particularly wish to do so, but his hold on the Jade Petal Throne was tenuous, based on many promises to many people. To break a promise made so publically before his reign was solidified would have been to risk rebellions within his court. The general who deposed this emperor honored the treaty as well, for this was one way he could make clear that his quarrel was with the immediately late emperor personally, rather than with his policies."

Nissa rubbed her forehead. "All these emperors and deposed emperors and former emperors. I'm having trouble keeping it straight. Just who do you serve, Righteous Drum?"

"As I said, I am of a faction made up of those who wished to restore things to the way they had been before the Orphans were exiled."

Riprap was quick to pick up on a certain hesitation in Righteous Drum's tone. "So you're not really related to our ancestors, are you? This restoring has more to do with restoring what the Thirteen Orphans took with them than with restoring the Cat's royal line to the Jade Petal Throne."

Righteous Drum did not bother to pretend he did not know who the Cat was. Once again, Pearl found herself wondering who had been his source for information here in this world, for the Cat was a title exclusive to the ranks of the Thirteen Orphans. This was not the time to ask. Later, though . . .

Righteous Drum was nodding in reply to Riprap's question. "Yes. What you say has an element of truth in it. Although much of the military support for the coup came from those who remember the reign of Albert Yu's ancestors with a nostalgic longing that is perhaps not merited, those who brought their magical gifts into the conflict and in time rose to take the role of the Twelve were all recruited from those who believed that—much as we did not like to face it—something had been lost when the Exiles left, something far more potent than an infant emperor.

"We hoped that when our own emperor was settled on the throne we would be able to research the matter at our leisure, to eventually venture across the divide between the Lands Born from Smoke and Sacrifice into the world of Origin, and once there to retrieve the soul-ch'i that had been taken away. However, if there is any truth in all the universes, it is that coups breed further coups.

"Brenda asked why our Snake and our Tiger are both so young. Simply told, the woman and man who held those titles and were in age closer to being my contemporaries were slain in the coup attempt that followed our rise to power. Their deaths, among many others, kept us in power, but that newly secured power is under siege. I convinced my allies that we could wait no longer to begin our quest for the soul-ch'i. I had hoped they would let me take as much as half of our number with me, but all they would agree to spare were these two half-tried, barely initiated youths.

"Even so, we did well, concentrating first on those we believed would pose either no threat or the greatest threat. . . ."

Pearl interrupted. "And how did you make these judgments? Shouldn't we all be perfect strangers to you?"

Righteous Drum looked at her with eyes too wide for perfect innocence. "I told you, the issue of what happened to the soul-ch'i is a matter that has been under study for many, many years. One of those who studied the matter discovered that we are linked, one might say, through our shared affiliations."

Too facile, Pearl thought. *By his own admission, Righteous Drum and his allies have been the appointed Twelve for a relatively short time. Still, I shall let it pass, for now. Let us see what else he may reveal.*

Righteous Drum had continued his explanation. "We employed our magics to exploit what you might term the harmonic resonances between you and ourselves, and so learned that not all of those who had inherited the soul-ch'i of one of the Twelve were aware of what this granted them. Even those who were aware were frequently less than well-trained. Then, too, there was the question of geographic proximity. All of these things influenced who we sought first."

Brenda cut in. "So when you'd finished your collecting I guess you were going to take the harvested memories back to your own land, and tough luck to the people who ended up with permanent amnesia?"

Righteous Drum clearly did not care for her flippancy. "We were very careful only to take what was connected to the soul-ch'i. Yes. In some cases this meant that the person concerned underwent a rather severe personality change, but not a single person was physically harmed."

Riprap's lips shaped a thin, rather nasty smile. "We've wondered about that, Mr. Righteous Drum, and we figure you didn't spare us out of any kindness. I think at some point you learned about how our ancestors had fixed things so that what you're calling the soul-ch'i would pass to an appropriate heir. Tough for you if you killed someone, thinking to swipe the soul-ch'i, only to find it was now wrapped up in someone else who would be difficult to reach—maybe a little baby, or someone living halfway across the country, or even in another part of the world."

Righteous Drum stiffened. "Think what you will. I continue to assert that the fact that we have not killed—or even seriously harmed—a single person is evidence of our high and noble intent."

Pearl glanced at the faces of her associates, and did not think that Righteous Drum had convinced any of them.

"So," she said, setting down her empty teacup, "we have what you have come such a long distance to collect, but as you mentioned, you also hold something we desire."

"The means to open the crystals and release the soul-ch'i, intact and undamaged," responded Righteous Drum with too eager haste.

"I still think we could work out how to break the spell in time," Des interjected. "Especially now that we know more than we did. Especially now that Righteous Drum and his partners are going to have a lot more trouble harassing us, and so we should be far less distracted."

"Perhaps," Righteous Drum retorted.

His mouth was opening as if he were about to say something more when his expression went momentarily blank. When it sharpened again, Righteous Drum was focused on something distant. Pearl immediately recognized the reaction as that of a sorcerer who has felt the unexpected tripping of a ward.

Righteous Drum surged to his feet, his hand outthrust, reaching upward into the space in front of him. The empty air had developed a curious solidity, a swimming, swarming texture, as if the air had condensed into a contained sphere of liquid that distorted the light while remaining itself transparent.

Then something brownish appeared within that distorted space, resolving almost as soon as Righteous Drum touched it into a human hand, long-fingered and bony, attached to an arm, equally long and equally skinny.

Righteous Drum gave a sharp tug and a skinny, long-armed, bow-legged Chinese man came sliding through the disturbed air. He emerged as if he were diving into water, but managed to twist in midair so that he landed neatly on his feet. The man's long hair and beard were both pure white, and his skin had something of the tissue fineness of age. His brown eyes and generous mouth were framed by laugh lines.

But the new arrival was not laughing now. His robes were shredded. The monkeys embroidered on the ivory fabric hung grotesquely dismembered. Blood splattered the fabric and oozed from numerous thin slices wherever the man showed exposed skin. More blood seeped into the fabric of the ruined robes, showing that the heavy robes' ability to protect their wearer had been far from complete.

The new arrival paid no attention to his surroundings, peculiar as they must have been to him. Nor did he seem to notice anyone but the Dragon.

"Righteous Drum, we have lost . . ." and then he fainted.

Righteous Drum barely caught him before he hit the ground.

Riprap had moved forward to help. Now, as he took the unconscious man from Righteous Drum and laid him gently on the ground, he sniffed the air.

"Gunpowder?"

"The Chinese invented it," Des reminded him.

Nissa stopped an impending lecture on the technological sophistication of the ancient Chinese by handing Lani to Des.

"Get her away. Distract her. She shouldn't see this." Nissa dropped to her knees and started inspecting the Monkey—for this could only be the Monkey—taking inventory of his numerous wounds. "Brenda, check the picnic hamper. There should be another thermos of hot water. Clean napkins, too."

Pearl did not intervene, but turned her attention to surveying the surrounding area. So far the Rosicrucians' protections were holding, but they would have been severely strained by this intrusion. She spoke without stopping her inspection of their surroundings.

"Nissa, can your patient be moved?"

Nissa did not raise her eyes, nor did her hands stop their expert motion as she catalogued wounds, tamping some with the napkins Brenda held out to her, rinsing a few that were encrusted over by something foul-looking with sterile water from the thermos.

"None of the cuts seem to have hit anything vital," Nissa replied after a moment. "Blood loss probably contributed to his fainting. We can probably shift him on the picnic blanket."

"Isn't someone going to notice?" Brenda asked.

"I'll do what I can about that," Pearl said.

Maybe the others expected her to work a spell, but instead she pulled out her cell phone. In a moment, she had the front desk in the temple's museum, and was relayed to a director who didn't need much explanation. He'd felt the surge that preceded the Monkey's appearance, and had been heading out to check on the disturbance.

"Don't bother ruining the picnic blanket," Pearl said after she had ended her call. "Someone will be out in a moment with a stretcher. Anyone who asks about the commotion will be told an old man fainted."

"When you lie, always stick close to the truth," Des said cheerfully from where he was holding Lani up so she could inspect the statue of Isis more closely. "Where are we taking him?"

"My garden," Pearl said. "I'm still a bit leery about letting these gentlemen into my house, but the area under the ramada should serve for now."

Righteous Drum had been too distracted by the Monkey's appearance, but now he turned and gave Pearl a stiff bow.

"I do have a domicile," he reminded her. "I would not be in your debt."

"I bet you wouldn't be," Pearl replied, knowing her grin was taunting as much as friendly, "but where he goes is the Monkey's decision, not yours. As he's in no position to express an opinion, we're taking him to my house."

"Because?"

"Because I am in a position to express an opinion. I know the people who are heading here at this very minute with a stretcher, and you are in no position to argue—domicile, debt, or not."

Righteous Drum still looked undecided, even though Pearl knew that he knew he had no real choice. She softened.

"Look, Righteous Drum. I'm not looking to force you to incur unwelcome debt. There's a man here bleeding. Didn't you just tell me we were all sort of related? If so, don't I owe hospitality to a distant relative?"

Righteous Drum sighed and rested his head in his right hand. He stood there for a long moment, sighed again, and nodded.

"You are right. Choice is just an illusion. Any other decision would be a bad one on my part, born of pride, not a desire to do the best for my old friend."

The Rosicrucian director arrived carrying a rolled-up stretcher under his arm.

He greeted Pearl with a nod, glanced at the unconscious, bloodied man on the ground, and set down his burden.

"You said you had matters under control so I didn't bring our resident emergency med people or someone to help carry the stretcher. Do I get to know more about this?"

"Later," Pearl promised. "Right now, we don't know much ourselves. The man over there came seeking his friend and almost immediately collapsed. He muttered a few words before he passed out, but nothing that makes much sense."

That's technically correct, Pearl thought. She saw the director glance at the statue of Isis and wondered what the goddess's representation might be prompted to tell. Well, that couldn't be helped.

"You're taking him to your house?"

"That's right. We'll carry him in through the side gate. Someone will bring you back the stretcher."

The director waved his hand in casual dismissal. "Take your time. Hopefully, no one else will collapse between now and closing."

"Thanks."

"And fill me in later. That was an astonishing surge, nearly triggered our defenses and blocked him out entirely. Glad they didn't go off. It would be a real pain to reset them."

With another curious—but not in the least rude—glance around the group, the director gave a nod that was almost a bow and departed.

Riprap and Nissa had no problem assembling the stretcher. Then Des and Riprap carefully raised the injured man, and Brenda and Nissa slid the stretcher beneath him. All of this was done with the minimum of words, even from Lani, who clung to Pearl's leg and watched in rapt fascination.

Beneath Isis's watchful gaze, the group formed a procession, walking slowly, almost solemnly from beneath the lotus pillars and Egyptian quiet to the tiger's jungle that was Pearl's garden.

When the old man emerged through the empty air and collapsed at the Dragon's feet, Brenda didn't wonder why everyone acted like this was the most normal thing in the world to have had happen. She knew perfectly well that all of them—well, at least other than Pearl and Righteous Drum and maybe Des—were simply in shock.

Dealing with the immediate and the essential, like stopping the injured man from bleeding to death, was something to do, something that made sense out of nonsense. So Brenda fetched hot water and handed Nissa and Riprap—who knew what they were doing—napkins and the like. When they had the Monkey on a stretcher, Brenda ran ahead because someone had to go in through the house and out through the garden to open the locked gate.

Hastings, the chauffeur, was in afternoon rehearsals for a bit part in a play, so he wasn't around. It wasn't one of the maid's days. Wong, the gardener, had left earlier, afternoon in the summer not being the best time for tending plants, so Pearl's garden was thankfully empty when the stretcher was carried around to the back and set down under the ramada on the veranda.

"When he comes around, the Monkey is going to be shocky," Nissa said. "Pearl, you have some old sheets and blankets in the basement. Mind if I . . . ?"

"Help yourself," Pearl said, "or rather, let someone else get them. I think you have the most medical training of the lot. I'd rather you stay with our patient."

Pearl glanced at Riprap when she said this, and the big man shook his head.

"First aid, some trauma. Nissa's better than me, though. I'll get the stuff."

Brenda did her part to help, and soon found that the best thing she could do was keep out of the way—and help keep Lani entertained. This wasn't easy. Lani was tired out after her day's ordeal, wanted her mother, and no one else would do.

No one else who was present that is. The little girl wouldn't stop asking about Foster, repeating her questions with the regularity and unvaried rhythm of a metronome until Nissa decided the little girl should be sent off to bed.

Brenda was drafted to attend to bath and bedtime. She was very glad when at last Lani was fed, bathed, and put down for the evening. Despite bedtime coming almost an hour early, Lani dropped off almost at once. Now only Brenda's own imagination could be blamed for the litany.

Where is Foster? What's he doing? Why isn't he here? Doesn't he like me anymore? Where is Foster?

"Foster is gone," Brenda said to the empty air in her room as she changed out of the T-shirt that had gotten soaked during Lani's bath. "Flying Claw is the only one who remains."

Brenda reached into the box on her dresser and pulled out a few fresh amulet bracelets. They weren't as strong as those she'd used earlier, but she felt better when she had them around her wrist. She suspected her allies had taken similar precautions on the excuse of running inside to use the bathroom.

When Brenda rejoined the others out on the veranda, she learned that Waking Lizard, as the Monkey was properly named, had come around about five minutes before. While not exactly energetic, he was coherent enough to give an account of the events that had led to his desperate dive through what he called the Last Gate to collapse in the Dragon's arms.

"You said we had lost," Righteous Drum was prompting. "You mean our armies have been defeated?"

"That's right." Waking Lizard's voice was whispery but still somehow resonant and strong. "I don't know what the other side had. They had weapons I've never seen before . . . Creatures . . ."

He began to shake and Nissa spooned something hot into him. The shaking stopped, but Waking Lizard's eyes remained wild.

"We knew our enemies had new tactics, new weapons, but this. I've never seen . . ."

He looked like he was going to start shaking again, but Pearl's voice brought him back into focus.

"If things were that bad, how did you manage to get away?'

Waking Lizard glanced at Pearl, but he directed his reply to Righteous Drum. "Why me? You know me, Righteous Drum. I'm no Stone Monkey, no frontline fighter, no warrior out of legend. I was directing staff in the palace. When things went to hell, when the word rippled through the ranks that the Horse was dead and the Ram badly injured, I decided I could do nothing more productive where I was. I ran."

He glanced back at Pearl. "And I didn't run *away* either, lady. I ran *to*. To Righteous Drum. I thought he needed to know what had happened. Also, along with the Snake and the Tiger, he represents a full quarter of our cabal's strength. The Tiger is young, but I thought he might be able to rally at least some of our troops. And what if the Dragon had discovered even part of what he had come to seek?

"Then, as I was readying the spell that would give me access to Righteous Drum via the bridge he used to come here, a group of soldiers burst through the door I had locked behind me. They threw a bomb of some sort. It bounced off my shield, but retained sufficient power to shatter the stone floor of the room. Most of my injuries came from flying stone."

Waking Lizard looked momentarily proud. "I'm not sure my attackers proved as hardy. I think I took one or two of them with me. Maybe more."

"So our enemies might not know what you were doing, where you were going?" Righteous Drum sounded anxious, almost hopeful.

"I think they'll figure it out," Waking Lizard said, "but they may take a while to follow. A month? Hard to say. Depends on if any of the others survived, and what they'll tell when questioned."

There was something in the manner in which Waking Lizard inflected the word "questioned" that made Brenda certain beyond a doubt that such questions wouldn't be restricted to words.

Riprap cut in. "So you're looking for sanctuary. Not just Waking Lizard, all of you."

Looking at the expression on Righteous Drum's face, Brenda realized that a face might hold both defiance and denial, but show surrender nonetheless. Righteous Drum clearly wanted to deny that either he or his could ever need help from those who only a few hours before they had been fighting, but the reality was that they did need help.

Nissa broke the uncomfortable silence.

"Waking Lizard, I'm a bit confused. Was the enemy who drove you here the same as the one you people were fighting when Righteous Drum and the others came here?"

Waking Lizard struggled to sit a bit more upright on the patio chair on which he'd been settled. Riprap obligingly adjusted the backrest and lifted him into place.

"Thank you," Waking Lizard said. "It is so hard to feel at all dignified flat on one's back. As to your question, Miss Nissa, the fighting started out that way. Has Righteous Drum told you anything of the ongoing contest to hold the Jade Petal Throne—a contest that was old before your ancestors were exiled?"

"He has."

"Well, for a time, even when our own position was the most desperate, the sense of the conflict was much the same, steps in a complicated and ornate yet still somehow familiar dance. I'm not sure when I began to feel something was different. It might have been when the usual truces were refused or when the Horse sent word of new weapons and tactics."

"Usual truces?" Riprap interrupted.

"To gather up the wounded, for the recognition of some feast," the Monkey clarified. "I can tell you're going to want to ask about the new weapons and tactics our enemies employed, but I'm the wrong one to ask. The details of battle meant nothing to me. I have always focused on the end result. Suffice to say that our enemies were winning ground, more rapidly, more efficiently than we had expected."

"Sounds as if your enemies made some new allies," Des said. "Surely that has happened before."

"Almost everything," Righteous Drum said, "has happened before. That makes it no less unpleasant when it happens to you. Your Dog has implied that since our allies have lost the war, we will need to remain here. I, for one, have no desire to remain in this universe. I have family in the Lands Born from Smoke and Sacrifice, as well as friends and students. I could not abandon them, especially if the situation is as dire as the Monkey reports."

Brenda nodded. She could understand this response. The uncomfortable beginnings of an idea were growing at the back of her mind. She was about to explore them further when almost simultaneously the doorbell rang and there came a rapping on the side gate.

"They'll wake Lani!" Nissa said, springing to her feet and moving inside the house to listen for cries from upstairs.

Brenda ran for the gate.

"Stop making all that noise! We hear you!" she called, keeping her voice low. A hammering in her chest told her before she'd even slid aside the panel in the door who would be there.

Honey Dream the Snake stood with her hand on the wrought iron ring that served as a knocker. Flying Claw, looking almost familiar in the clothes Foster had worn when he had left the house that morning, stood a few paces behind her. From the way he was glancing up at the windows on the second floor, Brenda realized that he had remembered that Lani was likely to be in bed.

The expression made him seem almost familiar, but the gaze he turned on her remained three-quarters a stranger's.

"Hang on," Brenda said, "and keep it down. I'll tell Pearl you're here."

She did. With a deep sigh and mutterings about letting enemies within her wards, Pearl said to let them come in, so Brenda went and opened the gate. The other two came in past her, and she couldn't resist sniffing just a little as Flying Claw went by, wondering if regaining his memories had changed his familiar scent.

Brenda thought it had, and wondered if the new odor blended in had anything to do with Flying Claw, or only that he'd spent the last few hours doing a lot of worrying and sweating.

As Brenda closed and latched the gate, locking a massive array of locks that made perfect sense on a movie star's garden gate, Honey Dream launched into her report.

"Flying Claw and I were talking, and I was filling him in on things that had happened when we both felt this surge. Flying Claw recognized right away that someone was attempting to establish a link to our bridge."

She's still trying to prove to her dad that Foster—Flying Claw—was worth coming after, Brenda thought. *Well, recent developments are going to make Righteous Drum really unlikely to argue the point. He said there were many Tigers, many Snakes. I guess that's not the case any longer. There's just these guys . . . and us.*

"We went back to the apartment and did some investigating." Honey Dream glanced over at Flying Claw. "This is really your part. You figured it out."

Flying Claw stood very straight. "Our bridge home has been broken. It is not merely barred against us. It no longer exists."

"You are certain?" Righteous Drum's question was snapped out in the tones of a commander seeking confirmation, not as an expression of either hope or doubt.

"I am."

"So we are stranded here," Waking Lizard said, his tone filled with disbelief.

"For now," Righteous Drum replied. "Only for now. There are other routes. That bridge was only the fastest and most efficient. Flying Claw, could you tell if the bridge was destroyed deliberately, or merely as a side result of our enemies pursuing Waking Lizard?"

Flying Claw reflected. "I think the destruction of the bridge was not done deliberately. After all, why should they create more labor for themselves when they come after us?"

Pearl cut in, forcefully interjecting herself into a conversation that had been—since Honey Dream's arrival—dominated by the four from the Lands Born from Smoke and Sacrifice. Brenda saw the others start, as if they had been so absorbed in their own problems that they had momentarily forgotten where they were—or that others were listening.

"Why should your enemies come after you?" Pearl asked, but Brenda thought the older woman already suspected. "Is the urge for vengeance so strong—or is it something else?"

"Why will they come after us? Think on it, Tiger Lady," the Dragon said, and his tone was not in the least mocking. "They will come after us for the same reasons we came after you—and with even greater reason. Four of the Earthly Branches have slipped their grasp: Tiger, Dragon, Snake, and now Monkey. Moreover, if they learn why we came here—as they surely will—they will almost certainly wish to come after the fragments that were already lost."

"Soon?" Nissa said, and something in the way she stood made Brenda think she was about to rush up the stairs and grab Lani, though where they could hide would be anyone's guess.

"Probably not too soon," Waking Lizard said. "When I fled—and I admit, that's what I did—our enemies had not yet consolidated their hold on the Jade Petal Throne. They will need to anoint their emperor first. Then there will be alliances to make, diplomatic ties to affirm. But they will come, never let yourself believe otherwise. They will come."

Brenda felt the thought she had been exploring snap into shape. "Not if we go after them first."

"Offer ourselves up in sacrifice?" Righteous Drum asked in shock.

Riprap laughed. "You don't know Brenda. She means we should go after them rather than waiting for them to come after us. I'm not sure I don't agree."

Nissa was slowly lowering herself back into her chair, momentary panic replaced with calculation.

"Count me in," she said. "Lani and I couldn't hide forever, and the others coming here would put my sisters and their children at risk."

Des smiled and touched the amulet bracelets encircling his wrist. "I, too, am a parent, and although my children are Brenda's age, I would not have them endangered."

Pearl shook her head. "Not so fast, my friends. I understand your impulse. I even share it, but there are two questions that must be answered before we can commit to anything."

Honey Dream sneered at the older woman.

"Like what you might face on the other side or how dangerous the journey might be?"

Brenda fought down an urge to punch the Snake, even though some wiser core within herself knew that Honey Dream was voicing her personal fears. Pearl must have realized that as well, for she shook her head and even managed a kind, almost motherly smile.

"No, young lady, not that at all." She turned to face Righteous Drum and Waking Lizard, but her body language did not shut out Flying Claw. Only Honey Dream was snubbed as if a child, unworthy of consultation.

Pearl says more with a gesture than I can with a thousand words, Brenda thought, swallowing a smile, *and the best thing is that no one can call her on it.*

"I must know two things," Pearl said, "before we can agree to help you."

"And if we refuse?" Righteous Drum retorted.

"I should think that would be obvious," Pearl replied, and her smile was dangerous. "If we do not aid you, then we must be against you. Do you really want enemies behind you, as well as in your homeland?"

Righteous Drum blinked slowly and scanned his small cohort. "Ask your questions."

"Very good," Pearl replied. "The first is this. If we agree to help you, will you agree to free those who remain trapped within your crystals?"

Righteous Drum opened his mouth as if to speak, but Pearl held up a slim hand for silence. The implicit command in the gesture held him.

"Second, we have arrived at the conclusion that someone advised you upon your arrival in our world. Will you tell us who that advisor was?"

★

Pearl paid great attention to the silence that followed her two questions. She had called the statements "questions," but she and all the others knew them for what they were: demands.

The silence stretched, but Pearl did not expect heated debate to break out among the four who might give answer to her questions. Three, in the case of the second matter, for she doubted if the Monkey knew the identity of the informant.

Debate was something that happened among equals, and the Chinese were not strong believers in natural equality. They had some of the finest hierarchical markers ever evolved by a society, with an elaborate system of academic examinations to provide a release valve to bleed off pressure.

An interesting contrast to how American society works. In the United States, we cultivate the illusion that all are equal, despite numerous indications that this is not so. The Chinese, in contrast, have long cultivated the illusion that anyone—in particular any man—might prove himself superior, never mind that an illiterate peasant would find reading a promotional examination, much less studying for one, impossible. Still, it is the release valves that let a society continue to function.

So Pearl waited, knowing that the Dragon would be the one to decide whether an immediate answer would be forthcoming. He outranked both the Tiger and the Snake in age and experience. The Monkey had come to him as a supplicant. She waited, and saw her own allies put aside their more contentious natures to imitate her. At long last, Righteous Drum the Dragon spoke.

"I can see why you would not wish to work with us while we held your friends and relatives as hostages against your actions—never mind that we have sworn not to harm them. You would be rightly concerned. Moreover, it is to our advantage that we release them."

Snake's mouth twisted in an ironic grimace. "Why should we make it easier for our opponents to collect the Earthly Branches? Let them do the work. Let them figure out how to parse souls."

"So you will free the remaining Thirteen Orphans?" Pearl asked.

"A compromise," Righteous Drum countered. "We will free some of your number—say half—as a sign of goodwill. The rest will be freed after the alliance between us is signed."

"Very well," Pearl said. "As long as we may choose the half who will be released. Now, as to the other matter . . . Who aided you?"

Righteous Drum met her gaze. "That is more difficult. I would prefer not to reveal that person's identity, but rather to assure you that since our informant would no longer need to inform us, any danger—or difficulty—this person could offer you is ended. Our informant acted under coercion. When that coercion is lifted, you would have no reason to dread further difficulties."

Riprap was frowning. "But how do we know that you wouldn't apply that same coercion again?"

"I cannot explain the nature of the coercion without revealing the identity of the one who acted as our informant and advisor. All I can say is that if we become your allies the source of the coercion will no longer exist."

Nissa's frown mirrored Riprap's. "Can you tell us at least this much? Was the one you call your informant one of the Thirteen—our Thirteen?"

"Yes."

"Was he—or she—one of those gathered here?"

"No."

Des looked no more happy than the others, but he shrugged. "Righteous Drum does have a point, Pearl. If their informant was one of us, and if we're going to need every one of us—as I suspect we will—then can we afford to reduce our strength?"

Brenda was nervously rubbing her hand along the edge of her jawbone. "But if we don't know—how can we trust each other, how can we trust knowing that someone was willing to help these people perform lobotomies on us?"

"Trust," Pearl said, hearing the acid in her voice and quickly moderating the tones, "is highly overrated. I prefer vigilance and carefully worded contracts."

Brenda looked at Pearl, startled, realized the anger that had touched Pearl's voice had not been directed at her, and relaxed.

"So you say we should agree to these terms?"

Pearl let herself smile a slow cat's smile.

"Rather, let me say that this can be a starting point on which we can base our contract."

She reached down and touched the sword Treaty, which, cased, had not left her side since she had regained her senses in that ramshackle apartment in Japantown. The hum of the blade underscored her words.

"I am rather good at negotiating contracts."

★

Some days later, it was all settled. Brenda did her best to help with the treaty that Pearl was working out with Righteous Drum. She knew that document was vitally important, that she should keep alert for loopholes like the ones that had slipped into the first pact.

But two things kept distracting her.

One was having Gaheris Morris back and himself again. Brenda had grown so accustomed to having her father not knowing what was going on that she found herself having trouble settling into their former relationship once his memory was returned. Unlike Pearl and Nissa, who reported having been somewhat aware of events going on in the immediate vicinity of the crystals, Gaheris and the others remembered nothing out of the ordinary.

They recalled the events of the intervening weeks—or in some cases, months—since their memories were captured, but other than a few, their Dragon and Albert Yu in particular, who reported unusually vivid dreams, the excision had been complete.

Gaheris Morris was no different from the others. He remembered nothing, and while this bothered him, he seemed to take it in stride. It was Brenda who had difficulty accepting his attitude. She realized she was being unfair, but she felt betrayed both by her father's lapse and then by his inability to see how difficult he had made things for her. He'd forced her into the Rat's role without the Rat's abilities. He hadn't been there for her, and wasn't that what parents were for?

Worse, he had no better guess than anyone else as to why Brenda should have maintained that tenuous connection to the Rat. In fact, Brenda thought—though she knew she could be wrong, could be projecting or something—that Gaheris even resented her managing not only to cope but handle her role as the Ratling with something of a flourish.

As much as it pained and confused her, Brenda found herself almost glad for this newly complicated relationship with her father. It almost managed to keep her from thinking about the other person who was troubling her: the other Tiger, Flying Claw, Foster.

He wasn't living at Pearl's house now. Pearl had arranged for the four refugees to have a nice suite at a rather exclusive local hotel. She intimated to the hotel manager—without actually saying so—that her guests were associated with the Chinese film industry. This covered their varying abilities to speak English and any oddities of behavior. After all, film people were weird already; being foreign was just a garnish.

But the four refugees in groups of various sizes came over to Pearl's house on a daily basis. Flying Claw had even agreed to swear to a preliminary treaty, agreeing to cause no harm while within Pearl's house, so that he could interact with Lani much as before. The little girl had been agitated and aggravated that "Foster," as she persisted in calling him, was no longer staying with them. When "Foster" had not been permitted to come into the house and play with her, her unhappiness had escalated to dangerous levels.

So not only did Brenda have to see Flying Claw every day, he was in and out of the house, the sound of his laughter mingling with Lani's, the entire situation making Brenda almost believe that things could go back to the way they had been.

They couldn't though. There was Honey Dream seated by her father, going over the terms of the treaty with a sophisticated knowledge and care that reminded Brenda again and again that, although they were within a few years of each other in age, Honey Dream had long been an adult, whereas Brenda—as her confused reactions to her father brought home to her more than ever—was still, at least in some situations, a child.

There was Flying Claw himself, for although he laughed and played with Lani almost as he had before, there was a reserve to him that had not been there. The competitive light that had shone when they played Yahtzee or basketball was present almost continuously now, a watchfulness, a tiger crouched and ready to spring.

Brenda couldn't decide how she felt about this new version of a man she had thought she loved. To deny the love seemed like treachery, but if Foster was truly gone, why should she love the stranger who had stolen his face and form?

By odd coincidence, the new contract was completed on the third of July. It seemed auspicious to everyone—even those from the Lands, once the significance of the date was explained to them—that the contract be signed on the fourth.

"Fitting," Righteous Drum said, "for the signing of this Declaration of Independence of which you speak was also in its way a formal declaration of war."

Waking Lizard grinned. "Also all the fireworks will be certain to frighten away the evil spirits."

The opposition—soon to be formally transformed into allies—arrived shortly before the appointed hour. Three of them—Tiger, Dragon, and Snake—were attired in their most formal robes. Monkey's had been shredded, but he was clad in a robe Des had loaned him. With his long white hair and beard combed, Waking Lizard looked much more formal than Brenda had ever seen him—even impressive.

Their own group was much less uniform. For her own private reasons, Pearl eschewed whatever robes she possessed in her role as Tiger, and instead wore a neat summer suit in pale green linen, much as she would have to a business meeting. Des had packed his Rooster robes, silvery white garments so elaborately embroidered that the under color was almost lost. Gaheris Morris wore one of his business suits, black, of course. Albert Yu, still a stranger to Brenda, although he had been at Pearl's house daily for the negotiations, wore what looked like emperor's robes.

The other four were less formal, partly because shopping for dress clothing had not been high on their list of priorities. Des, their fashion consultant in all things, said that as long as they wore something in which their zodiac animal's color dominated, even torn clothing would be appropriate.

Therefore, Riprap wore jeans and a pale yellow button-down shirt. Nissa wore a summer dress in a floral print with plenty of green foliage. Lani bounced around in overalls with a bunny on the bib front.

Brenda had dithered, partly because she couldn't help wanting to look good in front of Flying Claw. Also, she didn't know what color she should wear, since she wasn't really the Rat. Pearl had dismissed her qualms with an imperious sniff.

"They see you as one of us, and I think you are the one who makes Righteous Drum the most nervous. Your abilities are unpredictable. He'd probably back off if you didn't agree to take part."

So in the end, Brenda had worn a black skirt cut above her knees. With it she wore the red and gold brocade top she'd worn the night she and Dad had gone to meet Riprap that first time. Her now ruined jacket had protected the delicate fabric when she'd dived onto the garage floor.

Like me, like all of us, it's a survivor.

They signed their treaty out under the ramada. The air was fresh but still, as if the winds knew not to ruffle the important pieces of paper.

And maybe they do, Brenda thought as she wrote her name, hearing Treaty thrumming warning against taking this great step lightly. Out in the streets, firecrackers snapped and popped counterpoint.

Pearl and Des had made certain in advance that appropriate refreshments were ready, for in the Lands as in the China that had given them birth, food was an important part of all ceremonies.

Brenda hurried inside to get the first of the trays while the scrolls were being placed in their tubes. When she heard the kitchen door open, Brenda thought the new arrival was Riprap. She turned, ready to ask him if he'd carry out the heavier tray.

Flying Claw stood before her, resplendent in his tiger robes, balanced easily against the weight of the sword at his side. Brenda's breath caught in her throat, for he was as beautiful as he had been that first time she had seen him, a lifetime ago in that anonymous LoDo parking garage.

"We are friends now," Flying Claw said in English. "That's what the paper we signed says."

Brenda nodded, but for a moment she didn't trust herself to speak. Then she replied so softly that she wondered if Flying Claw would hear, "Yes. I guess we are, but what does that mean?"

"I wish I knew," Flying Claw said, reaching to take the heavier tray and speaking back at her over his shoulder. "With all my heart and soul, I sincerely wish I knew."